# THE MAIN MAN

## Jaen Hardy

Pen Press

First published in Great Britain

All paper used in the printing of this book has been made from wood grown in managed, sustainable forests.

ISBN13: 978-1-78003-552-9

Printed and bound in the UK
Pen Press is an imprint of
Indepenpress Publishing Limited
25 Eastern Place
Brighton
BN2 1GJ

A catalogue record of this book is available from the British Library

Cover design by Jaen Hardy

# THE MAIN MAN

# Nature or Nurture

## *Winter*

He kept 'escaping'. He did it nearly all the time. Years ago, it only happened when he was in the cupboard, but now it could be anywhere. He was doing it now: letting himself drift in and out of consciousness, letting words and sounds happen elsewhere, almost out of reach. He was permitting himself to surface momentarily, allowing Old Grimthorpe's voice to wash over him. Soothing words… cirrus… cumulus…

'Joel. Joel. JOEL!' He could hear sniggering – in and out – quite loud and then almost imperceptible, like waves crashing onto a beach and then drawing back, silently revealing bright, sparkly pebbles of light behind his eyelids. He felt a sharp pain in his ribs. He was back, and the Geography teacher was approaching him from the front of the class. Heads turned as his bulky form passed the other desks to where Joel was sitting, at the back. Joel swept the long swathe of dark hair from his face to reveal equally dark eyes, staring out with that early morning look of confusion when woken too suddenly. He shrunk into his chair, pushing his small frame hard against the wall.

'Don't flinch, boy. I'm not going to hurt you. It's more than my job's worth. Although sometimes I'm tempted, believe me!' The teacher was leaning over the desk, peering at him so closely that Joel could see right up his nose; he could have counted all the hairs if he'd wanted to. He was aware of Old Grimthorpe saying something about concentrating, about being away with the fairies. The teacher's nostrils dilated and quivered and then he drew away from him, sharply. Did he smell? Probably. It was Thursday after all and Friday was his day for a shower.

The sniggering had started again. Old Grimthorpe was back at his desk, and the bell was going. 'Quietly as you go out please, class. Jenna! Don't spoil my anticipation of this evening's jollities. No doubt I'll be seeing all of you again in a couple of hours… Before you go, Joel, take this note home please. And make sure your mother gets it this time. I don't think you remembered last week, did you?'

Joel couldn't remember if he had or not, or even if his mother had been there to give it to. His mother was like him. She escaped too, only in a different way. He hadn't a clue where to, or even when it would happen for that matter. She would be there one night when he went to bed, but would be gone when he woke up the next morning. Sometimes there was plenty of food, and some money left on the kitchen table, and other times there was just money. She'd be gone a couple of days and then she'd be back, often with an 'uncle' in tow.

Leroy was waiting for him in the corridor. 'Thanks for waking me,' Joel said.

'No problem. Are you going tonight? To the firework display?'

Joel shrugged. 'Might do. I'm not sure.'

'Please yourself.' Leroy turned his attention to Grace, a bright little girl from their class who sat in the front row. She was standing with her back pressed against the wall, allowing people to push past her. She smiled at Joel before whispering something in Leroy's ear. Joel felt a twinge of envy as they laughed, linked arms, and walked on ahead.

It wasn't far for Joel to walk home. The crumbling rows of Victorian terraces due to be demolished were situated towards the far side of town, on the eastern outskirts, along with the school, the industrial estate and town football ground. He always walked home alone. He turned right at the school gates, whereas everybody else turned left. His mum wouldn't allow him to bring anyone back, and because of this he never got invited to anyone else's house – although he had been to Leroy's once.

He let himself in through the back way, first down the alley between the houses, then through the rotting wooden gate to the concrete backyard. He automatically held his breathe as he passed the piles of rubbish that had been thrown over the fence – an old fridge, a mouldering mattress exuding ammonia fumes and anything else that was difficult to dispose of easily without incurring expense or effort – but he still experienced that catching in the back of the throat, making him gag. He unlocked the kitchen door with his key, took off his oversized second-hand school coat and hung it on the nail on the back of the door.

He ran his fingers across the grimy surface of the pine kitchen table. That would be the first thing his mum would clean when she got home, scrubbing and bleaching as if to remove all the stains and blemishes of their life. He put down his polystyrene container on it: burger and chips that he'd bought from the van parked on the corner of his road. He'd eat it later, but not much later because it would be too dark. He probably should've spent the last of his money on some more candles. At least it was light in here at the moment, not like in

3

the rooms at the front that were all boarded up. He'd better do that homework now.

He hoped that Mrs Colshaw wasn't going to make them do Family Trees in History on Monday morning. His was too confusing; he couldn't work it out. Who was this aunt that he was meant to be staying with in Scotland all those years ago, when they were living on the council estate? He'd never heard of her either then or since. At first he had assumed she was the sister of all the different uncles that drifted in and out of his life. Now he knew better. They weren't really proper uncles at all, not like the ones other people had. He opened the lid of his takeaway and started to pick at the chips, greasy, cloying and going cold.

And what about his little sister? Where would she fit in? His mum said that she belonged to someone else's family now. He could picture her standing in her playpen, stamping her little feet as she clutched at the bars. If that didn't work she would raise her arms in the air to be picked out, and then, when she wasn't, she'd start to scream. He couldn't help her because he wasn't very big himself then. He remembered how her screaming had annoyed the neighbours, making them bang on the wall next to theirs. And he remembered how his mum had told him to get into the cupboard when the people from the council had come round yet again.

He could visualise that cupboard now, from the inside. He could smell the mustiness of outdoor coats and muddy boots. He could see the ironing board and broom competing for space against the end wall. The front door to the flat had opened straight onto the dining room, and the cupboard was just next to it. It was quite large with louvre doors, and he remembered peering out between the gaps as his mum and the council people argued. He could hear his mum pleading with them –

4

and then shouting. Was it then that they'd taken his sister away, or later on? It was all a blur now.

That was the day when he had heard that he was living with his aunt in Scotland. That's what his mum had told the people from the council when they had asked where he was. After that the cupboard had become a magic place rather like Dr Who's TARDIS. Once in it he would be transported to Scotland, or anywhere else for that matter. High up on the back wall, above the coats and the shelf that held all their bits of junk, he could see the controls, with all the knobs and switches in a special box behind a transparent plastic door. He couldn't reach them, but he didn't need to. He had his remote control: a special tin with a picture of a Scottie dog on it, with thistles all round the edge. It had always made a clinking noise when he shook it, but he'd never been able to get the lid off. His mum said that it had the meter money in it.

Every time he came out of his TARDIS he was somewhere else. All he had to do was to blank out the real world and he could be anywhere: the Moon, Venus, Mars, or even planets that nobody else had ever even heard of, planets he'd discovered all by himself. Those were the best because he was the boss in these worlds, and he always won the battles.

When his little sister was taken away his mum had started to leave him alone for longer. It was also the time when the man had vanished, the one he assumed was his dad. And then more and more uncles came round, and some of them used to shout a lot and the neighbours started complaining again. That was when his mum had decided that they would have to move. That's when they ended up in this squat.

His mind returned to the matter of the Family Tree lesson. Was he the only one in the class who didn't even know who his dad was? Some of them had stepdads, but at least they saw their real ones sometimes. He tried to conjure up an image of the man, the one that might have been his dad, but it was too long ago now to recollect his features. He remembered all the arguing though, before the man left for good. Perhaps he was just another uncle after all. For a while after he'd left, this man had featured in his games in the cupboard. He was Dr Who making a special visit. But then his image would fade along with the vanquished aliens. But he soon found that he didn't really need him. He could look after himself. Perhaps he'd never even met his real dad. Perhaps his real dad didn't even know he existed.

He'd missed that cupboard when they had first moved to this dump, but not anymore. He'd learnt the trick. All he had to do was to let his mind go completely blank and he'd feel a click, and the door to a secret part of his brain would open, inviting him in. First he'd do it when his mum was away, when it was all dark and he couldn't get to sleep. But now he was doing it more often.

The yard gate was opening, and he could hear two pairs of footsteps approaching the back door. He recognized the uneven clickety-click of his mother's high heels on the cracked concrete path, but the more solid sound of the other pair of shoes was unfamiliar. He'd better get his burger finished. He didn't want to share it with anyone.

'Oh, you're home then, Joel. This is Len, your new uncle.'

A squat, stocky man came in behind his mum. 'Alright?' he said, giving Joel a cursory nod. 'What a dump, Jeannie. You can't expect me to stay here.' He took a bottle of whiskey out of a pocket of his donkey jacket. Joel noticed a four letter word tattooed on the fingers of his right hand, a letter just above each joint. The word was upside down but he could still make it out: HATE.

6

'Got any glasses, doll?' Len said. 'Just a quick drink and I'm outa here. It's bloody freezing!'

Joel sighed and swallowed the last mouthful of burger. Nothing had changed, but at least his mum was back for now. Anyway, he was feeling better about things already, even without her. Darren, a boy in his class, had just offered him a Saturday job, and he was proud of the way he'd handled himself. He knew Darren was a bully, particularly around the smaller boys like him, but he hadn't let that faze him. He'd stuck out for a good rate of pay. He'd show everybody that he could get on very well by himself. After all, he was fourteen and a quarter.

Len had finished his drink and was on his way out.

'Hey Mum,' Joel said. 'There's a firework display at the school later. We could go if you like.'

Jeannie fumbled in her handbag and retrieved a packet of cigarettes. 'Not this again, Joel. You know I can't stand school dos.'

'That's alright, Mum. We can watch it from here. There'll be a great view from the upstairs window.'

## *Spring*

It's the end of class, and Old Grimthorpe's getting up from his seat at the front. I catch his eye; easy from where I'm sitting. I like to be close to the front. The teachers can spot me quickly when they ask a question, then I can get in first with the right answer. But today I catch his eye for a different reason. Today I glare at him. All that talk about the forces of nature – tornadoes, earthquakes, volcanoes and tsunamis – is bound to start my nightmares off again. If I don't get a good night's sleep I won't be able to concentrate in the Geography test tomorrow morning, and then whose fault will it be when I don't do as well as usual, when I don't come top? I see this sudden wall of water approaching, sweeping me up, swirling me round, dragging me down.

I must try to think of something else. I turn to look for Joel and see him struggling to push past the other losers from the back of the class. I try not to glance at the empty seat next to Joel's, the one that's been empty now for a few weeks.

'Do you want me to help out on your Dad's stall again on Saturday, Darren?' Joel has to bend his neck upwards as he asks me this. He's a good head and shoulders shorter than me, but I've got a lot of respect for him, in spite of him being a runt. The thing with Joel is that he knows the value of things. He'll do anything that I tell him to, of course, but he always expects to be paid, and at the going rate. Now Leroy was totally different. He'd agree to anything I suggested, but only to try and gain my respect and friendship, and for that reason he'd never got either. But Joel can read me; he knows where I'm at. He's OK is Joel.

We walk down the boringly long corridor together in silence, out of the wide double doors and into the car park. The light is hazy and fading behind the stark leafless trees. We walk right to the school gates that lead onto the top of East Street before I answer his question. It's a little game of mine. I like to keep people guessing.

'I'll let you know tomorrow, mate,' I tell him. Joel shrugs and turns away in the opposite direction to where I'm going. I've no idea where he lives. I didn't know anyone lived in that direction. But it's not important. I can tell by his scruffy appearance that it won't be anywhere worth knowing about.

8

I glance through the window of the electrical shop on the corner leading to Mortimer Road. The jaded looking stock that's displayed hasn't been touched for yonks; everything looks ancient and grimy. I'm reminded of those new computer games I've been saving up for. I've got enough money on me to buy one, but not from this dump of a shop. I cross the road and head for the Shopping Mall. The concourse in front of it is all bleak and windswept, and I kick at the scudding detritus made up of other peoples' waste: empty crisp packets, crushed and oozing takeaway boxes, dented drink cans. I'm outgrowing this place, this out-dated backwater, this dung heap. I feel my new blazer pinching me under the armpits. I must be having another growth spurt. I'd better have a snack after I've bought that game. I need to keep my strength up. Which game shall I get? It needs to be one that'll take my mind off things, help to stop all these bad dreams.

Once in the café, I trace my fingers over my prized purchase and bite into my muffin. The bubbles in my glass of cola fizz and pop as they fight their way to the surface. They remind me of Leroy.

None of it had been my fault. I've got nothing to feel guilty about, so why all the nightmares? Leroy had been just as eager as ever to join me that day, and I'd shown him how to do it first, hadn't I? It wasn't as if I'd expected him to do anything I wasn't prepared to do.

I relax as the shot of double choc chip kicks in. I allow myself to recall that Saturday…

You're on the market stall with Joel and there's Leroy peering at something or other further up the row. There'd been torrential rain all week, but now it's all sunny and bright, and you feel a sudden surge of energy. You leave Joel to man the

9

stall alone, and push through the crowd of punters, sweep Leroy up, and the next thing is that you're on the bus out of town.

The terrible weather over the last few days has made the river very high and fast flowing: essential for the game you have in mind. You manage it easily. You lie on your stomach on the small footbridge where the river narrows, and hook your toes over the far edge to brace yourself so that you don't slip into the water. You lean out head first and touch the surface easily with your hand. You manage to grab a number of interesting, but as yet unrecognizable, objects out of the water as it froths and swirls below, and it isn't a problem for you to lean back and put them onto the bridge. You'll inspect it all later, decide if anything's worth keeping.

It's Leroy's turn now. He's having to lean further and further out over the edge of the bridge. As he's so short he's finding it difficult to touch the water, and his legs aren't long enough to help secure himself with his toes. The sky suddenly darkens and you're aware of the rain slanting in towards you from the direction of the town like a grey, all enveloping veil. You hear a crash as part of the river bank collapses and then a great swooshing noise as a great rush of water approaches. It's bringing more debris in its wake. Everything goes the colour of slate, like in an old black and white movie.

It isn't your fault that Leroy's arm has become entangled in a piece of netting and that he's being pulled into the river. It's hardly your fault that Leroy is such a runt, or that the weather has changed so suddenly.

You stand on the bridge watching him struggling to get free, but only making it worse. You could jump in and try to save him, but why risk your own life? You're safe and dry, and it isn't as if Leroy's your brother, or even your cousin. That

10

would be a different matter altogether. You wait on the bridge until you can't see him anymore, until he has become part of the swirling mass of flotsam and jetsam careering towards the sharp bend in the river, and then you run back to the road to catch the bus, before the rain finally catches up with you.

I lick my finger, gather up the remaining cake crumbs, and pop them into my mouth. Actually, that heavy downfall had saved me. When I finally got back to the market place it was deserted. All the traders were huddled inside Eric's café trying to keep dry. The punters had long gone and nobody had taken much cash, so I'd never had to explain myself to Dad. If he'd found out that I'd left Joel alone on the stall he'd have gone ballistic. I know exactly what Dad thinks of Joel: a waste of space. He noticed straight off how Joel's always out of it – on another planet even – ignoring the punters, and only taking any money if it's thrust into his hand. Dad can't understand why I bother with him. I don't think he really likes me mixing with boys like him. But actually, the runt has proved invaluable for a number of reasons – helping me with my bit of business with Crunch for instance – but not least when people started asking questions, wanting to know about what had happened to Leroy. When we were asked, we knew nothing. We'd both been on the market all day. Joel's the only one who knows any different, and he's not going to say anything, is he? He's given me his word. Joel's good like that.

I'm feeling a lot better now, so I might as well go home. I won't look down as I cross the town bridge. The palms of my hands are starting to go sweaty, and I feel a bit giddy and sick. I've developed a slight case of vertigo recently, but I'll be OK if I take a few deep breaths. I walk up the steep hill to our house on Western Heights, and look back over the town below.

From here I can see the scruffy little independent shops lining the riverfront, with the shopping mall, school and industrial estate snaking off behind them. I glimpse the council estate where I used to live. The high-rise blocks loom up out of the shadows, trying to snatch the last rays of sun. Beyond them, right over to the east, I can just see the boarded-up terraced houses due for demolition in the summer. Dad reckons his firm will get the rebuilding job. The sun is quite low in the sky, and as it catches the surface of the water, the river appears red, like an open wound dividing west from east – the 'haves' from the 'have-nots'. And now that I'm at my front gate my nausea has completely gone.

Anyway, I know exactly what Dad would have said if I'd told him about what happened that day, and of how Leroy had drowned. He would have said what he always says:

'It's dog eat dog in this life, son. You have to look after number one. How do you think we managed to get off the estate and move here, eh? You have to be ruthless sometimes to survive – to get on in life – and if that means that others have to fall by the wayside, then that's just the way it is. Nature red in tooth and claw, and all that.'

I crunch along the gravel drive, past Dad's gleaming white van, and down the side passage to the kitchen door. Mum's hideous plaster gnome's leering up at me from the clump of daffodils, so I give it a sharp kick; I hear it crashing onto the path as I go inside.

I'm greeted with familiar sounds floating in from the living room across the hall. Mum's watching that old 1960's film again, *Breakfast at Tiffany's*. She loves watching daytime TV, particularly the old films that Nan used to like, and especially this one. She's gone a bit soppy since Nan died. I'll go and watch it with her in a minute, although it's not really my kind

12

of thing. Mum says that Nan used to fancy the leading actor, but I reckon it's her that does really, which is incredibly sad of her considering he died ages ago. Mum says that I look a lot like him, and she keeps saying how handsome I am, so she must fancy him, mustn't she? What does she see in Dad then? I can't think of anyone more unlike him. But I suppose I'm no better. That Audrey Hepburn chick is completely hot and she must be dead by now as well. All the same, if I had to go out with a girl, she'd have to look like her.

'Darren. Is that you? Put the kettle on, will you, my beautiful boy. And then come and give your old Mum a big kiss.'

'In a minute, Mum.'

I reach into the cupboard for a bag of crisps, and remember the lesson Old Grimthorpe gave us last week, all about Charles Darwin and the survival of the fittest. I'm obviously one of life's survivors, and Leroy wasn't.

In the end that poor little runt just couldn't hack it, could he?

## *Summer*

Grace had finished the end of term test with twenty minutes to spare. She had read all her answers through and double checked everything for errors, and felt relatively confident that she had done well, although she didn't consider Geography to be her best subject.

Since studying her family tree with Mrs Colshaw back in the autumn term, Grace had developed a passion for English Literature and History, particularly in relation to Jamaica. Mrs Colshaw had picked up on her growing interest, and had suggested that she read a book called *Small Island*. She had devoured the story of Gilbert and Hortense, and how they had left Jamaica for London on the ship the *Empire Windrush* in 1948 in order to start a new life, because this was what her great grandparents had done. They had of course both died before she was born, but they had brought their small daughter with them: her Nan, who although now not in very good health, was still a very important part of their small family.

Grace remembered how the family had scrimped and saved to be able to take them all to Jamaica last Christmas for Nan's 70th birthday. It had been Nan's greatest wish to go back once more, to seek out old friends that she hadn't seen for decades. Grace and her brother had been introduced to them, and whilst talking to these people over copious convivial cups of tea and cold drinks, she had managed to find out a lot more about her family's past, right back until the time when slavery had been abolished. She remembered with affection the interest her elder brother had taken, even though it had really been her project. Her great grandfather, and his father before him – in fact everyone dating back to the 1830s – had been tailors. Grace had been shown some old sepia photographs of people smiling and showing off their new suits, and she could imagine her unknown relatives measuring, tacking and stitching with immaculate care. She supposed that was where she got her attention to detail from, her perfectionist streak – particularly with regards to her school work. She had been impressed by how much respect her Jamaican ancestors had commanded in their own country. Unfortunately, that respect now seemed to have evaporated. Nobody seemed to respect anybody on their estate.

Grace felt her head nodding forward. She must try to keep awake. The soporific heat from the glass next to her desk was intense, and she leaned to her right to open the window a crack, giving access to a half dead bee together with the welcome flurry of air. The bee buzzed and juddered against the glass, then expired on the window sill. Turning her head slightly to her left, she was not surprised to find that Joel was in one of his trances. He reminded her of a much scrawnier version of the little statue of the Buddha that she'd seen the other day in the corner shop by the river: his eyes lowered, and the palms of his hands turned upwards in his lap.

She could see that Joel had only got up to question six, so she jabbed him in the ribs, just the way that Leroy used to do. It was obviously not hard enough as it just extracted a soft moan. She prodded him harder and with more conviction, fearful that the slight noise might attract the attention of Mr Grimthorpe. She had moved to this seat at the back of the classroom at the beginning of term because she couldn't bear to see it empty any longer, and also because Joel needed looking after. She glanced at him again out of the corner of her eye. He was leaning over his work now, his unruly dark hair falling over his face. She imagined his high, pale forehead obscured beneath it, together with his large brown eyes with their exquisitely long lashes, delicate like a girl's. A bond had gradually grown up between them. They were both slight for their age and were also the youngest in the class, neither of them fifteen until August. She was beginning to love him. He was almost like a second brother.

Mr Grimthorpe's eyes were upon her. She had to look busy. She started doodling on a spare piece of paper, creating intricate patterns involving large loops and interlocking spirals. When it was safe to do so, she allowed her eyes to wander towards the front of the class, seeking out Darren, one of the oldest and definitely the most mature boy in the class. She felt sure he was the only one who really needed to shave, although some of the other boys professed to. His strawberry blonde hair had been cut so short that she could see the pink of his scalp beneath, and the back of his neck was burnt from sitting outside on the market stall on Saturdays.

She looked at the skin of her right arm as her hand continued to draw patterns across the page. From her extensive and avid reading habits, she had just discovered a new word, *quadroon*, which was a term used during slavery for someone that was a quarter Negro. Although obviously a racist expression, she liked the sound, and it applied to her. Her grandpa had been white, and so was her dad. She thought of how Darren had said her skin reminded him of a tasty cup of latte. She felt a new and unnerving tingling sensation spreading from the pit of her stomach, into her crutch and then right down the backs of her legs to behind her knees. She blushed as she remembered him licking her arm from the wrist to the fold of her elbow, and then right up to her shoulder, whilst all the time staring at her with those pale blue eyes, the colour of icy water.

She was finding it difficult to fill in the small spaces her patterns had created. Her hand had started to shake slightly, so she gripped the pencil, making jabbing movements in her attempts to make small dots and cross hatching. But she was not producing the precise, delicate strokes she wanted.

What Darren saw in her she had no idea. The other girls in their class were much more grown-up than her, much more *buxom*. This was another new word she had recently discovered in the novel she was currently reading, and she loved the full-bodied sound. She wished it applied to her. Her classmates all wore their regulation summer blouses with the top three buttons undone to reveal their cleavages, but she had hardly anything to show, so she kept hers buttoned up to the neck.

Darren was taking her out again tonight. They were going to the cinema, and the film being shown was one that he had referred to as 'soppy'. She hoped he wouldn't want to snog right through it as usual. She really wanted to see this film. He never paid her so much attention when there was a war or action film on, the sort that she had very little interest in. Then he would lean forward in his seat and hold her hand very tightly, particularly during any particularly violent scenes, making it very difficult for her to eat her popcorn. Then the snogging had to be done in a more concentrated and frenetic manner, somewhere on the way home. After the film tonight however, he'd said that they were going back to his house as his parents were going out, and because they had some unfinished business left over from their last date. She knew exactly what he had meant. That was the reason for these new and overwhelming sensations she kept experiencing today. It was all her fault of course. She must have egged him on, but not on purpose. She shouldn't have allowed him to go so far before, but she didn't know how to stop him. She felt a sudden rush of blood to her cheeks. Would it be easier after this evening, less embarrassing? She didn't think so. Her face was burning now. She opened the window a little more.

She looked down at her work again, but she couldn't concentrate. All she could hear was her mother telling her to be careful, not to jeopardize her future by doing anything foolish, not to end up like her elder sister Faith, marrying too young and spoiling her academic chances. This time next year she would be taking her GCSEs, and if she did well, her parents expected her to stay on at school to do A Levels. Perhaps she might even get a place at university – to be the first person in their family to do so. All her mother's hopes were focused on her alone now.

The timer on Mr Grimthorpe's desk was going off, summoning them to put down their pens. Darren was already standing up and was looking towards the back of the room, but his attention was on Joel. She followed them outside, a few steps behind, and saw Darren put his hand on Joel's shoulder. She thought she saw him discretely handing Joel a small package, and also some money. He was always looking out for Joel. That was one of the things that she liked about him; that, and the fact that he was the best-looking boy in the whole world.

Darren was striding on ahead of her. He didn't look back. She turned off at the shopping mall and headed for the estate. She would go straight home. Her parents encouraged her not to loiter with the other children from the flats. The lifts were broken again, so she climbed up the six flights of concrete steps to the small flat that she shared with her parents and Nan.

'Would you like something to eat, Grace?' her mum asked, as she bustled around the small kitchen.

'No thank you, Mum. I'm not really hungry.' She still had that strange feeling in her stomach from earlier on. 'I'm going to my room for a bit before I go out. I'll have something to eat later.'

'Going out again, Grace? Is that wise? Where are you off to this time? Is it with your friend Lauren? I hope you're going to do your revision for next week first.'

'We're going to the cinema, Mum.' That wasn't a complete lie, was it? 'And yes, I will do my homework first.' She wondered if Darren had to work as hard as she did to always be top of the class. She suspected that he didn't need to do any work at all.

She remembered her mother's advice about being careful around boys. Her mum would die if she knew what she was really up to. Anyway, how was she meant to be careful? Surely it was up to Darren to take care of all that. It wasn't really something she felt she could discuss with him. In fact she never discussed anything with him. Talking in general didn't really figure in their relationship. It had always been purely physical.

Would Darren stand by her if anything were to happen? Would he look after her if she got pregnant? She pictured how Darren had put a protective hand on Joel's shoulder after school, and felt reassured. If only Darren had been with Leroy on that fateful day last term instead of at the market with Joel. Darren would have saved him from drowning. He would have kept Leroy safe. She missed him so much, older than her by only eleven months. He hadn't even reached his sixteenth birthday. It would have been this September, the same as Darren. He hadn't only been her brother; he had been her best friend.

# PART I

# Starting Out

# Chapter 1

## Grace's Coming of Age

Grace had been waiting for what seemed like ages. She was positioned just inside the foyer, next to the large glass doors forming the entrance to the cinema. From here she had the best view of the bridge over which Darren would have to come from his home at Western Heights. The place was filling up quickly now as the film was scheduled to start in five minutes. Should she buy the tickets while there were still some left, or would that annoy him? He always insisted on paying for everything when they were on a date, even the popcorn. She wished that for once he would ask her which sort she preferred. He always bought the sweet variety even though she much preferred hers salted.

There he was, hurrying over the brow of the bridge. They should still be able to make the start of the film as long as the traffic lights didn't change.

'I've decided we're going straight home,' Darren said, entering the foyer without any other form of greeting. 'I don't think I can face sitting through that film at the moment. It's bound to be just a load of romantic crap. We've got much more interesting things to do.' He grabbed her hand tightly and led her out of the foyer and onto to corner of Broadway and East

Street. His grip on her hand became tighter as they crossed the road to the town bridge. 'Anyway, my parents have already gone out, so we'll have longer before your mother expects you home. I'm on a promise, remember.'

Grace had been looking forward to seeing the film. She had already bought the book in readiness for next term, and had even begun to read it. It was one they would be studying for GCSE. And she hadn't remembered actually promising him anything, although she had to admit that neither had she raised any objection when it was alluded to the other day.

Darren increased his stride as they crossed the bridge, and she almost had to run to keep up. He put his arm around her and sheltered her from the traffic by swapping sides with her, allowing her a view of the river. This was considerate of him, of course, but her longed for romance with him wasn't turning out quite the way she had imagined it. She had always had a crush on him. When Leroy was still alive she would sometimes look around in class from her seat at the front, to catch her brother's eye. Darren sat behind her in her direct line of sight, and she always made sure that she got a surreptitious glimpse of him as well. He was the most perfect looking boy that she had ever seen, like a Greek god. She had seen pictures of their marble statues showing their lithe and muscular bodies, and she was mesmerized by the power behind their strange, otherworldly, emotionless eyes.

She was reminded of the time when he had first come to the door of her flat, and of how she had felt when she'd seen him standing there framed in the doorway, staring both at and through her as he'd asked for Leroy. She'd felt like a small animal in the middle of a narrow lane, trapped motionless in the glare of the approaching headlights. She had been both relieved and disappointed that it was not her he had come to see, and from then on she had started daydreaming about the next time he came, and how it would be her that he wanted. Her daydreams had become more and more elaborate, but they had been rather like scenes from a Jane Austen novel. Grace imagined herself as little Fanny Price in *Mansfield Park*, having to wait patiently for Edmund to fall out of love with someone else first before noticing her. But it hadn't been like that at all. Darren had suddenly just latched onto her without any prior warning. And sex had never been involved in any of her daydreams.

They had crossed the bridge and Darren was slackening his pace. He held her hand tightly again when they crossed the main road as the line of traffic stopped for them at the lights. They entered his house by the kitchen door, and after grabbing some bottles of cider from the fridge, Darren led her upstairs to his bedroom. Grace sat stiffly on the edge of the bed as requested. His room was much larger and more comfortable that hers, as was the bed. Everything was also incredibly tidy. There were no piles of clothes heaped on the floor like in her room, and his school books, together with his laptop, were arranged neatly on his table under the window. Everything looked very clinical. The décor was plain, sporting only natural earth colours and black, and the walls were completely devoid of pictures or posters. She couldn't even see any photographs.

It was only just after six o'clock and therefore still light and warm, but as she watched Darren drawing his heavy curtains, she suddenly felt chilled. He turned on the bedside light and opened one of the bottles of cider. After taking a swig himself, he passed it to her.

'Drink that, it'll help you relax. And don't look so scared. You'll like it, I know you will.'

'I've never had alcohol before. I probably won't like it,' Grace said, tentatively taking the bottle from him.

'I didn't mean the cider. I meant the other thing, silly. Anyway, I'm sure you'll like the cider as well. It's sweet and fruity, just like you.'

He kissed her neck as she took her first sip. He was right, she did like it. It was rather like fizzy apple juice, only tastier and the bubbles made her nose tingle. When they'd finished the first bottle, he opened another one, and then another, and then to both her consternation and relief he got some sort of packet out of the bedside cupboard. It looked like the one they had been shown in that rather uninformative sex education class they'd been given the other week at school, just before Darren had started taking an interest in her. They had been told not to do anything until they were ready, and preferably not unless they were in love. Well, she was in love, and Darren was definitely ready, so she supposed that was alright. At least she would be safe, and he had been right about her liking the cider. Perhaps this wouldn't be so bad after all. He'd already started undressing her, and she instinctively drew away and clenched her shoulders forward. He'd have to turn the light off first.

Grace lay in the dark, flat on her back as stiff as a board, the bedcovers drawn right up to her neck. He had been wrong; she hadn't enjoyed it at all, and was relieved that it was all over. It had been surprising painful, but mercifully very quick.

Darren turned on the bedside lamp and got out of bed. 'I've got to have a slash,' he said.

Grace watched him retreating to his ensuite bathroom, and was transfixed by the sight of his nakedness. She had been right. He looked exactly like a Greek god: broad shoulders, well defined muscles, nice tight butt. She wondered what he looked like from the front. Why had all the Greek gods had their willies broken off? She had never seen a boy without any clothes on before, except when Leroy and she had shared the same bath when they were little, but that had stopped when they were about five or six, and she was sure that didn't really count. The copious amount of cider that Darren had just plied her with, together with her lack of food, was beginning to take effect, and she could feel both her thoughts and vision blur. She began to giggle at the thought of the broken off willies.

Darren turned the bathroom light on and left the door wide open. At home, all bathroom activities, however minor, were undertaken behind a firmly locked door. Although she was finding it more and more difficult to focus properly, she was quite aware of what he was doing. He'd told her, hadn't he? It was taking him ages. The cider had obviously gone straight to his bladder, not to his head like it had with her. She found herself giggling uncontrollably. Darren was flushing the toilet over and over again. Why was he doing that?

'I can't get the thingy to go away,' he complained. 'I'll have to fish it out later.' She could hear herself giggling again.

She was aware that he was walking back to the bed and she wished that her vision wasn't so impaired. Everything had become disjointed and blurred. Her head and body were now feeling very light, and she began to arch her back and wriggle, pressing her head and shoulders deep into Darren's thick luxurious pillows.

He was standing over her now, pulling the bedclothes off, and telling her it was time to go home. She didn't want to go home just yet. She wanted to lie here in all her nakedness, with him looking at her with his penetrating stare, her Greek god.

'I don't want to go yet,' she heard herself saying, as if from somewhere else, up near the ceiling. 'I want to stay here with you.' She was beginning to slur her words, and was saying a lot more things, although she wasn't sure what. Had she told him that she loved him, and that he was the most beautiful boy in all the world? She was patting the mattress and encouraging him to get back in.

She could sense that he was staring at her tiny, pointed, pubescent breasts which she had tried to hide from him before. She pushed her shoulders further back into the mattress so that he would get a better view. She was asking him what they reminded him of. Were they as tasty as her latte-like skin?

'They remind me of those lovely little coconut pyramid cakes,' he said, kissing them very gently, 'the ones that are cooked to a delicious shade of brown, each with a cherry on top. I always leave the cherry till last.'

'Do it to me again,' she heard this new Grace saying. 'But this time leave the light on.'

≈

We're on our way back to her home. I wrap my arm around her shoulders; she's definitely my girl now. That second time was ace. She was so yielding and welcoming just like I reckoned it should be.

'You see, I was right. You did like it, didn't you?' I say. She smiles up at me and nods.

She really reacted badly to all that cider though. She'd sicked up in my loo for ages afterwards, but she's fine now. I'm getting a massive headache. It's as if someone's using my head as a drum kit. We've reached the entrance to her flats, and I'm feeling as if my kidneys are on fire. I nip round the side of the building and prepare to relieve myself in the nearest flower bed. Through the thundering noise in my head I can just hear

Grace pleading with me to stop because I'm killing off all her dad's plants, and anyway someone might see, but it's already too late. I feel like a wild animal scent-marking my territory against any mangy looking ferrets that might come sniffing around her. Nobody else can ever touch her, particularly not that little runt Joel. I can see him and Grace sitting too close together at the back of the class. Everywhere I look, there he is with her: during break, at lunch, doing their homework together in the library, everywhere. She can't do that anymore. She's got to learn that she belongs to me. I drag her to me and pin her against the wall. I'm pushing her back, and I can feel the rough concrete biting into my knuckles. I pull at her flimsy summer skirt and pants and try to force myself inside her, but it's as difficult as the first time, when she was still a virgin. Perhaps she hadn't been a virgin. Perhaps she'd deliberately held herself rigid just as she's doing now. Perhaps that runt Joel's got there first after all. She's beginning to cry out, so I kiss her even though her mouth smells and tastes of sick.

It's over and I let her go. I see her looking up at me like a faithful but confused puppy that's just been whipped. She's whimpering.

'Please don't do it like that again. You really frightened me – and hurt me.'

I hold her to me as gently as I can. I move the strands of wavy hair from around her ear and whisper that I'm sorry. I've never said that to anybody before, but I feel that it's what she wants to hear. I know she loves me, she told me, so why would she want anyone else if she can have me? She puts her arms around my waist and buries her face in my shirt. I can feel the wetness from her tears penetrating the material, but she's calmer now.

'We'll go and see that film of yours on Sunday if you like. If we go to the matinee, we can get some Chinese takeaway and eat it in my room. Dad will be playing golf and Mum will be watching some old film. We'll tell her that we're studying for our exam next week if she bothers to ask. I promise we'll do everything the way you like it best. You do still love me, don't you?'

She nods eagerly up at me, and allows me to kiss her lightly, but this time I keep my lips closed. She's still watching me from the entrance to the flats as I turn the corner into East Street.

The evening air freshens as I walk back over the bridge. The heat of the water below rises and dissipates along with my headache. It won't be so bad seeing that soppy film. We're doing the book for GCSE next year anyway, and with any luck I'll only have to speed read it afterwards. I must remember to buy some more thingies tomorrow; I wasn't expecting to use them all up at once.

I lie on my bed and wallow in the tangled mass of sheets, usually so smooth and clinical; Mum sees to that. I'm definitely going to start locking my room. I don't want her sniffing around in here anymore. I inhale Grace's smell: slightly sweet, a mixture of coffee and coconut. But I can't completely relax, not yet. Even though my head doesn't hurt anymore, it's still reeling. I try to fight my way out of the confusion over how Grace had reacted. It threw me a bit after the first time when she wanted more. It wasn't really meant to be about her at all. I just didn't want to be a virgin anymore. It sounds rather gay if you think about it. I wanted to be a man. All that guff about her enjoying it was just to encourage her. How was I meant to know if she'd enjoy it or not? But I had to say something, didn't I? I didn't want her to suddenly change her mind. And drinking all that cider was for my benefit as much as for hers. I was petrified that I might be rubbish. That's why I chose Grace in the first place, and not that mouthy cow Jenna. They were both blatantly up for it. They both fancy me rotten, but Grace's only friend is Joel, and I can't really see her discussing me with him – particularly not about whether I was any good or not. But the whole world would have known if I'd hit on Jenna – well, Lauren and Kelly at least, but that would have been bad enough. I've heard them whispering about me after class, calling me 'Pretty Boy', 'The Nerd', 'Teacher's Pet'. But Jenna had said that even so, she'd still be up for it if I asked.

And why the hell had you virtually raped Grace outside her flat? If Grace was only a means to an end, why does it matter to you what Joel has, or hasn't, done with her? Why do you always feel this sense of rivalry where he's involved? He's nothing. But for some unknown reason, if something is important to him, then you always want to get in there first.

Anyway, now that Grace says she loves me, Joel's definitely off limits. I've never felt like this before, and I don't much like it. I've never had to share anything before, – ever. Mum and Dad always give me what I want, and that's it; but somehow, things seem to be changing. Perhaps that's what happens when you become a man.

I'll have a word with Joel tomorrow morning: try to get him to open up a bit – tell me what he really thinks about Grace. I can't stand the fact that I can't read him. What, if anything, is going on in that head of his? I'll try and find out tomorrow.

# Chapter 2

## The Morning After

'You're sluggish today, son, and you can't blame it on the weather. The sun's been up for ages.' Ronnie picked at a piece of toast. 'And if you don't get that fry-up down you pronto we'll be late setting up – much less me missing my golf lesson.'

Ronnie knew that he had to reduce his handicap considerably now that he had finally been accepted at South Meadows golf club. He was aware that 'standards had to be maintained'. As part of the emerging nouveau riche in the town, he had to be extra vigilant on this point. The golf club was to be his scene from now on, and he had to be seen to fit in. He had outgrown the dog track, along with the petty criminals who had been useful to him a few years back.

'Hello. Anybody there? You're not even listening, are you Darren? Right: two more minutes and then we're off.'

But Darren was not to be rushed. He was savouring every mouthful of his mum's cooking. His eyes had taken on the soft hue of a lily pond, and his mouth was set in a permanent smile even when he was chewing.

When they finally arrived at the Saturday market on Broadway, Joel was already there waiting for them. Fortunately for Ronnie, Joel was quick and alert this morning, and began arranging the stock on the table in a logical and eye-catching manner as soon as Darren started handing him the boxes from the back of the van.

Ronnie no longer needed the stall at the Saturday market. It no longer fitted his newly constructed image. Its purpose had changed for him over the years. The under the counter-type goods to which his police buddies had either turned a blind eye or had benefitted from had gradually been exchanged for perfectly legal stock for the home improvement enthusiast, and it had become a useful platform on which to advertise his own emerging building company. He was quite aware that he was not a popular figure in town. He knew too much about the people in high places. But knowledge was power, and Ronnie knew how to use this to his advantage. So he usually got what he wanted: controversial planning permission for sensitive sites, being made a Justice of the Peace, and latterly being voted into the golf club.

Although Ronnie no longer needed his stall, for some reason his son seemed to. They'd had a blazing row a few weeks back over keeping it on, but what Darren wanted he invariably got. In defence of his weakness over this, Ronnie argued to himself that in just over a year, when Darren was old enough to drive the van, Ronnie could leave the running of it completely to him. And he'd been heartened by – but rather surprised at – Darren's sudden entrepreneurial spirit.

Ronnie had come over to England from Ireland at the age of sixteen, at the height of the Thatcher era. She had already won a second term in office, along with the Faulklands War. When he'd arrived, the then Secretary of State for Employment had already made his 'get on your bike' speech, encouraging people to take responsibility for their own future success, and this had still been the mood of the government: to look after number one. Ronnie found that this philosophy suited him very well. He'd found buried inside him entrepreneurial skills that had not been allowed to flourish under the dictatorial hand of his father. At first, he had taken a job as a humble labourer with the construction company engaged in building the new Shopping Mall on East Street, but by a twist of fate, everything was to change, first for the worse, and then for the better.

The accident he'd had on the building site some years back had actually proved to be a godsend. From then on life had suddenly begun to improve for Ronnie and his family. His back injury had made it impossible for him to continue in a job that required a high level of physical strength. However, the pay-out from his employers' insurance, together with some dodgy deals – including the selling of illegally imported goods – soon made it possible for them to exchange their council flat for a house on the newly constructed estate on the west side of the river, the development named Western Heights. For a while he had also become a police informant, not one of his proudest moves, but 'needs must' sometimes to keep oneself out of trouble. In one way or another he had gradually begun to mix with the rich and influential members of the town: businessmen, councillors, the constabulary, the Mayor; and his growing prosperity and position had made it possible to start his own building company. He was indeed a typical product of the Thatcher era, although she may well not have condoned his methods used to gain success.

He'd attained the position and standing that his family back in Ireland held, as respected members of the farming community, but he still had ambitions. He was going to take this backwater of a town out of the last century, and bring it up to the present day – in fact, propel it into the future. It had hardly moved on since he'd first arrived. Thanks to the dissatisfaction and greed of an acquaintance of his who worked for the Housing Association, he now had one up on the other building firms in the area. He was made privy to his competitors' tenders ahead of the deadline. But it wasn't just the renovation of old buildings that he had his sights on, he also had plans to buy up any failing shops in the town, refurbish them, then hike up the rents to encourage more profitable businesses into the area.

From where he was standing behind his stall, he could just see part of the premises that he particularly had his eye on. It was a grand Georgian edifice that formed part of a parade of shops fronting Broadway. This one however was at the end of the row, and sported shop fronts on both Broadway and East Street. Apart from the cinema, an even grander building on the opposite corner that had once been a theatre, this shop held the prime spot in town. It was the first one you saw as you crossed the bridge into town. Until recently it had been a drapery shop and gent's outfitters, a business that had been in the same family for generations but had become out-dated and eclipsed by the modern chains housed in the Shopping Mall. Ronnie's dream of one day owning this building had been momentarily dashed when, a few months previously, a 'Sold' sign had gone up in one of its large and prominent windows. But the new owner was, to Ronnie's mind, not a businessman. The shop's potential was not being maximised, and would be back on the market in a year or two, just when Ronnie would be in a position to make an offer for it. He could see an empire building up around him. He would become the most influential man in this town. One day he might even become Mayor.

Ronnie had been surprised when he'd found out who the new owner of the magnificently situated shop premises was: his old friend Theo. He hadn't seen him for over fifteen years.

He hadn't even been aware that he was back in the country. He'd been somewhat offended that Theo hadn't contacted him. He knew why Theo had left: to break free of his old lifestyle of which Ronnie had been a part. But if Theo had cared to do his homework, surely he would have found out that his old friend had changed, that he wasn't the Ronnie of old but a respectable, and respected, businessman? So Ronnie had made the first move. It would give him an excuse to have a good look round his future premises. But Theo had been off-hand and dismissive. 'Ronnie. I wondered how long it would take you to find me.'

'You could have looked me up. I'm not exactly invisible in this town these days.'

'So it would seem. And still with Lorraine, I gather?' Theo had raised his eyebrows while saying this, and Ronnie had bristled, finding him offensive and 'holier than though'.

And that had been it. Ronnie had cast a cursory glance over Theo's jaded and inappropriate stock, and had made his excuses. 'We'll have to meet up sometime, Theo,' he'd said. 'For old time's sake.'

They had started out together as angry young men impatient to discover what they wanted out of life, and frustrated by not finding it. But now that they had, they couldn't have turned out more differently. Theo had become so spiritual that he seemed to Ronnie as no more significant than his superfluous pieces of stock in his equally superfluous shop. What a waste of prime real estate. But he'd keep his eye on the Emporium. Unless Theo bucked up his ideas, his shop would soon be yet another 'white elephant' along with all the other unsustainable businesses in this town.

As he started sorting out the empty boxes in the back of the van, Ronnie watched the two boys as they sat together, and caught a few snippets of the rather one-sided conversation. So that's why Darren had found it so difficult to get out of bed! He hadn't wasted the fact that he and Lorraine were going to be back late last night. How different these two boys were: Darren and Joel. Darren had so much confidence and charisma – a sort of presence – not something that could be applied to this other poor lad. Darren was certainly a son to be proud of, a real 'chip off the old block' – not in looks though, he had to admit. Darren looked exactly like Ronnie's father – tall, blonde and well built – whereas Ronnie himself looked more like his mother. Alright for a woman of course. She'd been considered 'a bit of a cracker' in her day, apparently: slender, with a fair, delicate complexion, dark hair and eyes to match. How Ronnie missed her, but he had vowed never to go back home to Ireland while his father was still living.

Joel was looking distinctly uncomfortable at the turn of the conversation, and Ronnie wasn't at all surprised. The details concerning Darren's conquest were becoming rather graphic, and the less Joel was responding, the more graphic they became. Ronnie couldn't recall ever having conversations quite as informative as this in his day, certainly not with Theo. Ronnie remembered seeing his son with this little girlfriend kissing, and who knows what else, in the alley next to the Off License the other night. No doubt he was taking her home after the cinema. She was the sister of the boy who had drowned a few months ago, wasn't she? Ronnie inwardly shuddered and he could feel his lungs constrict at the memory of the local newspaper headlines: *Local boy missing for three days – discovered drowned.* Apparently he had been washed up a few miles downstream, on the other side of the narrow, fast-flowing section of the river known as 'the rapids'. He would have stood no chance along that stretch. The case had remained a mystery.

There had even been talk of possible suicide. The thought of that boy being swept along in all that water filled Ronnie with anxiety. He instinctively looked over to Darren and Joel, fortunately both very much alive.

The tightness in Ronnie's chest was increasing, making it difficult for him to breathe. The pain behind his eyes was becoming unbearable. He took in a few gasps of air. Like him, Darren was not particularly fond of water, but for a much less sinister reason. Ronnie could still recall all too clearly what had happened on that first family holiday with Darren at the seaside, when he was still a toddler. Lorraine had been nagging him to take Darren down to the water's edge for a paddle. He could hear her now, calling to him from the safety of her sun lounger. 'Go on, get in both of you. You're nothing but a couple of wimps!'

Lorraine knew how to annoy him, how to get him to do something he didn't want to. He had carried Darren to the water's edge, and had sat him down. He could see him now, playing with the fine, wet sand and chuckling with glee as his plump little fingers dug down into it, creating little pools of water around him. At first, the waves had been very gentle, and the water had barely touched his son's toes. Suddenly, a much larger wave had broken and had swept up the beach, knocking Darren over and covering him, salty water filling his mouth and nose. He was choking and unable to scream as Ronnie had carried him, rigid in his arms, back to his mother. After that, they had contented themselves with building large sandcastles, and damming small streams as they meandered lazily to the far-off shoreline. Later on at school, Darren had learnt to swim, but he'd never had the desire to go in if it could be avoided. And he would never jump in, but would slither in from the side of the pool.

'Do you swim at all, Joel?' Ronnie said, as he got his folding bike and golf clubs out of the van.

'Yes, I do actually, Mr O'Donnell,' Joel said. 'I go every Friday after school.'

So that's what the smell was when Joel was around: chlorine. Now he really must get going; he'd have to cycle in record time down Broadway to get to Southern Meadows in time for his golf lesson. Perhaps he'd book one up for Darren as well. It would do him good to try something different, and also give him the chance to make some more suitable friends. What had attracted Darren to Joel: the boy he called the runt?

≈

Joel had been surprised at Darren's father's question. Ronnie rarely spoke to him at all. And of all the things he could have asked him, why that? Joel always went swimming immediately after school every Friday, partly because it was half price, but mainly because he could make sure he was clean for the weekend. There was only cold water at the squat, so after his swim, Joel made good use of the hot showers not only to get himself clean but to wash his shirts and underclothes as well. After washing them with the shower gel provided, he would wring them out in the small tumble drier specially designed for swimwear, and then, if there was no one else in the changing room, he would attempt to dry them off a bit under the hand drier before slipping them into a plastic bag. Later on at home, he would peg them out on the old fashioned overhead airer in the kitchen, ready for school on the following Monday.

But Joel had welcomed Ronnie's rather unexpected question. He was pleased with the natural break it had created from Darren's conversation. He was getting increasingly uncomfortable by all Darren's talk of 'pert little boobs' and other parts of this girl's anatomy that he found even more unfathomable, and also faintly repellent. Didn't Darren realise that he wouldn't even be fifteen for another ten days? He was nearly a year younger than Darren. There was still plenty of time for him to become interested in that sort of thing.

'Can I go for my breakfast now, Darren?' Joel said. 'I'm starving.' His mum had been out all night with Kyle again, and she hadn't been shopping lately either; although, to be fair, she had left a tenner for him on the kitchen table.

'Off you go then mate,' Darren said. 'I can man the stall by myself for a bit. I'm not really hungry at the moment. I'm expecting a visit from Crunch, as it happens. Actually, on second thoughts could you get me a latte to take away, and a couple of those coconut macaroon thingies?'

Joel crossed the street, and entered Eric's steamy café, as he always did on a Saturday morning now that he was working for Darren. He was greeted by the sight of the proprietor, a small, ever diminishing man of about sixty with grey, thinning hair, shuffling around behind his counter, his head permanently jutting forward from many years of stooping over a hot frying pan.

'Full English and a large mug of tea please, Eric.'

Danny, Eric's sullen and expressionless son, was leaning over the tables, brushing off yesterday's crumbs from the seersucker cloths before the morning rush started. The place would be packed in half an hour; the holiday season had already begun. This area of the Wye Valley was popular in the summer. The B & Bs and the camp site just past the golf club were filling up with tourists intent on exploring the river and surrounding countryside: canoeists, kayakers, fishermen and ramblers.

Joel sat down near the window. From here he could get a good view of Darren. He was sitting upright in his chair now, not leaning back as he had been when he'd been boasting about this girl: how she'd been 'gagging for it', and how he was going to give her an even better 'seeing to' tomorrow. Joel had instinctively turned his head away when he'd noticed the bulge growing in Darren's already tight jeans. His old feelings of insignificance had enveloped him again. Darren wasn't really trying to engage him in conversation. He was just trying to put him in his place. Darren was quite obviously the main man, the alpha male.

'How far have you got with your little friend Grace then, mate?' Darren had asked him, with what appeared to be interest laced with a hint of sarcasm.

'It's none of your business, actually,' he'd managed to reply, avoiding Darren's gaze. 'And anyway, that's all she is: my friend.' How could Darren think of such a thing with Grace? She wasn't that sort of a girl.

Danny plonked Joel's breakfast down in front of him, the contents of the plate moving around in the grease in a distinctly unappetizing way. If he made this meal last the whole day, he'd have enough money to go to the cinema later, once Darren had paid him for today's work. They'd be packed up by three o'clock, and he could go to the matinee. He'd invite Grace, and then they could come back here afterwards to discuss it. He couldn't ask her back to the squat. Grace was always so eager to talk, and he found conversation much easier with her than with boys, particularly Darren. Recently, his mind was only ever on one thing.

He could tell Grace about how he was going to lose his home soon, something he hadn't mentioned to anyone yet. She'd understand. She may even be able to suggest what to do. He couldn't imagine that living in a mobile home on the campsite with his mum and Kyle would last very long. Grace would help him. Joel mopped up the last drop of grease with his bread.

'I might see you later, after the cinema, Eric,' he said, as he got up to pay.

'With that pretty little girlfriend, I hope. Not too much snogging on the back row, now.' Joel sighed at Eric's wink as he handed him his change.

# Chapter 3

## The Golf Club Barbeque

I replace my weights under my table next to the window, piling them up neatly. I don't want to go tripping over them. I go back and inspect my naked body in front of my full length mirror. I always work out naked. I have to make sure I don't overdo it. I want my body to be nicely toned, not all sinewy and muscle bound. I look at myself from every conceivable angle. Everywhere has to look good, not just the bits I can see. I inspect Percy as well. I was a bit worried when I discovered that extra thingy in my bedside table. If I'm going to catch anything off Grace, then I want to know straight away.

I dress myself slowly and meticulously in the new lightweight summer suit that Mum insisted on buying for me. She considers it 'essential to be correctly dressed for an occasion such as the golf club barbeque'.

'You're bound to be introduced to some influential people, after all,' she'd said. Actually, now that it's on, it's not too bad as suits go, but my hair's a disaster. What the hell did that tosser of a barber think he was doing last time? It'll take weeks to grow back to anything approaching OK.

'Hurry up now, son. What on earth are you doing up there, you nancy boy?' Shut up Dad, give us a break!

'Oh, don't you look handsome! Doesn't he look handsome, Ronnie? You look about eighteen in that suit, maybe even nineteen,' Mum says as I come down the stairs.

'Yes, yes, my love. I'm sure you're right. But can we just get a move on?' Dad's fidgeting at the front door.

Mum's started to smooth down the material over my shoulders. I wish she wouldn't do that sort of thing anymore. It makes me cringe. I'm a man now, for Christ's sake. I'll end up like that Oedipus character if she doesn't stop handling me.

'You'll be turning all the girls' heads tonight, my beautiful boy,' Mum's saying, in that soppy voice of hers. She's stroking my cheek now, to check if I've had a shave like she told me to. 'I wouldn't be surprised if you found yourself a nice girlfriend.'

'I've got a girlfriend already Mum, as it happens.'

'Have you darling? You've kept that quiet. What's she like?' She's still fussing over my suit, but I manage to shrug her off.

'Tiny little thing she is,' Dad's saying, 'all puppy dog eyes and pouting lips. Now hurry up you two, for Christ's sake. I've got people to see, deals to make.'

But Mum just won't be hurried. 'Tell me about your girlfriend, Darren. I'm sure there's more to her that what your dad's just said.'

'There's lots more actually, Mum.' I glare at Dad as I say this. 'In fact she's the cleverest girl in our class. We're in love, if you want to know. When we've been to Uni, I expect we'll get married.' I'm not quite sure why I say this, but perhaps it'll keep Mum off my back – stop her trying to pair me off with one of her friends' hideous daughters.

I can see Dad making a gagging gesture behind Mum's back, pretending to stick his fingers down his throat. 'Come on now, son. You don't have to go that far just because you've had your wicked way with her.'

'Ronnie, really! You don't have to speak like that to Darren. I think it's really sweet that you're so much in love, my darling. I'm sure she's a lovely girl, and I'm longing to meet her,' Mum says. 'But I hope you're being careful. And you're still rather young – you're not even quite sixteen, you know.'

'Yes Mum, I know. And of course we're being careful.' I could kill Dad for that. 'I'm sure you'll meet her soon. I'll probably be bringing her back here quite a lot, actually. She hasn't got a computer, so we can do our homework together upstairs.'

'That's my boy,' Dad says, and gives me a sly wink. 'Now hurry up and get into the car, will you? Come on Lorraine; leave the poor boy alone. You'll be wearing a hole in that suit if you rub away at it any more.'

We're late as usual. We're on the large paved area in front of the clubhouse and everyone's turning to stare at us. The whole place has been decked out with fairy lights, even on the trees protecting the eighteenth green from the car park, and there are candles on saucers scattered around on small tables ready to be lit later, when it gets dark. It's a perfect evening for a barbeque, still warm, with just a light breath of wind. I don't really need my jacket, but I can't see anywhere obvious to leave it. I don't want some rat-arsed old fart spilling red wine over it or crushing it if I put it over the back of a chair.

There's so much food laid on. There are all these long tables set out to one side, next to the barbeque. They're positively heaving with loads of different types of salads and puddings. The aroma of cooking meat hits my taste buds, making me salivate. Waiters are dodging in and out carrying trays of wine,

45

cider and beer. I take a glass of cider and swig it back before Mum can say anything.

Dad's started introducing me to all these different people, mostly with daughters, but I don't even bother to listen to their names, much less try to remember them. Why should I be interested in any of them? They all look completely up themselves, and either chinless or horsey looking – or both – and none of the girls are even half as fanciable as Grace. I wish she was here now, as it happens. I feel really awkward and out of place. I'm no good at talking to people at the best of times, much less with people I don't know. I excuse myself and stroll over to the barbeque area. If I help myself to a load of food and sit quietly somewhere, perhaps people will just leave me alone.

'All by yourself, darling? I don't think we've been introduced. I'm Fiona Sutcliffe.' I look up from my half empty plate to see this tall, snake-hipped woman sidling up to me on razor sharp stilettos. She leans over to shake my hand, and gives me a view right down the top of her low cut dress, almost to her shoes. She's as thin as a board but goes in and out in all the right places. I'm boiling. I wish I'd taken my jacket off now.

'Pleased to meet you; I'm Darren O'Donnell,' I say, putting my plate down and getting up to shake her proffered hand. Her hands are slender and long, but she has a vice-like grip.

'You're surely not Ronnie O'Donnell's son?' Fiona says. 'I wouldn't have guessed it. Where have you been hiding?' She's giving me a bit of a look that I'm not sure how to interpret. She's tilting her head back, pouting her lips and peering at me with her eyes half closed.

'Well, I'm not actually a member here yet, but I'm thinking of starting lessons soon.'

'Oh, you simply must, darling. I'm sure you'd be very good, a big strong lad like you.' She leans across me to take a glass of wine from the tray of a passing waiter, and I get a blast of expensive smelling perfume. She's invading my personal space, but for once I don't mind.

'Come on now, darling. You must have a little drinky as well. It's impolite not to keep me company,'

Obediently I take a glass. I don't really like wine, but this is a woman you have to obey. I glance at her as I sip my wine, and decide that she's pretty fit for an old bird. I look at her long dark hair that's pulled back off her high forehead and secured with a sort of tiara. Her lips are bright red and match her finger nails, and as she smiles at me, I can't help but see her very white, even teeth.

'What beautiful blue eyes you have, Darren,' she drawls. She knocks back her wine in a couple of gulps and grabs another from the waiter as he moves off. 'Now drink up, my sweet, as I've got a little job for you to do. I'm suddenly feeling rather faint, in fact not very well at all.' She drains her second glass and sits down on the next seat, ending up half on my lap.

'The thing is Darren, my husband will be getting up in a minute to make the longest and most boring speech, and then there'll be the interminable prize giving…' She hiccups slightly. 'So you see, darling, I need someone to escort me home. Do you drive, Darren?' I shake my head. 'I'm surprised at that,' she continues. 'Well never mind; we can walk. The fresh air might do me good, and if I suddenly feel faint I can always lean on you, can't I?' She gets up to go, and takes my hand in one of her ferocious grips again. 'Clive will be ages before he gets home. After all the boring stuff, he's bound to have a few more drinks with his pals. You're not in a rush are you? You'll keep me company, darling?'

The way she says it, I don't think I've got very much choice. She's having these fainting fits quite a lot on the way to her house and I have to keep propping her up, but the fresh air seems to be reviving her, the closer we get to her front door. Now we're inside she's positively frisky, and the way she's dragging me upstairs makes me wonder what's brought about this miracle cure. And the speed with which she's taking my clothes off is quite a revelation. Memories of Mrs Robinson in that old classic film *The Graduate* come flooding back. It's another one of Mum's favourites… I'm not sure I'll be able to watch it with her any more.

'We must do this again,' she says when she's finished with me. 'But ring first, won't you darling? During the day, when Clive's at work.' She doesn't give me her number, but it won't be that difficult to find it.

I get back to the golf club and find Mum and Dad are preparing to leave.

'Where were you, son?' Dad says. 'We're just off. You nearly missed us.'

'Oh, I mingled for a bit, and then I went for a walk. All those speeches went on a bit. Can I change my mind about that golf lesson tomorrow afternoon, Dad?' I'll be great at golf, I just know it, and Fiona reckons I will be too. I'll get my handicap down in no time, whatever that means; I'll just be relying on myself. I hate all that team sports rubbish. None of the wankers at school ever pass me the ball when we're forced to play football, so how can I ever be expected to score any goals and show anyone what I can really do?

Suddenly I can't face seeing that stupid film with Grace, not after what I've just experienced with old Fiona. I'll tell her that

Dad's already booked the golf lesson for me without saying, and I can't get out of it. She'll have to wait to see me another day. We'll be breaking up from school at the end of next week, and then there'll be plenty of time. I'll ring her up tomorrow morning and tell her.

'I've got to see you, Grace. I've changed my mind; I can't wait until next week to see you after all.'

That golf lesson this afternoon was ghastly. It's not quite as easy as I thought, although to be fair, it wasn't my fault that I was so rubbish. That boy in my group who kept coughing just as I was preparing to take my shot didn't exactly help. I'm sure he was doing it on purpose.

I can hear Grace breathing over the line, but she's not saying anything. 'Tell me again what you told me on Friday,' I say.

'What was that?' Grace says. 'I'm sure I said more than one thing.'

'Say what you said when you made me get back into bed.'

'I can't. There's people listening.'

'Whisper it then, or go into another room. Please Grace.'

I wait for ages until I hear her again, but she's speaking so softly that I can only just make out the magic words.

'You're the best and most beautiful boy in the whole world,' she says.

'And what else did you say after that?'

'That I love you.'

That's even better than what she'd said before. 'And you're my very best girl,' I say. 'I'll meet you outside the Shopping Mall in half an hour. I'm treating you to a pizza at Luigi's.'

# Chapter 4

## Grace Continues her Education

Grace sat on Darren's bed, decidedly more crumpled than the first time he'd brought her here. In fact the whole room had assumed an air of neglect. She supposed that he must have tidied up especially for her that first time. She watched him opening his end of term report and test results. Hers were still unopened in her bag. She was always tempted to have a peek before giving it to her parents, but she never did. After all it was addressed to them. Darren was studying his intently. A flicker of annoyance crossed his face, and he snatched at her bag, took out her envelope and ripped it open.

'Darren, you've ruined it. My parents will kill me for opening it before they've seen it.'

'Oh, don't be such a wimp. Of course they won't kill you. Mine couldn't care a toss, so why should yours?' His eyes kept flicking from his set of results to hers. His eyebrows and mouth were both set in a hard, straight line that Grace didn't find very attractive. She leant over to see what was bothering him. On his sheet, he had been placed first in every subject except two: English Literature and Geography, where he had only been placed second. When she looked at her results, she found, amongst her usual seconds and thirds, two firsts.

'English Literature and Geography!' Darren was saying. 'Eng. Lit's fine, you can have that. In fact it's rather embarrassing to be top in that. It shows that you probably enjoyed reading all that crap. But Geography! That's one of my best subjects.'

'I've only beaten you by one mark, Darren. Look.'

'You're a complete and utter swat, Grace. You don't even like Geography much, do you? You're not going to do it for A Level, so why bother? It's so embarrassing the way you suck up to Old Grimthorpe. Anybody would think you fancied him, or something. It's disgusting, actually. No one likes you for it, you know. They all think you're a bit of a joke. The only person that'll even talk to you in class is that stupid little runt Joel, and he only tolerates you because you help him with his homework.'

'Well, nobody likes you either, Darren. They all jeer at you behind your back, and call you 'Teacher's Pet', 'Toady' and even 'Arse Licker'. They all joke that you must have done it with Mrs Jenkins to get such good marks in English.' It had all come out in a rush and Grace immediately wished she could retract it. By now, Darren had her wrists in a vice-like grip, and was pushing her down onto the bed. The look of hatred in his eyes scared her.

'You're such a little nerd. I don't know what I see in you, always rushing home to do your homework when you could be here with me for a bit longer. That's why I don't want anyone at school to know that we're going out. Anyway; what if I had done it with Mrs Jenkins? She's fitter than you. You're not exactly sexy looking, for that matter. You're just an embarrassment.'

51

Grace struggled to stop herself from sobbing. 'You're hurting me, Darren. Get off! You found me sexy enough yesterday. You can't have forgotten.' Yesterday had revealed a creativity in Darren that was completely unexpected. Things were done to her, and also asked of her, that she would never have thought of herself. Yesterday he was the perfect boyfriend, but now he was spoiling everything. She struggled to try and free herself, but the more she did so, the more his grip tightened. He was on top of her now, pinning her down.

'I can't help it if I have to work hard. I'm not clever like you, and I have to do well, especially now Leroy's gone. My parents expect it.' She struggled again, but it was only making it worse. She would have to think fast before Darren did her any serious damage. 'You're lucky, you're so good at everything; it's not fair! And you're so... so sexy as well as being clever.' She felt him relax his grip on her wrists, now nearly numb with pain. This was the second time this week that he'd frightened her. Although the reason for his anger that first time outside her flats was still a mystery to her, this time she was beginning to understand what he did, and did not, like to hear.

'I still think you're the best boy in the world,' she continued, 'even though you're hurting me. Please be nice to me again. I still fancy you, even if you don't fancy me anymore.'

'Of course I still fancy you, you stupid thing.' He finally let go of her wrists and rolled over on his back next to her. 'But you're just so annoying sometimes. It's all your fault that I get so cross. You shouldn't have said all those things. It's really nasty of you, and they're not even true.' He got off the bed and went to look out of the window, his back to her. 'Tell me again that you still love me, and I'll forgive you.'

'Of course I still love you,' Grace said. 'Please be nice to me. I've got to go home with this letter soon, or Mum will be panicking. She always does at the end of term before she sees my results.' She folded her now crumpled letter back into its damaged envelope. 'I could come back again later though, if you want me to.'

Darren re-joined Grace on the bed, and began to kiss her neck and hair. Grace still held herself rigid. The moment had passed and Darren was himself again, but it was still too soon to completely relax.

'I'm busy later,' he said. 'I've got things to do. I'd better be *nice* to you now before you have to go home to Mummy. We don't want her to worry about what her good little girl is up to, do we?' He started to tickle her rather roughly, and they rolled about the bed together laughing, Grace almost hysterically. She hated being tickled. She had detected a slight note of sarcasm in his voice just now, but she chose to ignore it.

# Chapter 5

## Joel Takes a Chance

'Come on, Joel. You must have packed everything by now. It's not as if you've got very much anyway, is it? Kyle's waiting for us outside.'

It was August 2nd, Joel's fifteenth birthday, and eviction day for him and his mother Jeannie. The weather was oppressive and humid. The low lying clouds pushing in from the south-west were streaked with charcoal-grey, presaging a storm.

The pavement outside was filling up with the belongings of their neighbours of the last dozen or so years: dilapidated sofas, beds, tables and chairs, along with cardboard boxes of clothing and knick-knacks. Jeannie had already disposed of what little furniture they had. There'd be no room in Kyle's mobile home for any of it. The estate, which amounted to a couple of streets of identical late Victorian two storey houses, had originally been built by a local factory owner to house his workers, selling them on ninety nine year leases. When the leases ran out, the ownership reverted to the factory owner's great grandson, himself an elderly man at this stage, who had emigrated years ago to Australia, and who took little interest in his inheritance. Squatters, including Joel and his mother, had quickly moved into the empty buildings, successfully avoiding

54

the half-hearted efforts of the new owner's agent to secure them. The local council had had their eye on the properties for years, but it wasn't until they were left to the owner's niece that they were able to purchase them.

Originally, the houses had been earmarked for demolition, but the Housing Association had finally been instructed to refurbish them, and let them out at 'affordable' rents. A large sign had been erected on the corner of the street, displaying an architect's impression of the finished result, and at the bottom of the sign, in large letters, was the name of the building firm that had won the tender: R. O'Donnell Construction Ltd.

'Not that the likes of us could ever afford the rent,' Jeannie had said with a toss of her head, although Joel had eventually managed to persuade her to put their names down on the council waiting list for one.

'Is that it then, Jeannie?' Kyle said, after loading their meagre possessions into the back of his car.

'Joel, wait!' He turned to see Grace hurrying towards him. She handed him a small, beautifully wrapped package. 'Happy birthday. It's nothing special – a bit silly really. What else did you get?'

Joel shrugged. He hadn't been given anything else. He supposed that his mum had been too stressed to remember it was his birthday.

'Nobody told me it was your birthday, Joel,' Kyle said. 'Why didn't you say? Jeannie and I are going for fish and chips later. I suppose you'd better come too. Anyway, who's this, your girlfriend?'

'This is Grace, my best friend from school. And Grace, this is Kyle, my mum's boyfriend,' Joel said, not addressing Kyle directly. He'd never had to introduce anybody to him before, and he wished he didn't have to. He encouraged Grace to move further down the street, out of earshot.

'I don't think my moving in with Mum and Kyle is going to work,' he said. 'He doesn't like me very much, and his caravan's really too small for three. Have you managed to think of anywhere else I can stay? You said you might.'

'Well, there's somewhere that could just do as a last resort, I suppose; but it's really small, with no loo and nowhere to wash. Try and give Kyle a chance first. It might not be too long before you can move back here anyway.'

'It'll be a few months, at least. I don't think I'll be able to put up with it that long.'

'Text me soon and we'll meet up. You know I'll help if I can,' Grace said. 'You'd better go; they're glaring at us. Have a good birthday. I hope you like the present.'

Joel had had enough of his new home after two days. The weather hadn't helped. The rain had continued to lash down on the metal roof of the caravan, creating small explosions of sound that reverberated around everything inside. Nothing seemed stable – or permanent. Fortunately, Jeannie and Kyle spent most of their time drinking in the clubhouse bar, leaving Joel alone with his thoughts. The space was cramped for two people, impossible for three. Joel particularly hated the night time. His banquette seat that served as his bed in the kitchenette area, was separated from Jeannie's and Kyle's sofa bed by only a curtain, giving visual but not auditory privacy, and not even that if one of them needed to use the bathroom. Joel was weary and fractious through lack of sleep. Jeannie and Kyle both drunk heavily into the night, becoming more vociferous the later it become, and also needing the loo regularly. Joel had tried to 'escape' on numerous occasions, but somehow he seemed to have lost the knack.

He would leave tomorrow morning. See what Grace had managed to find for him. He wished she'd answer her phone or at least reply to his texts. What was she doing? He needed to talk to somebody. He'd even tried Darren, but he'd had no luck there either.

He started to pack, ready for an early start. He couldn't stay any longer, not after the conversation he'd just overheard. 'I've got to move on in a few days,' he'd heard Kyle tell his mum. 'There's no work for me around here at the moment. My mate John says to go west, to meet up with him on this fruit farm. We could both get a job there for a couple of months.'

'What about Joel?'

'What about him? He's fifteen now, for Christ's sake, Jeannie. He must have friends he can stay with. He'll have to go back to school in about four weeks, anyway. I can't guarantee we'll find another caravan site near a school that'll take him. It's illegal for him not to go to school at his age, isn't it?'

'Yes, I suppose it is,' was all his mum had said.

Joel rolled his clothes up neatly before putting them into his rucksack. He found that he could get more in that way, and they didn't get so creased. He'd have to leave his winter coat behind though. His mum was sure to be back before it got that cold, wasn't she? Perhaps they'd be in their new flat by Christmas. He looked at the present Grace had given him one more time, before packing it safely between his sweatshirts. He remembered how she'd told him of the little carved figure of the Buddha that she'd seen, and how it had looked like him when he was in one of his trances. Did he really look like that? The face looked so peaceful and serene, a faint smile playing around his full lips. The nose was long and straight, and the eyes, although closed, were obviously large. The face was neither definitely male nor female, although the figure as a whole looked male. Joel went into the tiny shower room and looked into the mirror. Yes, Grace was probably right. There was a resemblance, except for his long hair that nearly reached his shoulders, the fringe flopping over his face like a curtain. Perhaps Grace would cut it for him. She had said she would.

He tried her mobile again, and this time he got through. 'I'm leaving tomorrow morning, Grace. Can we meet?'

'Sorry Joel, I can't hear you; the line's really bad.' Joel could hear noises in the background: a boy's or possibly a man's voice, interspersed with Grace's. 'Stop it. In a minute…' Grace was whispering and giggling. 'Look, I've got to go now. Ring again tomorrow. Bye.' He heard a rustling sound, and then the line went dead.

Joel was showered, packed, and ready to go by eight thirty the next morning. He'd already counted out the money he'd saved: quite a satisfactory amount. Most of it was from Darren, for both his Saturday job at the market, and for the extra he got for delivering Darren's packages – plus the odd bung he gave him now and then. Joel knew very well that the packages were illegal and involved drugs, but he never looked inside before delivering them. He'd rather not know. Anyway, it all made him feel rather grown-up, almost as grown up as Darren himself. Joel had seen the man called Crunch who came to the stall in the early mornings sometimes when they were setting up. He could tell that he had something to do with it. He would meet Darren at the back of the white van carrying a couple of small boxes with the name of an electrical firm on them. Darren would always put them straight in, right at the back, and would never open them to put the contents on the stall to sell. Money would then change hands, a discussion would take place, and then later that day Joel would be given his instructions as to what he had to deliver and to where.

Joel couldn't remember Darren ever asking him if he was prepared to do this extra work. He'd just said something like, 'Here mate, I've got another job for you. Not a bad little earner as long as you're careful.' Joel knew why Darren made him do the deliveries. It was too risky for him with his distinctive appearance. And Darren had made it quite clear that if he ever got caught he was on his own. Joel didn't mind though. He liked helping him, and was proud to be asked, and anyway he wouldn't be caught, he was sure. He could go anywhere at all and not be noticed. Sometimes he felt as if he didn't really exist. He was never acknowledged in the lifts on the housing estate, or on the wide, sweeping staircases of the mansion flat buildings in the grander parts of town. It was always the same places, always the same routine. He would be ushered into a kitchen where the packages would be weighed and checked off from a list, then he would be handed an envelope to give to Darren. Darren paid well for everything that he wanted him to do, and seemed to be pleased with the results. Joel blushed a little. He was afraid that he might have developed a bit of a crush on him.

The synchronised snoring had stopped, and Joel could hear sounds of movement behind the dividing curtain. The sofa bed was being folded away.

'Are you there, Mum? he said. 'I've decided to go and stay with my friend Grace for a bit. We might even go and see her sister in Wales.'

Jeannie popped her head around the curtain. 'Wait a minute, Joel, won't you? Give us a chance to get up. Hurry up, Kyle.

Joel's going.' Shortly afterwards, the curtain was drawn back to reveal a rather dishevelled and hung-over pair.

'I'll need some money, Mum. I can't expect Grace's mum to feed me the whole time, can I?'

'I haven't got any,' Jeannie snapped. 'Kyle, what've you got?'

'Me? I'm not his dad. It's not my job to feed him.'

'Well, if I knew who my dad was, I'd be asking him for some, wouldn't I? But I don't.' Joel glared at his mum, and earned himself a slap on the face from Kyle. Its force projected him onto the corner of the sink unit, its sharp edge making contact with his shoulder.

Jeannie flushed. 'I might find you something, I suppose.' She rummaged in her bag and took out a twenty pound note. Joel took it, but kept his hand out. She miraculously found another. 'That will have to do. You've completely cleaned me out now.' She gave him a peck on the cheek as he moved to the door. 'Keep in touch. We'll be back before you know it.'

Joel stepped outside and breathed deeply, expelling the acrid air of confrontation. Once free of the campsite gates, his pace slackened. The rain had at last stopped, and everything smelt fresh and new, just like his life was going to be from now on. He was entering a new phase, where he could decide what to do. Head down, he tentatively negotiated the towpath into town, his trainers sinking and squelching in the mud. High bushes crowded in on him, then suddenly dispersed as he reached the riverbank. A breeze lifted and clawed at the tangles in his hair. He raised his head and the sun caught him a blow on the side of his head. Snatches of this morning's argument returned but were soon pushed away, although the burning sensation in his shoulder was beginning to trouble him.

He shifted the weight of his rucksack and leaned over the embankment wall. A single pleasure boat bobbed in the water, its long shadow moving restlessly to and fro. What if he just jumped into it, freed the ropes, and allowed it to transport him somewhere – anywhere? But then a family emerged from the cabin and his fantasy shattered.

He needed the comfort of food. By now he'd reached Broadway, where the embankment widened to allow space for the Saturday market stalls. He'd have breakfast in Eric's Café, courtesy of his mum. As he opened the café door the steamy air, replete with the cloying odours of yesterday's cooking, enveloped him like a wet towel. He chose a chair next to the counter and sat down, allowing forgotten crumbs to stab through his threadbare jeans.

'Full English and a mug of tea as usual please, Eric.' The clock above the counter announced 8.30am, still too early to ring Grace.

'Coming right up, young man. You're early today. Going somewhere? First coach will be in soon.'

Joel shook his head and allowed his eyes to wander around the empty space. Reluctant rivulets ran down the windowpanes, only to morph into unwanted puddles. It had always looked the same in here, as long as he could remember. The pictures hanging on the walls – of places he didn't recognize – had gradually faded to an unearthly shade of pale blue, while the walls had done just the opposite. They were getting a darker shade of yellow by the day. The only exception was a patch left by a picture now vanished, his favourite, the one of the *Chinese Lady* with the bluish green face and red lips and the far-away look in her eyes.

'How long have you owned this place, Eric?'

'Ooh, donkey's years, son. Ever since my old father died, God rest his soul. I must have been working here for nigh on forty years in all, and it hasn't changed a bit. Except for this new-fangled contraption, mind.' Eric thumped the side of his hot drinks machine. 'My pride and joy, that is.' It spluttered and hissed in response.

'You were lucky working with your dad,' Joel said. 'I've no idea what I'm going to do next summer when I leave school.'

'It's not easy these days, getting a job,' Eric said. He flipped the already scorched rasher of bacon over in his pan. 'There must be something you fancy doing though, a bright young lad like you. I've seen you and your mate Darren setting up his stall on a Saturday. I've watched you arranging all the stock. You do a lovely job at that, Joel. Much better than Darren. You've definitely got the eye.'

Joel turned around and tried to imagine how the stall looked from here on a Saturday morning. He could see Darren sitting behind it, so confident, and somehow glowing. Of course, it was his dad's stall really. All these dads helping their sons. Where was his, and why did his mum refuse to talk about him? All she'd ever said was that one day he'd decided that there were more important things in his life, and he'd just upped and left. Once, when he'd tried to ask her again after she'd been drinking, she'd shouted at him and told him to mind his own business, and he hadn't liked to mention it again. He flinched as the burning sensation in his shoulder returned. Darren and Grace were more like a family to him than anything else he'd had. Grace looked after him better and took more interest in his welfare than his real mum did. Darren wasn't really like how he thought a father should be, but he certainly looked out for him in his own way.

Eric slapped down his overcooked offering in front of Joel with a flourish, and shuffled back behind his counter in his slippered feet. A solitary mushroom broke cover from behind the sausage and floated away in a sea of oil. Joel teased the sausage with his fork. A spurt of fat shot upwards, only to expire on the stained tablecloth. Joel knew that Darren was a bully and a coward, of course, but he still respected him. He never physically assaulted the smaller boys like him. He'd seen him give Ben a good kicking after school once, but he'd probably provoked him, and anyway, Ben was nearly as big as Darren, so that didn't really count. He'd also seen Darren make a quick getaway when there was more than one of them on his case. He could remember him locking himself into a cubicle in the boy's changing rooms once throughout the whole of break, but he didn't blame him for that. There was no point in getting a pasting if you could avoid it. He was also aware that Darren had only homed in on him because he was small and easier to boss around, but he didn't object to that. He was quite happy to be told what to do by him – not by anybody else though, especially not Kyle.

The coach had arrived, its breaks hissing like a wildcat. A horde of raucous holidaymakers were jostling amicably for empty seats. Eric's surly son Benny miraculously appeared with cloth in hand, scattering leftovers from seersucker folds.

'Are these seats taken, son?' A burly prop forward moved towards his table. A chunky shoulder made contact with his as chairs were rearranged. He flinched and moved closer to the wall in an attempt to protect his injury.

It was 9.00am; his mum and Kyle would be on the road, but it was still too early to ring Grace. What if she didn't pick up? What if he hadn't got anywhere to stay tonight?

'Cheer up, Joel, it may never happen,' Eric said, catching the boy's mood as he got up to pay. 'Something will turn up. It always does. See you on Saturday, my lad.'

# Chapter 6

## Joel Meets Theodore Kitchen

Joel decided that he'd hang around in the Shopping Mall for a while. There must be something in one of the shops that he could spend his mum's hard fought money on. He probably actually needed things anyway: toothpaste for instance. Where was he going to be able to clean his teeth though? Even if Grace had got somewhere he could stay, she'd said that there were no washing facilities, not even a loo. He could use the public toilets by the town bridge in the mornings, but he suspected that they closed quite early in the evenings. He'd better buy some chewing gum just in case.

As he was turning the corner from Broadway into East Street he saw him sitting there in the shop window, his little Buddha, only this one was massive, about ten times the size of the one Grace had given him. The hair on his head had been intricately chiselled to reveal little spiky tufts, and the wood had been burnished all over to give him a soft golden glow. He had been placed at a slight angle so that he could look out onto the bridge and to the river beyond. Joel cast his eye over the rest of the display and decided that 'display' was the wrong word for it. It was just a hotchpotch of unrelated items thrown in to fill the space. Everything looked dusty and abandoned, except for the few areas where stock had been taken out and not replaced, rather like Eric's missing picture. Joel had never even noticed this shop before, and he wasn't really surprised, although the building itself was magnificent, taking advantage of its position by sweeping around the corner in a flamboyant curve, and mirroring that of the cinema opposite.

The entrance to the shop was set half way along the shop front, and enjoyed the same views over the river as the gigantic Buddha. Joel looked up at the sign over the door: The Emporium: Proprietor, Theodore Kitchen… followed by a series of capital letters that meant nothing to him. Joel rolled the proprietor's name around on his tongue and decided he liked it, but he liked the magnificent Buddha even more. He would have to go inside.

The first impression that struck Joel as he entered wasn't visual, but olfactory: something exotic, strong, and decidedly heady. As his eyes grew accustomed to the gloom he was able to pinpoint the source of the smell to a bunch of incense sticks. They were in a carved wooden container rather like a giant pencil pot that was placed on what Joel took to be the proprietor's desk. He read the label sitting next to it, written out in the neatest and most artistic handwriting that Joel had ever seen: *19th century Japanese brush pot – £25.*

'Good morning, young man!' Joel turned to see a rather short man about the same age as Kyle coming out from the back of the shop, carrying a cup of coffee. Joel liked the look of him at once. He liked his neat goatee beard, and his smart, snappy-looking clothes, stylish but still managing to look comfortable. He was sporting a yellow waistcoat over a long sleeved, open necked shirt, finished off at the wrists by a pair of wooden cufflinks carved in the shape of an elephant. He had to be the author of the handwritten label. But why were the man and his labels so neat, when his shop was such a shambles?

'Can I help you at all, or are you "just browsing," as they say?'

'Oh, I suppose I was just browsing, although I came in because of the big Buddha in the window. My friend Grace has just bought me a smaller one for my birthday. She says that I remind her of it sometimes.'

'So you're the mystery birthday boy are you? I was hoping to meet you. Your friend told me quite a bit about you. I'm Theo, by the way.' Joel took his proffered hand and shook it; it felt compact and dry. 'Now, tell me about these trances of yours. They sound fascinating. I'm into meditation myself. I took it up when I stayed at a Buddhist monastery a few years ago when I was living in Thailand. In fact I did a lot of travelling back then – Laos, Cambodia, China. I even got as far as Tibet. I had lessons in meditation from the monks, but it seems to me that you've taught yourself a form of it all by yourself. When did it all start… and why?' He sat down behind his desk and blew lightly across the surface of his coffee before taking a sip. 'Put your rucksack down and take a seat. Would you like a coffee?'

Joel refused the coffee, but gladly took the seat. He suddenly felt weary after his early start. He'd never really discussed his 'escaping' with anyone – not even Grace – but Theo not only seemed genuinely interested and knowledgeable, he also appeared to consider Joel's behaviour quite acceptable. So he decided to confide in this stranger. He smiled for the first time today. He'd left home less than two hours ago, and he'd already found a new acquaintance, someone who'd noticed that he actually existed. So he told him how it had all started just as a game in the cupboard and of how it had gradually changed into a retreat from the world, a world that invoked boredom, loneliness and fear, and often a feeling of inadequacy.

'The trouble is,' Joel said, 'I can't seem to control when it happens any more. It gets me into a lot of trouble at school. I don't think I'm going to do very well in my exams next year because of it, and then I won't be able to get a job.'

'What you need is some discipline, young man. In fact, what you need is to come back here this evening for one of my meditation classes. It sounds to me that what you're doing is more a form of self-hypnosis, and that will only push your fears deeper into your subconscious. True meditation will help to free you of them altogether. Don't worry, the classes are absolutely free. I just like to spend my time with like-minded people... and hope that they'll buy some of my books! Here, take this.' He handed Joel a small book with a picture of the Buddha on it, entitled *Meditation for Beginners*, which was hiding amongst the general detritus on his desk. 'You can have it. It's a bit shop-soiled so I'll never be able to sell it. But you must promise that you'll be back here at 6.30 this evening. Make sure you come on an empty stomach, mind. Afterwards, there'll be a few nibbles and drinks: non-alcoholic of course. You'll be the youngest, but we're a friendly crowd. Your Mum won't mind you coming along, will she?'

'Oh no, she's away at the moment, so I can do what I like.' Joel picked up his rucksack and headed for the door clutching his new book. 'Thanks for this. I'll see you this evening.'


'It sounds great Joel, but you don't know anything about this Theo bloke, do you?' Grace said, when Joel told her all about it.

Joel felt his excitement dissipate at Grace's apparent lack of enthusiasm. 'He had a poster about it on the door, so I'm sure it'll be OK. It only lasts about an hour and a quarter. I'll be out before eight.' Was this what mothers were meant to be like?

'I'll walk along with you as far as the shop door then. As you say, I'm sure it'll be fine. Hey, we haven't seen your new home yet. Come on, you'll need this. I got a spare one cut.'

Joel took a large key from her. It looked more suitable for a cupboard than a front door. He followed her down on the lift to the ground floor and was directed to a brown painted door with the number twelve painted on it, one of the many in a row that circled the staircase and lift shaft. Joel put the key in the lock, and on opening the door he found that it was indeed a cupboard, but quite a large one. He reckoned it must be at least two metres long by nearly as much wide, and one of the side walls was completely taken up by floor to ceiling shelving housing paint pots, jam jars full of screws and an assortment of garden implements.

'I'm afraid it's not very exotic, Joel, although it does have an electric light. Of course there's no window, but there are grilles on the outside wall and the door, so you won't suffocate. It's my dad's store, but so long as you've tidied your stuff away and don't use it during the day, I'm sure he won't notice. They used to be for people who had an allotment, but they all went after they built the Shopping Mall. My dad just has a flower bed to look after now.'

'It's great,' Joel said. 'I like cupboards. They make me feel safe. Is there anything for me to sleep on? The floor looks a bit hard.'

Grace pointed to a faded sun lounger sporting large yellow sunflowers folded up against the back wall. 'I thought you could use that, although you have to be careful getting on and off it. It's a bit unstable. And I've found you a sleeping bag as well. I think it was bought for Leroy when he went to Scout camp, but he only used it a couple of times. You'll have to fold it up into the bag each morning though, which can be a bit tricky. Right, let's get back upstairs now. I'm longing to cut your hair. We must get you looking smart for this evening.'

Joel sat very still as Grace wielded her mother's hairdressing scissors. He hoped she knew what she was doing. An awfully large quantity of his long dark locks seemed to be ending up on her kitchen floor. She'd assured him that her elder sister Faith was a hairdresser, but he wasn't sure if that made any difference.

'I love the way that bit of hair grows at the front,' Grace said. 'It looks really cool now it's short.'

Joel's hand automatically went up to his forehead to discover an unfamiliar tufty bit of hair sticking upright. He'd never really been interested in his appearance before, but because Grace obviously was, he suddenly found that he was too.

'Now, go and wash your hair in the shower, Joel. You can use my towel. It's the pink one.'

When Joel had showered, he buried his head in Grace's pink, fluffy towel and breathed in her scent. She was the kindest and most wonderful person in the whole world. She always knew exactly what to do for the best. As he dried himself on her towel, he imagined her kindness and concern entering every pore of his body.

Grace was knocking on the bathroom door. 'I've left some of Leroy's clothes outside the door for you. They were Christmas presents for him last year. You might as well have them. They've hardly ever been worn. It seems such a waste.'

Joel could hardly believe what she had sorted out for him: a pair of fashionably faded jeans, a brilliant white T-shirt and a rather expensive looking leather jacket – all the sort of clothes he would have chosen for himself if he'd had the chance. When he was dressed in his new attire, he applied some hair gel that he saw sitting on the shelf over the wash basin. He paid particular attention to the newly constructed quiff. Yes, he agreed with Grace, it was definitely very cool.

Later on, when they were walking down East Street on the way to Joel's meeting at the Emporium, Grace teased him.

'You can't stop looking at your reflection in all the shop windows, can you Joel, now that you're looking so hot!'

'You said I looked really cool earlier. Make up your mind,' Joel said, laughing for the first time in ages. The smells from her towel and bath products were still encompassing him, making him feel special. He pulled himself up to his full height of five foot three inches and imagined himself as tall and impressive-looking as Darren.

'I might not be able to see you again this evening, Joel. But I'll get up really early tomorrow morning and knock on your door. I'll look forward to hearing all about this meditation business.'

The door to the Emporium had the 'Closed' sign showing when Joel arrived, and he almost turned round to catch up with Grace, but Theo had already spotted him from inside the shop.

'Come on in, young man. Nice and punctual I see. We're all here now except for one, but I'm afraid she's usually a little late. Come and meet everybody. You've only missed one week, so I'm sure you'll manage just fine.'

Theo led Joel to a part of the shop that he hadn't noticed before. Some chairs had been placed in a circle around a table that appeared to be a library area, created by a bank of bookshelves laden with books on Comparative Religion, Meditation, Greek and Roman Mythology, Theosophy and other strange sounding subjects that Joel knew nothing about. He stood still as Theo introduced him to the other members of the group, trying desperately not to let his mind wander as he was told their names in turn. He knew he wouldn't be able to remember any of them. However, the general overall impression of the group was favourable. Although he was obviously the youngest, the age range was so vast that somehow it didn't seem to matter. There were a couple of men who looked between twenty five and thirty and several middle aged and elderly women. The old boy who looked about eighty five didn't seem to mind that he was the oldest, so why should it matter that he was the youngest?

'Ah, good! Here's our latecomer. Come on in and join us Phoebe. Meet our new member, Joel, a recently acquired friend of mine.'

Joel was introduced to a slightly flustered looking girl of about twenty whose wild, wavy, rather unkempt locks reminded him of Grace's when she'd been out in the wind. He liked the look of her at once and complied with alacrity when she suggested that they sit together. Joel had decided to concentrate as hard as he could this evening. There would be no 'escaping' if he could possibly help it. Everyone was taking a seat as Theo prepared to address them.

'Welcome, all of you. I'm glad that our first session didn't deter anyone from continuing along our quest for enlightenment. Obviously, we all have our different reasons for taking up meditation. Some of us will be going along the spiritual route, others will be hoping to relieve the pressure brought on by the demands of their job and a third group will be trying to release the demons stored away deep in their subconscious minds. Now, as I explained to you last week, this personal journey will not necessarily be an easy one, but like everything else in life, meditation becomes easier with regular practise at the same appointed times each day, preferably first thing in the morning and again in the evening. But not on a full stomach, or you're likely to get indigestion. Don't make it a chore though, and finish the session if you're unable to relax, or if you feel you're going to sleep. The first thing is to get into a suitable sitting position. Only the very fittest and most agile of us will be able to maintain the Buddha's pose for very long, so I suggest we all sit upright in our chairs.'

Joel longed to sit cross-legged on the floor just like his little wooden statue, but for now he would go with the flow, and try to concentrate on what Theo was saying.

'Draw yourself up and relax your shoulders, and be aware of nothing but your breathing. Breathe in slowly and deeply through your nose and then out even more slowly through your mouth. If you feel any tension anywhere in your body, try to release it with your next outward breath.'

After what seemed to Joel like an age, Theo began to speak once more.

'This week we are going to use a different visualization exercise, one that we should all be familiar with. First, close your eyes and direct your sight upwards to a position in the centre of your forehead. Imagine a fast flowing river running through the middle of your brain, flowing in one ear and out the other. Allow whatever thoughts coming into your head to flow along the river. Be mindful of their existence, but do not dwell on them. Concentrate your attention on the far bank of the river and allow your thoughts to be taken along with the current. Gradually, the flow of the river will diminish. It will become narrower and will finally dry up. You will then be able to cross unimpeded to the far bank. Be open, alert, and just allow this to happen, and don't worry if at first you fail. In fact, getting to the other bank could take weeks.'

Joel could imagine this type of river very well; the type in which Leroy had drowned. He could imagine him being buffeted around against the rocks. He was aware that his palms were becoming sweaty. It hadn't been his fault, he hadn't known that Darren was taking him to that dangerous stretch that day, and even if he had, he wouldn't have known that it would all end in disaster. He was conscious that his breathing was becoming shorter and shallower. This wasn't working at all. Theo's calming voice was telling them to remember their breathing: to relax into any tension that they may be experiencing.

Joel concentrated on the far bank of his raging river and soon Leroy was out of sight, only to be replaced by other demons, all fighting to be recognised and acknowledged: his mother and Kyle arguing with each other whilst ignoring him, his absent and unknown father, his sister long gone to who knows where, his lack of a proper home. Grace's cupboard was alright in the summer when it was warm and light in the evenings, but what was going to happen if his mum didn't come back when the days begun to shorten – when it started to get cold and dark? He breathing was becoming faster and more shallow, his head felt light and his whole body was starting to feel cold and clammy. What if Grace decided for some reason that she didn't have time for him anymore? What would he do then? She'd obviously got other friends that he didn't know. Who was she giggling with on the phone yesterday? She was often off doing other things where he wasn't included. Where was she going to this evening for instance? If he kept concentrating on the river he might see her flowing by, out of his life for ever.

'If you're finding it difficult to let go, return to your deep breathing, relax, and try to become nothing but an observer. Watch your thoughts flow along the river and out of your line of sight. Concentrate only on the far bank. You are the maker of your destiny. Be open, aware and accepting, and those things that really matter in your life will become apparent. Everything else will just melt away.'

Joel tried again, but he was beginning to feel pins and needles pricking his hands and feet. He shifted in his chair, trying to make himself more comfortable, but the more he tried to relax the more impossible it became. But at least he wasn't escaping into one of his trances.

'Now, in your own time; open your eyes, stretch your arms and legs, and then release all tension and relax.'

Joel knew that he hadn't done it right at all, and had ended up giving himself a headache, but because of this he was determined to persevere. He accepted a drink of apple juice and some nuts without thinking. Things around him were becoming blurred and diffused. He was aware that people were talking, but it was all just noise to him.

Theo was approaching. 'Don't despair just yet, Joel. I could see that you were struggling. You've obviously got a lot of issues to work through, but it will get easier if you allow it to. Actually, I've just had a totally unrelated thought. How would you like a few hours work in the shop? The stockroom is getting extremely cluttered and I'm expecting another delivery in the next few days. I could only give you the minimum wage I'm afraid, but it would be cash in hand. Just say though, it if doesn't appeal.'

'Oh yes, I'd like to help, if you think I'd be any good,' Joel said. He was sounding too eager, he must slow down. 'I could come tomorrow if you like... although I might be away next week.'

'Excellent. I'll expect you at about two o'clock tomorrow then. I'll say goodnight now. I think your friend Grace is waiting for you outside.'

'I'm not doing anything after all this evening,' Grace said as he went to greet her. 'Something "came up" apparently. I guessed you'd be hungry, so I've got us some fish and chips. Let's cross the road and eat it on that bench by the river. Quick, before that couple beats us to it. How did it go, by the way?'

'Oh, fine,' Joel said. 'I think I've got myself a holiday job.'

Looking back over the events of the day, Joel feels his spirits lift. It seems as if Eric was right this morning. Something has turned up already. His confrontation with his mum and Kyle seems light years away. They are both just a speck on the distant horizon – about to vanish over the edge of his world – and this thought no longer frightens him. He feels his constant need to 'escape' melting and diffusing into the fast cooling atmosphere of the evening. The traffic lights are changing from amber to green.

'Come on then, I'm starving! I hope they put salt and vinegar on the chips.'

# Chapter 7

## Joel's Holiday Job

Joel's alarm on his mobile phone is going off. He grabs it from under his carrier bag full of clothes that acts as a pillow, and turns it off. It's 6.45am: time to get up. He'll try his hand at meditating, and then he'll get dressed, tidy up the cupboard, have a wash at the public conveniences, and afterwards wait until 7.30am when Eric opens up for breakfast.

Last night, he had found out just what Grace had meant when she'd told him that the sun lounger was unstable. Your weight had to be distributed just right, otherwise you would find yourself either being tipped suddenly backwards against the end wall or alternatively head-first towards the door. This morning, when he's confident that he's found the strange contraption's centre of gravity, he tentatively crosses his legs, closes his eyes, and puts his hands palms upwards on his upper thighs. He concentrates on sitting upright and observes the rise and fall of his breath as he waits for the thoughts going through his mind to become stilled. But he knows within a very short time that it isn't going to work. Try as he may, he's unable to quieten the demands of his bladder. He'll have to dress first, have his ablutions, and then come back and try again.

By the time he gets to the town bridge conveniences it's just coming up to 7 o'clock, and much to his relief the cleaner is in the process of opening up. However, by the time he gets back to the flats, several of the occupants are already on the move, leaving for work. So great was his need to relieve himself earlier, that he has failed to pack his sleeping bag and bed away, although luckily he does have his rucksack with him. What if Grace's dad needs to go in for something before he goes to work? This really isn't a good start. Grace may decide that it's all too risky, that he's not worth the hassle after all. He's aware of the pain in his shoulder once more as he adjusts his heavy rucksack that carries all his worldly goods. He moves away from the entrance to the flats. He'll have to give Grace a ring.

'I think you may have got away with it today, Joel. My dad's just leaving. He has to get to work early this morning, so I doubt if he'll look in the store. I'll meet you at Eric's in half an hour,'

Joel walks back to Broadway and sits on the bench that he and Grace occupied last night. He's surprised at how many other people are up and about: joggers, dog walkers, commuters, shop owners. There's no way he can meditate here. With some relief he decides he'll have to forgo this morning's session.


Two o'clock couldn't come quickly enough for Joel. He'd been hard pushed to know what to do with himself after breakfast. Grace had told him that she was going out for the day, but from tomorrow she would be free all the time for the next two weeks. Luckily the weather was fine, and he'd gone for a long walk along the river in the opposite direction to the campsite, but his heavy rucksack was becoming an encumbrance.

'Why don't you come with me to Cardiff for the weekend, Joel?' she'd said. I'm catching the coach tomorrow at about 5 o'clock. I'm sure my sister won't mind. We can make up the sofa bed for you. I don't know what my parents would make of it, but they don't need to know, do they? And it's my birthday on Saturday. We can go out and celebrate.'

Joel had readily agreed. Darren wouldn't need him on the stall this Saturday because he was going to Greece with his parents for ten days.

Two o'clock finally comes, and Joel is shown into the stockroom at the rear of Theo's shop.

'Put your rucksack down in the corner, Joel, out of the way. Are you going away this evening then?' Theo says.

'No, not until tomorrow evening, but there's things in it I'll need later on.' Joel looks around the badly neglected stockroom. The shelves surrounding the walls are half full of mismatched items of stock: candles of all colours and sizes, table lamps and shades, carved wooden boxes and Buddhas, cushions, throws and much else; and the bare wooden floor can hardly be seen for piles of sealed cardboard crates.

'Where do I start?'

'A good question, my boy. I've been rather remiss of late, what with all the new orders coming in after the Trade Fair. If you could just try and put some logic into it all, that would be great. Oh, and empty as many crates as you can, and feed in whatever you can onto the shelves somewhere. I'll leave it all in your capable hands. We'll have a cup of tea in an hour or so.'

The next morning, Joel is again on his way to the Emporium, this time to Theo's flat over the shop. Although praise had been heaped upon him for his efforts of the day before, there's still a little more to sort out before the next influx of orders are expected, and Joel has been invited to breakfast before starting work. He walks past the shop-front as it sweeps around the corner into Broadway and looks once more at Theo's window display. That's the job that he wants. Arranging the tools and boxes of DIY equipment on Darren's stall is all very well, but hardly challenging – not compared to this. After his stint in Theo's stockroom yesterday, he knows every item for sale personally. He imagines sweeping everything away and allowing light to flood into every gloomy recess of the shop. He would transform the place with brightly coloured, coordinated displays. He can't quite visualise the finished result yet, but he's itching to give it a go. Joel steps into the arched porch recess next to the newsagents and rings the bell.

'Is that you, Joel? Come on up.' Joel hears a click as the catch on the door is released. He enters a long narrow hallway with a staircase going straight up, and there's a matching doorway at the far end, presumably giving access to a back yard. Theo is waiting to greet him at the top of the stairs.

'Good morning. Another early riser, like me. Let's go into the dining room for a few minutes and meditate, and then we can have some breakfast. It'll be nice to have some company for a change.'

Joel is led past a series of doors, all slightly ajar. The first is obviously Theo's bedroom. Joel detects a manly, musky smell as they pass. The second belongs to what appears to be a storeroom filled with boxes and the third leads to a small, rather chaotic looking living room, crammed with an eclectic mix of chairs and sofas. Next up is a rather poky dining room completely filled by a large, antiquated oak table and matching chairs, and Joel assumes that the kitchen and bathroom are beyond this at the far end. Joel is ushered into the dining room and he takes a chair near the window. From their position off the landing, he can tell that each of the principal rooms affords a view of Broadway embankment and the town bridge. He is overwhelmed by a vision of himself relaxing in a large, light and airy space, the evening light streaming in through the three big sash windows.

'Have you ever thought of knocking any of these rooms through, Theo?'

'Quite the architect, I see. I did think about it actually when I first moved in, but what with the shop and my antiquarian books, I don't seem to be able to get round to anything like that at the moment.' Theo sits down on the seat opposite Joel. 'Now, I could tell that you struggled a bit with the river visualisation we did in class the other night, so this time why don't we just get used to the breathing exercise? Don't fight any thoughts that come into your head, but then again, try not to let them take you over.'

But Joel's thoughts refuse to be cast aside. Why, for instance, is Theo living alone? Has he ever been married? Is Theo really happy with the chaotic mess that surrounds him everywhere? He and his mum have never actually owned enough objects to really make a mess, he supposes, but when she's actually at home she's forever scrubbing and tidying what little they do have, even more so after she's been away for a few days. Is it because she feels bad about leaving him alone? Is she somehow trying to wash away her guilt? And of course, another question springs to mind: how long ago did Theo leave to go on his travels? Can he be the man who left his mum because he had 'more pressing things to do with his life'? Joel considers most men as a possible contender, even famous people he sees at the cinema or on TV. He and Theo look a bit alike. They're both short with dark hair, but he knows that doesn't really prove anything. He always looks at the other pupils' fathers at Parents' Evening near the end of each term, and is surprised at how unalike most of them seem to be. This he finds disconcerting. Perhaps he won't even recognise his dad if he ever meets him. He won't ask Theo how long ago he first went away though. He doesn't want to spoil his dream too soon.

After what seems like an age, breakfast is prepared and eaten in the tiny kitchen: freshly brewed coffee, muesli soaked overnight and topped with yoghurt and various types of fruit, followed by wholemeal toast and yeast extract. It doesn't quite live up to Eric's gigantic fry-ups served with mugs of tea, but at least it's free.

'If you don't mind helping out for another couple of hours in the stockroom this morning, Joel, I think that will suffice until you get back from your holiday. Have you anything planned with your friends this afternoon?'

'Grace is busy all day today, and Darren never seems free either at the moment.'

'Is that Darren O'Donnell by any chance?

'Yes he's my friend. Do you know him then?'

Joel can't imagine that he does. Darren's never mentioned him, or the shop for that matter. It's not the sort of place that Darren would have any interest in.

'Not really,' Theo says, 'but I knew his dad Ronnie quite well, years ago. I only saw Darren once, when he was a couple of months old. In fact, it must have been just before I went on my travels.'

Joel cannot contain the broad smile that is spreading across his face; even he could do the maths. Darren is eleven months older than him, and eleven minus two is nine. Not definite proof, he has to admit, but it certainly doesn't rule out Theo as a possible contender on the father front. And if it was him, then he wouldn't have even known that his mum was pregnant when he went away. And she wouldn't have been able to contact him if he was in some Tibetan monastery, would she? So it wouldn't have been his fault. Joel has no idea if Theo and his mum have ever even met, and he certainly won't ask, not yet anyway. He'll keep his fantasy alive for a little bit longer.

# Chapter 7

## Darren and the White Water Rapids

'Darren; how come you're brown all over?' Grace asks. 'Even Percy's brown.'

That had surprised me as well, as it happens, what with the amount of factor 50 I'd slathered on him every time he was exposed to the sun.

'Well?' she persists.

'Don't be such a prude, Grace, how do you think? Anyway, you are.'

'I'm what?'

'Brown all over.'

'That's hardly the same.' She allows the cool water from my ensuite shower to cascade through her hair, onto her shoulders and beyond. She starts to soap my shoulders and chest with my sponge.

'Most of the beaches in Greece are nudist,' I say. 'Didn't you know that?' Of course, she doesn't know one way or the other. She's never been abroad at all, much less to Greece. I remember how difficult it was to find that particular beach. The ones to either side of the harbour by the main town definitely weren't nudist, and in the end I'd had to catch a bus right to the other side of the island. There were all these old grannies with their weekly shopping sitting on the bus too, covered from head to foot in black, giving all us potential 'naturists' very disapproving looks. And then the first beach I tried was obviously reserved for gay men.

Grace is looking up at me, rather worried-looking. She's stopped sponging me down, so I add, 'Anyway, this nudist business is completely non-sexual. You just don't think of that sort of thing when everybody's got their kit off.' It's true; nothing ever happened on the actual beach, but that wasn't to say that nobody hooked up later, back in town. But Grace has nothing to worry about. Those other girls have definitely given my confidence a boost, which must be a good thing. I had to find out for sure if I was OK at it or not. After all I'd only experienced a virgin and a frustrated 'Mrs Robinson' type before, and the girls on holiday were no threat to Grace. None of them lived anywhere near here. She still doesn't look completely convinced so I add, 'and there wasn't anybody as fit looking as you there. You're my best girl, you know that.' That's true, as it happens; this 'being in love' business is definitely improving her looks. I bury my nose in her wet hair. Her distinctive smell of coffee and coconut has gone. She smells of my shampoo and shower gel. 'We're like one person now,' I whisper. I tickle her and make her shriek.

'Darren! Stop it. What will your mum think?'

'Oh, she knows what we get up to. Dad guessed and said something. But she doesn't mind. I told her that we're in love, and we're going to get married after we've been to Uni. Oh, and I also told her that you're the cleverest girl in the class.'

'Darren. You really told her that?' Her eyes have gone all wide and shiny.

'Of course I told her that. It's true isn't it?'

'And then what did she say?'

'Her exact words were,' – I put on Mum's annoyingly gushing voice –'"I think it's really sweet that you're so much in love, my darling. I'm sure she's a lovely girl, and I'm longing to meet her".' I grab the sponge and throw it at her, laughing. 'Oh, then she added "but I hope you're being careful".'

'I've missed you so much,' Grace says. 'At least we've still got nearly another three weeks left before we go back to school. We can do this every day.'

'Ah, about that,' I say. 'I've just booked up another holiday actually. I'm going on a white water kayaking course for a few days next week. It's something I've been meaning to do for ages.' She looks surprised and rather upset, so I add, 'I want to do it because of what happened to Leroy.'

'Whatever do you mean?'

Oh shit! I'm going to have to admit to being a coward when it comes to water; something I've never told anyone before. Admitting to any sort of weakness isn't really my thing.

'Well, it's just that if I'd been with Leroy that day when he drowned, I don't think I could have helped him. I just can't bear the idea of jumping into deep water, or of having my head submerged. It gives me a panic attack. Apparently, it's because of something that happened to me when I was little. I can't remember it, of course, but that's what my dad's told me. I know it won't bring Leroy back, but I just feel that it's something I have to do.' Her expression has softened, and she's put her arm round my waist, so I continue. 'It sounds really scary, actually. Before you start, they strap you into this kayak, and then you have to deliberately turn yourself right over so your head's underwater.' I've made that bit up, but it sounds suitably scary. The thought of it's made me feel a bit weak, so I grab my towel and go and sit on the bed, and Grace joins me.

'That's so brave,' she says. 'To admit you're scared of something is brave enough by itself, but to go through something like that is amazing. You are just so lovely, and Leroy was very lucky to have a friend like you.'

So that's how girls' minds work, is it? I'll have to remember that, and I was so convincing that I nearly believed it myself. I know I'll have to do a deliberate capsize at some point, but at least they'll be people there to help me. I remember all the activities I missed out on in Greece this year: water skiing, snorkelling and riding the banana being just three. If I get this course over with now, I'll have much more fun next year. But Grace is more than satisfied with my alternative explanation about doing it for Leroy, so that's fine. It's my job to make her happy, after all.

I'm sitting in Mum's car on the way to Kayak Camp. It's not very far, only about thirty miles downriver, but with her driving no doubt it'll take for ever to get there. I turn my head and look out of the window, although there's nothing much to see – only high, neatly clipped hedges. But I keep looking so as not to encourage her to start yacking.

I'm surprised at how impressed Dad was when I booked up this holiday. He was as impressed as Grace, or even more. Then he said that he wouldn't come with me on such a course even if I paid him, which I've got no intention of doing anyway. He's much too old, as it happens. You have to be between eighteen and twenty four to be in my group. All the ones for my age group were full up, so I put down that I was eighteen on my cousin Ryan's birthday, 14th July. I'll be sixteen on the 8th September, and Mum keeps saying that I look at least eighteen, so I reckon what I put is about right – and I said that my name was Ryan as well, just in case they bother to check. And my slight Irish twang is quite convincing now. After all, I've had to listen to Dad all my life. And if anyone asks, I'm starting a Law degree at Oxford in October. That should cover it.

The scenery is changing. Fields are opening up before me and cows and sheep are glaring at me from behind gates. I ignore Mum's incessant chatter and close my eyes. Nature red in tooth and claw isn't really my scene. I'm a natural city dweller – I'm sure of it – and one day I'll prove it. I imagine the tall buildings housing museums and theatres and night clubs and multiplex cinemas and shops stocking all the latest clothes and gizmos. And all the up market restaurants with their Michelin starred chefs, and not a seersucker tablecloth or fake coffee machine in sight.

We're here at last. I get out of the car and go to get my rucksack out of the boot. Mum follows quickly and looks as if she's about to give me a hug and a kiss, but I manage to dodge her.

'Don't you dare, Mum,' I say. 'Just get back in the car and go. I'll see you on Thursday.' I see this group of people, about nine or ten of them, lolling about in a circle on the flat grassy floodplain next to the river. The other bank rises steeply upwards. The trees covering it appear stark and sinister looking in the shadows. A single buzzard soars overhead, its mew snapping the silence. Now that I can see the river stretched out before me, the reason why I'm here has surfaced and gives me a sudden blow to the solar plexus. I'm walking down the slope and suddenly all eyes are upon me. I'm like an actor entering centre stage. I'm in the spotlight, exposed, and I don't remember the script. What is it? I stretch and clench my fingers, but my shoulders and ears have permanently bonded. I remember now, I'm my cousin Ryan.

This wiry old geezer is standing up, beckoning me over, looking at his list. 'I'm Mike. And you must be Ryan. All the way from Ireland, I see.'

'That's right, sir,' I say. I hope to hear Dad's soft voice, but what comes out is more like a bark. I sit down cross legged in the only space left in the circle and clench my knees. This girl next to me smiles, but all I can manage is an upward movement of the chin. She reddens slightly and turns away. A pity. She looks alright – and vaguely familiar.

'Now that we're all here,' the instructor is saying, 'let's introduce ourselves. Firstly, I'm Mike. I've been involved with the sport of kayaking for nearly twenty years, and will be guiding you at every step to help you gain confidence in handling your craft in the water so that we can progress from navigating in calm waters, such as we have here, to the more testing conditions further upstream. Firstly, we'll be learning to lift, carry and launch your kayak. We'll be doing that in pairs. Then I'll split you into two groups and we'll learn some elementary paddling skills, forwards to start with. After lunch we'll do a bit of theory, followed by a session in steering and controlling your craft, as well as making a safe exit onto the bank. And most importantly, at the end of this session we'll be covering rescue skills, which will include a safe and controlled capsize.'

I'm beginning to feel very hot, but I've got nothing I can really take off. Mike's still talking. 'Tomorrow we'll run through everything again before you're assessed, and then for those of you who are ready, we'll attempt a simple roll. How quickly you progress is up to you. Some of you may have to spend your last day of the course repeating what we've learnt, whist those of you who have managed a reasonable roll will be able to progress to the next stage. Now, although the craft you will be using are one-man kayaks, that doesn't mean I won't be expecting a feeling of team spirit amongst you. Helping others in difficulty on the water is part of the course, and it's essential that you are prepared to assist and encourage others if needed. Right then, before we take to the water, I'd like you all to introduce yourselves, and give us your reasons for enrolling.'

I try to listen as they start, but I can't shift the image of performing this roll thingy. Perhaps I won't be good enough to get that far. Even the thought of this capsize business is playing havoc with my concentration. I didn't think we'd be doing it so soon. Anyway, why should I care a toss about these other people and why they're here? This is all about me – and, actually, why I've come is none of their business, is it? But it seems as if I'll have to tell them something. The two sets of couples have had their go, something about them all being on some work-related scheme arranged by their manager to help 'bonding' or some such nonsense. They couldn't look more closely bonded if they'd used superglue. Then there's a couple of gay guys who work in a bank somewhere or other and who probably like the idea of sleeping together under canvas. Now it's the turn of these two girls who look desperate to hook up. Sorry girls, those two won't be interested, and I'm definitely not in the mood right now.

Mike's addressing me now, but I can't think of what to say. That pretty girl is looking at me again with an encouraging look in her eyes – very big and brown – so I give her my best attempts at a smile and she blushes again, but this time she doesn't look away. She definitely looks familiar. I know what I'll say. All that guff I told Grace. It feels like the truth now I've said it once. I straighten up, unclamp my knees and fold my hands together in my lap. I wait to hear Dad's voice in my head before I start.

'I've come over to stay with my aunt and uncle for a couple of weeks. It's not far from here, you see, and I thought this course sounded just the thing to relieve the boredom.' Why did I just laugh? 'But there is another, more important reason, of course.'

'And what is that then, Ryan? Please share it with us,' Mike says.

'Well, it's not that easy, actually. I've not told anyone this before, and I feel rather ashamed.' My fingers are rubbing relentlessly together, up and down.

'In your own time, Ryan. We're all friends here.'

'Well, I had a friend once – actually he was much younger than me – the brother of my girlfriend. He drowned in the river near my home back in Ireland, and if I'd been there when it happened, I know for sure I wouldn't have been able to save him. I have a terrible fear of putting my head under water, do you see, and I've decided that I must conquer it once and for all, just in case I'm in a similar situation, where I need to act decisively.'

'Very laudable, I'm sure,' Mike says. 'You're just eighteen I see, Ryan. What are your plans for the future?'

I've practised this bit. 'I'll be going up to Oxford at the end of October, to study Law.'

'Well done,' Mike says. 'Now Kaye, how about you?'

The pretty girl gives me a rather wistful, but approving look before she starts. 'I'm going travelling in Australia and New Zealand for eight weeks after this,' she says. 'I'm meeting some school friends who're already out there. They're all into extreme sports, and I wanted to do this course so that I won't be lagging too far behind them. And as soon as I get home, I'll be off to university to study Medicine – at Oxford, like Ryan.'

Oh shit! I wish she'd gone first. She might start quizzing me about what halls I'm in, and who knows what else? Why didn't you say Dublin, or Liverpool, in fact anywhere else but Oxford? She's smiling at me again but my features have frozen into that of horrified surprise. Her face flushes an even deeper red.

'Don't worry, Ryan,' she hisses at me. 'Oxford's a big place, you know. And I wasn't trying to flirt with you when I smiled just now. I have noted the fact that you've already got a girlfriend.' What was all that about?

We're being told to get up and collect by the riverbank. Kaye has moved away from me and has joined the shop girls and bank clerks. Mike's begun demonstrating the correct method of lifting the kayak into the water. We must keep the load close to our body without twisting. He's chosen me to help him as he says its best to do it in pairs. Then he shows us how to get in, making sure that the paddle is within reach.

'Now it's your turn,' he says. 'You'll find wetsuits in the changing block over there. Off you go. We'll assemble back here in ten minutes.'

We've been put into pairs, and I find that I'm lumbered with the short, top heavy blonde girl, but she's not much help so I have to do most of the work myself. She can't stop looking over towards the dark haired gay bloke who's been put with Kaye, except that he doesn't look quite so gay anymore. Now that we're all safely in our kayaks, we've been split into two groups of five. I'm in the back line together with the two 'closely bonded' couples, and Kaye's positioned just in front of me. The dark haired slime ball has insinuated himself between her and the dumpy blonde. Mike's encouraging us to move forward together in a straight line, using the correct grip on the paddle. He says we must try to maintain an active but upright posture while rotating our bodies. Kaye and the dark haired bastard are pulling away and I manage to keep up, but Mike is alongside, telling me to keep in my line.

I eat my lunch on the fringes of the group. I feel very young and alone. Mum's made me up a great picnic, so I concentrate on that. As I bite into the slice of homemade cake I suddenly miss her. I shouldn't have been so short with her in the car park. The thought of the capsize that we've got to do later is making my throat constrict. I can't swallow. What if I chicken out and they send me home? What if I have to ring her up and ask her to come back and collect me?

I get through the rest of the day in a state of numbness. I'm taking it all in, but on a subliminal level, just waiting for the signal to get into pairs for the capsize. And then there she is – Kaye! The dark haired lunatic seems to prefer blondes. She manoeuvres her kayak in my direction, and I'm transfixed by her lithe and athletic body. It's accentuated to perfection by her wet suit. She's exactly my sort of girl, as it happens. Why is she so familiar? I'm sure I've never met her before. I hope that whatever I did to offend her hasn't completely blown my chances. Luckily she seems to be softening her opinion of me. She can feel my fear, I'm sure.

'I'm sorry I snapped at you earlier, Ryan,' she says. 'Just for the record, I think your attempting this is really brave. It's not that difficult. You just have to think of yourself and the kayak as one entity, and the centre of gravity being your stomach and hips. So if you lean over too much to one side, you'll automatically capsize. Once you've done it, you'll wonder what all the fuss is about.' She's not convincing me. I'm more interested in staring into her enormous dark eyes.

'I'll go first,' she says. She does it perfectly. She's completely calm and relaxed as she hits the water. Then she collects the boat and paddle swims to the shore on her back exactly as Mike has shown us. She gets back in and returns to me straight away. She's smiling, completely elated.

'Now it's your turn,' she says. 'If I can do it, then I'm sure you can. You're certainly strong enough. If you don't master this, they'll keep you down with the beginners. It's some Health and Safety rubbish I expect. We don't want to end up in different groups, do we? That would be a shame.'

Perhaps all that blushing and strange behaviour earlier on means she fancies me. I'm surprised I didn't pick up on that before. My fear must have addled my brain. I'm going to do this, if only for her sake. I set my face, close my eyes for maximum concentration and tip myself sideways. But now my head's underwater, and it's invading my mouth and nose, I'm coughing and spluttering, I can't breathe. Time stands still and I know that I'm going to drown. I try to shout 'Help' but it's only making it worse. Where is everybody? Why isn't somebody saving me? But then I hear a splash. Someone's manhandling me, lifting my head and shoulders up and I'm being transported through the water. Someone's helping me to the bank, slapping me on the back and massaging my shoulders. Echoes of being on a beach return. I'm tiny and there's a large wave. I'm choking, gasping for air, and Dad's carrying me up the beach. Mum's thumping me on the back and saying 'my poor darling'.

I open my eyes but it's not Mum that's standing over me. It's Audrey Hepburn. She's squeezing water out of her hair and twirling it into a knot on top of her head. That's why this Kaye girl's so familiar. She's not Kaye at all. She's the actress in that ancient 1960's film, the one I used to watch with Mum. She's the girl I used to have all those embarrassingly messy dreams about before I hooked up with Grace.

'Audrey,' I whisper.

'Audrey?' she says. 'Is that your girlfriend? She'll be so proud of you for doing this.'

'Oh, she's not my girlfriend anymore,' I say, after my brain's clicked back into gear. 'After Leroy died she and her family moved away, and she's never contacted me since.'

'I'm so sorry, Ryan,' she says, although I can tell from her face that she's not.

Mike's coming over, asking us if everything is OK.

'You did that perfectly, Kaye, but you're ahead of yourself,' he's saying. 'The rescued capsize was meant to come later. Ryan was meant to swim to the shore that time.'

'My fault,' she says. 'I got carried away. But he can do the other method now, can't he? You don't mind, do you Ryan?'

'Of course not,' I say. She's squeezing my hand. I've stopped shaking now, so I entwine my fingers in hers. Is some silly business that happened on the beach when I was a toddler the only reason why I've been afraid of putting my head under water all this time? Why did Dad fill my brain with all that crap about some horrendous accident? Was it to justify his own stupid fear?

I perform the capsize and swim exercise, with Kaye close by just in case. But everything's just fine. We spend the rest of the day on the river together. The only time we're apart is when we have to change out of our wet suits. She even sits next to me at the evening barbeque. I have to deflect her questions concerning me, by asking her to tell me all about herself. I've never had to do that before.

95

Now it's time for bed and we go and look for our tents. They've all been taken except for one. We are the only people that haven't come as a couple.

'I'm so sorry about this,' I say. 'I hope it isn't going to be awkward for you having to share such a small space. I'll try not to knock into you in the night, but I am rather large and clumsy, as you can see.'

'That's fine,' Kaye says. 'Anyway, I trust you completely, otherwise there's no way I'd agree. You'll probably think me a bit old fashioned and even a bit of a prude, but I'm saving myself for that 'special person'; and anyway, we've only just met.'

'My sentiments entirely, although I thought at one time that I'd found her – my special person. You know that boy I told you about who drowned last February? Well, his elder sister Audrey and I had been going out since we were fifteen. We were childhood sweethearts, I suppose, although we didn't actually make love straight away of course, as we were so young. I wish now that I'd waited… for someone like you.'

She kisses me lightly on the cheek, but that's it. I settle myself down next to her, my sleeping bag as close to hers as I can manage without causing her offence. For now, I'm quite content just to lie next to her. I was with Grace only yesterday, and I can still sense the coffee and coconut aroma of her skin. But Grace was with somebody called Darren, and Ryan will only ever want to be with Kaye.


It's our last night together. Mum will be picking me up tomorrow morning. Everything has gone brilliantly. Even the roll was a doddle. Only four of us out of the original ten were good enough to attempt some white water stuff today: the two single guys, me and Kaye. Our new instructor said we were all well on our way to getting our 3 Star Award. It's just a pity that we haven't got more time to complete it. Dean and Lee aren't actually that bad, as it happens. Quite a laugh once they got the message to stop flirting with Kaye – that she's definitely my girl.

I lie next to her, my arm cradling her head; I stroke her bare arm with my fingertips. She's admitted that I'm her special person now, although she still won't allow me to prove how special I really am. She needs more time. We're to wait until after her trip and then we can be together properly, she promises.

I watch her as she lies there. Her face is lit by the eerie glow of the moon as it filters through the canvas roof of our tent. Her cheeks glow silvery white like an ethereal, beautifully carved statue of some Greek Goddess or other. I kiss her lightly.

'I wish I wasn't going to New Zealand now,' she murmurs. 'I'd rather stay here with you.'

'I won't be here myself,' I say. 'I'll be back in Ireland. Anyway, you'll have a great time; I just wish I was going too. You must email me with all your photos.'

'I'll make you my friend on Facebook,' she says, 'and I can change my status from "single" to "in a relationship".'

'Oh, I don't bother with all that Facebook nonsense. It's much too time consuming. Emails are better,' I say.

'And we'll be together again as soon as we go up to Oxford, won't we Ryan? At least I've got that to look forward to when I'm away. I was really dreading going to Uni and not knowing anybody. We will be together won't we? You won't find someone else while I'm away?'

How have you got yourself into this situation? One or two tiny lies to get onto this course have ruined everything. How can you possibly tell her the truth now: that you're only fifteen, your name isn't Ryan and you won't be going to any university, much less Oxford, for ages?

'Of course we'll be together,' I say. 'I'll contact you as soon as I get there. But it seems such a long time to wait. It'll be years and years.'

I know it'll seem like years,' she says, 'but it'll only be a few weeks.' Her finger traces the faint line of freckles over the bridge of my nose and under my eyes. She kisses my tears away. 'You silly big baby,' she whispers.

It's now that I makc up my mind. I'm definitely going to Oxford, even if it means actually doing some work. It won't be this October though, or the next one, or even the one after that, but as soon as it happens she'll definitely be the first person I'll contact. She'll still be there. A degree in Medicine takes at least six years.

# Chapter 9

## The Picnic

Grace sat paddling her bare feet in the water. The flow of the river was faster at this point, the width being restricted owing to the obstruction of a partly submerged tree that had been wrenched from the opposite bank during the winter storms of earlier in the year. But now it was late summer, and a perfect day for a picnic. The water rushed over the boulders in a laughing, playful manner, sending pearls of refracted light shooting upwards into the warm September air.

But the gnarled and twisted roots of the dead tree, as they pointed bleakly skywards, served as a reminder of less balmy times. How different it must have appeared to Leroy last February. The river would have been a torrent then, the sounds created by the forces of nature deafening and terrible. Had he passed this point on that last day of his – the stretch known as 'the rapids'- or had he entered the water further downstream? Why had he ended up in the water at all? Grace had not been oblivious to the rumours of suicide that had circulated at the time, but she'd never believed them. Leroy had never shown any evidence of the depth of despair needed to deliberately end his own life. She needed to know why he died before she could mourn him properly. She looked at the flow of the river once more. It was confident and smooth midstream, but confused and uncertain in the shallow areas around the rocks, swirling back on itself before continuing its relentless journey downstream. Had he felt confused as to the direction his life was taking that day? She felt ashamed at how little she thought of her brother now: every day still, of course, but not nearly enough. Once he'd been her only friend – and everything to her. But now was not an appropriate time to mourn. Now her attention should be completely focused on Darren.

Grace stretched out her legs and allowed the sun to play along her wet shins. She always thought it such a shame that they had to go back to school while the weather was still so warm. But today was Saturday, Darren's birthday, and she was determined to make the most of it. He had brought her to this quiet and secluded spot that he said he'd found especially for her. It was completely overgrown with trees and bushes except for this one clearing, and he had assured her that they would have complete privacy to do whatever they wanted.

She breathed deeply, allowing the fragrant scent of the large, dense clumps of Himalayan balsam to invade her nostrils. She watched as the breeze shook the purplish-pink, slipper-shaped flowers. The sounds of the ever-moving water were being echoed by the animated chatter of a pair of dippers, the female wadding in search of food and her mate exhibiting himself on the adjoining rock – cocking his tail and displaying sudden flashes of white as he bobbed his head.

'Grace?' Her reverie was broken by the sound of Darren's voice, coaxing, entreating. She turned round and was unable to prevent herself from laughing out loud. Darren was lounging on the picnic rug, his right knee bent up, and the corresponding arm outstretched to her, the sunlight through the tall, densely packed trees casting dappled shadows on his naked body.

'What's so funny?' Darren raised a questioning eyebrow as Grace tried to stifle her giggles.

'I'm sorry, Darren, but isn't that taking your Art Appreciation homework a bit far? You must have spent ages lying on your bed in front of the mirror to get it right, but it's wrong in one important detail. Good try though. I'm sure Miss Harris would give you top marks for effort!'

'What detail have I got wrong then, Grace… and why is it so important?' Darren still had one eyebrow raised, his full lips turning upwards in jest.

Grace visualized Michelangelo's picture, *The Creation of Man*, that they were shown in class last week. It was a special, one-off class to mark the beginning of a new school year. She could see the figure of God reaching out his hand to Adam, while at the same time protecting a timid and rather awestruck Eve as she stared at her intended mate.

'You've got Adam's pose the wrong way round. He had his left knee bent. That's what comes of practising in front of the mirror.'

'Surely that's not the only thing that's different,' Darren said. 'Look harder.'

'No. It's all exactly right: the tilt of the head, everything.'

'Well, thanks a lot, Grace!' She watched with surprise as Darren hurriedly replaced his clothes. He was obviously seething with rage, but in a suppressed, damaged sort of way that she had never seen before. His head and shoulders were hunched forward stiffly, his movements clumsy.

She tried to remember what Miss Harris had said about the picture. She recalled something about Michelangelo's Adam being 'the quintessential image of what the artist thought to be the ideal of male beauty'. Then she remembered the over-loud whispers from Jenna and her friends, said deliberately to embarrass the teacher while amusing the rest of the class. She'd said something like 'his six pack's not bad, shame about the lunch box'. She hadn't really taken much interest in, or fully understood, Jenna's comment at the time. But visualising the painting again, she remembered Adam's tiny, inconsequential member.

Darren had lost that roguish, questioning look. It had been replaced with something altogether much harder. His eyebrows and mouth were set in straight lines, his jaws tightly shut. She had obviously not given Darren the right reply to his question. Was he really that vain, and also that insecure about himself? Could she redeem herself with an addendum? She didn't think so, not from the look on his face.

She had already found out, to her cost, that he had no sense of humour, unless it was directed elsewhere, and preferably laced with malice, so there was no point in trying to make a joke out of it. She longed to go and put her arms around him and say she was sorry, but she was afraid of his reaction even to that. He had deliberately brought her to an isolated spot. What if he decided to turn violent?

'Hurry up and help me pack up this stuff. I've lost my appetite all of a sudden,' Darren whispered, his hands shaking slightly as he started to fold up the rug. Grace felt herself emboldened as she detected no viciousness in his current mood.

'Certainly not,' she said. 'Not until we've eaten your birthday lunch. I've got all your favourite things. I've even got those little coconut cakes you like so much.' She grabbed the rug off him and quickly spread it over the grass. 'Come on! We're in ancient Rome. You're the emperor, and I'm your serving girl. Lie down and let me pamper you, my illustrious and mighty Emperor Percy, the best and most powerful ruler in the whole world.'

Although Darren submissively did as he was told, allowing her to feed him, to stroke his hair and to lightly kiss him between mouthfuls, she felt a vast gulf of emptiness had opened up between them. His obvious embarrassment and feelings of foolishness had somehow diminished him. His shoulders were no longer drawn back, his chin was no longer held up. He reminded her of an exquisite piece of porcelain, strongly glazed on the outside, but brittle and easy to shatter if not handled with care.

'You are the best, you know that, don't you?' she said as she wiped his lips with a birthday napkin. She felt like a mother trying to calm and console a petulant and rather silly child.

After they had eaten, they packed up the picnic things in silence, and retraced their steps in single file along the neglected path that led to the little bridge. All sounds were stilled, apart from the plaintive call of a lone buzzard as it glided and soared overhead. Back on the bus they sat together without touching. Grace wanted to hold his hand, but it was forever moving, trying to erase an imaginary mark from his sweatshirt.

'I'll ring you,' he said when they got to her stop. 'You'll have to take the picnic things home by yourself. I'm going on to the golf club. I've just remembered I'm expected there this afternoon.'

This was not what he'd led her to believe before, but she was getting used to these sudden changes of plan, along with his deep bouts of depression. Some days, she felt that, in his eyes, she couldn't get anything right at all.

Grace waited all day on Sunday for his call, and tried to catch his eye at school on Monday, and although they never acknowledged their special friendship around other people, he appeared to be deliberately orchestrating his avoidance of her. She was unsure what to do. Should she text him, ring him, or just ignore him too?

On Tuesday however, she managed to catch his attention, and from his slight nod of acknowledgement she knew to her relief that her period of punishment was over. That evening, in his room, he was as frisky and inventive as ever. It was if the incident had never happened. The cracks in the porcelain had been filled and the varnish had been re-applied. But the wardrobe door housing the full length mirror was left firmly shut.

# Chapter 10

## Fiona Sutcliffe's Toy Boy

Fiona Sutcliffe still couldn't believe her luck. What had she ever done to deserve this vision of male loveliness lying next to her? He was stretched out next to her on her bed naked, flat on his back with his hands behind his head, staring at the ceiling. The way he had positioned himself invited her gaze, invited her admiration. He had such an air of confidence for one so young, and why not feel confident looking the way he did?

She had always fancied the idea of a toy boy, of course, but had never actually believed that it would ever happen, that she would manage to seduce someone so much younger than herself – in fact exactly half her age. But there had been such a look of vulnerability about this boy sitting all alone at the Golf Club barbeque that, in her state of inebriation, she just couldn't help herself. She'd had to exploit the situation. She had expected it to be just a one night affair, but for some reason he kept coming back.

He was completely relaxed now as he lay next to her. The violence of his earlier mood had dissipated after the sadomasochistic force of their sexual activities of earlier. His alternating desire for dominance and submission excited her. It had aroused a dormant desire for role-play that she knew Clive would never agree to. But although invigorating, she was looking forward to some gentle, more playful lovemaking before he left. Sometimes he would be angry like today, but on other occasions he would just want to be mothered by her, as on the day of his sixteenth birthday. On such occasions she would have to work hard to get him interested in sex at all. She had been surprised and slightly horrified, when she'd discovered how young he was. She had been convinced, when she first set eyes on him, that he was at least eighteen. For the first few weeks of their affair, not only was she breaking her marriage vows, she had in fact been committing a criminal offence. He was under the age of consent. She turned away from him momentarily and reached for her wine glass on her bedside table. She drained it. She was drinking too much, she knew that. Perhaps she shouldn't in front of this boy.

Before her marriage to Clive she had always attracted older, invariably married, men. At first this had suited her. She'd enjoyed the freedom and lack of commitment that this brought. But eventually she had come to her senses. She'd realised that these married men were all shallow, egotistic and thoroughly unpleasant. Clive had come along at just the right time. He was attentive, unattached and the proud owner of this lovely home near the golf club, courtesy of his departed mother. But the proximity of the golf club was the problem with their marriage. He had gradually started spending more and more time there, made worse after his appointment as Club Chairman. That was Clive's trophy, Darren was hers.

There was a definite frisson in the thought that her lover had to leave her bed to go and finish his homework, and it wouldn't be just his school teachers who would be awarding him straight A's for diligence and creativity. But he was so cold and unreadable. She longed to break the carapace that protected his soul. Although inscrutable, he was undoubtedly beautiful. She must feast her eyes on every aspect of his body now. She must consign it to memory for when he'd grown tired of her. She would need to reproduce this image when all she had left to look forward to were her husband's rare and inadequate advances.

She ran her hand over his taut stomach to try and catch his attention. What thoughts lurked behind those other-worldly eyes? They were not thoughts of romantic love, she knew that. But surely that was a good thing, wasn't it? She wasn't looking for the attentions of some lovelorn youth who demanded that she must leave her husband. She didn't want a boy who threatened to kill himself if she decided to end the affair. Not that she would ever be the one to end it. You didn't do that sort of thing to the likes of Darren O'Donnell, however young they were. The thought of crossing him was unimaginable.

He turned his gaze upon her, and a bolt of electricity shot through her. His eye colour had changed from the ice cold blue of earlier to something iridescent, almost luminous. His eyes were like unfathomable pools of water, changing colour not only with the quality of the light, but with what lurked in the depths beneath. But instead of returning her caress, he got up and headed towards her bathroom. Why did he always leave the door open, she wondered? It was as if he forgot she existed. If he couldn't actually see her then she was no longer there. She wouldn't mention the door business again though, not after the last time. And it was quite true what he'd said. It wasn't compulsory to watch if she didn't want to.

Surely this stallion of hers wasn't really from that weasely looking little Ronnie's stable? He was an only child, so perhaps he was adopted. Or perhaps he was Lorraine's but not Ronnie's. Lorraine was just the sort of woman Fiona loathed, with her overworked hair and make-up and her profusion of expensive but inappropriate accessories. She started to chuckle at the thought of this ridiculously pretentious, social climber of a mother having an affair with a delicious-looking relief milkman. The regular ones were certainly not up to producing a specimen such as Darren.

'What are you laughing at? Nothing I've done, I hope.' Darren was coming back, his eyebrows puckering.

'I was just wondering what I reminded you of today, my darling,' she said, as coolly as she could manage. She liked this childish little game of his.

'Today, my sweet, you are like a silky-smooth, creamy yoghurt,' he said, kissing her wrist, his lips continuing their passage up the inside of her arm. 'With an exotic hint of vanilla,' he added, licking the crease of her elbow. 'But much as I'd like to stay and devour you, I have to go. I've got things to do.'

She didn't want him to go. She wanted to be devoured. He reminded her of Cleopatra in male guise. The quote 'But she makes hungry where most she satisfies' suddenly came to mind. She remained silent, gazing at him.

'Actually, I suppose I could stay a little longer,' Darren said, pulling the bedcovers back.

'No, off you go. I mustn't get in the way of your studies,' she said. She mustn't come over as too desperate. Perhaps she should take a leaf out of Cleopatra's book. Fiona watched with regret as he started to get dressed, inwardly mourning the sight of his ever decreasing nakedness.

'Are you studying Shakespeare at school, Darren?'

'Yes, worst luck, but not after my GCSEs. English Lit.'s a load of bollocks. It'll just be Maths and the Sciences for me in the Sixth.' He had turned his back on her. He laced up his trainers, and with that he was gone, without even so much as a backward glance.

≈

What the hell was that all about? She must know the rules by now. I make as if I'm going home, and then she begs me to stay. I hate the way she made me change the script like that, trying to make me look like the needy one. Grace never does that. Even that first time she got it right. And what was all that crap about me studying Shakespeare? If she'd started quoting any at me I think I'd have decked her, especially after humiliating me like that. I don't know why I bothered to go round now. She was meant to calm me down. And why did she start laughing when I was having a pee? What's so funny? Surely everybody has to at some time, even her? Grace did that once, but only on our first night, but then she said she loved me and that I was the most beautiful boy in the world, so that was alright. She didn't turn me away.

I'll ring Grace now and tell her I can see her after all. We can do our homework together, and she'll look at me in her special way, and everything will be alright again. I've completely forgiven her for the way she humiliated me on my birthday, and ruined the whole day for me. Well, I've nearly forgiven her.

Unless Fiona ups her game, I'll have to give her the push. It's not all that exciting with her anymore, as it happens. That pathetic excuse of a husband never comes home early. I've never had to hide or anything, so what's the point? She'll have to think of something extra special to spice things up if she wants to keep seeing me. She's quite fit for her age, I suppose, but way past her sell by date. 'Silky smooth, creamy yoghurt!'

How had I thought that one up? More like lumpy soured cream. Yes, I reckon I've had enough of that particular dish.

I want to lash out, push some rubbish bins over, but I mustn't attract attention. There might be nosey neighbours watching – curtain twitchers. I'll wait till I'm somewhere more private then I'll kick the crap out of whatever's there.

# Chapter 11

## The School Outing

Grace had been sick before breakfast, and hadn't felt like eating afterwards. She was more than just 'late' now, and her breasts were beginning to feel strange and tingly.

'You look terrible, Grace,' her mother said. 'You must have food poisoning. You can't possibly go on the school trip today. What if you suddenly feel sick on the coach, or even worse, need the loo?'

'I am feeling rather tired, Mum. I think I'll go back to bed for a bit. Then I'll catch up with some homework.'

'You've been going out too much recently, my girl. I don't know what you and this friend of yours, Lauren, have to talk about.'

Grace went back to her room and lay on her bed. She hated lying to her mum about seeing Darren, but she knew that she'd only put a stop to it. Anyway, it might be too late. What if she was pregnant? They'd always been careful, but what about that one time outside the flats? Later on, when she felt a little better, she'd go and buy a pregnancy test. She'd catch the bus and go to the chemist near the hospital. She wouldn't be recognised there. And then on the way home she'd get off at the stop by Western Heights and go and see Darren. She'd text him to say

111

that she wanted to see him when he got back from the school trip, then they could do the test together. Darren would know what to do for the best, and everything would be alright because they loved each other, and they were getting married one day, after they'd been to Uni. He'd told her. He'd even told his mum.

He wouldn't be angry and blame her for making it happen sooner, would he? They could still both go to Uni even if they did have a baby. She was sure other people did. She hoped he wouldn't say it was all her fault that time when he'd been careless. She hadn't meant to annoy him and she still had no idea what she'd done. She often seemed to be annoying him recently. She was always doing or saying something wrong. But then he'd forgive her and say that she was still his best girl, and he'd be so kind and gentle again, that she'd forgive him for being so rough. After all, it always seemed to be something she'd said or done.

As Darren hadn't replied to her text, Grace decided to wait for him at his house anyway. His mum would be out as it was Thursday, so she'd wait for him in the shade of the front porch. The sun was still very hot for late September, so she sat on the cool flagstones as far in as she could manage. She couldn't see the drive from here, but she'd be able to hear Darren's footsteps on the gravel. While she was waiting, she read the instruction leaflet for the pregnancy test once more. She wished he'd hurry up. Surely the coach would have got back by now? She was getting drowsy, but after what seemed like an age, she heard him at last, but he was obviously not alone.

'It's your lucky day. My mum goes out on Thursday afternoons, so we won't be disturbed.'

Somebody was giggling. 'What are we going to do then, Darren?' Grace could hear a continuous rustling sound against the wall behind her head. They had obviously stopped.

'What do you think? Don't you want to then? You seemed well up for it earlier. Don't tell me you've never done it before.'

'Of course I have. I did it with Ben once. It was rubbish though.'

'I'm not surprised with that little wimp. I'm amazed he could even manage it at all. What you need is a real man, someone experienced.' Grace heard some more giggling, and then a long silence.

'How many girls have you done it with then, Darren?'

'Who's counting? But at a guess about seven or eight. Actually, one isn't really a girl. She's the wife of a friend of my dad. She calls me her "toy boy".'

'Err. That's disgusting, Darren! Are you still seeing her, then?'

'Every now and again, yes. I fit her in when I can. I've learnt most of what I know from her as it happens, so really she's doing you a favour.'

'Who was your first, Darren? Was it Grace? I saw you snogging her in the cinema last term.'

'Well, yes she was, actually. I used her as a trial run. There has to be a first time for everybody, even me. Anyway, she was gagging for it, so I thought it only fair. I still see her now and again, as it happens, when I've got nothing better on.'

The girl was giggling again. 'I can't imagine a nerdy little swot like her being interested. Mind you, you're no better yourself: always top of the class.'

'I'm not a swot. I'm just naturally brilliant at everything. Let me prove it to you.' The rustling sound had started again.

'Stop it, Darren. Someone might see.'

'Nobody can see us from here. Anyway, it'll make it more exciting.'

'I'm not doing anything with that evil looking gnome staring up at me. One of its ears is broken off. Take me upstairs to your room or I'll go home right now.'

'Why do you want me to take you upstairs then, Jenna?'

'Because you're the hottest boy I've ever seen, and I've fancied you for ever.'

'Then how could I possibly refuse. I thought you'd never ask.'

Grace had sat completely rigid throughout, not wanting to hear. She just wanted to creep away, but she couldn't leave without being seen. As soon as it was obvious that they had gone inside, she rushed blindly home, her eyes on the ground so as not to see anybody she knew. She wouldn't allow herself to cry until she reached the safety of her bedroom. Once indoors, she hurried past the kitchen where she knew her mother would be, closed her bedroom door firmly behind her, and threw herself onto her bed, burying her head in her duvet. She allowed her tears to flow noiselessly, her fingers gripping the sides of her pillow.

Later on, she was aware of her mother knocking on her door. 'Are you alright now dear? Do you want your tea yet?'

Grace turned herself onto her back and pulled herself into a sitting position. 'In a minute, Mum,' She had completely exhausted herself with crying, but she was determined to pull herself together. She had to keep this to herself. She got up and put the unused pregnancy test right at the back of the drawer where she kept her winter jumpers. She wouldn't be needing it. Of course she wasn't pregnant. She wasn't even quite fifteen yet, and she was often late. And her boobs just felt funny because they were growing. They weren't going to stay at 32A for ever. And anyway, they'd only done it once without anything, and she was sure somebody had told her that it didn't really work if you were standing up.

It was all her fault that Darren needed other girls as well. She obviously wouldn't be enough for someone as gorgeous as him. She was just a boring, nerdy little swot after all, and not even very pretty. How could he possibly love someone like her. He'd never actually said that he loved her anyway, only that she was his best girl. She should have guessed that she wasn't the only one.

She couldn't possibly go to school tomorrow. All Jenna's friends would know, even if Darren had told her not to say anything, and they'd all be talking about her and laughing behind her back. She'd tell her mum that she was too ill. At least it was Friday tomorrow, and then she'd have the whole weekend to decide what to do. She'd turn her phone off just in case Darren tried to ring or text her. She couldn't trust herself not to start crying again.

That night Grace had a dream. She was being tossed about in the fast flowing river. She was being both pulled along and dragged under by the currents and whirlpools created by the rocks beneath. Leroy was up ahead of her, just out of reach, with one arm up in the air, trying to keep afloat. While he was progressing very fast, she was hardly moving. Something was preventing her, even though she was trying with all her might to keep up.

Leroy's head kept vanishing under the water, only to surface again a few moments later. He kept shouting 'Help me, help me!' over and over. He wasn't calling to her though, but to someone further upstream, someone she couldn't see. She kept trying to turn her head, but it wouldn't move. They were approaching a steep bend in the river, and as Leroy disappeared round it, she was flung to the bank. She was soaking wet and gasping for air. She turned and saw him standing on the bridge. It was Darren.

Suddenly, he was beside her. They were in a clearing surrounded by large, dark trees. It was the place he had taken her to on the afternoon of his birthday. The sun was trying to penetrate, but the trees were too thick and densely packed. She was completely naked, and curled up into the foetal position for fear of what he might do. He was fully clothed and staring in her direction, staring but not really looking, as if he was thinking of something, or somebody, else. On closer inspection however, she realised that he was looking at himself, at his own reflection in the stream.

Grace woke up drenched in perspiration. She was gasping for breath, and choking on the taste of salt from her tears as they flowed into her mouth. Darren wouldn't stand by her if she was pregnant, and she didn't even want him to, and he wouldn't have helped Leroy that day last February, even if he had been there with him. He was just a coward and a bully who made people do things. Nobody really liked him. He didn't have any real friends at school. He was just a horrible boy who told lies and used people that were weaker than him. He was hardly a real person at all, he didn't care what anybody else felt, he'd never asked her what she wanted to do, but just told her what he'd decided, and then if something more interesting came up, he'd stand her up without any warning and refuse to tell her why... She'd never even look at him again just in case he got the wrong idea. She'd completely ignore him. She would go to school after all today. He wasn't going to dictate her behaviour any more.

# Chapter 12

## Darren Gets Dumped

Grace got ready for school much earlier than usual. She needed some fresh air. 'I'm feeling much better today, Mum. I'm going out for a walk along the river, and then I'll have something to eat at Eric's.'

'Make sure you do, dear. You hardly had anything yesterday. Are you coming straight home from school, or going to your friend Lauren's? You could always ask her back here if you want to.'

'I don't really like Lauren very much anymore, Mum. She's not my friend now. I'll see you at about three thirty.'

On her way out, Grace knocked on her dad's storeroom door. 'Joel. It's me, Grace.'

Joel opened the door a crack. 'You're early, Grace. I'm not dressed yet.'

'Well hurry up; I'm starving. I'm off to Eric's for the biggest, greasiest breakfast he can possibly produce.'

'Doesn't sound like your sort of thing at all, Grace, but it sounds great. Wait for me.' In hardly any time at all, Joel was out of the door, fully clothed, with his rucksack. He ran his hand through his heavy fringe, already flopping over one eye again after his haircut in August.

'I'll cut your hair again after school if you like. It's beginning to lose its shape,' Grace said.

'It'll have to be later, I'm afraid. Theo's given me a couple of extra shifts in the shop after school, and one of them is today. In fact, he wants me to do lots more hours, including all day on Saturdays. I don't really know what to do about helping Darren on his stall though.'

'What would you prefer to do, Joel, work for Theo or Darren? Also, who's going to treat you more fairly and give you more money?'

'Theo, of course, but it's not as simple as that. I feel I owe Darren some sort of loyalty. I've been working for him since last Christmas.'

'You don't owe Darren anything, Joel. He'll ditch you just like that if it suits him, and for no good reason, believe me.'

'You're probably right,' Joel said. 'But it's going to be really difficult. But how do you know what he'd do? I didn't know you knew him that well.'

'I don't,' Grace said. 'I don't think anybody does, and I can't imagine there's anything worth knowing.'

As Joel and Grace sat at the table by the window mopping up the last scraps of grease with their bread, Grace caught a glimpse of Darren walking over the bridge from the direction of Western Heights. He was fiddling with his phone. He was probably trying to contact her again. She'd turned hers off yesterday afternoon after she'd got home, and she'd turned it off again this morning after she'd noticed that he'd left her several messages. She hadn't bothered to read them. He was either dumping her, or telling her a pack of lies.

As he waited to cross the road, she caught his eye for a second, so she swiftly turned her attention to Joel. 'You must let me cut your hair again soon, Joel. You've lost that really

118

cool tufty bit again.' She ran her fingers through his fringe and tried to tuck it behind his ear, but it fell over his face again. She looked over to where Darren was standing, still waiting for the lights to change, but as he looked at her she blanked him.

'Come on now, you two lovebirds. Isn't it time you were in school?' Eric said from behind his counter. 'And no smooching allowed in here. It'll put the other customers off their food.'

'There's nobody else in here, Eric. Anyway, Grace and I are just good friends.'

'Is that what you call it nowadays?' Eric said. 'Come on now; pay up or you'll be late. Are you paying for your little *friend* as well, Joel?'

'I'm sorry about that, Grace,' Joel said as they left the café. 'That Eric's got a one-track mind. He's heard Darren shooting his mouth off about all his conquests so often that he thinks we're all the same.'

'That's all right,' Grace said. She felt her face burning with anger and shame. 'But we're not just good friends are we Joel? We're best friends.' She linked her arm in his as they walked up East Street, just as she'd seen Jenna, Lauren and Kelly do and just how she used to do with Leroy.

Grace and Joel were the last into class, and in spite of what she had feared, she was aware of a decided lack of sniggering. Jenna was sitting with her head down, fiddling nervously with her nails. All her cocky flirtatiousness had vanished and she seemed oblivious to her friends' usual banter.

≈

I'm just coming out of the boys' cloakrooms, when I see Grace. She's still avoiding me, so I grab her arm and drag her through the door. It's quite safe. I was the only one in there just

119

now, but I lean against the door to keep it that way. I lose my rag with her a bit and start shouting. 'What the hell are you playing at, Grace? Why won't you answer my calls? You're my girl and you're meant to be there when I need you, and I really did need you yesterday.' I'm giving too much away. I must control myself, try and stay calm. 'Anyway, I was only really replying to your text. You said you wanted to see me. It sounded pretty urgent.'

I still have hold of her arm, and she's shaking. She still won't look at me; without eye contact I feel completely powerless. 'What is it, Grace? Don't you want to be with me anymore?' She just stands there staring at her feet, so I tighten my grip on her arm, and finally she says something.

'Unlike some people I know, I don't approve of going out with more than one person at once, especially if you're having sex with them,' she says, but she still won't look at me.

What the hell is she going on about? Then I remember her and Joel in Eric's earlier, cozying up over breakfast. Something's going on between them. This lack of eye contact business means that she's feeling guilty.

'Oh, I get it. You're dumping me for the runt are you? He's finally managed to get his leg over. Well, it was bound to happen at some time, I suppose. But why now when you've got me? Can't you take a real man anymore?' My grip on her arm tightens even more.

'You're hurting me, Darren. Let me go.'

I'm tempted to really hurt her, but this isn't the place to do it. 'Go then,' I say, and relax my grip. 'It makes no difference to me. I was ringing to dump you anyway, as it happens.' I feel pressure on the door, so I move away and a sixth former comes in.

'I should hang fire for a bit if I were you, mate,' I say. 'There's some girl in here. She came barging in when I was having a slash, and refused to go. She said she was meeting her boyfriend, or something.' I turn to look at Grace and finally catch her eye. I give her the steeliest stare I can muster, but her puppy dog eyes just stare back.

I've got to get out, away from her. I need some fresh air. Why is everything going wrong at once? I really needed Grace yesterday after that disaster with that stupid Jenna girl, but she wasn't there for me then and now she doesn't want me at all. And what the hell was all that about with Jenna? She'd been flirting with me all day on the trip, and then she positively begged me to take her up to my room, so what was I supposed to think? Was it some dare she'd had with those equally stupid friends of hers? Perhaps they thought I was all talk, and that such a nerdy 'Arse Licker' wouldn't actually be able to manage it even when it was offered up on a plate. But it was all her fault. If she hadn't really been up for it then she should have called a halt earlier, not after you'd put a thingy on and everything. Well, at least she can't accuse you of rape. You haven't left any evidence. And why did she pretend that she wasn't a virgin? It's lucky I managed to wash and dry my sheet before Mum got home. I've never seen so much blood. Thank God I'm not squeamish. Grace didn't leave that much, but then she wasn't struggling. She wanted me then. She used to love me.

I'm round the back by the bike sheds, so I'll kick in as many bikes as I can, which should be a fair few, there's at least five minutes before the bell goes for the end of break. It's a good thing that those third formers broke the CCTV last week when they were mucking about with a football.

Now that I'm back in class I feel much calmer, particularly when I notice that the seat next to Joel's is empty. No doubt Grace is having to explain herself to the Head. Serve her right for being caught in the boys' cloakroom. After all, some boys feel the need for a bit of privacy. Mrs Jenkins is simpering over me as she hands me back my English homework. 'Excellent marks again, Darren,' she says. She's positively gleaming, and I can hear groans from all those losers sitting behind me. 'But not quite top of the class this week. Where is Grace, by the way? Has anybody seen her? Joel, how about you, do you know where she is?' Kelly and Lauren are sniggering behind me, and whispering 'Grace and Joel are in lurve,' but Jenna remains completely silent. Luckily for me, I don't think she's talking to them anymore.

I'll ring old Fiona up after school. She'll probably be at a loose end, and anyway, I've got to see this equipment she's ordered over the internet. She's getting a bit kinky for my taste, as it happens. I'm not surprised that her pathetic husband refused to try it out, even though she can be really persuasive. But I like it when I don't always have to be in the driving seat. Fiona can be very assertive, and incredibly inventive, for an old bird – and I'm more than happy to be ordered about by her on occasion. And she always manages to deflect my anger.

Mum comes into the dining room as Dad and I are finishing our breakfast, looking as if she's seen the proverbial ghost. She hands Dad the local newspaper and tells him to look at the headlines. Dad takes the paper, brushes his mop of hair out of his eyes, and puts on his reading glasses. 'Golf Club Chairman's Wife Found Asphyxiated. An ambulance was called at 6.30 last night, but the paramedics were unable to revive her. Her husband is at present helping the police with their enquiries, and – '

'You don't have to read out the whole article, Ronnie,' Mum says, 'not in front of Darren. It's disgusting, perverted. I always knew there was something odd about that woman. She was obviously a sex maniac.' She gives Dad a decidedly odd look as she leaves the room.

Dad refolds the paper and pushes it aside. 'She's never forgiven Fiona for that *brief encounter* I had with her,' he says. 'But it's nothing to worry about, son. It was about ten years ago, when your mum and I were going through a rough patch. We're solid now. It was just before Fiona got married. I always thought she married Clive on the rebound. I never reckoned he was red blooded enough for her – but reading that... well, I'm shocked.'

I feel my mouth drop open. The thought of Dad doing it with Fiona before me is positively revolting. It's almost as bad as me sleeping with Mum. Has Dad done all the same things with her as I have? Perhaps she learnt all she knew off him. Dad sees my horror and slaps me on the shoulder. If he does that once more I'll deck him.

'As I said, no worries son. Everything's been just fine between your mother and me in that department for years now.'

'Too much information, Dad.' I've still got all these images of him and Fiona chasing about in my head, and now he's adding images of him with Mum. 'Anyway, we'll be late setting up the stall if we faff around here any longer,' I say. 'And you've got your golf lesson, remember. By the way, could I have private lessons in future? The other people in my group are all rubbish. They're holding me back.' I ram another piece of toast into my mouth as I leave the table.

I'm all cold and clammy as I approach the van. I feel sorry about old Fiona in a way, but it was her own fault. Mum's right. She was perverted. If she'd wanted to be dominated – get a good thrashing – she didn't need to introduce all that bondage crap. But she insisted, so what could you do? And she was completely rat-arsed when you got round there. Empty bottles of wine everywhere. Saying that Clive had refused to even give it a try. She was wheedling – 'I'm relying on you, darling'. Then she was shouting, demanding you put her in those hand and ankle cuffs. And you were already seething yourself. What with all that business with Jenna and then Grace, you felt like a volcano ready to blow. And anyway, how were you supposed to tell when she'd had enough. She'd said she wanted to be dominated. How could you be expected to know what that struggling and gasping meant? She shouldn't have insisted on that mouth corset thingy. And then when her face started to go blue, it wasn't your fault that you couldn't undo that tightening devise thing round her neck. You tried, but you just couldn't. Your fingers kept slipping. There was nothing more you could have done; it all happened so fast. The only thing you could do after you'd wiped away your fingerprints was to get away as quickly as possible. It was better that you weren't on the scene when Clive came home. He wouldn't have welcomed the embarrassment of knowing that his wife had a toy boy. He certainly wouldn't have wanted that sort of information splashed across the front of the local rag. It's unfortunate for Clive that he's a suspect in her death, but that's how it goes sometimes. He should have gone along with her, been more responsive to her needs.

Anyway, I'm too busy for any of that sort of nonsense at the moment. I'd have stopped seeing her anyway. She was getting way too extreme. All that kinky bondage stuff just wasn't on.

I'll actually have to do some extra work if I want to get my English marks up; I can't let Grace keep beating me all the time. It's a pity that the war poetry's turned out to be such crap. I'd been looking forward to that. But it was all written by either poofs or head cases – or both – so what can you expect? And Joel can have Grace for all I care. All those visions that Dad's just planted in my head have put me off sex for life. I was getting bored with Grace anyway, in fact she was beginning to really get on my wick. I kick the gravel under my feet.

'Come on son; don't sulk. It was over between me and Fiona years ago, and your mum never really knew the half of it.' He tries to put his hand on my shoulder again, but I manage to dodge him and jump into the van. I squeeze myself tight up against the passenger door, as far away from him as possible.

'Chop, chop. I'm not going until you've got your seat belt on, Darren. You've got to do the right thing when you're with me; I'm a magistrate, remember.'

As if he ever lets me forget.

# Chapter 13

## Darren Feels Superfluous

'What's up with you, Darren?' Eric asks. 'Not your usual self at all. What can I get you this morning?'

I slump myself down at the table nearest the counter. 'I don't know what I want at the moment, Eric. Give us a minute, will you? I'm feeling a bit depressed today, as it happens: a bit superfluous.'

'Superfluous, eh? You boys with your long fancy words.'

'It means not needed, Eric – surplus to requirements.'

'No girlfriend to perk you up then?'

'No, mate. I've decided to become a monk.'

'Well if it isn't your lucky day, son! Here's someone that needs you.'

I turn my head to see Joel laden down with his rucksack. What's with that thing? He's never without it.

'No Grace today, young man?' Eric says.

'She always has a lie-in on Saturdays, Eric. You know that.' Joel is about to sit at another table, but I won't allow it. I'm intrigued. I push back the chair next to me and pat the seat firmly.

'What's all this then, mate? How do you know about her lie-ins? Are you living with her or something?'

'Well, sort of,' Joel says.

'Come on then, spill.' This I've got to hear. This runt has more to him than meets the eye, but then he must have if Grace has chosen him over me. 'What do her parents think, then? Don't they mind?' This was insane; Grace hadn't allowed me to go further than the entrance to the flats. She wouldn't even let me go up in the lift with her just in case anybody saw us together.

'Oh, they don't know. I've got my own key. I have to wait until they've all gone to bed, and I have to leave early in the morning. Nobody's spotted me so far. Then I have to wash in the public loos over by the bridge.'

'Doesn't your mum say anything?'

'She couldn't care less. Can I have my usual please, Eric?' Joel bends down and gets his maths homework book out of his rucksack.

Eric leans over the counter at us, his neck jutting forward like a turkey's. 'Oh, I forgot, Darren. That's what I meant by you not being *superfluous*. You can help Joel with his homework. A little bird tells me that you're the main man at school.'

I look at Joel's work, with his funny numbers all sloping the wrong way. 'Of course I can help, mate,' I say. I have to lean right over him because he's cack-handed, and I put what I hope is a brotherly hand on his shoulder to steady myself. 'Well, you've got that one wrong for a start, mate. This is how you do it.' I've always wanted a brother. Any sort of one would do, even a nonentity like Joel. He's alright actually. We've got quite a lot in common. And I don't mind a bit about him and Grace. She's old news.

'Are you and Grace engaged, then?' I say, as I correct one of Joel's calculations.

'No. They're *just good friends*. Isn't that right, Joel?'

'Do you mind, Eric. This is a private conversation, mate.'

'No, he's right, Darren. I don't think I'm the marrying type. I'm like my mum in that respect.'

'Don't you have a dad then, mate?' I know almost nothing about him.

'Well, I must do, I suppose. But I've no idea who he is. I've got a sister somewhere, as well. She's been adopted by some other people though, and I don't even know where she lives.'

'Didn't you find anything out when we were doing our family tree thingies last year?' I say.

'I didn't have to do it. I had to do extra Geography with Old Grimthorpe instead. I would like to find out though.'

'Why don't you come round to my house sometime, and I can help you; you can use my computer. I can help you with your homework at the same time. We won't have old Eric here to contend with.'

'Not so much of the "old" if you don't mind, son. Anyway, aren't you eating anything today, Darren? I can't just let you sit here for nothing, you know. You're hogging that chair from my other customers.'

'We're your only customers, Eric.' I lean over Joel to try and see what he's writing down. I put him straight, and then glance over my shoulder and look out of the window. From here I can just see Susie from the year below us at school who's replaced Joel behind the stall. Joel was quite right to resign. On reflection, what he said about it getting too dangerous, what with our bit of business with Crunch, was spot on. As he says, if we're seen together too much, we might accidentally implicate each other if one of us ever gets caught. I'm surprised it was him and not me that thought of it first, as it

128

happens. And anyway, if he hadn't resigned, then I wouldn't have the lovely Susie for company, would I?

I can't stop looking at her. The sun's dancing in and out of her blonde curls, creating bubbles of light, and she suddenly looks very soft, sweet and inviting as she sits there waiting for me to return.

'Actually, I've decided what I want now anyway, Eric,' I say. 'I'll have a ring doughnut and a bottle of lemonade. No, not that kind, mate; I want the yellowy coloured sort.'

'You mean the old-fashioned lemonade. What's happened with the latte and the coconut macaroons then, Darren, my man?' Eric says.

'Keep up, Eric, that was ages ago. And I want two of each mate, and make it a takeaway. I'm going to treat my young assistant.' I've definitely decided to treat her, and not only to a drink and a doughnut. I'm going to make Susie's day and ask her out, put her out of her misery. If she blushes any more when I look at her, she'll do herself a mischief: self-combust or something. I'll only be doing the decent thing after all. Anyway, I've never had a blonde before, and I fancy a change. It's like that old saying 'a change is as good as a rest' and I've had enough of a 'rest' from girls. Celibacy doesn't suit me at all.

I give Joel a conspiratorial wink as I get up to leave. 'And give me a bell before you come round, Joel mate. Something might have come up.'

# Chapter 14

## Jeannie with the Light Brown Hair

Joel settles back into the passenger seat of Theo's car, and stretches out his legs. The creased and slightly worn leather material is yielding under his buttocks and back. The car may be old, but – unlike the Emporium – Theo keeps it spotless and Joel approves of it heartily. He knows nothing at all about cars, but he loves the clean curvature of the body and the stylish circular dials on the dashboard.

It's the last Sunday in November and Theo is taking Joel to a furniture warehouse he knows, situated a few miles out of town. Joel's mum is coming back home at last and – much to his relief – by herself. It seems that she and Kyle are no longer an item. He remembers the phone conversation he'd had with her a few days ago.

'Joel. At last! I thought you'd never answer. Where have you been?'

'I've been working actually, Mum. I had to switch my phone off,' he'd said. That was just typical of his mum. She didn't bother to contact him for ages, and then when she couldn't get through, it was suddenly his fault.

'Well, I'm glad to hear you're getting on with your homework. You've got GCSEs in the summer remember.'

'No, Mum; I haven't forgotten. But I was *working* working. You know: the kind that you get paid for. How else do you think I've been paying for my food?' Joel now has a regular shift at the Emporium on Wednesdays after school as well as all day on Saturdays, plus other times when Theo needs him. This suits Joel very well, as Darren often invites him back to his house on other days so that he can help Joel with his homework, but never on Wednesdays. Apart from seeing Susie on Saturdays and Sundays, Darren is always with her on Wednesdays. He'd told Joel that it relieved the pressure to space his dates out like this, which had surprised him, as he wasn't aware that Darren ever felt any pressure with his schoolwork at all. Then Darren had leaned back in his chair in that annoying and embarrassing way of his, the way he'd done after telling him of how he had scored with his first girlfriend, and Joel wondered if he was talking about pressure of schoolwork after all.

When they've finished their homework, or Darren has become bored, they usually end up playing computer games together, which of course Darren always wins. Joel doesn't mind never winning. At least it's nice and warm in Darren's house, and Darren's mum has taken quite a shine to him, and is always plying him with food. Darren's dad invariably keeps a low profile though, which is fine because Joel feels a bit awkward around him. He's so sullen and quiet. Darren insists on helping him with all his subjects now, except for English. That, he reluctantly had to admit, was definitely Grace's domain. Apart from Grace, of course, he reckons that Darren is his best friend now.

'Anyway, Joel, we've finally got the keys to the flat!' Jeannie had said. 'The Housing Association has just rung to say that we can pick them up this time next week. We've finished digging up the vegetables now, thank God. It's much too cold. You're not the only one who's been working, you know. So I'll be back in a few days.'

'That's fantastic news, Mum.' The sudden change in the weather after half term is making sleeping in his cupboard increasingly uncomfortable, and although Grace often manages to sneak out in the evening with a hot thermos of soup, Joel is worried that his health may succumb to the extreme cold. He's already developing a bit of a cough. He's used to a degree of discomfort from living for so many years in the squat, but the weather is more extreme this year than he can remember; and his mum has never thought to come back with his winter coat. Luckily for him, Leroy's old one just about fits him.

'Anyway Joel; I was ringing to ask you if you could find us some bits of furniture. We're being given a cooker and fridge, but that's it, apparently. The rest of the flat's completely unfurnished, and we got rid of all our old stuff, remember. We've got to have beds and a few chairs at least. I think there's a second-hand furniture warehouse somewhere you could try.'

'I'll try and find out about it then, Mum. Perhaps Theo could help.'

'Theo, did you say?' Jeannie had said. 'That's an unusual name. How do you know someone called Theo?'

'He's my boss; didn't I say? Why; do you know anyone called that?'

'I might have done once,' Jeannie had replied, after what had seemed like a particularly long interval.

Joel had felt a thrill of satisfaction running through him on hearing this. He wouldn't ask her any more questions yet, though. At the moment his fantasy was still intact. And he certainly wouldn't mention his mum's name to Theo.

Theo had known just the place to find some furniture: a once derelict farm building about two miles out of town. He'd offered to take Joel there the next day, as the Emporium is closed on Sundays.

'I might even find a few interesting things to sell in the shop,' he'd said.

Joel had inwardly sighed at this idea. The shop is a hotchpotch of totally unrelated items as it is, and he wasn't sure that this would improve the image. In fact, the Emporium doesn't really have an image at all, other than that of random mayhem. He longs to bring some logic to it. He's itching to be allowed to sort out the shop as well as the stockroom. What he particularly longs to do are the window displays. The areas of the shop that the customers never see or notice are immaculate now. The spare stock is all arranged neatly in a logical fashion, all the shelves have been dusted and the floors have been swept. Theo was so impressed with his work that he now allows Joel to check the new stock off from the delivery notes before it is put on the shelves. He's told him that he has a very tidy and methodical mind, and can therefore be entrusted with this important job. Joel knows however that his main talents lie elsewhere; even Eric has told him that he's got 'the eye'.

The furniture warehouse turns out to be a large open space enclosed by corrugated iron walls and a pitched roof, divided into smaller areas like rooms, created by the furniture on sale. Joel's eyes flicker about the space, trying to take it all in. He's entranced. The whole place is crammed full of mirrors, lamps, side tables, pictures and all sorts of things that he reckons might come in handy. He's never been asked to choose anything before, the situation has never arisen. But he supposes he'd better stick to his mum's list. He quickly spots a couple of comfy looking armchairs with rather loud, floral patterned loose covers that could easily be replaced with plainer ones at some stage.

His eye is suddenly drawn to a rectangular table and three chairs a few stalls further down. It's made of a light coloured wood and the table legs stick out from the top and curve over in an attractive, sinuous fashion.

'Very stylish, Joel!' Theo says, when Joel points them out. 'I think this might be the real thing.' He starts to feel the underside of the table top, and then he suddenly bends down and looks underneath. 'Bingo; it's even got the original makers metal sign: Finmar.'

The dealer is approaching them, a confident swagger to his gait. Joel sees Theo pretending to fumble with his shoelaces before straightening up.

'I can do that for a very good price, if you're interested,' the dealer says. 'I've had it for some time because it only has three matching chairs.'

A deal is struck, Joel hands over the cash, and is given a receipt along with a promise that the set will be delivered, along with the armchairs, to his new address on a suitable day next week.

'Now, let's go and get a cup of coffee somewhere before I give the game away,' Theo says, when the dealer is out of earshot. 'We can always come back later when I've calmed down. You've just landed yourself a very stylish and sort after bentwood dining room set from the 1930's, Joel my boy, designed by a famous Finnish architect. There have been loads of copies made, of course, but yours is the real thing. It's worth more than ten times what you've paid for it. Well done!'

Joel smiles broadly and feels himself growing by at least two inches in height. Theo thinking that he's got 'the eye' is way more important than anything Eric might say. 'And I don't

134

mind at all that it only has three chairs,' he says. 'It's not as if my mum's going to hold any dinner parties or anything.'

'What's your mum's name, Joel? You haven't told me anything about her at all.'

Joel doesn't really want to say, but he has to now. 'It's Jeannie.'

'Jeannie? That's an unusual name. You don't meet someone with that name very often. It reminds me of an old song I heard somewhere: I think my Granny used to sing it to me when I went to stay, and I couldn't get to sleep:

> *"I dream of Jeannie with the light brown hair*
> *Born, like a vapour, on the summer air*
> *I see her tripping where the bright streams play...."*

I don't remember any more. Was your mother ever a barmaid, Joel?'

'I've no idea,' Joel says, and he has no intention of finding out just yet. The comforting smell of old leather enfolds him as he settles back into Theo's car and he allows the echoes of Theo's clear baritone singing to reverberate over and over again in his mind. The pearls of knowledge that he longs for are dripping like tiny beads of water into an ever-growing pond all by themselves, and he isn't going to cause any unwanted ripples just yet.

# Chapter 15

## Grace Leaves Home

Grace felt exhausted both physically and mentally. She lay back on her bed and surveyed the growing mound that used to be her ultra-flat stomach, the shape only too visible through her cotton nightdress. She had calculated that she must be about five months pregnant by now. It could only have happened that time outside the entrance to the flats on their first night together. Darren had been scrupulously careful both before and since.

She had finally put her hand into the back of her jumper drawer and retrieved the pregnancy test a few days after Darren and she had split up, the day when she'd spent an embarrassing half hour with the Headmistress trying to explain what she was doing in the boys' toilets.

She laid her hand gently on her bulge and felt the baby kick. She loved it already in spite of its father and she still loved Darren in spite of herself. She was surprised that she'd managed to keep her condition a secret for so long. Luckily for her the weather had suddenly turned bitterly cold after half term, making it quite reasonable to wear several layers of clothing under a baggy jumper. She'd managed to let out the sides of her school skirt with strips of elastic and had insisted that she did all her own washing. It was the least she could do considering how busy her mum was looking after Gran – before they'd had to move her into the hospice a week ago. She knew she'd have to tell someone soon, but she just didn't know how to, and the time never seemed quite right.

'Grace!' Her sister Faith had come in without knocking, and quickly shut the door. 'Oh my God; when's it due?' Faith and her four year old son Dylan were staying for Christmas, made possible now that Gran's room was empty.

A wave of relief flowed over Grace. If anyone had to find out, then she'd rather it was her big sister. She'd know what to do. 'About the end of April, I think.'

'Well, you've left it too late to have an abortion. Whatever do Mum and Dad think? At least I was sixteen when I had Dylan, and old enough to get married. I presume its Joel's.'

'They don't know yet. I didn't know what to say. And of course it's not Joel's. It's his best friend's.'

'That's a pity, he's really cute, and he's obviously completely smitten on you. What does he think about it then, and more to the point, what does his best friend think?'

'I don't know and I don't care. I don't want anything to do with him.' Grace was beginning to cry, her shoulders heaving with each sob. 'I don't want to stay here anymore... I can't go back to my old school... please let me come and live with you... I could help you now that Eddie's away so much. I could go to that school near your house where nobody knows me... I wouldn't be any trouble, honestly. And can you tell Mum and Dad? Please Faith!'

Faith put an arm around her and Grace buried her face in the reassuring texture of her thick woollen jumper. 'Of course you can come and live with us if Mum and Dad don't mind, but you'll have to tell them yourself why you want to. And you'll have to do it now. Get your dressing gown on and come with me. I'm sure they'll be more upset than angry with you.'

It was the day after Boxing Day, and Grace was doing the last of her packing. She worked swiftly, folding her clothes with a neatness and efficiency she usually reserved only for her schoolwork. She remembered with a sense of relief how, with Faith's help and encouragement, she had at last told her parents of her predicament.

'Grace has something very important to tell you,' Faith had said. Her father had remained reading the newspaper, head down at the kitchen table, while her mother had continued to make him a cup of tea.

'Just for once, can't you just concentrate and listen to what she has to say?'

They'd both turned their gaze on her simultaneously and Grace had felt like that naughty five year old all over again, the one who had had to pluck up courage and admit that she and Leroy had accidentally spilt blackcurrant squash on the new sofa.

'I'm pregnant,' she'd whispered, head down, hands folded to protect her bulge.

'Speak up Grace. I don't think I can have heard you right,' her mum had said.

Faith had come to her aid once more. 'Yes you did. She said she's pregnant.'

And then there had been complete silence: no shouting, no questions, so Faith had filled the void with information as to the due date and of how Grace was to come and live with her.

'And don't worry about her going to school and getting her exams. I'll make sure she gets a place at the school near me.

The Headmistress and the School Secretary are both clients of mine. I always do their hair. She can stay with me as long as she likes. And I'm sure Grace will get a glowing report from her old school. She'll be fine.'

'Yes, I suppose so,' her mum had said, ignoring Grace completely. 'Once the baby's adopted, and she's got satisfactory GCSE results, she can come home, do her A Levels, and go to university. Who's the father, by the way?'

'Don't go there, Mum,' Faith had said. 'It was just a one-off mistake with a boy she doesn't even like, in fact she positively dislikes him. He doesn't know, and its best left that way. He would only complicate the situation, cause trouble even.'

Her mother had said no more on the subject. And her father, as usual, had said nothing.

Grace clipped the catches on her case shut, and looked around her bedroom one last time. It had never really been hers at all; it had always been Leroy's. She had shared the larger bedroom with her gran before Leroy's death. The décor in this smaller room hadn't changed at all since she had moved in. It was still the rather gloomy black and grey palette typical of a teenage boy. The only thing that brightened it up was the red and white frieze encircling the walls above window height, depicting the strip worn by the local football team. She had taken all the team posters down, but hadn't replaced them with anything else, no images of the latest boy bands. She hadn't felt the need when she'd been with Darren.

She bent down once more to give a final check under the bed for her elusive bedroom slippers. Although completely taken up with boxes, nothing else under there belonged to her. Her mother was still unable to throw anything of Leroy's away, but had folded up all his clothes and packed them neatly away under the bed to give Grace some space for her things in the

139

chest of drawers and wardrobe. She'd only really been camping out in here, rather like Joel had in her dad's storeroom downstairs.

She still hadn't told Joel that she was leaving. She'd just slip away without any goodbyes. She'd ring him up or better still text him when she got to Cardiff, but she wouldn't tell him the real reason why she'd left. She wouldn't tell him about the baby. He'd only want to know who the father was, and then he'd go and tell Darren. Darren was Joel's best friend now, not her. She hardly ever saw him out of school anymore. Now that his mum and he had moved into their new flat together, and he'd got all those extra shifts at the Emporium, she'd been side-lined.

Her mum looked around the half-open door. 'Have you finished packing, Grace? I think Faith wants to get off before it gets dark. It'll take at least an hour to drive back.' She helped to carry the case to the front door. 'We will miss you, you know, but I suppose you're doing the right thing. If you really don't think this boy, whoever he is, would be a very good father, then it's probably best for you to get away. And at least you'll be able to continue your education without any distraction after the baby's adopted.'

Grace knew exactly what her mum really meant. If she went now, and said it was because she'd be company for Faith while Eddie was away with the Royal Navy, then none of the neighbours need ever know of her shameful predicament. If they were ashamed of her, then she would keep away. That suited her perfectly. She would never have her baby adopted and she would never come back to live with them. She'd be sixteen in August and no longer their concern anyway. She'd be quite old enough then to look after both herself and her baby.

140

# Part II
# Caught Midstream

# Chapter 1

## The Old School Photograph

The visit home had been a success of sorts, Ronnie supposed. After nearly a quarter of a century he hadn't been sure what to expect. He had noted the enjoyment his wife Lorraine had gained in choosing the inappropriate Christmas presents for her unknown relatives. Unfortunately, they appeared to show off their recently acquired wealth rather than her good taste, but they were received in good part and without adverse comment. He had also noted how his son Darren had enjoyed himself – on more than one level. Not only had he become acquainted with his Irish roots, but also he had become good friends with several of his numerous cousins, enjoying impromptu jam sessions on his guitar with Ronnie's youngest sister Deirdre's sons Ryan and Finn, and enjoying an altogether different activity with her daughter Dawn.

Ronnie raised his eyes to the overhead luggage rack, and visualised the care Darren had taken in placing his prized guitar there. No one else was to touch it, or help him in any way. Although insisting on having it for his Christmas present last year, he hadn't shown any interest in it until a few weeks before his sixteenth birthday, just after his kayaking adventure. Then suddenly he was on the internet taking online classes on how to play and, as with everything else, he had picked it up quickly. Now he was writing his own material. Ronnie could often hear him in his room alone, and could gauge his mood from what he was playing. Sometimes it would be light and whimsical love songs about finding that 'special girl', at other times the electric amps would be turned on, and the walls would vibrate with the heavy metal sounds of anger and frustration, all dark and jagged. Then would come the soulful, depressing sounds of confusion as he ploughed through the pointlessness of his life. Until now his music had been a very private thing, but Ronnie recollected the look of joyful concentration on Darren's face as he bent over his guitar while playing with Finn and Ryan over Christmas, every now and then giving an enraptured Dawn a brooding look from beneath his eyebrows. Ronnie stifled a chuckle as he recalled the way Darren had started to hold a spare plectrum between his teeth at the side of his mouth. No doubt the look had appealed to Dawn as being rather cool, but it was fortunate that he hadn't swallowed it. Ronnie had then noticed Dawn and Darren's coinciding absences. A slight stare and an almost imperceptible nod of the head towards her before Darren made his exit would be followed, a few minutes later, by Dawn's. Well, good luck to them. He didn't suppose it was actually illegal. They were both sixteen after all. He wasn't going to get involved in the subject of the likely deflowering of his sister Deirdre's youngest daughter by his son.

He looked across at the seats opposite to his where Darren and Lorraine had positioned themselves, sitting close together almost conspiratorially, Darren leaning into Lorraine so that their shoulders touched even though he was a good head taller than her. Darren always insisted on sitting in the forward-facing seats on the train, which prevented father and son from ever sitting together because travelling forwards always made Ronnie feel sick. So Ronnie had found himself looking backwards as the train left the station at Fishguard; had been made to relive the apprehension he had felt on the outward journey to Cork, first on the ferry and from there to the O'Donnell family farm. He had been compelled to confront once more the memories of his growing up. The feeling of restriction in his chest was returning. He held his breath until the pain behind his eyes and in his ears became unbearable. Then he took great gulps of air to try and compensate.

He wouldn't have gone back home at all, if it hadn't been for his father's funeral. It had been fortunate that his sudden death had been so close to Christmas; it meant that Ronnie could spend more time with his estranged family. His eldest brother Ken had collected them off the ferry that first day and driven them back to the farm in the Landover. They had been welcomed by freezing conditions. Lorraine and he had squeezed in at the front next to Ken, while Darren had been obliged, rather unwillingly, to travel in the back on a hay bale surrounded by their luggage. The farmhouse had appeared to have changed little as he caught his first glimpse of it, the windowless north wall hugging the lane and forming a barrier against the outside world: to some a fortress, but to him a prison. All the principal rooms faced south over their rolling farmland, away from prying eyes.

Apart from the attendance of their large family, the funeral had been a quiet affair of which Ronnie now remembered little. His father had never gone out of his way to make friends, and apart from several elderly ladies sitting quietly at the back of the church, the only other attendees were business acquaintances: auctioneers, feed suppliers and the local vet. The only memories that remained of the service were the sudden, and until then forgotten, choking smell of burning incense as they entered the church, and then the biting cold air surrounding the newly dug grave causing moisture to form at the corner of his eyes. He hadn't been crying for the loss of his father, but for his inability to mourn his loss.

It had been the sight of the old school photograph that Ronnie's mother had shown to Darren on Christmas Eve that had started Ronnie's asthma-like attacks off again, only partly compensated for by his son's look of satisfied recognition when he was first invited to inspect it.

'Can you find me, Darren?' Ronnie's mother had said, and he'd found her almost immediately: a small child for her fourteen years – dark with large intelligent eyes.

'Which one's Grandad? I can't see anyone like me in your row, Gran. Dad's told me I take after him.'

'You're the spit of him, and no mistake. But you won't find him on my row. He was always so tall for his age; even sitting down he would have masked the child behind him. No, he's standing at the back with the teachers and the sixteen year olds. Look, there he is, and he's still the tallest.'

Darren's face had brightened as he followed his gran's finger. 'Were you two childhood sweethearts, Gran?' he'd asked.

'I wouldn't say that exactly, Darren… Not really.'

Ronnie had inwardly sneered. Sweethearts? Not at all! Ronnie knew how soon after his parents' marriage his eldest brother Ken had been born. At that time, and in most 'good' Catholic families even now, abortion wasn't an option, any more than the use of contraception. Ronnie had long been aware of the air of resentment emanating from his father when he was in his mother's presence, only to be confirmed when he began to openly move a succession of girlfriends into the

146

family home. Why had his mother put up with it? On reflection, of course, she had obviously had no choice. The farm and her children were her life. She had nowhere else to go. But that was all in the past, before his father's death.

Ronnie glanced at his son again, leaning even closer onto his mother's shoulder owing to the rocking motion of the train taking them home. The physical contact with her was unintentional, Ronnie was sure. Darren usually rather shunned it now that he had discovered girls. He wondered what had become of his son's first, rather timid, girlfriend Grace, who had been almost seamlessly replaced by Susie, his current choice. Darren did indeed look like his grandfather, and all through Darren's growing up, Ronnie had watched for other signs – other genetic traits. The boy had always been wilful and egocentric, and his violent and destructive tendencies over the last couple of years had given him some cause for concern, but this behaviour seemed to be the norm these days. Some of Ronnie's first building jobs had been repairing damage to hollow doors and partition walls, inflicted by boys growing up faster than their years. But Darren's behaviour had improved greatly of late, his violent outbreaks being dissipated by his music making. He had certainly inherited his grandfather's build. He was never to suffer the insults inflicted on Ronnie – the runt of his parent's overlarge litter.

'You weren't even an afterthought,' Ronnie's father would say when he was angry with him. 'I don't know what we were thinking of at all when you were conceived.' But the verbal abuse had been the least of his worries. He could just about tolerate that. That wasn't what made him finally slip out of the house with only a rucksack one day after he had turned sixteen to take a job on a building site in England, arranged by a friend of his cousin. It was the culmination of the cowardly acts of

147

violence that he could no longer endure, acts done in private when he and his father were alone and unobserved, acts that left no physical evidence, only psychological scars, acts predating those of a somewhat similar nature that came to light in Iraq and Guantanamo Bay.

Ronnie felt himself beginning to hyperventilate again, just as he had done as a child. He must try to take slow, deep breaths. He remembered how at first, his mother had told him to blow into a paper bag, and when that hadn't worked he'd been given an asthma inhaler. There was no psychoanalysis offered in those days. Of course, breathing deeply would not have been appropriate when his father's anger was aroused. In fact it would have been fatal. How did his father always know when to stop? Was it careful judgement or pure luck that he always managed to time it just right? But each time there was always that fear that his luck would finally run out.

Again he heard his father's raised voice, saw his eyes as their colour turned to steel. 'Why can't you do anything *right* for a change? Why can't you be more like your brothers, you little runt? Why do you always think you know best? Just do the job *my* way, why can't you?' Again he felt his father's knee in the small of his back, felt his thick hair being grasped by a large hand, and as his face touched the water in the drinking trough, his one thought had always been – *don't breathe in*.

Darren was sitting upright in his seat now, his hands behind his head, a faint smile playing about his lips. Once more Ronnie could hear echoes of the insults he had endured in his youth: *the runt, the little runt, the stupid little runt…* How he hated the expression, and how he hated the way his son was using it to describe his friends: Joel, and before him Leroy, the boy who had drowned in the river under such mysterious circumstances last February.

148

# Chapter 2

## Joel Samples the Stock

It has started to snow again as Joel approaches the junction with East Street, the flakes descending like large pieces of dandruff, settling conspicuously on everything they touch, and the icy wind bites into him even through his heavy winter coat, the strength of it making his progress slow. He's still wearing Leroy's old school coat – regulation brown – not a colour Joel reckons suits him. He can see himself in navy. Now that his Mum's working, perhaps he can spend more of his money on himself. He's already started planning his new wardrobe. He'd nearly hugged his mother when she'd told him she'd got a job as temporary bar staff at the King's Arms, but physical contact had never really been their thing.

'You never know, Joel,' she'd said. 'They may take me on permanently after the New Year. After all, I do have plenty of experience. I worked in the Nag's Head for years before I had you. But that's a young people's pub. It always has been.'

The man called Crunch had been to see Darren again at the market, just after he'd got back from his holiday in Ireland, and so Joel is making his deliveries as usual. As he turns left up Walpole Street, the effects of the wind lessen, making headway less strenuous. He finds the doorway easily enough. He's been here plenty of times over the last year. The large apartment is

149

situated on the second and third floors of a Georgian building that forms part of a terrace of shop and office buildings: solicitors, estate agents, alternative therapists and dentists. He rings on the door and is answered with the usual hissing-sound of the intercom.

'It's Jay, mate,' he says. He hears the familiar buzz and click.

Joel mounts the two flights of stairs, savouring the warmth both of the decor and the air temperature. The walls below the dado rail that snake up at the same angle as the stairs is a rich vermillion colour, fading to a lighter shade above it. Although the paintwork is chipped and scuffed, it exudes the grandeur of a former, more glamorous age.

'Come on in, Jay. Get in out of the cold, so I can shut the door.' Mickey, an unhealthily thin, tall and stooping man, leads him up a few more steps to his massive, dark kitchen facing onto the courtyards of the closely surrounding buildings. The temperature inside is oppressively hot, although Mickey obviously doesn't think so. He's replaced his usual bandana with a knitted hat with intricate repeating patterns around it. His long, greasy strands of hair hang wispy beneath the rim.

'It's brass monkeys today and no mistake, Jay. Come and meet my flatmates. I don't think you've met many of them before, although they all know and love you already of course. We've all had quite a heavy time over Christmas, and could do with your offerings.'

Joel is introduced to the assortment of people sitting around the large, ring-stained table: Frankie, Lance, Carol, Jude, Wendy – but as usual he fails to register any of the names. Mickey shuffles over to the worktop for his old-fashioned kitchen scales, his large, rather flat moccasin-covered feet sliding awkwardly over the tiled floor.

'Put the kettle on won't you, Cerise?' he says. A slim woman, probably in her twenties, with almost white coloured hair and black roots gets up from the table as Mickey sits down opposite Joel. Joel tenses slightly as he watches him weighing out each bag from the package he's placed in front of him. He's never had a problem so far, but it could well happen at some time, he supposes. He longs to open one of the bags and just smell the stuff, but he's never dared tamper with any of them. Someone was bound to notice.

Mickey reaches for a tin with some tobacco and cigarette papers in it. 'Let's give it a try then, Jay. It better be as good as the last batch. That was first-rate, I must say.' Joel watches with fascination as Mickey's thin and misshapen fingers fill a cigarette paper with a mixture of tobacco and some pinches of stuff from one of his bags, rolling it up deftly, licking the paper's edge and forming it into a neat tube in a matter of seconds, making a sort of filter with an odd scrap of card. He lights it, takes a drag, and passes it to Joel.

'Oh, I don't smoke it myself, mate,' Joel says. He'd tried a cigarette once when his mum had left an opened packet on the kitchen table, but it had left him feeling decidedly nauseous.

'OK, have a slice of cake then, if that's what you'd prefer. Hurry up with that tea, Cerise, and give Jay here some of that cake you made.' He takes another drag on his spliff and passes it around the table. Joel eagerly accepts the cake with his cup of tea, and wonders if Cerise always wears bright red to match her name. His mother hardly ever does any baking and the stuff from the supermarket always tastes rather like aerated cardboard. As his teeth sink into its firm but light texture, he notes a flavour of cinnamon with overtones of something slightly herbal.

'This is delicious,' he says. 'It's the best I've ever tasted. You'll have to give me the recipe.'

'Well, thank you Jay,' Cerise says, as she bites into a slice herself. 'I'm flattered. But it's all to do with the quality of the ingredients, and as Mickey has already said, last month's batch was quite exceptional.'

Joel knows he will sleep well. He's never felt so relaxed in ages. He doesn't feel the need to do any deep breathing or meditation at all before bedtime. He'll have to have a word with Mickey next time he gets him on his own. It seems a bit ridiculous to have to ask him really, seeing as he delivers the stuff to him in the first place, but the only way he's going to get his hands on any of this wonderful cake-making ingredient is to buy some back off him. He can't possibly put an order in for himself via Darren. Darren has quite strict moral principles when it comes to actually taking drugs. He says it's a filthy habit, and not to be contemplated. Darren considers his body to be a temple, and probably his biggest asset.

Joel doesn't reckon that baking a cake can be that difficult. Cerise had said that it's all to do with the quality of the ingredients. Quantities may have something to do with it as well, he supposes, but didn't Mrs Aitken say something about doing cake-baking with them in Food Technology next term…?

# Chapter 3

## The Right Price

Theodore Kitchen sat watching Joel as he busied himself in the shop window facing East Street. He was becoming a real asset to his business, and – he had to admit – to the rest of his life. He had been drawn to the boy as soon as he first met him that day last August, with his thick mop of tousled hair and heavy rucksack. He had looked so familiar somehow. Reflections and echoes of the past had flashed and reverberated in his mind. Joel had seemed like a kindred spirit, even though they had never met before. He fingered the form that he'd put ready on his desk to give him.

As usual, Joel was causing quite a stir with the pedestrians in the street. Many of them had stopped to watch him as he commenced his window display. First, he had removed all the old stock from the wide shelf area that formed the window sill, and placed each item neatly in a row against the wall below, so as not to inconvenience the customers already inside. Then he had climbed inside and dusted and cleaned the whole area, even the inside panes of the large window. Theo employed a cleaner for two hours once a week, but she refused to clean anything other than the carpeted area of the shop, together with the staff kitchen and toilet. She was too nervous to dust the shelves and window areas where there was stock. She was afraid she might break something.

Quite a large crowd had gathered outside the shop now, of which Joel seemed completely oblivious. It was a wonderful way to advertise the place. Paying Joel to perform this feat of magic made much more business sense than placing a boring ad in the local paper. Joel was making an ever-decreasing tower of empty cardboard boxes that he'd salvaged from the stockroom and was transforming it into a ziggurat by draping it with a piece of light coloured material that he'd found in a charity shop. At each change of level he was tucking in the material and placing small pieces of stock on the ledges he had formed: Buddhas, candle holders, small boxes and anything else he could find that would be colour and theme co-ordinated. He'd suggested to Theo that they might buy in some small pieces of furniture both to sell and to help with his displays. By arranging everything better, he reckoned that he could make the stock look more desirable and therefore more saleable.

Theo took his eyes off Joel for a moment to survey his shop. The boy was transforming the place, changing it from a frowsty, dusty and dark cave, only frequented by people interested in his esoteric books that he could just as easily sell over the internet, into somewhere bright, modern and thoroughly inviting. The sundry small items of stock that had previously filled the odd gap were no longer gathering dust, but were being sought out and purchased. But Joel's artistic touch was not the only asset he was bringing to the business. Theo had allowed him to work on the shop floor on occasion and was surprised at how well he connected with the customers. He knew every piece of stock intimately and was able to communicate this with enthusiasm. He made Theo smile

154

secretly on occasion, at the way the boy could invent several reasons for buying a particularly useless item. He had also started to take an interest in the books, particularly those on Greek and Roman myths and religion, and would sit, during his breaks, reading them. Joel was no longer that nervous boy who hid behind his hair or made frequent trips into his subconscious. Theo took pride in the fact that the meditation classes were obviously working. Joel had even started to keep a notebook on the counter in which he wrote down the details of frequently requested items, and Theo had started to buy things in specifically to order.

Theo felt a sudden emptiness. If only he had a child like Joel who could take an interest in this business of his, someone who would benefit from it, someone who would inherit everything one day. Perhaps he did have a child somewhere. It was not impossible. He was not proud of the sort of life he had lead before he had left this town. In fact his chaotic drug and alcohol-filled lifestyle was the very reason that he had left. He had had to change, before it changed him irrevocably. His past was filled with a string of failed relationships, and he had left very suddenly without any means of being contacted. The monasteries that he had stayed in had no modern forms of communicating with the outside world. Perhaps he was a father without even knowing it.

Joel had finished his window display, and his enthralled spectators were beginning to file into the shop. Theo put the application form that he'd continued to finger into a drawer of his desk that acted as a counter. He'd show it to Joel after the initial rush. Later, over coffee, Theo breathed deeply before confronting Joel. 'Have you had any more thoughts on what you're going to do after your GCSEs, young man?'

'Not really,' Joel said. 'I'm finding it much easier to concentrate in class now, thanks to you, and my friend Darren's giving me a lot of help with my homework, but I've just left everything a bit late, I'm afraid. I don't think I'll get good enough grades to be allowed to stay on and take A Levels. I don't know what I'm going to do really.'

'I was hoping you were going to say that, Joel, just as much as I'm hoping you'll say yes to what I want to propose. You're doing such an excellent job here that I was hoping that you might agree to come and work for me full time. I've looked into it thoroughly and I can apply to get a grant for you to come here and learn everything about the business. It's called a Retail Apprenticeship. You'll get a proper rate of pay and you'll get a qualification at the end of it. You could have a look at the form now, even fill it in if you like, but I won't send it off until you've thoroughly thought it over.'

'Of course I want to work with you,' Joel said. He took the form and started to fill it in straight away.

'Now off you go and show me your customer handling skills,' Theo said. 'I'll keep your form safe until you've talked it over with your mum.' Theo glanced at Joel's strange, rather endearing, backwards-sloping handwriting before he put the form back into the drawer. His full name jumped out at him: Joel Price. So Jeannie Price really was his mother, the Jeannie who'd worked in the Nag's Head, the Jeannie who everybody was in love with back then. He hadn't been the only man who had dreamed of 'Jeannie with the light brown hair'. His thoughts flew back to that morning when he woke up in her bed. She was leaning over him in her dressing gown offering him a cup of tea. He remembered the distinctive smell of recent lovemaking that lingered on her skin and hair. It was the last morning he had spent in England before leaving for Asia.

His initial instincts had been right about that boy now serving his customer. No wonder he had looked so familiar. But of course, he would say nothing about any of this to Joel. It was Jeannie's place to tell him really, he was sure. But the boy should be told. It was his right to know. Theo would once have felt anger over this, but that was back then, before he went away.

Theo imagined that wonderful Art Deco table that Joel had found, sitting against the wall of Jeannie's living room, its three matching chairs arranged around it, and wondered if they were all used on a regular basis.

'Joel, if you do decide to take up the apprenticeship, we'll have to go out for a meal one evening to celebrate – with your mother, of course. Do you have a stepfather, Joel? He'd obviously be welcome as well.'

'No,' Joel said. 'She had a boyfriend called Kyle at one time, but we haven't seen him since we moved into our new flat.' Joel beamed at him and his eyes seemed to grow even larger, just like his mother's. 'I'm sure she'd love to meet you.'

Theo however, was not quite so sure.

# Chapter 4

## At Eric's Café

Joel eyes his usual Saturday lunch with satisfaction. He lifts off the top slice of bread and smothers the sausage with a thick layer of ketchup.

'Has Darren been in for lunch already, Eric?' Joel bites into his sandwich, and savours the sudden explosion of grease and tomato as it hits his palette.

'He came in earlier for a coffee, but he hasn't been back for his lunch yet,' Eric says, swabbing down the counter with a decidedly grey-looking cloth. 'In fact he was in much earlier than usual today. Said he was "bored and disgruntled". Do you know a geezer called Percy?'

Joel shrugs and shakes his head. He's still chewing.

'Well, it seems that this Percy character has got Darren's little assistant Susie into a bit of trouble. Her mother got hold of her private and very personal diary, and was horrified at what she was getting up to with him. She'd used some very graphic descriptions apparently, so she's been grounded for nearly a year until her sixteenth birthday. She's not even allowed out on Saturdays to help Darren on the stall. It appears he's rather missing her. I think he rather fancied her himself. In fact I'm sure he had more than just his eye on her on several occasions, if you get my drift. You'd be surprised at what I can see from behind this counter.'

Joel's interest in Darren's love life – or lack of it – is not uppermost in his mind at the moment, much less on the exploits of this unknown character called Percy. He wants to talk to Darren on a much more important subject: how he's got on in helping him trace his sister Zoe. Clues as to his parentage have dried up for the moment, but as Joel is quite happy as to the direction in which they appear to be leading, he has turned his attention to another puzzle in his family tree. Darren has promised to look a few things up for him on the internet if he has time. He'd understood why Joel had wanted to find her.

'I know how crap it is to be an only child,' he'd said, 'and knowing that you have a brother or sister out there somewhere must make it even worse. I envy my cousins in Ireland. There are loads of them all living close together, but I'm miles away from all of them, and I won't be seeing them again until at least next Christmas.'

The door rattles open and Darren comes in. 'Give me a cheese sandwich and another cappuccino, will you, Eric,' he says. 'I need something to perk me up. I didn't get a wink of sleep last night.'

'What have you been up to then, Darren? My old mum used to say that insomnia was the sign of a guilty conscience,' Eric says, giving Joel a wink.

'I've done nothing recently, that's the trouble,' Darren says, slumping down next to Joel. 'I suppose Eric's already told you about Susie?'

'Yes. I was surprised to hear that she was two timing you.'

'That as well, eh? That's news to me. It's probably for the best that I can't see the little slapper anymore then. How's Grace, by the way? Have you been to see her yet?'

'No, but I'm going to stay for a couple of days next week, when we break up for Easter. I keep asking if I can go, but she's always had some excuse or other before now. I think we're still friends though. She's always texting me.'

'So you're not actually going out, or anything?' Darren says.

'They're *just good friends*; that's right isn't it Joel?'

'Shut up, Eric. But yes, he's quite right. We are just good friends,' Joel says.

Darren looks down at his immaculate fingernails and picks at some imaginary piece of dirt under one of them. 'Where does she live now then, mate? Cardiff, wasn't it? How do you get there? By coach?'

'Yes. It's not a bad journey really. It only takes about an hour and a half. I'll be back by Saturday if you have anything you need me to do.' Joel knows that Darren is expecting Crunch sometime soon, the man with the boxes purporting to hold electrical goods. 'By the way, how did you get on with the business of tracking my sister?'

'Not good news, I'm afraid,' Darren says. 'It looks as if you'll have to wait until she's eighteen, unless your mum gets in touch with her step-parents via the adoption agency, and comes to some arrangement with them. But then your sister still has to actually want to meet you. It's a bit of a bummer really, isn't it?' Darren resumes the inspection of his nails for some time. 'Have you got any of those coconut macaroons today, Eric? I just fancy a couple today, for old times' sake. And give Grace my best, won't you, mate.'

# Chapter 5

## Hope and Expectation

'What do you think then, Grace? Should I go for it?' Joel was sitting on Faith's rather battered, once cream coloured sofa in her lounge, looking eagerly up at her as she stood in the kitchen doorway. This was the first time they'd actually seen each other since just before Christmas, although they'd communicated nearly all the time by text, and in one respect he hadn't changed a bit. He still seemed to need her opinion on really important matters, she'd noticed.

'Definitely go for it! I think it's a brilliant idea. You'll always be able to get a job in retail. It's a bit of a strange shop though, but as long as you're learning how to run a business, I don't suppose it matters which one.'

He had changed in one respect though. Although still slim, he no longer had the gawkiness of a child, and she noticed that his new-found confidence had in fact made him rather attractive. His thick mop of dark hair had grown quite long again, but she rather liked the way he swept it out of his eyes occasionally and tucked it behind his ear. Before, he'd just hidden behind it. When Faith had met him again yesterday she'd pronounced him *really cute*, and once more expressed her disappointment that he wasn't the expectant father. In a way, Grace wished that he was. She was so fond of him, but there had never been a hint of sexual attraction between them. She'd never felt that churning in the pit of her stomach that she'd felt with Darren. She would have to tell Joel about the baby soon. She was surprised that he hadn't noticed yet, although to be fair to him, she was one of those girls who carried her pregnancy evenly distributed around her middle and hips, and not just out in front, on her stomach. And she was sure the mini dress she was wearing over her elasticated jeans helped. After all, it did look quite fashionable – very 1960's retro. His absorption in his own affairs had no doubt made him less observant than usual, and she had tried to make sure that he didn't catch a sight of her side-on. But she felt that she must really tell him now. 'Joel…'

'… and Theo says he doesn't really mind what grades I get in the summer, although good passes in English and Maths would be useful, and possibly French, and I'll probably do quite well in Art. My maths is actually getting OK now, especially my mental arithmetic, which was useful when we went to the Trade Fair at the NEC last month. I could work out really quickly what items we could make a good profit on. Darren's been helping me a lot. We're still really good friends.'

'I'm glad, Joel. Actually, there's something I have to tell you.' Grace began to feel an unexpected weakness in her legs, and she had to lean against the doorway for support. Somewhere far behind her she heard the click of the electric kettle as it turned itself off and she was aware of the whoosh of steam subsiding. She'd just rest here for a while. She could make the tea in a minute. Suddenly she was aware of a hot liquid pouring down the insides of her legs and splashing onto the lino.

'Help me Joel, quick! I need an ambulance!'

Joel remained where he was, staring at her. 'You've wet yourself, Grace,' he said.

'For Christ's sake, Joel; my waters have broken!' Grace doubled up and let out a moan as her stomach muscles clenched together. 'I'm four weeks early, and I haven't even packed a case. I'm having a baby, Joel!'

Joel jumped up from his chair, grabbed his phone from the sideboard and dialled 999.

'We need an ambulance, quick. My girlfriend's gone into labour and she's four weeks early.'

Why had he said that, Grace wondered – called her his girlfriend? Without a doubt he was her best friend, but they had never even held hands. They were only children really, innocents... well Joel was at least. She felt a sudden surge of affection for him. He was trying to protect her honour.

'Name and address, please. And who is her midwife?'

Joel gave the answer to the first question mechanically. He looked over to Grace, but got no response.

'I don't think she's got a midwife, I'm afraid.'

Grace got herself to a chair, and strained to hear the instructions being given over the phone. He was to make a note of the time between contractions, he must try to make sure that she did her breathing exercises and, above all, he must make sure that her case was packed.

Grace was still doubled over with pain when Joel put the phone down.

'Try and breathe,' he said.

'I am breathing. What do you think I'm doing?' Grace shouted.

'Breath slowly, and deeply, and concentrate on just that. Try not to focus on anything else at all,' he said. 'It's what I do when I meditate.'

'I can't any more. It's getting too bad,' Grace wailed after only a short while.

'You need a mantra – a single word or note. Or part of a song would do. You could hum it to yourself,' Joel said.

Almost at once, Grace could hear Gran singing and humming to herself as she worked in the kitchen back home before she'd become ill. It was always the same thing – something about raindrops – the melody interspersed with the odd line of words that Gran happened to remember. To Grace, it had always sounded very up-beat and optimistic. She concentrated on Gran's voice, her barely perceptible Jamaican accent coming through. She hummed along with her until she reached the last couple of lines: *'Because I'm free / Nothing's worrying me.'*

'It's working,' she says, smiling up at Joel as the contraction fades. Like the words of the song, she suddenly feels completely free. She no longer cares what anybody thinks about her, or expects from her. Joel is looking after her and she only has one thing to worry about right now and that is getting this baby born.

≈

Joel wakes up next morning to find himself still in the reclining chair that has been placed next to Grace's bed in the delivery room. He is holding her hand. The baby was born just after midnight, and although perfectly healthy, she has been taken to the nursery as she was premature and underweight. As it was so late, the hospital staff left them where they were.

Joel remembers the midwife saying that as the baby weighed more than 5lbs she would not need to be put into an incubator. They would be carrying out blood tests however, as she would probably get jaundice, but they were not to worry as this was quite usual, and easily dealt with. Joel feels a glow of pride as he recalls the midwife saying 'Come on, Dad. It's your turn to hold your daughter. Mum needs a rest after all her hard work,' and he remembers Grace's encouraging smile as she held the baby out to him. But now he must be going to work. It's Saturday, and Theo will be expecting him at the shop bright and early as usual. He'd love to stay longer and see the baby again, but Faith will be coming in soon. If he leaves now he'll be in time to catch the 7.15 coach and be back home by 8.45, leaving him time for breakfast at Eric's followed by a quick wash in the public toilets. He kisses the sleeping Grace lightly on her forehead. The night light over the bed is casting a golden glow over her. She looks like an angel lying there, her mass of tight, unruly curls framing her face like a halo. In their rush to pack her case, they had forgotten her hairbrush.

Joel catches the coach from outside the hospital and sits at the front. The coach terminates outside Eric's Cafe, so he can catch up on his sleep without fear of missing his stop. There are few stops on this particular route and Joel soon relaxes into a deep slumber helped by the gentle rocking motion of the coach as it negotiates the winding country lanes. When he wakes up, the coach is descending out of the early morning mist and is already heading towards the river crossing, and Joel sees the start of Western Heights ahead of him – the estate of executive homes that have been built a few years ago for families going up in the world: for families gaining status in the town, families like Darren's.

He looks out over the river and to the town to the east where the sun is rising, painting great swathes of horizontal bands of differing shades of red across the horizon. He can just make out the Shopping Mall and the three towers of the council flats where Grace's family live as their top storeys begin to tentatively emerge into the sunlight. As the coach reaches the crossroads with the river and is beginning to turn left over the town bridge, Joel gets a view of the stallholders setting up their wares along Broadway, all the way along the river embankment on the east side. The coach begins to slow down as the traffic lights into town are changing to red, and Joel rises to get off the coach around the corner. He catches a glimpse of Darren a few stalls in, leaning back on his chair between his stall and his dad's van, and suddenly all becomes clear. In the hurried confusion of the birth, he hadn't even considered who the father of Grace's baby was. He adds four months onto March, and comes up with July – July of last year. He rushes to the door and waits impatiently, ready to jump off as soon as the coach doors open.

Memories of the conversation between him and Darren at the end of the summer term come flooding back. Darren is leaning back in his chair in that confident way of his, his thumbs tucked into his jeans pockets. He's telling Joel about how he has 'scored' with some girl in their class at school, and how she'd been 'gagging for it'. Joel remembers how he'd tried not to show any interest, trying to banish the images of Darren and this nameless girl from his mind. And there he is now, sitting in exactly the same position, his thumbs in his pockets, and his chair tipped at just the right angle so as not to fall over. Joel rushes over the road and weaves deftly in and out of the mass of early morning punters until he reaches Darren's stall. He's on him in a flash, both of them landing in a heap between the stall and the van. Joel is on top, punching and pummelling him, his hot tears splashing onto Darren's startled face. Quickly, Darren's strong hands encircle Joel's slim wrists, preventing him from moving.

'What the hell are you playing at, you moronic runt!' Darren demands. 'Get off me, for Christ's sake. People are beginning to stare.' A few of Darren's fellow stallholders have started to gather round them. 'There's nothing here I can't handle, mates. It's just a bit of harmless horseplay.' Darren is already on his feet, brushing himself down.

Joel stays sitting on the ground, and refuses Darren's hand to help him up.

'What is all this, mate? What on earth have I done?'

'Grace. That's what you've done. She's just had a baby. She's in Cardiff maternity hospital.'

Darren's features become still for a moment before he says, 'There must have been somebody else before me then, the little slapper. I thought I was the first.'

'She's not a slapper, and it was you, you complete bastard! The baby was four weeks early. And you said that she was gagging for it. Well, she wasn't. She's not like that.'

'I can assure you she was. They all are. There must be something wrong with your technique.' Darren tries to help Joel to his feet again, but he pushes him away, sobs of impotence racking his body.

'You've got to go, mate. Everybody's still looking,' Darren says. 'I can't give you any more stuff for the moment, either. We can't be linked, it's too dangerous. I told you not to come to the stall anymore. That's why you don't work here anymore, remember.'

Joel gets up and moves slowly over to the embankment wall. He feels weak with exhaustion as he leans his elbows on the parapet. He mops at his eyes and takes in great gasps of chilly air. He stares blankly at the row of pleasure boats tied up in readiness for the Easter holiday season. A couple of squabbling mallards are chasing after a female as she breaks

167

cover, swimming into the centre of the river. Not looking back, he leaves the market area, crosses Broadway and heads for Eric's Café.

Joel sits down in his preferred seat nearest the counter and orders a mug of tea. 'Make it extra strong will you, Eric?' Joel's sudden feeling of exhaustion has made him lose his appetite. 'I might have something to eat in a minute,' he adds, answering Eric's questioning look.

'You look rough this morning, Joel,' Eric says as he reaches for the tea pot. 'Had a hard night?'

You could say that,' Joel answers, trying to remain sitting upright.

Eric gives him a knowing look and taps the side of his large nose with his tobacco stained index finger. 'You boys, eh!'

For the second time this morning, Joel is reminded of his naivety and lack of experience, and it isn't even nine o'clock. Perhaps he's the freak, not Darren. He cups his cold hands around his scalding mug of tea, and looks absently over to the table by the window where the only other customer is sitting, speedily demolishing his fry up. His small terrier is occupying the chair next to him, standing alert, watching the elderly man's quickly emptying plate with interest, his head cocked. Is he like the little dog, only ever getting the scraps?

He suddenly feels very alone. Grace was always saying that they're best friends, and he thought that he was getting somewhere with Darren, but neither of them had bothered to tell him about this. He wasn't important to them at all. They had loved each other once, enough to do that together, and he hadn't even suspected. He hadn't even noticed that Grace was pregnant, so what sort of a friend was he anyway? His reaction just now, when he had tried to attack Darren, hadn't been jealousy over what had happened between them, but sheer misery because they hadn't told him. Because he hadn't been important enough to be told.

The door opens and Darren strolls in. As Joel watches him approach the counter in that confident way of his, shoulders back and hips gyrating slightly, Joel wonders if he still has a crush on him. His feelings for Darren are so confusing. Does he just admire him and want to be like him, or does he actually love him? Is he in fact gay and is that why he doesn't think of girls in the same way as Darren?

'A latte and a bacon sandwich to take away please, Eric. Actually mate, make that a cappuccino. A latte brings back graphic memories of a super-hot chick I had last year, and I've got to work today.'

'Coming up Darren, my man.' Eric's finger hovers from one button on his coffee machine to another, and gives it a smart press. He then slaps a couple of rashers into his already smoking pan.

Darren sits down next to Joel. 'This sprog of Grace's, then, what's it called?'

Joel's brain and body feel completely numb. He is beyond rage. All he feels right now is misery and embarrassment. Quite calmly and evenly, but avoiding Darren's stare, he says, 'She's not an "it", she's a little girl. And for your information she's called her Hope. Not that you'd care.'

'Hope! What sort of a dumb name is that then, mate? Hope! Fat chance of her finding any of that around these parts!'

'Your order's ready, Mr O'Donnell, sir,' Eric says, placing a brown bag and polystyrene cup on the counter. Darren gets up and pays, and with a 'Keep the change, Eric mate,' he swaggers out of the door and into the welcoming light of a beautiful, crisp Spring morning.

≈

I mustn't run across the street, Joel might be looking. Anyway, I don't particularly want to get run over, not now that I'm a Dad. I can't believe it. I've got a daughter! I must go and see her. Where is that blasted tarpaulin? I'm sure I put it in here somewhere. Ah, there it is, hiding under that pile of boxes right at the back of the van. I'll just fling it over the stall and fasten it down, and then I can go. These spring clip thingies are even stiffer to open when your hands are shaking. Why is that always the case when you're in a hurry?

The gorilla on the next stall is staring. I'll have to say something. 'Something's come up, Gerry mate. I have to be somewhere, but I should be back before lunch.'

I cross the road again, but this time further up, next to the bridge. I'm running up East Street. I can't go and see Grace and the baby empty-handed. I'll get something from the Mother and Baby shop in the Shopping Mall. Good, they're opening up the giant metal shutters. I mustn't look into any of my favourite shops, I haven't got time.

My breath comes in gasps. I hear myself gabbling almost incoherently at this startled, middle aged assistant, about how my daughter has just been born four weeks early, and I don't have anything for her, and I don't even know what she'll need.

'It is a shock of course sir, when they are born so unexpectedly,' she's saying. 'The standard size baby clothes that you've probably bought already will be much too big. How much does she weigh?'

I shrug. How am I meant to know? She's showing me the tiniest little romper suits I've ever seen. They would barely fit my hands. Quickly I chose three of them: one white, one pink, and one yellow, all with a rabbit motif on the front.

The assistant's directing me to other, larger necessities: carry cots, baby baths, prams and push chairs. It seems as if I need to buy everything in the shop. I feel completely overwhelmed. I sit down on the chair next to the counter and try to catch my breath. I can't afford all this, and anyway, I can't take all of it to the hospital, can I?

'Don't feel as if you have to buy it all at once, sir. I'm sure your partner will have her own preferences. I suggest you take the clothes now together with the carry cot. She'll need that when you collect her from the hospital. You can bring her in for the rest of what the baby needs after that. It sounds as if they'll be in for at least a week.'

I pay for the suggested items, together with a small, soft rabbit I see sitting next to the till. I'll bring Grace in next week and let her choose the rest. I'll find the money from somewhere and Crunch has just paid me for delivering the latest drugs consignment so that will help. I'll give all that up now, of course. I've been thinking of it for ages. After all, I only got mixed up with Crunch because Dad was getting so up himself when he was made a Justice of the Peace. And we'd just had some stupid row. It seemed a laugh at the time. I was getting my own back.

Back at the stall, I rummage for the spare keys to the van that Dad keeps in the glove box. I'll have to drive to Cardiff. So what if I'm not old enough to have a license? It's lucky that Dad's been teaching me to drive on that large building site of his. I'm quite good enough to pass the test, so there's no problem so long as I don't get pulled over by the police. I haven't got an option. I just don't have time to take the coach there and back if I'm going to be ready for Dad when he comes back from golf.

'I'm sorry Gerry, but there's been an emergency, mate. I'll be back before you know it.'

I wish now that that stupid bitch Susie hadn't let me down. I could have left her in charge. I set the satnav to get me to the hospital. It looks quite a straightforward journey: fifty eight minutes. I'm sure I can do it in forty five.

I'm on the road at last, and 'Deirdre' is shouting out instructions: 'turn left over bridge, turn right at the lights', but I can hardly hear her over all this stuff that's going on in my brain. Why didn't Grace tell me she was pregnant? If it's my baby I've a right to know about it, haven't I? And why did she suddenly decide to turn against me like that? She must have known she was expecting by then anyway, so why ditch me just at that particular moment? Why decide that she'd rather be with Joel? Has Joel known all along, and if so why the hell hasn't he said anything before? I thought we were meant to be friends. And I do love Grace, I really do. It wasn't my idea for us to split up. It's just not fair.

'Deirdre'! What the hell are you playing at? I've never practised filtering onto a dual carriageway. Well, it can't be that difficult. Even morons drive, don't they? Take him for instance. Yes, alright, no need to hoot quite so loud, mate. And what's with the flashing headlights? This is actually quite scary.

I just can't stop the same thoughts about Grace and Joel from going round and round in my head. It's a bit much to put up with for nearly a whole hour. They've almost made me miss the Hospital turning, even though 'Deirdre' is shouting at me at the top of her voice, just like the real Auntie Deirdre did when she virtually caught Dawn and me 'at it' at Christmas. I'm livid over being kept in the dark all this time. I can't get out of the car. I'll have to sit here in the car park and calm down, decide what I'm going to say. I take a few deep breaths and quietly construct my speech.

I'll tell her that I love her, and that I've got the right to be with them and look after them, as it's my baby. We'll get married as soon as she's sixteen, and we'll live happily ever after, just like in those crap novels she's always reading. And if she'll only say that she loves me, and that I'm still the best boy in the world, then I might even watch a few of those soppy films with her. I've really missed hearing her saying all those nice things. Nothing's really been the same with anybody else. I know I love her. I must do.

I'll have to go in. I've wasted too much time already. Oh, shit! I've only just noticed the sign. 'Drop off point only. Waiting limited to 20 minutes'. I'll just have to risk it. The rest of the car park's completely full and there's a queue of cars waiting for spaces. I grab Grace's things out of the back of the van and go down the steps to the main entrance.

There's this officious old broiler on reception telling me that visiting hour doesn't start until 2.00pm. 'I'm the dad,' I say. 'The baby was born prematurely while my partner was on holiday visiting relations. She only gave birth a few hours ago and it's taken me all this time to get here.' I show her the carry cot.

'In that case I'm sure it will be alright for you to go in,' she says. 'What's your partner's name?'

'Grace Bradshaw,' I say. Lucky I remembered her surname.

'That's fine.' She's smiling now, and directing me towards a corridor on the left.

It's a lovely new building, as it happens: all bright and fresh looking, but why is it that all institutions smell of cabbage and custard, and it's not even lunchtime? It's as bad as school. The corridor's about a mile long. Every time I think I've got there I'm confronted with yet more double doors. I look into a side ward and see this old geezer hitched up to a machine with tubes going in and out of him. Suddenly I feel cold and drained. The soles of my trainers squeak impotently on the hard, unforgiving floor tiles.

At last I've found Grace's ward. It's massive! There must be at least forty beds in here. I scan the place quickly but I can't see her. She's not here. There's just a sea of thirty year old Fiona Sutcliffe lookalikes, and they're all staring at me accusingly. Ah, there she is, sitting up in bed right over by the window. She looks exhausted, dishevelled and very, very young. I want to put my arms around her and kiss her better, just like she used to do to me. Then I notice it. Everyone's got a crib by the bed except for Grace. I panic. 'Where's ours?' I say. I can feel a dull pain building up behind my eyes. Surely she hasn't had it adopted. Could she actually do that without my consent? Grace says nothing. She just draws the covers up around her.

'Oh, it's alright dear, they'll be bringing her down soon,' the woman in the next bed says. 'So you're the father, are you?'

Grace is staring at me, but not in the way I'd hoped she would. She looks hard and hostile. She's still gripping the bedclothes.

'What are you doing here? Who told you?' she says.

'Joel did, just now. Why didn't you? Didn't you think I had the right to know?' It's all coming out wrong. I'm sounding too aggressive. All the old crones surrounding us are leaning forward, straining to hear, and Grace is getting her scared look.

174

'I think you'd better go now,' she says. 'They'll be bringing Hope down soon and I'd rather you weren't here. I don't want her upset.'

I want to show her the things I've brought her. I want to see her smiling up at me the way she used to. I want to hear her saying that she still loves me and our breaking up had all been a big mistake. Instead, she's dismissing me.

'I've got some things for you. I'll just put them by the bed,' I mutter. 'And you'll need some money. Look after it. Don't let any of these old witches steal it. They'll be a lot of things you'll need to buy.' I reach into my jacket pocket and draw out the tatty envelope of used notes Crunch has just given me. I want to bend down and kiss her, but I know she won't let me. Her once full and welcoming lips are pursed tight shut.

I rush out as fast as I can, but it's not fast enough. I can't run in here, can I? It'll be like school, just like the horrid smell. I want to lash out: vandalise everything that's getting in my way, but there's cameras everywhere – inside and in the car park. I climb into the back of the empty van and sit down. I lean back against the side panelling, scrunch my fists into a ball and press them into the floor. It's making my knuckles ache. My eyes are welling with tears. I'm howling like some wild animal, like a wolf that's just been banished from the pack. I've always wanted a brother or sister but a baby would have been even better, something that really belonged to me. And I did love Grace once, I'd sure I did, even though I never got round to telling her.

But I've been here too long. I can't mope around anymore, it's nearly 11 o'clock already. If I go now I'll be back in time for lunch. I'm starving. I never ate that takeaway, did I? I'll quickly sort out the stall and then I'll go to Eric's. I feel much better about everything after that cry. I don't really want to be tied to some girl who's egging me on one minute, and then pushing me away the next. Only two more years and I'll be going to university, and then everything will be different. I don't want to be lumbered with some frigid little bitch and a sprog called Hope now, do I? I can't wait to escape from my ridiculous parents and all the other pathetic excuses for people who're surrounding and suffocating me. I've outgrown everything that dump of a town can offer. I'll just put my head down, pass all my exams with distinction, and then I'll show them all what I can do. I'll show them what real living is. And I'm bound to get into Oxford now that I've persuaded Dad to pay for me to go to private school.

I'm back on the stall, and I see Joel going into Eric's for lunch. I give Gerry a cursory 'Won't be long, mate,' cross the road and follow him in. Joel doesn't seem very pleased to see me, but I sit next to him anyway.

'Give me what Joel's having, Eric, and put it on my slate.' I'm not sure I have one, but I realise that I've just given all my cash to Grace. Eric obliges, taking a biro from the pocket of his repulsive-looking apron.

'I don't suppose you'll be going to the hospital to see the baby, then,' Joel says.

'Not much point really is there, mate. They all look exactly the same.' I've no idea if that's true because I've never bothered to look, but that's what everybody says.

Eric slaps something positively vile down in front of me. I bite into it and a great spurt of grease shoots onto the lapel of my jacket. Thanks for that, Joel. Good choice.

# Chapter 6

## Theo at The King's Arms

'How did you get on at the bowling alley last night, Joel? Had a good time?' It was a Saturday in mid-May, and Joel had just come back into the Emporium after an early lunch with Darren at Eric's Café.

'It was fine thanks, Theo. I didn't do too badly for a beginner, actually. We met these two girls as well. Darren's asked his one out tonight, but her friend and I didn't really hit it off.'

'Isn't that always the way?' Theo said. 'It's seems impossible to meet a couple of girls that'll suit you equally. I've been there myself. It's a pity your friend Grace moved away. Now you're back, I think I'll go out to lunch myself. I haven't got much food in at the moment, so I couldn't make anything today. I won't leave you alone for too long. Ring me if you get inundated with customers. I'll only be round the corner at the King's Arms.'

Theo hadn't been in the King's Arms for years and even then not very often. It was always considered the place for the older generation to go. The Nag's Head had been his principle watering hole in his youth, but all that loud music wasn't really his scene anymore. The King's Arms was a large and rather oppressive edifice on East Street, situated on the other side of the road to the entrance to the Shopping Mall that incorporated the new library. Theo remembered the old library, and indeed the new one, very well. He had worked in them both for several years after leaving school, studying for an NVQ in Librarianship. Books had always been his passion. Working there had been the means to his meeting Darren's father Ronnie – not through Ronnie's love of books, but because he was working as a labourer on the project to replace the old library building. They'd gelled straight away. They'd started going to places together out of town, picking up girls just like Joel and Darren were doing now. But just like Darren, Ronnie always seemed to end up with the more attractive of the two. Although both Ronnie and Theo were short, slim and dark-haired, Ronnie's brash confidence and soft Irish accent seemed to act as a magnet to members of the opposite sex, while his underlying youth and vulnerability brought out the mothering instinct in all the girls they met. Theo had never found a girl who he could really relate to until he'd met Jeannie, the barmaid in the Nag's Head. But that had not worked out as he had hoped. He'd started drinking too much, and his studies had suffered. His best option had been to leave the country and start afresh.

When Ronnie had come into the Emporium a few months ago, Theo had been bitterly disappointed in how his old friend had turned out. However sly and circumspect the Ronnie of old had been, he'd had an underlying friendly honesty about him. They'd always been privy to each other's inner thoughts, feelings and hopes. But this new Ronnie was different. Theo remembered his look of barely disguised contempt as he'd cast his eye over the shop. To Ronnie, Theo was just another insignificant businessman with no power or influence, someone who couldn't help Ronnie's cause in self-promotion. And Theo sensed that he had plans to take the Emporium off him.

The large portico, which acted as the entrance to the King's Arms, stretched out over the pavement, the roof of which was supported by two columns: a popular place to shelter on rainy days. Once an old coaching inn, the place had been revamped in the Victorian period, but it appeared that very little had been done to it since. The interior decoration was made up of dark and dismal red walls, an oppressively patterned carpet of black and green leaves, complemented by heavily varnished oak furniture. The only means of illumination, apart from the windows facing onto the street, was from electric wall lights purporting to be candles. Theo walked up to the bar and ordered an orange juice and a cheese sandwich on wholemeal bread from the man he assumed was the proprietor.

'Jeannie, can you serve this customer please? I'm sorry sir. I'm just going off duty.'

Theo recognised her straight away; older of course, but still the same Jeannie – alert and wary like a little sparrow.

'Theo! It *is* you. I wondered when you'd be in. Joel's told me all about you. He never stops. You're his hero, if you want to know.'

'Jeannie,' he said. He felt almost speechless. 'Jeannie, about Joel…'

'And thank you so much for giving him this great chance of a career. He hasn't had much help over the years: not from me, or anybody.'

'Jeannie, about that…'

'Not now Theo. Don't spoil things. It was all such a long time ago. And anyway, I'm meant to be working. I'll get you your order and then I must get on. It's really filling up in here.'

'Before you go rushing off, Jeannie, why don't I take you and Joel out for a meal tonight to toast Joel's future? His friend Darren's got a date with a girl tonight, so I'm sure he'll be free.' Theo stared into her eyes, trying to read her reaction.

'That would be great, Theo. I'm sure Joel will appreciate it. It's a lovely gesture. But no talk about – you know – anything in front of Joel, mind.' She turned her eyes quickly away.

'I'll book a table at Luigi's then. Is 7.30 alright?'

'That's fine by me,' she said, pouring him his orange juice, but she didn't raise her eyes to him again. 'Till tonight then, Theo. Your sandwich will be over in a minute. And about that other business. If we've got to talk about it, you'll have to take me out by myself next time.'

Their surprise meeting had been so sudden and unexpected that Theo was left wondering if it had actually happened. His sandwich was brought over by a young waitress and all sight of Jeannie evaporated. There was so much he wanted to ask her concerning the past and so much he wanted to know about their possible future together. But she had given him hope, which was more than he'd been given all those years ago.

# Chapter 7

## Darren's New Home

I'd had to talk Dad out of buying the Sutcliffe's old house.

'It's a lovely place, Darren,' he'd said. 'I know your mother was never keen to go there on the rare occasions we were invited: understandable really. But I'm sure that deep down she'd love to be the mistress of a house like that, to be able to entertain in the same way that Fiona and Clive used to.'

I'd just stared at him, speechless for a moment.

'OK, son, I know what you're thinking – insensitive of me and all that, on account of my past history with Fiona. But that was years ago before they'd even moved there, and it's not as if she can come back for a bit more of me now, is it?'

'That's just my point, Dad. It's because someone you both knew died there, and her husband's likely to be banged up for her manslaughter, that Mum won't fancy it. That's the reason why she won't want to live there. To sleep in the room where all that *perversion*, as she sees it, took place.'

'Bravo for being so sensitive, son. But that's why the house is the price it is. With a little tweak of the finances, we could just about afford it. I'd have thought you would be jumping at the chance of living there. It's only about five minutes' walk from the golf club.'

Of course, that was just the reason why I didn't want to live there. It's a great house, and a definite step up from the pretentious estate we're on at the moment. The houses at Southern Meadows are massive, detached 1920's piles set amongst spacious lawns. They are the homes of the well-established families of the town. With my intimate knowledge of Fiona's bedroom and her accompanying ensuite, I just know that Mum would love it there, and it would be great to live so close to the golf club. But it was the proximity that was bugging me. The trouble is, I always seemed to be round at her house last autumn, twice a week after my private golf lessons, and also at other times if something, or someone, had upset me. Old Fiona was great at helping me out of my bad moods. She hadn't minded my rough handling of her on these occasions. In fact she'd positively revelled in it. That was what had given her the idea of buying that kinky fetishist equipment in the first place. It was the possible curtain twitchers that I was worried about, the dried up old crones who had nothing better to do than watch who was going in and out of the Sutcliffe's house. Nothing had ever been mentioned in the papers to suppose someone like me had ever been spotted, and I wanted to keep it that way. I didn't want memories to be jogged.

I stare at my face in my bedroom mirror. Although often an advantage with the opposite sex to have such a striking appearance, it can definitely have its drawbacks. My strawberry blonde hair doesn't help. It's so noticeable, easy to remember and recognise. And wearing a hoodie somehow makes it worse. It accentuates my steely blue eyes and can make me look decidedly menacing. I'll practise those facial exercises again, the ones I've been working on to try and stop girls freaking out when I'm angry. The trouble is, if I see fear in other people's faces, it seems to make me angrier and more violent than ever.

You're reminded of the time when there'd been that bit of difficulty with that girl from school, the one who had suddenly left at half-term – that slag Jenna. She'd wound you up with all her giggling and teasing, and then when you'd stared at her in your usual way she'd become tense and then she'd started to struggle. You'd really had no choice in what you'd done to her after that; she'd led you on just a bit too far, but it hadn't been your finest hour. And then of course, there'd been that business with Grace at the hospital, and her not allowing you to see Hope. You'd never have harmed the baby. Surely she must have known that?

The thing with these facial exercises is that it's all to do with tensing up and then relaxing, a bit like what Joel does before he meditates. I tighten my jaw muscles, and also the ones around my eyes and forehead, and then relax everything. That's it; it's working already. My eyes have taken on a softer colour, and I now appear sort of wistful instead of vicious. The girls seem to like this new look. Instead of being frightened, they mother me – much more satisfactory all round. I must have looked like this when I was with Kaye that last night, but then I really was wistful, sad that I'd lost her after telling her a couple of fibs…

We're still moving to Southern Meadows though, but thankfully not to the Sutcliffe's old home. The one we're buying on the other side of the golf course suits me much better. It's a bit smaller than Fiona's, and the same price, but it's got the advantage of having a sizeable plot at the side. With a slight over-estimation of materials on his other jobs, Dad reckons that he can build an extension on it for virtually nothing. The advantage to me of this new house though, is that it's in an area I've never been to before. So even though I'm bound to turn a few heads in our new neighbourhood, nobody will recognise me as a frequent visitor of Fiona's.

'Darren, my love?' What the hell does Mum want? 'Can I come in, sweetheart?' Mum's barging in carrying a couple of heavy books of curtain samples together with what look like colour charts. I'm going to have to keep the door locked even when I'm here. She's in her element at the moment. She's gone completely over the top with this obsession with interior decoration. She hardly watches any daytime television anymore.

'Now, you really must help me to decide on the colour scheme for your new bedroom. It won't be long now before we move, and it must be just how you want it. You deserve it, my beautiful boy.' She leans over and tries to give me a peck on the cheek, but I'm too quick for her. Can't she get it into her head that I've outgrown all that nonsense?

'Mum, its ages away. It's at least five weeks before the end of term, and we're not moving until after that, anyway.' I remember Diane's favourable reaction when she'd first been given the privilege of coming up to my room a couple of weeks ago. 'Very stylish and sophisticated,' she'd said.

'Actually, I've decided to take my old curtains with us to the new house.' I say. 'I'm sure they'll fit. And the walls can be the same colour too. There's no point in spoiling a winning combination, is there? But a cup of coffee would go down well, if you're putting the kettle on.'

I lie back on the bed, my hands behind my head. Diane's quite fit as it happens, in both senses of the word. I could tell that when I first set eyes on her at the bowling alley. It was the action of her hips when she was preparing for her shot that gave her away. It was a pity about her friend. I don't blame

Joel for not fancying her. Why is it that you never see two great looking girls together? It was the first time I'd managed to persuade Joel to go out on the pull with me, as well. The trouble is, when you've had someone like Grace, as we both have, you're bound to be a bit fussy. Grace had been pretty-well perfect really: slim, lithe and incredibly athletic – definitely my type of girl. I shouldn't have let her go that easily. I still don't feel as if I've quite finished with her yet. My imminent cup of coffee that Mum's bringing me reminds me of how tasty she was. I'll allow myself the luxury of lying still a little longer, so that I can remember her creamy brown skin with that sexy smell of coconut.

# Chapter 8

## How to Win Friends

Is it really only a year since I was last standing here all by myself? It seems like a lifetime. So much has happened. I'd only just lost my virginity with Grace the night before, and I wasn't a dad then. Although, come to think of it, I must have been an expectant dad by then. And this year there's no Fiona Sutcliffe to rescue me from all these boring people. I still haven't got a clue how to conduct myself around people I couldn't care less about. There's no Clive here either for that matter, so no boring speeches to avoid, although I don't suppose the new chairman will be much better.

God knows why I came, but Dad insisted – said there'd be some people I should get to know who already go to my new school. It's alright for him though. There he is, over by the beer table, at the centre of a group of men, engaging them all in lively conversation. They're all asking him questions, and he's slapping them on the back and laughing. How does he do it? Going by looks, Dad should be the one in the shadows, not me. All I can see when I look at him is a short, wiry little man, with slightly bandy legs, whose nose is too long. What do they see in him?

I glance around, and the more I look the more depressing it all is. Everybody except me is talking to someone, either in a group or in couples. There are two girls not far off who are eyeing me up the way girls always do. Even they're together, although I don't think that's their plan. I could easily separate them, I know that, and hook up with one or other of them. But all we'd end up doing was kissing and possibly more, and I'm not in the mood right now. Even Mum's in a group of women – on the fringes it has to be admitted, but she's still there amongst other people.

I spot a group of boys of about my age or a bit older and walk over to them as casually as I can. I recognise a couple of them from those disastrous group golf lessons I had last year. They're talking about handicaps, matches and the like so I try to join in, but nobody can hear me, nobody has even noticed I'm here. It's like I'm a goldfish in a bowl, opening and closing my mouth, banging against the glass. They're all wankers anyway. It obviously makes you deaf as well as blind.

'What's wrong with you, son, all on your own?' Dad's broken away from his group and is coming over.

'I sometimes think I must be invisible, Dad, except to members of the opposite sex.' I'm aware that the two girls are still eying me up, whispering together.

'That's bad news, son. Nobody wants to be too pally with a ladies' man. Makes them feel nervous for the safety of their wives and girlfriends. No, what you've got to do to get noticed is to develop the knack. It's a trick, son. A game.'

'A game? How do I play it then?' I like the sound of this.

'The thing is son, you have to pretend you're interested in them. Ask a lot of questions – not too personal of course, you don't want your head punched in. And then if they know the game as well, they'll start asking about you. Let's face it son, most people are only interested in themselves, so you have to milk that knowledge. The hardest part is to concentrate, but that's the most important part of all. You have to listen, learn and remember. You never know when you might need to use the information to your advantage.'

Dad's steering me away from our present spot on the fringes. We're heading for the barbeque.

'Now, there's my old friend Bill over there with his son. Don't know the boy's name, but that's easily solved. What I do know is that he goes to that new school you'll be starting at soon. He's been there for years, so you'll have plenty to ask him about. But remember; make it personal, but not aggressively so.'

Now I'm being introduced to this character called Wills. Wills? That's just typical. He looks a bit like the 'Royal Wills' as it happens, but when he had more hair. No doubt his parents are pretentious tossers who've named all their children after royalty. This 'Wills' probably has a sister called Beatrice or Eugenie or some such nonsense. I can imagine the names of all the other posers in my class at this private school I'm going to: Harry, Edward, George, Charles. How the hell am I going to fit in with that lot? But I'm going to have to try, aren't I? After all, it was my idea to go there.

'I hear you're starting at Hazelwood this autumn,' this Wills person is saying. 'What subjects are you taking? Perhaps we'll be in the same class.' His voice sounds royal as well as his looks. He's asking me all these questions. Is he doing it because he's interested, or is he just playing the game? I decide to go along with him and play too. I'm sure I can pick it up with a bit of practise. Don't make it too personal to start with though, that's what Dad's just said. I remember my time with

Kaye, how I'd kept asking her questions about herself to try and deflect awkward ones directed at me.

All is going fine to start with. I'm finding out all about the teachers and their strange whims, the extra-curricular activities on offer: bridge, chess and the debating society. But now it's all starting to go wrong. We've somehow got onto the subject of girlfriends. Wills has just spotted a girl he fancies, and tells me that he's thinking of asking her out.

'Don't ask her, mate. Just tell her where you're taking her. It always works with me.'

'Where's your girlfriend then Darren, old chap, if you're always so successful?'

I don't like his tone. I feel a bit riled as it happens and forget myself. 'She's only fifteen. I didn't think she'd enjoy it amongst all these posers.'

'Fifteen!' he says. 'What's the point in that? What if you want to… you know? You could get locked up for doing it with a minor.'

I've never thought of that. 'It's a bit late not to now, mate. She expects it. It would hardly be fair to suddenly deny her.'

'Well, be careful old chap, that's all I can say. I had a friend that made a fifteen-year-old girl pregnant. He had real problems after that. No one wants a kid at that age.'

'I've got a kid already actually, mate. She and my ex live in Cardiff now. Nobody knows about her as it happens, not even my parents.' Why am I telling Wills all this? This bloke's obviously too good at this game. He's got something on me now, in fact two things: Hope and Diane. I'm rubbish at this game. What the hell am I going to do? Thank God he's moving off.

'See you next term, Darren.' He emphasises my name with what sounds like a sneer. 'I'm off to try my skills on the lovely

Emily.' He gives me a strange, questioning look before he moves away.

'So how did it go, son?' Dad's come over again and is slapping me on the back. I've got to stop him doing that.

'Rubbish, as it happens. I told him things I didn't want anybody else to know.'

'Whatever did you tell him, that you're a rapist and a murderer?'

'Not quite, Dad. I told him that Diane's only fifteen.'

'Nothing wrong with that as long as you're keeping it in your trousers, son. But knowing you, you're not. You've got to let her go, Darren. You know that, don't you. Go for a girl your own age for a change – or even older if needs be. But whatever you do, you've got to finish with this Diane girl. Is that all you told him? It doesn't sound too bad.'

'Just that I've got a daughter, Dad,' I mutter, looking down at my feet. 'Do you remember Grace, the one that moved away rather suddenly last Christmas?'

'Darren, Darren, Darren.' Dad's started to act concerned; his feet are shifting about. 'That's not the sort of information you should be spreading around. What if he tells his dad? I've got my reputation to think of, son. I can just see the headlines in the local paper: *Respected Justice of the Peace's son caught up in underage sex and paternity suits.* Who else knows you're the father – her parents, her friends?'

'Only Joel, Dad, and he won't say anything. Grace and I broke up after some sort of misunderstanding, and she doesn't want anything to do with me now. I gave her quite a bit of money just after the birth, and she's never contacted me again since.'

'You've done the right thing, son,' Dad says. 'You don't want any repercussions. A clean break's best. No contact; no mess – just what I should have done in your situation. But why does Joel know? Are you two still friends?'

'Oh, he and Grace were an item for a while after we split up. He still goes to see her sometimes, as it happens.' What did Dad mean by 'should have done'? Does he mean that he shouldn't have married Mum? I know they got married in a hurry, I saw the relevant dates when we were doing our family trees. Dad's still talking, but I've missed some of it.

'What's he up to now? Has he left school?'

'He's working full time in that weird Emporium shop,' I say. 'That Theodore Kitchen's given him an apprenticeship.'

'He's working for Theo? Well that's rich. I looked him up some time ago, but we don't seem to have anything in common any more. I hadn't seen him for years, not since he came back from Thailand, or wherever it was. We go way back. We used to drink together in the Nag's Head, amongst other things. He used to have the most horrendous temper, as I remember. He was always getting into an argument with someone or other. That's why he took off and got interested in all that meditation malarkey. Let's hope it's calmed him down. I'm not sure I like the idea of Joel working for him.'

'Oh, Joel's into all that "meditation malarkey" as well now. They seem to get on really well actually, and Theo's going out with Joel's mum. But Dad, what should I do about Wills? Should I just ignore him and hope he forgets?'

'Worst thing you could do, son. You'll have to become his best friend. Find out a few choice things about him and then you'll be quits. Never become an enemy of anyone that has something on you. On reflection, the best thing you can do is try and retract what you've told him. Arrange to have a round of golf with him, I should. Now, I've got to circulate, "win friends and influence people", as they say. And ditch that little girlfriend of yours first thing tomorrow, for Christ's sake.'

I manage to catch Wills' eye. He's standing talking to the fitter of the two girls who were ogling me earlier. The other one's hovering, looking as uncomfortable as I'd done earlier. I'll make it her lucky night. She's not really my type, as it happens; she's taller and much larger framed than the girls I'm used to handling, and with much fuller breasts – although I'm not completely averse to the idea of handling them. I leave Dad and walk over to them.

'Hey, Wills old chap. I hear you're pretty handy with the golf clubs. How about a round tomorrow? A tenner says I win.' I see a strong glint of competitiveness in his eyes.

'You're on. 2.30 suit you? Let me introduce you to Emily and her friend Jessica. Girls, this is Darren.'

'Call me Dan,' I say. 'Everybody does. It's only the olds that call me Darren. I nearly fooled you with all that rubbish I was telling you just now, didn't I Wills? As if I could have fitted all that in over the past year.' I laugh and slap him on the back. 'I've been living the life of a reclusive monk, as it happens. I've had my head down over my books making sure I got good enough grades to get into Hazelwood.' I turn my attention to Jessica. She's got a very pretty face, I suppose… shame about the body.

'Nicely done, my boy,' Dad says on the way home. 'For Christ's sake let him win though – just by the smallest of margins of course – otherwise you may not get a rematch. And that girl Jessica's a good choice. Lovely girl isn't she Lorraine? She's a few months older than you, but that's just fine. Be careful with that one, mind. Her father's in the Town Planning Department. I'm in and out of his office all the time.'

I lean back in the car seat and put my hands behind my head. I allow myself a smile of satisfaction. The evening has turned out surprisingly well, as it happens. The lovely Jessica has agreed to come out on a double date with me, Wills and Emily. It seems that 'Dan' is just as much of a babe magnet as Darren is. Although not at all my usual type, she's already seventeen and the idea of legal sex has suddenly become quite an aphrodisiac. Also very much in her favour is the fact that she's a year ahead of me at school. She'll be off my hands in less than a year at the most. She's bound to be going to university. Girls like her always do.

I won't get rid of Diane yet though. I don't want to be too hasty, do I? I'll wait until Jessica agrees to do the business. I'll cut Diane's hours down though, phase her out slowly. That's the least I can do, considering how much in love with me she is.

# Chapter 9

## Future Plans

'Look Grace, I still can't believe it.' It's August, and Joel is pointing at his GCSE results sheet. 'Five passes – English, Food Technology, Art, Woodwork and Maths. Mum and Theo are so proud of me. We're going out for a meal on Friday to celebrate. We're going on a hiking holiday after that, did I tell you? We're staying in a lovely little stone cottage for a whole week. And then I'm starting work full time at the Emporium.'

'Yes Joel, you said. You're doing so well. I'm not surprised that everyone is proud of you.' She fingers her results envelope, inviting Joel's question.

'Well, come on Grace – spill. I bet you aced them all, just like Darren – millions of A and A stars. He's off to that posh private school in September. He's got a bit up himself, actually. Everyone has to call him Dan now.'

Grace recalls seeing the boys from Hazelwood getting off their private coach that takes them the few miles out of town. She's been past it a few times. It's housed in what used to be a large country pile, belonging to Lord Someone or Other. She imagines Darren in the smart light grey suit worn by the Sixth Formers. The colour will complement the blue of his eyes. She passes Joel her GCSE results.

'That's brilliant!' he exclaims. 'Eight passes, and five of them at level C. So you'll be able to stay on to do A Levels then.'

'That's right,' she says. No As or Bs as once predicted though. Darren has seen to that. And she won't be exactly 'staying on' either. The school she transferred to in January doesn't have a Sixth Form. She's got a place at a Sixth Form College from September to do English, French and Art – English so that she can immerse herself in literature, French so that she can immerse herself in even more and Art as an escape from her life as it is. Art has never been one of her strengths. History was always to be her third subject, but she won't have the energy for three academic subjects now. How she's managed to do as well as she has is a surprise to her. She hasn't learnt anything new from the day she left home. Academically, the new school was hopeless. On the surface, the children it catered for were just like her: pregnant girls and underage mothers, along with troublemakers who have been excluded from anywhere else. Although Hope had been assigned a place in a crèche, some days Grace and the baby just stayed at home. There didn't seem much point going into school. Grace never fitted in there. She still doesn't think of herself in those terms, a single mother with no prospects. In her mind she's still a clever girl who has a burning desire to achieve something in her life. But when she'd complained to Faith, she'd dismissed her. 'What did you expect, then? Welcome to the real world. You're in the big city now, not some protected little backwater. Anyway, no other school would have taken you.'

'What have your parents said?' Joel was saying. 'I bet they're pleased with your results.'

'I haven't told them yet,' she says. And as yet they've failed to ask. Very different from last year when her mum had gone ballistic when she'd been handed Grace's end of year report without its regulation envelope. But she's sixteen now, so she doesn't have to bother with all that anymore. In fact she hasn't heard anything from her parents at all since her birthday two weeks ago, not since she told them that she definitely wasn't going to take their advice and have Hope adopted. They can't make her do anything now. She's an adult.

She observes her beautiful, blonde daughter, bouncing happily in her special canvas sling chair as they sit in Faith's tiny back garden. She's gurgling and waving her little fists at the butterflies as they flutter around the long purple buddleia fronds hanging from the nearby bush, the staccato movements of their wings creating kaleidoscopic flashes of colour. Sometimes when she looks at Hope, she wonders if she's really hers at all or just on loan, and then a cold fear runs through her and she has to pick her up and clutch her tightly to prevent her from vanishing. Grace can see nothing of herself in her daughter. Her Jamaican genes seem to have been totally overlooked. She wonders if there's a word for someone who is only one eighth Jamaican. She'll have to look it up.

Joel is playing with Hope now, dangling the soft toy rabbit in front of her and allowing the long ears to tickle her laughing face. It's the one Darren left for her in the hospital. It's her favourite toy. She always pulls at the silky ears as she goes off to sleep; she screams if she can't find it. Her chubby hands are trying to grasp it as Joel snatches it away. Her Michelin tyre legs kick and thrust strongly. The Health Visitor was so impressed with her progress the last time she weighed her. 'For a baby born one month prematurely, she has caught up magnificently,' she had told Grace. 'You're obviously a natural mother. Well done, my love. But don't overdo it, or she'll become overweight.'

But Grace can deny her nothing. She picks her out of her cot in the middle of the night to feed her at the slightest indication of a whimper. Joel has told her about how his little sister Zoe had been taken away for adoption because she'd cried so much and the neighbours had complained.

'Oh, I mustn't forget this,' Joel says, fishing a brown envelope out of the back pocket of his jeans. 'It's from Darren.'

Dirty, used notes again, but at least they're in a clean envelope today, not like that first time. 'There's no note, Joel. Does he ever ask after us?'

'Not really. I'm surprised he hasn't wanted to come and see her.'

She wished she'd let him see Hope that time when he'd come to the hospital; he'd come a long way. And she'd been wrong not to tell him she was pregnant. He'd had a point. If he was the father then surely he had the right to know. He hadn't shirked his responsibilities or pretended that it hadn't got anything to do with him. A lot of the girls at school were having to arrange DNA tests on boys who were denying everything, calling them slags, saying it could have been anybody's – anybody's but theirs. And he was giving her money. He'd looked so nervous when she'd seen him standing at the door of the maternity ward. If he'd stayed like that she'd have definitely allowed him to see her. If he'd said the right words she would have forgiven him.

'Where does he get all this money from, Joel?'

'His family are rolling in it now. They've just moved into this massive house in Southern Meadows. You know, the ones by the golf course. And his dad's building an extension. Darren's shown me the plans he's drawn up. There's going to be a snooker room on the ground floor, and over the top, he's getting his own sitting room and bathroom. It'll be like his own little flat.'

'Surely this money he gives me isn't coming from his dad though?'

'Of course not,' Joel says. 'I shouldn't think they even know about Hope. Darren earns all that… on the stall.'

'I can't imagine how he can take so much just on selling the odd screwdriver,' Grace says. 'But then I suppose he could sell anything to anybody if he had a mind to.' Either through charm, coercion or bullying – no doubt she wasn't the only person to believe everything he said.

Her mind flies back to that time last August, almost a year ago to the day. Darren had just got back from his holiday in Greece and their lovemaking had been even more frenetic than usual. The day had been hot, humid and overcast, and they'd taken a cool shower together afterwards. She catches her breath at the memory. She'd loved him so much then. His body had glowed the colour of deep gold as the water flowed over him, and his hair had been bleached to that of the finest sand. He'd held her tight and whispered, 'We're like one person now.' Then he'd said that he'd told his mum, 'We're in love, and we'll be getting married after Uni.' She'd believed him then. These words echo through the chambers of her mind every day, and then again every night when she's awake feeding Hope. If she keeps them alive within her, then perhaps one day they'll come true.

'If he ever does ask after us,' she says, 'tell him he's welcome to come and visit. He can come and see his baby any time he likes.'

# Chapter 10

## Joel's Wishes are Answered

'You're not really expecting us to climb that one today, are you Theo?' Jeannie is looking out of the living room window that sports a magnificent view of the nearby mountain. 'You reckon we're up to it, do you?'

'Of course we are,' Theo says. 'That's nothing compared with some of the ones I climbed in Asia. It can't be much more than a couple of thousand feet. And we've got all the right gear now. I'm not expecting you to attempt it in high heels.'

The first day of their holiday had been spent in the Mountain Centre where Theo had kitted them all out with climbing boots, anoraks, water bottles and small rucksacks. Joel's old one was deemed much too big to cart around all day. Theo had said that they'd only need one big enough to carry a packed lunch in, together with an extra pullover and light cagoule just in case it turned cold or wet – or both. Even in August you had to plan for such eventualities.

'Get the sandwiches from the kitchen, will you Joel?' Theo asks.

The kitchen of the cottage that they're renting is Joel's favourite room. The cottage, converted from an old stone outbuilding into a two bedroom holiday let, stands on sloping ground, so that the surrounding countryside abuts this side of the cottage at window sill level. As he enters the kitchen he can see sheep grazing nearby. One approaches him as he reaches for the sandwich bags. It comes right up to the window and stares down at him through its small beady eyes, its head cocked inquisitively – brazenly.

As he re-enters the living room, Theo and Jeannie are still discussing the merits of mountain climbing.

'To be truthful, that mountain you can see out there isn't quite as easy to climb as it looks,' Theo explains. 'You can only see the lower slopes from here. And it's not all grassy like that. It'll be stony and quite steep in parts, and it could be a bit boggy around the lake. You won't see the actual summit until we're nearly there. Didn't you notice when we were going up Snowdon yesterday? Every time it looked as if we were almost at the top, another peak came into view.'

'I could hardly see anything yesterday,' Jeannie says. 'It was too misty. Anyway, we were on the train so I didn't really notice. I was reading my magazine.'

'You are such a townie, my love. Never mind. I'll break you in before the week's out. There's no going back now that you've agreed to become a Kitchen. Isn't that right, Joel?'

'It certainly is. That was a bad move, Mum. You should have waited until we got home.'

Joel's smile grows broader as he recalls the events of that first day away. After their shopping spree, Theo had taken them on a walk along the woodland path running past the Mountain Centre. 'Just to break us – and the new boots – in', he'd said. They'd followed a rocky, fast running stream and had seen it transform itself into a waterfall as the spume cascaded over a precipice. They'd clambered down the rocks to the lower level, and walked behind the sheet of water. It hung like a translucent curtain in front of the mouth of the tiny cave. The roar of the water was deafening, and the spray it produced invigorating, and they'd all laughed out loud. Joel had never seen his mother so happy. The stone floor was wet and slippery, but Joel had felt safe in his brand new boots. He'd decided to give them a good clean when they got back to the cottage. He wanted to keep them in their pristine condition forever, just like he was going to cherish this day in his memory.

'Back in the car, you two,' Theo had said on their return to the car park. 'We'll get a takeaway on the way back, and a bottle of wine. We'll make it a bit of a celebration. Your Mum and I've got something to tell you, Joel. I hope you'll be pleased.'

Joel had hardly been able to breathe. He had sat rigidly on the back seat, head completely still but his eyes flickering and darting about. He had caught Theo's reflection in the rear view mirror and Theo had given him a wink.

'You're very quiet son. Frightened of what we're going to say? Honestly, if you don't like what you hear, then just say so, and we'll say no more about it.'

Son! Theo had never called him *son* before. So his suspicions were right, he'd known it all along really but had pushed it to the back of his mind just in case he was disappointed. And now they were actually going to tell him on their own account, without him having to ask.

'Why can't you tell me now?' Joel had said. 'Why do we have to wait?'

'All in good time, Joel.' His mum was smiling and leaning over the passenger seat. She'd briefly held his hand. 'We want to do this properly, don't we?'

Shortly after getting back to the cottage, the takeaway meal, in its tinfoil containers, was sitting in the centre of the table, and plates and cutlery had been laid. Theo had poured three glasses of white wine and had passed them round.

'To us as a family,' he'd said, raising his glass. 'Come on Joel. Don't tell me you've never had a glass of wine before.' Joel had shrugged, shaking his head.

'Well you're sixteen now, and plenty old enough, I reckon.'

'Get on with it, Theo. Joel doesn't even know what we're celebrating yet.'

'I'm sure he must have guessed, Jeannie. But anyway, here goes. Your mother and I are getting married. We haven't set a date yet, but it'll be quite soon I hope.'

Getting married? That hadn't been the news he'd been waiting for, although he'd admitted it was a step in the right direction.

'Nothing to say, Joel?' Jeannie had leaned towards him, smiling. 'I thought you'd be pleased. You don't mind us getting married, do you? It'll be a bit of a squash in our little flat, but it won't be for long. Theo's finally getting round to updating the flat over the shop, knocking down walls and all sorts, and when it's finished we can all move in there.'

'I was hoping for your input with that, actually,' Theo had said. 'Do you remember your suggesting it all that time ago, when you first came round for breakfast? You're OK with it, aren't you Joel? You don't mind us getting married?'

'Of course I don't mind,' Joel had replied. 'It's about time, if you ask me.'

'About time?' Theo had laughed. 'I didn't take you as a prude, Joel. Not with the way you keep going to Cardiff to stay with your girlfriend. Don't tell me you sleep on the sofa.

202

Anyway, sit down both of you and tuck in. I hate Chinese when it's gone cold.'

Joel had felt his face burning. Why did everybody assume he was sleeping with Grace? Should he have been by now? Was it somehow unnatural for them to be just friends? He'd kissed a girl now – that friend of Diane's that he didn't fancy – but he hadn't enjoyed it much and he didn't think she had either.

'Of course I'm not a prude,' he'd said. 'I didn't actually mean that. Why won't you just tell me what I guessed ages ago? I just want you to admit it.'

'What do you want me to admit, Joel?'

'That you're my dad, of course. What do you think?'

Joel had watched as Theo turned to look at his mum. He'd raised his eyebrows and pulled down the corners of his mouth, but had said nothing, waiting for a reaction from Jeannie. After what had seemed like forever, Jeannie had given Theo a slight nod.

'Is that what you really want me to say – that I'm your dad? You're quite sure?'

'Of course I'm sure!'

'Then I'll admit it,' Theo had said. He'd stretched his arm across the table and grabbed Joel's hand. 'I didn't want to spoil everything son, especially as we're going to be working together full time now. I know how much you've resented not having a dad around. I thought you might have ended up hating him, whoever he turned out to be.'

'Of course I don't hate you. You didn't know about me when you were away all that time. You didn't even know I existed. It's exactly how I wanted it to be. I didn't want a dad who'd abandoned me because I was too much trouble.'

'You'll never be too much trouble, Joel. You're a great asset to me, in the shop and everywhere else. We'll be like proper partners once you've learnt the business. In fact I'm thinking of leaving you to run it single handed eventually. It'll give me a chance to concentrate on my antiquarian books.'

Joel had beamed. 'In that case, Dad, I'd like to do a course in Interior Design as well as this Apprenticeship Scheme thing. There's an evening class I could go to. I've researched it all and everything. If I'm to run the business by myself one day, I know exactly how I want it to be.'

'Sounds great to me. You don't hang about, do you, Joel? But none of the "Dad" thing if you don't mind: Theo's just fine. I haven't got used to the idea yet, much less the title.'

'Tell me about this girlfriend of yours, Grace,' Jeannie had demanded. 'Why haven't I ever met her?'

'It's a long story, Mum. She's fallen out with her parents and she never comes home. She's settled in Cardiff with her elder sister Faith and her family now. And she's not actually my girlfriend as such anyway. She's always been keen on somebody else, even though they broke up ages ago.'

'You're obviously very fond of her though, Joel,' Jeannie had said. 'Haven't you spoken to her about it?'

'I don't like to, Mum. As I said, she's still in love with this other boy. If I say anything yet it might spoil everything.'

'You're doing the right thing, Joel,' Theo had said. 'Bide your time, and if she's really the one for you, you'll know when the time's right to tell her. Just like me and your mum. Now come on. We haven't drunk that toast. To the three of us!'

Joel remembers how he had shuddered after taking his first sip of wine, and how Theo and his Mum had laughed. It appears that they have now finished their discussion on the merits of mountain climbing. Theo is folding up the Ordinance

Survey map he's been poring over and is putting it safely into the front pocket of his rucksack.

'Come on, you lot, let's get going,' he says. 'The weather looks great at the moment. With any luck we'll get a brilliant view today once we've reached the summit. Apparently, on a clear day we should be able to see thirteen peaks without even turning our heads.'

In that moment, Joel sees the rest of his life laid out before him. The feelings of confusion and frustration that have clouded his brain for so long have lifted. The peaks and troughs are levelling out so that he can see a clear way through at last, and everything begins to appear surmountable. But what about his future with Grace? Theo was right. He needed to bide his time. Surely Grace's feelings for Darren would fade? She hasn't even seen him for eight months.

# Chapter 11

## Crunch is Taken Out

'Hey, Darren, what's with the designer stubble – new image?' Gerry's come over from his stall, leaning over, invading my personal space.

'No mate. I just didn't have time to shave this morning.' My three day stubble feels nice and rough under my hand now. It's not my fault strawberry blonde hair takes longer to show than most. Anyway, it's none of that gorilla's business. I've got to look tough today, and older than seventeen, at least twenty-one or two. One of Crunch's superiors might come asking questions.

I shift in my seat. Where is everybody this Saturday? The metal structures over the empty stalls look like skeletons without their protective awnings, standing out all stark against the sky. The few remaining stallholders are dotted about, exposed. The only stall with any customers is the one giving out free samples of food. The punters are all having their pre-Christmas panic in the Shopping Mall. It's warmer in there, more choice. I wish I'd stayed in bed, but it would've looked a bit suss if I hadn't showed. But it's all good – it was an accident – the papers said so.

Only one more week after this, then I'll be free of the stall, free of the drugs business. It's just getting too dangerous. Perhaps nobody will come looking for me today, or next Saturday, and then I'll definitely be in the clear. Crunch's next drop would have been next week.

A fit, smartly dressed looking chick of about thirty's come over. She's giving me the once over. She's running her long slim fingers along the screwdrivers, chisels and rasps. She doesn't look like your average DIY enthusiast, not with that immaculate red nail varnish. I catch her eye, give her one of my steely stares. I raise the corners of my lips slightly. That usually gets them going. She runs her tongue around the inside of her teeth in response. She likes what she sees, and why not? Mum says I have the timeless good looks of a film star.

'Dick, I presume?'

Oh shit! I wasn't expecting a woman. I nod. Why Crunch always called me Dick I've no idea, nobody else ever does.

'A definite improvement on your predecessor, I must say,' she comments. My mood goes from seduction, through surprise to fear. My smile fades, my head shoots forward, and I feel sweat forming. She colours slightly then stiffens.

'I've got a bit of business for you.' She hands me her card. 'Give me a ring later to discuss it.' She moves off quickly without looking back.

Is she really Crunch's boss, or is she just a trap? Will she be surrounded by a bunch of heavies later? Even by herself, she doesn't look the type to mess with. Perhaps Crunch wasn't old at all. Perhaps she'd been hot for him as well, and worn him out. And what did she mean by my 'predecessor'? I don't want to be promoted. I just want to be left alone. My heels are drumming the ground beneath my chair, so I clamp my knees down with my hands. I'm burning up and shivering. I'm being transported back to that night eight days ago, like in that old film Groundhog Day.

It's 7.45pm and you're sitting under the arch of the bridge next to the water. It's almost pitch dark, but you can see the entrance to the Nag's Head on the other side of the main road. It's lucky it's right under a street lamp. You shiver and twitch. You just want to get it over with so you can get ready for your date with Jess.

There's Crunch, suddenly illuminated against the darkness. He's going in without turning round. He's much bigger and handier than you remember. Pins and needles stab at your fingers, hammers pound your chest, your body's a furnace, heat turns to ice on your exposed skin, cold sweat under your clothing sweet-smelling then sour. Horrendous! You'll need a shower before going out again. You take deep breaths and exhale what looks like cigarette smoke. Filthy habit, smoking. Stains your fingers, makes your clothes reek.

Crunch's safely inside, so you're not hanging around here. You'll give him an hour to get hammered before coming back. You're hurrying up the steps to the main road. The place is like a stage set, empty, ready for the action to start. You're cutting up East Street. Balls of light hang from sky hooks, extras flit in and out of the spotlights. Everything's in place, waiting for you, the main attraction.

The aroma of coffee outside Luigi's embraces you, draws you in. The warm air enfolds you, leads you to the one remaining table. You're caressed by the airwaves, something by Vivaldi. It's as if the whole place is giving you a motherly hug. You sink into the soft, yielding seat and breathe deeply and evenly. You begin to relax. You order a double espresso and some spaghetti carbonara. That waiter Antonio's looking uglier than ever tonight. His greasy, badger-like hair's bristling from his scalp like a bog brush. What his wife ever saw in him you've no idea.

'Maria not working tonight?' you ask. Of course she's not. Friday's her night off. So close to him, should you feel guilty about your legover with her last Friday? You don't see why; he was working, wasn't he. It wasn't as if he could have been with her that night anyway.

You breathe deeply once more and allow the profusion of smells from other peoples' food to meld in your nostrils. It masks your body's unacceptable whiff. You prod at your pasta, move it around the plate. It's all Crunch's fault that it's come to this. You're not taking orders from flotsam like that anymore. And it's Dad's fault as well. If he hadn't got so up himself when he was made a JP and then got all heavy with you over nothing, then you'd never have got into drugs dealing in the first place. It would've served him right if you'd got caught. But you weren't thinking straight then, the future was just a blur on the horizon. No way are you risking a prison sentence now. You're going to get brilliant A Levels and get a place at Oxford. You're going to be something big in the City or politics, the top job even, and nobody's going to stop you. Crunch really shouldn't have reacted like that when you'd told him you were pulling out.

'Can't allow that, old son,' he'd said. 'Once you're in, that's it. You made me that promise, remember? My superiors wouldn't take kindly to it at all.' Then he'd coughed violently before lighting up another fag.

'I would never renege on a promise, Crunch. But I'm giving up the stall. This is my last week.'

'Then we'll do our bit of business elsewhere.' Then he'd coughed again and gobbed, nearly hitting your new designer trainers.

'Get in touch before the next drop, Dick.' He'd spat out your alleged name as if he'd had something unpalatable between his teeth. 'And if you don't, I'll find you, believe me.'

That was it! If he wasn't going to release you, Crunch would just have to go. He may have been something in his day: short but stocky, with a tree trunk of a neck, and the size of his fingers was obviously the reason for his nickname, but now they're all bent and twisted. He's knackered from booze and drugs, and he's no spring chicken anymore. You could take him out quite easily – it would all be 'an accident'.

Crunch had fallen for your plan to meet in the Nag's Head when you'd rung him yesterday. There'd be a live band, the place would be heaving, no one would notice you. Your heart's racing. You must stop gobbling this food. You must chill out, get a grip.

Back under the bridge and you feel strangely calm. You give Crunch another call. 'A change of plan, mate. I forgot it was twenty-one and over tonight, and I haven't got any ID.' You tell him where you are and hang up.

You're in the shadows watching the pub door, and there's Crunch, looking suitably wasted. He's weaving precariously between the lines of moving traffic. Why can't he just get run over, make it easier for everybody? You hear Crunch's uneven footsteps negotiating the stone steps. You hear his wheezing breath. This will be a doddle. You've never killed anyone before. The time when Leroy drowned was a complete accident. Although, to be fair, you're not planning to actually kill him, just to facilitate his death.

The sky is clear, the moon's new and everything's coming into sharp focus: the high embankment wall, the promenade edge – knife-sharp against the shroud-like sheet of water.

'Over here, mate.'

Crunch puts out his hand to do his usual high five and you're on him immediately, forcing his arm into a half nelson and bringing him to the ground face down. It's as if time is folding in on itself, like some giant accordion expelling air and sound. The whole world exhales at once, and waits for the director to shout 'action'. This is your moment. You're the main man. You grab the rock you positioned earlier, raise your arm high and give Crunch's head a decisive blow.

Sounds start to return. Crunch is moaning softly, twitching. You rummage in the inside pocket of his coat and extract the package he's brought for you. Joel will have to deliver it as usual. You come across his mobile phone. You'll take that too. You roll him to the edge and let him go. The roar of the traffic muffles the splash. Crunch's body swirls out of view, caught in the currents. He'll have more than a bash on the head once he gets to the rapids. He'll get battered against the rocks.


'Darren.' Gerry's still here, leaning over the stall. 'Who was that? A bit out of your league isn't she?'

What does he know? The nymphomaniac drugs baron is inspecting fabric a few stalls down. She turns and stares, indicates for me to ring her. I picture the headlines in last Monday's local paper: *Body Found on Riverbank by Jogger. Charlie Hines – local character and father of four – drowns.*

I'm still clutching her card, now all damp and crumpled. So it's not all over, is it? Dick's still here. He hasn't gone the same way as Crunch.

# Part III

# Home and Dry

# Chapter 1

## Darren's New Future Backfires

I look at the card, once all white and pristine. I try and straighten it out on the table top, but my sweaty hands are making it worse. All it says on it is 'Alicia Mason' and a mobile phone number. I wish I knew how this drugs business works. Apart from Joel, I've only ever had dealings with Crunch. What sort of people was Crunch dealing with, and how much do any of them actually know about me? I think back once more to Crunch's answers to my questions the other week, when I'd asked him what would happen if I moved away. I can hear his gruff, sandpaper-like tones as clearly as if he's here, saying them to me now.

'Don't worry about that until the time comes, my old son. You'll get your orders, believe me.'

'Who gives the orders, mate?' I'd said.

'Too many questions, Dick. What is all this? You know the score. We only answer to our direct superiors. It's safer that way.'

There are still hardly any punters around, so Gerry's still hovering, still asking questions.

'You still haven't told me what that bird wanted from you,' he complains.

'Oh, just a bit of private business, mate,' I say. I try to sound casual, but I feel as if I might shit myself.

'You OK, Darren?' he says. 'You don't look too good to me – quite "green round the gills". You haven't got that tummy bug again, have you?'

I'm reminded of last Saturday when I'd told Gerry I had to make an urgent visit to the public toilets. I'd just got my takeaway breakfast from Eric's when I'd got a phone call. It was Diane and she'd sounded more whining than ever.

'Darren, I'm ringing from a public phone. My mum's confiscated mine. She's got really suspicious about who I'm seeing. She doesn't believe it's always my girlfriends anymore. Not since she found some fruit flavoured condoms in my drawer.'

'Oh shit, Diane,' I'd said. 'You should have been more careful. You'd better have deleted all my messages first, before she took it off you.'

'Of course I did, Darren. I always do that straight away, just like you told me to.'

'Well that's something, I suppose. But don't for Christ's sake come and see me today. Do a bit of shopping, or better still, actually go and see one of your girlfriends, and then go straight home. Perhaps even take her home with you, why don't you.'

'But I want to see you, not anybody else. I can't wait another whole week. A week's too long as it is. Why can't you see me more often? I love you so much.'

'Well, I can't help that,' I'd said. 'We've been through all this, Diane. I'm too busy at the moment. And it's all your fault anyway; you should have been more careful. I'll ring you later. Oh, silly of me; I can't now, can I?'

'Don't be nasty to me. I'm so sorry, Darren. I love you.' Diane's voice had gone all high and blubbery, so I'd ended the call.

'Look after the stall a minute, Gerry,' I'd said. 'I must answer an urgent call of nature. Back in a minute.'

I'd hurried to the public toilets by the town bridge. I'd just remembered the episode with Susie and her diary entries concerning Percy nearly a year ago. I'd gone into a private cubicle and made an invigorating video on Crunch's phone, with the aforementioned Percy in the starring role. Then I'd added a text: CUDNT W8 2CU LUV PERC XXX, and sent it on its way. That was bound to do the trick. No doubt her mum would ground her for ever after she'd opened that particular message. Anyway, it had served Diane right. Slappers like that were a danger to mankind. Wills had been right. I could have gone to prison for two years because of her, even if she had been gagging for it.

I'd kept her on too long; I should have taken Dad's advice and got rid of her in July. She'd been getting to be a real pain, as it happens. She was forever moaning about having to restrict herself to only seeing me on Saturday afternoons. The snogging in the cinema during the matinee performance, followed by the bit of business in the back of the van amongst the boxes, didn't seem to satisfy her at all. I'd had just about enough of the constant battering she gave my eardrums as I was dropping her off at her bus stop. 'Why can't I come home with you anymore?' she'd kept asking. Of course she couldn't come home. Dad would have gone ballistic. Anyway, I'm busy with Jess on Saturday evenings now, aren't I?

The picture quality on Crunch's phone had been ace, much better than on mine. It was a good choice for an old geezer, the latest thing in fact. The urinals had just started their flush cycle

217

when I came out of the cubicle, so I'd taken out the SIM card and sent it on its way along with the flow of water, just like I'd done with Crunch. It was about time that Crunch went AWOL. He'd already had a couple of missed calls on his phone already.

I take his phone out of my pocket and inspect it. Only the select few of 'Dan's' friends have been given its brand new SIM card's mobile number. My old phone has gone now, so I'll never hear from Diane again. My old life as Darren is fading fast, but now that this Alicia bird has turned up, I just can't seem to shake my Dick character off. I just want to be Dan now. I just want to wipe out everything that's happened and start afresh. I prefer my new persona, and so does everybody else that matters.

'Hey, Gerry, its brass monkeys out here. I'm going to warm up in Eric's for a while. If anybody shows an interest in any of this crap, let them have it half price. Next week's my last one ever on the market.' I find a large piece of card in the back of the van, write a sign in large italics and clip it onto one of the metal uprights surrounding the stall.

Once in the café I look in the cake display cabinet, but the thought of Jess doesn't inspire me the way other girls do. Lardy cake is a step too far.

'An Americano and whatever you recommend, Eric,' I say. I move to a seat by the window, as far from the counter as possible. I'm not in the mood for Eric's banter today. This Dan character I've created is a great chap – much more well-liked than Darren ever was. I'm not just a pompous nerd anymore. I'm actually popular amongst my peers at the new school. People are taking me seriously. I'm doing great at both the bridge and chess clubs, and I'm positively shining when it comes to the debating society. Everyone hangs on my every word. Of course, the subject matter under debate is always of secondary interest to me, also the point of view I choose to take, but I always seem to be able to sway people to my supposed way of thinking. That was what cemented my decision to go into politics. Obviously I'm still going to Oxford, but studying Law is not my preferred subject anymore. I don't ever want to be a solicitor. I couldn't really give a shit about people's rights or getting them a fair deal. Saying I was studying Law was just something I said to shut that Mike character up on the kayak course. I've definitely decided to study PPE now. I could become a journalist with that, perhaps with a media company, get myself known before I try for Parliament. I can see myself in the House of Commons. These MPs are masters when it comes to being interviewed. The way they deflect uncomfortable questions by the use of counter-questions is something I'm taking on board. And they all have a 'selective memory'. Downright lying isn't usually an option though. People in the public eye usually get rumbled at some stage, so it's best to be 'economical with the truth'. And watching the Daily Politics show is the best, particularly on Wednesdays when it's PMQs. I don't budge from the Sixth Form common room at lunchtime when that's on, however good the weather. I love the insults thrown across the House, and the way each side always apportions blame. No situation is ever their fault. It's always the effect of the legacy left by the previous incumbents. This is something that I can readily relate to. I've thought that way all my life. And a valuable lesson I've learnt is never to show you're riled. It makes you go bright red and consequently makes you look ridiculous.

All in all, I'm very satisfied with the direction in which Dan is heading, but the 'born again' virginity I've been forced to adopt will finally have to go. Now that I'm not getting any with Diane, the occasional 'brush' with the likes of Maria is not going to be enough. The situation that Jess had put Dan in on that first date was a bit tricky, as it happens, but I think I conducted myself admirably, and my self-control over the ensuing months has been highly commendable. But what else could I do? She'd made it clear that she wanted her first time to be with someone in as pristine a condition as she was.

Actually, I've found that faking my innocence is not as difficult as I'd imagined. As long as I always allow her to take the lead, we're getting nowhere fast, apart from the odd chaste kiss. But her total lack of experience, combined with my new found state of purity, is proving just a bit too big of a barrier to progress. I'll have to think of something to change all that now, even if she isn't really my type. The trouble is, if I make the first move I might get carried away, and then she'll guess I'm not exactly an innocent.

I look down and see that not only has Eric delivered my order, but that I've almost finished it. The coffee mug is completely empty, and there are only a few crumbs of lardy cake left. That is actually quite scary. Eric hasn't even met Jess. This is the last place Dan would bring a prissy girl like her to.

Back at the market once more, and I find that my half price notice has done the trick. I've hardly enough stock left to cover the stall. News has carried fast around the other stallholders, and Gerry's waving a stack of cash at me. I'll pack up early and have a shower and shave before contacting that Alicia woman. I'm starting to feel petrified again. I sit down and try to control my breathing, try and relax my shaking limbs. There's only one thing for it. I'll have to tell Dad. He'll know what to do. He'll probably kill me, but that must be preferable than being killed by these drugs dealing characters. They've probably guessed that I took Crunch out. I've got to find some way of freeing myself from all this.

My new phone of Crunch's is ringing. It's Dad. 'Get over to the golf club right now, son,' he's saying. 'I'd kill you with my bare hands if I could. And don't go home and ponce yourself up first. Come as you are, however scruffy and repulsive.'

The club bar is virtually empty when I arrive. What the hell does Dad want with me? I feel decidedly ill dressed for the place. My stubble's beginning to itch and all that fear from earlier has made me horribly sweaty. I see Dad sitting at the furthest table from the door, and when his companion turns round I nearly go straight back out. It's none other than Inspector Wilkes, Dad's golf partner. I remember the video message I'd sent Diane's mum last week. Surely she didn't know it was from me? I've never met the woman. Did Diane say something? Am I going to be subjected to some bizarre form of ID? But what Dad says next makes me realise that this matter is something of a completely different nature.

'My friend Bernie here has just told me what you've been getting up to in your spare time, son, and as you're still a minor he came to me first. This is my concern too, apparently, as your guardian.' I've never seen Dad look so angry. His face is all white and hard looking, and his mouth is just a straight slit.

'We've been watching you and your goings on for some time now, lad,' Inspector Wilkes says. He's interrogating me with his hang-dog eyes, his jowls quivering slightly. 'Did you happen to see the news item about the drowning of a man called Charlie Hines a few days ago?

I shrug and start to bite the inside of my cheek. Oh shit, how long will I get for murder? But Dad's said I'm only a minor. Perhaps that will make a difference.

'My team knows all about your involvement in drugs dealing, Darren. And we also know that the unfortunate man I've just mentioned was in it with you. He's been under surveillance for some while now. In fact we've been keeping an eye on both of you at the market. Quite a good idea to take the stuff off him in boxes with brand names on. Making him look like a supplier of legitimate merchandise fooled us for a while. But his area was a large one, and his other contacts weren't so clever, I'm afraid.'

I realise that I'm finished, and I just stare at the floor. Even if my involvement in Crunch's death isn't known, I could still be put away for a long time. Even if I escape with just a conditional discharge, will I even be offered a place at a crap university, much less Oxford?

'But don't worry, lad. I'm not going to press charges. In fact, that's exactly what I don't want to happen.'

I look up quickly. 'I don't understand,' I say.

'Oh, you soon will, I can assure you of that. Don't think you are getting away with any of this. I'm confident that you'll be contacted soon. You're going to be promoted, my boy. We'd been planning on how to remove this Hines character for some time now, and it would appear that he's helped us with that little problem all by himself. How fortunate! He was no use to us at all. He was the last person to agree to becoming a grass.' Inspector Wilkes chuckles. 'Sorry about the pun, boy; I couldn't resist it.' I've no inclination to laugh though, and neither, it seems, has Dad. 'They'll choose you to replace him because of your patch's squeaky clean record. We've deliberately chosen never to catch you or your little friend "in the act", so to speak. So, what do you say; will you help us?'

'I really don't want this, sir. I was hoping to give it all up. I've just started my A Levels, and I'm planning to go to Oxford.'

'Very laudable I'm sure, lad. But I'm afraid I'm not actually giving you a choice. You either agree to help us, or I charge you right now. But don't worry. If you do what we want, I'll make sure your name stays out of all this. You won't get a criminal record. You'll have to watch your back with your drugs cronies, though. Remember what happened to your predecessor? We're treating his death as an accident for the time being... although we suspect from the nature of his injuries that this may not be the case at all. We'll be following that up later. We're surprised at our findings. This particular organisation has been non-violent up until now.'

'But I won't have time, what with all my school work, sir.' I've come out in a cold sweat. I put my hands in my jeans' pockets, but I can't stop my feet tapping as if to some ghastly rap music. But I still try to give the Inspector the most piercing stare I can muster.

'Then you'll have to delegate, lad. I'm sure your little sidekick can take over the more menial tasks. Good choice, by the way. He's very forgettable. One last thing: let me know as soon as you're contacted and we'll give you your instructions.'

'I already have been,' I say. 'I'm meant to be ringing her right now.'

'A woman, eh? That's interesting. In fact it couldn't be better. I hear you've got quite a reputation with the ladies. There would certainly be no harm in promoting "friendly relations" with her, if you get my drift. What is it they say? "Keep your friends close, and your enemies closer".' He slaps himself on the knee and laughs.

'Oh, I mustn't forget your little present before I go.' He reaches down and brings out a large, flat package from under the table. 'A spare set of number plates for your van. Just clip them on when you're on a job. The numbers are very similar to your official ones, so if your associates have already made a note of them, they'll just think they've made a slight mistake. With these ones on, you'll never be stopped by the police, and you'll be untraceable with them if anyone thinks to try.' Inspector Wilkes stands up. He looks larger than I remember. 'Well, that's about it, lad. Your dad has my contact details. Let me know what happens today and I'll fill you in on your duties. Good luck!'

Dad's expression from earlier has completely changed – 'positively radiant' comes to mind. 'You've got the luck of the devil, son, you really have. Now do what the nice man says, and make that call. I'll see you at home later before you go off gadding with Jessica. 'By the way,' he adds, when his golf partner's no longer in earshot, 'I'm glad you saw sense with that other little girl when I suggested it. You can't afford any more run-ins with the police now, can you?'

'Certainly not, Dad. I gave up Diane yonks ago. Jess is the only girl for me now.'

'Good boy,' Dad says, and he can't resist slapping me on the back. 'I knew you'd do the right thing eventually. And mind your back this afternoon, for Christ's sake.'

# Chapter 2

## Darren's Brush with Alicia

I'm really not in the mood for all this. Why does this Alicia woman have to live so completely out in the sticks? I should have turned 'Deirdre' on earlier than this but I just couldn't face her officious manner. I'm going to get enough of that from the drugs baron woman when I finally get there, aren't I? Why do all these narrow country lanes look exactly the same, and why don't they go in for sign posts at junctions anymore? I'm not psychic. OK dear, so you're *recalculating* are you. Well just get on with it, will you?

This must be it – at last. Wow! This is some place. She must be making a packet. A double fronted Georgian pile in the centre of a prosperous village: not bad. I'll just have a quick look in the rear view mirror. This stubble's looking good, as it happens, but it feels terrible. I'll probably end up with a hideous rash. But at least I look old enough to take on all this extra crap.

Everything about this Alicia chick's house is really tasteful: cast iron railings, gravelled front garden, two large ornamental pots, each sporting a neatly clipped bay tree guarding the front door. She'll get those nicked if she's not careful. I use the brass knocker shaped like a lion's head. I hope she hurries up. Now the sun's sunk so low it's freezing out here.

'Ah, there you are, Dick,' she says. She's running her tongue around the inside of her teeth again. 'Well, hurry up. Quick, quick.'

She ushers me into a large, elegant room full of packing cases. All the furniture has been placed in the middle of the floor and is covered by dustsheets.

'I've just taken this place over,' she says. 'Once it's been done up I'll move on. It's better that way, I find.'

I'm impressed. No doubt as builders come and go, I'll be able to do whatever I have to do in their shadow. My unmarked white van won't be conspicuous at all. She's giving me a guided tour of the house, showing me where the new kitchen units are going, pointing out which walls she wants demolishing, complaining about the limitations because it's Grade II listed. At each turn I'm expecting to come across some other ring members. Is she stalling because they haven't turned up yet? I'm feeling brain dead. The events of earlier – the memories of what happened with Crunch, and then that business with Inspector Wilkes – have completely drained me. She's taking me upstairs now. I hang back so she leads me by the hand. They're up there, waiting for me, I'm sure of it. If she's leading me to my doom, then so be it. I've no fight left in me, not even if my life depends on it.

She leads me into what must be her bedroom. The bed and chest of drawers are the only pieces of furniture without dust covers on. I sit down on the bed. She's starting to tell me where she wants her built-in wardrobe to go.

'Can we just stop all this faffing about and get down to it?' I say.

She must have misunderstood me. She's raising her head and giving me a provocative sideways look. She pretends to look startled, but that won't wash. Why else would she have brought me up here?

'I don't usually mix business with pleasure, Dick,' she says. 'But in your case, I'm sure I can make an exception. Why not? After all, I've had a pretty stressful year; I deserve some fun.'

She pushes me back onto the bed. 'Let's dispense with the pleasure first, she says. 'Then we'll be able to concentrate on the real matters in hand.'

She's undressing me, and I'm just too knackered to resist. Is this some sort of initiation ceremony that all her minions are put through? Surely this could be classed as rape? But I'll have to go along with it. Presumably this is what Inspector Wilkes had in mind when he suggested promoting 'friendly relations'. I close my eyes and allow her to take the initiative. Poor Percy's not at all happy about this. This must the worst performance of his whole career.

Alicia appears to be putting her 'business' hat back on along with her clothes. 'Downstairs with you now, Dick,' she says, 'and let me show you my plans.'

Once back in the living room she goes to the topmost packing case and pulls out a pile of paperwork: maps, details of contacts, perhaps even photos, I'm assuming. But no, they appear to be plans of a very different nature: architect's drawings, colour swatches, mood boards, catalogues of kitchen fittings: the sort I've seen Dad poring over. She's going through them all in detail, and I just sit still, numb with confusion.

'What's the matter Dick? Don't you think you can handle this? Your uncle assured me that you could.'

My confusion turns through embarrassment to joy. Dick Winslow's obviously the guy she's really after. For some reason he hadn't turned up at the market this morning. He's just taken over his uncle's building business. And yes, I'm a definite improvement on that miserable old git.

'Of course I can handle it,' I say. 'I'm in partnership with my father now. This size of job is no problem. I can get you a quote on this almost immediately. I'll make it a priority. I'm sure we can give you a very good rate.'

'Especially for cash, eh, Dick? Now, you look exhausted. I'm sure you had a very early start this morning. How about you go and have a nice shower while I make us both some coffee. I'll bring it upstairs. There's a bathrobe on the back of the door. Its miles too big for me, so it'll probably just about fit you.'

I'm sitting up on Alicia's bed feeling refreshed when she finally comes up with the coffee. It's taken her ages. It's obviously not the instant variety. We chat amicably about colour schemes. She has the same taste as me, as it happens: everything nice and neutral. She suddenly jumps up and starts frantically undressing. I'm not really surprised. I always seem to have that effect on women, and I'm sure that this time round Percy will make a better showing. With the same urgency, I rip off the bathrobe she's lent me.

'Oh, thank you Dick,' she says, grabbing it off me and putting it on. She's looking at her watch. 'I'm running late. I must have a shower myself. Be a dear and see yourself out, won't you? I'll see you again if you get the contract.'

Back in the freezing van, I make a quick phone call to Dad. I've got to hear someone's voice. I've never felt so humiliated in my life.

'Darren, where are you? I've been worried sick. What's happened, son?'

'Everything's fine, Dad. I'd got my wires crossed over that woman. It appears that she's a property developer, not a drugs baron. I've had quite an informative time, as it happens. And I think I might have landed you a very lucrative job. Oh, and Dad, keep Jess entertained if I'm not back by 7.30, will you?'

I wonder how Dad will fare with Alicia. No doubt the 'organ grinder' will get the same attention as the 'monkey'. For Dad, a woman like that is probably just a perk of the job, not worth a second thought, much less a mention. And certainly not something to feel guilty about as far as Mum's concerned.

I turn on 'Deirdre' for the journey home. I don't want to be late. I must have a shave and a change of clothes. 'Deirdre's' tone seems to have changed from dull resignation to that of joyous expectation. She's obviously caught my mood. I've decided to ditch all this passivity with Jess. From what's just happened with Alicia, it's obviously a turn off. No other chick's ever been satisfied with just one bout with me before. Of course my passivity has all been based on fear. With Alicia it was all about who she was and what she knew. With Jess it's been fear of who I am and what I know.

But all that is going to change. Once the olds have gone out this evening, the entertainment will begin. Dan's 'virginity' will finally be lost. I'll risk Jess realising my true state. This is going to be her lucky night.

# Chapter 3

## Darren Meets the Master

So it's all happening at last. I'm sure he's going to be the one. He's looking at all the surrounding stalls, paying more attention to them than any of them warrant, but I can tell that he's got me in his sights. And he's even less of a DIY freak than Alicia. He's similar in type to her though: smart suit, well groomed, about thirty. Should I have grown this wretched stubble again? But Crunch never looked exactly suave, so I reckon I'll do.

He's at the stall, but instead of running his fingers up and down the screwdrivers and suchlike in the way Alicia did, he's fiddling with them, lining everything up neatly. An anally retentive control freak – or is he just stalling for time, sizing me up?

'You must be Dick,' he says at last.

I raise my eyebrows slightly. 'Who's asking?' I say.

'I believe we have something to discuss concerning a departed colleague,' he says.

I'm not one hundred per cent sure that I like the sound of that. The word *departed* has a sinister ring to it. We can't talk at the stall with Gerry the Gorilla's ears flapping, and Eric won't be any better. The café will be empty at this time in the morning, and he'll hear every word, and no doubt he'll address me as Darren. I suggest that we sit in the front of the van. As its facing the river, we'll be away from prying eyes.

'Hey Gerry, mate,' I say. 'Keep an eye out, can you? Won't be a tick.' I doubt if this character will try any funny business now that the ape's clocked him.

He brushes the passenger seat down with a gloved hand and sits down. 'No doubt you read about how Crunch met his end,' he says. 'A sorry business. Crunch was always a loyal and reliable member of the team. He'll be sorely missed. Other than drinking too much, his only other vice was overindulgence in the stock. He can't have made anything out of it financially. I suppose he was only in it to feed his habit. He always had a good word for you though: quick learner, good memory, excellent work ethic, and most importantly, creative. That's why I'm offering you the chance of promotion. Are you a user if you don't mind my asking you Dick? Or are you just in it for the money?'

'Definitely the latter,' I say. 'My only vice is women, my only overindulgence, so to speak.' I give Mark what I hope is a manly wink. I'm glad about my stubble now. It makes me feel, as well as look, older, but I wish my jeans weren't so scruffy looking.

'Good man!' he says and gives me a friendly, but infuriating, slap on the back. 'My sentiments entirely. Why sap one's health and strength on anything else? Let's have our first proper meet in a club. I'll fill you in on your duties, and then we can get down to the more serious business of pulling some totty. But before I forget, I must give you this.' He hands me a new mobile phone even flashier than Crunch's. 'Only use it for business mind, and never store any numbers. Memorise them as and when you get them. Here's mine for starters.' He hands me a business card: 'Mark Hensley – Specialist in Horticulture & Pharmaceuticals', followed by a phone number.

'I think we'll get on very well,' he says. 'I'll contact you again in the next couple of days. We must sort this out before Christmas. Our supplies need to go through as usual.' He shakes my hand, gets out of the van and walks swiftly away in the direction of the bridge.

Well, that's it then: a doddle so far. There's absolutely no point in me hanging around anymore. Its bloody freezing. I put all my remaining stock into the back of the van and just drive off. I'll sell it all on eBay. Home for a shower, shave and a change of clothing, and then I'll contact Dad, get him to arrange a meet with his friend Inspector Wilkes.


I look at the clock above the bar of the clubhouse: 4.00pm. Dad and Bernie should be finishing their game soon. It must be getting too dark by now. Should I call him Bernie now I'm on board? The double doors swing open and they're approaching my table. My mood today couldn't be more different from this time last week. My bizarre brush with Alicia seems to have cured me of fear. I lean back in my seat with my hands behind my head, and give them a smile.

'Well I've met him, and it all went surprisingly well actually,' I say as they sit down. 'He seemed like a really nice chap, quite ordinary really, more like a businessman than a gangster.'

'That's exactly what I expected,' Inspector Wilkes says, raising his continuous, incredibly bushy eyebrow. 'I hoped I'd satisfied your dad on that score. I would never have allowed you to get involved with hoodlums. It would have been kinder just to have arrested you. Ronnie and I go back a long way, you know. We respect each other.'

'It all seems safe enough, son, as long as you don't blow your cover – or start nicking the stock of course,' Dad says. He gives me a stare rather like the ones I give people sometimes. 'It appears that they're businessmen, not gangsters, but then again they're not angels – but I'm going to the bar for some beers. Bernie will fill you in on the details.'

'That's right, Darren. They're not money launderers, or gun runners involved in importing illegal drugs from South America or anything. We believe that the top men in this cartel are indeed businessmen, making money from actually growing cannabis on a large scale in this country and also from employing chemists to illegally manufacture prescription drugs. The top men will probably be members of the same family. The next link down in the chain will be trusted friends and the lower echelons will be people that they trust, but are disposable. How long have you been working for them now… about two years isn't it? That's a long time for someone in your position. Six months is considered pretty good. No wonder they trust you.'

'That would explain what it says on his business card,' I say, handing it to him. 'I've got to memorise his mobile number and then throw it away. He's ringing me on this new phone he gave me in a couple of days, and then we're meeting in a night club. How far up the chain do you think he is? Is he a family member?'

'Hard to say,' he says. He looks at the card, and pockets it. It's lucky I've got a photographic memory. 'I shouldn't think that's his real name anyway. We're assuming that he takes his orders from someone of importance, but not directly from the top man. They'll be a number of people like this 'Mark' character, each one responsible for their own area, and each with several people like you under them. If you were to draw it out, it would look like a family tree. But getting back to your role: his wanting to socialise with you is a stroke of luck. Meeting somewhere in a night club couldn't be better, in fact. It will allow us to send a plain clothes man in: keep an eye on him, follow him if he gets a taxi home, or even get his car registration number. Contact me as soon as you know when and where you're meeting him, and I'll get someone onto it. I know just the right man.'

I scowl. I don't reckon such a person exists – not in the police force. Bernie seems bright enough, but he's an exception. This will ruin it. Mark will realise that he's a cop, and I'll find myself in a ditch somewhere with certain vital bits of me missing – chopped off. My hand automatically goes to my crutch.

'I know exactly what you're thinking, Darren, but the Drugs Squad will find just the right chap. He'll be well trained in surveillance. We're not all brain dead in the Police Force, you know. Some of us actually have degrees.' Dad's come back with the drinks, and Bernie stops to take a swig. 'Hopefully your duties as our inside man will be over before you know it. I'm not saying that we'll be moving in anytime soon though. We suspect that it's a pretty extensive organisation you're involved with. And if your contact proves to be not very high up in the pecking order, it may take months, even years to wrap the whole thing up. We mustn't move too soon and just snatch at the fringes. We want to close down the whole operation in one fell swoop, which means people in your patch will feel the fallout. But you won't need to know any of the details just yet. We'll let you know when the time comes – when it all kicks off. All you'll have to do for the moment is carry on as normal. And keep socializing with Mark if you can.'

Months or even years, he's saying. That's not on. I don't want to be Dick anymore. What the hell do I have to do to get rid of him? I can't facilitate any more deaths. I've decided that's not really my style. It had been a real drag walking all the way along the embankment from the bridge, to where it ends further downstream. It was brass monkeys for starters. But I'd had to memorise the positions of all the metal ladders that went down into the water – the ones people use to access their boats. I'd needed recognisable landmarks along Broadway so I'd know where they were in the dark, just in case the worst possible scenario had happened and I'd ended up in the water instead of Crunch.

It had been interesting as an exercise, I suppose, but incredibly time-consuming to plan and both physically and emotionally draining to execute.

# Chapter 4

## Joel is Taught a Lesson

'Now that Crunch is no longer with us, we've both been promoted, mate. We're one step up the ladder. I've become Area Manager, and you've got my old job of District Distributor.'

Darren has instructed Joel to meet him in the car park of the industrial estate next to the Council flats where they both used to live. It's completely empty, it being a Sunday morning, but Joel is surprised that the entry barrier is up.

'Nice new wheels,' Joel says, getting himself comfortable in the passenger seat. It's a black Mini Cooper with two white stripes running down the bonnet. It's about three years old from the registration number, and very smart indeed: immaculate even. 'Where are we going, and why meet here? Why couldn't you just pick me up from home? It's freezing.'

As to the matter of Crunch's demise, Joel has his suspicions. He'd been surprised at how Darren had needed to come round to his house every day for a week just before Christmas, insisting on practising a series of manoeuvres on him. For some reason Darren needed to find the best way to force him to the floor with the least amount of effort. When he'd finally decided on the 'high five and half nelson' technique, it all had to be tried out on both sides to see which hand Darren preferred to keep free for the final blow to the head. Nothing was ever explained to Joel as to why this had been necessary, or why it had stopped as quickly as it had started.

Joel isn't surprised that Darren may have had some part in Crunch's death. He's more bemused by the reason for it. Surely it wasn't so that he could slip into Crunch's shoes? Why would he want promotion? It wouldn't be for the money. He's never short of that, his dad's loaded. It must be for the power. What Darren says next confirms this, but also confuses Joel even more.

'We're staying right here for the next hour, mate. I don't want the extra workload as it happens. So when the time comes I'm delegating most of it to you. It will mean a lot more cash for you, of course. It's just a pity your birthday isn't till August. Right then – out you get. We're swapping seats. I'm teaching you to drive this baby.'

'But I'm not old enough, Darren. I won't be seventeen for nearly seven months.'

'Exactly. It'll take me that long to get it all into your thick skull, mate.'

Joel bristles at this. He knows he's not as intelligent as Darren, but he's certainly not stupid. He's observant, and not just of his physical surroundings. His antennae are finely tuned to the vibrations of a situation, and everything he picks up is stored safely away for later, like a squirrel storing food.

'Why on earth do you want me to drive your new car? I might wreck it for starters. What's the point?'

'The point, my slow witted little friend, is so that you can take over the running of my area ASAP. You'll take your driving test as soon after your birthday as possible, and then your duties will increase, mate. You'll be practising on the roads with me as well soon, as soon as I reckon you're up to it. I'm quite sure nobody will stop us as long as you don't do anything stupid. This car's got magic number plates.' He laughs at this but Joel can't see the joke. 'I'm taking you on the rounds after this lesson, mate. Introducing you to all the other distributors in our area. Then when you've passed your test you'll be virtually taking over my job. You're bound to pass first time with me teaching you. I did, didn't I? This promotion has come at a bad time for me, as it happens. I've got too much on right now. So come on, mate. Change places.'

Obediently, Joel gets out and slips into the driver's seat. He runs his hands over the steering wheel. It feels good, the leather is warm on his freezing hands. It's still only just after 9.30am, the January sun is still low in the sky, and there was a piercing east wind following him all the way from his house courtesy of the Urals.

'Well come on, short arse, and change your seat position or you'll never reach the pedals. And alter the mirror so that you can see the whole of the rear window.'

Joel obeys orders with a growing amount of both excitement and trepidation. What if he crashes into something and alters the pristine appearance of Darren's 'baby'? He looks around the barren, litter-strewn wasteland that's the car park. There's actually nothing to crash into other than a few empty beer cans and the odd takeaway container.

'You won't be taking over all my duties though, mate. I'll still be providing you with the gear, but now I have to collect it from a warehouse instead of from Crunch. But some of my newly acquired perks are just too good to give away – like my meetings with our immediate boss. That club he took me to last week was pretty special, as it happens, as were the female clientele. And our new boss is the Master when it comes to pulling. Even I'm learning a few new tricks. If it was an Olympic event, he'd definitely get gold. Anyway you're too young. They wouldn't let you into such places.'

'You're too young as well then, aren't you?'

'Only in years, mate. Only in years. But enough of all that. Let's get started. Listen, learn and remember: lesson number one coming up.'

Joel wonders whether he could swing it to borrow the car for other things like going to see Grace for instance. All that waiting around for coaches that are never on time is getting to be a bit of a pain. If only he was as confident around girls as Darren. He's still not sure how he feels about Grace. In fact he's not even sure how he feels about girls in general. The subject of his sexuality is still troubling him. His connection with Darren has an unfathomable strength, although it's true that no other boy has this effect on him. And he'd be wasting his time trying anything with Grace anyway. He's sure she still has feelings for Darren. She's still asking after him, after all this time.

# Chapter 5

## Hope's First Birthday

Grace is having a difficult time with Hope today, but no worse than usual, and nothing she hasn't learnt to handle. It's the Easter holidays and she's busy this morning tidying up after her sister's last client. Some of them prefer to have their hair styled here instead of in their own homes, and after having it washed in Faith's downstairs bathroom, they are invited into the front room to have it cut and dried. Grace is sweeping up the fallen hair and tidying away the tools of her sister's trade: the mousse, the gel, the hairspray and, most importantly, the scissors. Grace has resorted to putting Hope into her playpen, something she hates doing, but Hope is becoming wilful and disobedient if she doesn't have her own way, and her inquisitive little hands are not safe around Faith's things.

Hope, a year old today, is a danger to herself now that she has learned to toddle. She always wants the most hazardous and inappropriate things to play with, but when put in her playpen out of harm's way she screams, stamps her feet, shakes the bars and finally puts up her arms for Grace to lift her out. It's at this point that Grace invariably weakens. Each time Hope behaves like this she's reminded of what Joel had said the day he'd first seen it happen. He'd said it was identical to one of his first childhood memories and the last time that he'd seen his baby sister Zoe. Her incessant screaming had led the neighbours to complain to the Council, who in turn had taken Zoe into care, after which she had later been adopted. Grace is petrified of the same thing happening to Hope, so she always picks her up as soon as she makes a fuss.

Grace looks at her daughter with awe. Even in a temper she's so beautiful. Hope has stopped screaming now and is looking at her in that defiant yet pleading way of hers that makes Grace's heart ache. She lifts her out and carries her to the sofa by the window. She's smiling so sweetly, and playing with Grace's hair so gently, that she can't stop her eyes filling with tears. She's reminded of the times when she'd given in to Darren after one of his sudden and unexplained rages; of how she had soothed him and whispered encouraging words to him when he was upset, just as she is doing now to his daughter. 'You're the prettiest and best girl in the whole world, and Mummy loves you so much,' she whispers.

If only Darren hadn't misunderstood her that day after the school trip and thought she had given him up for Joel. She'd said the wrong thing and it was all her fault. She should have replied to his messages and given him a chance to explain about Jenna. It wasn't as if Jenna and he had seen each other again. In fact at half term Jenna had mysteriously left. Their form teacher had told them that she had moved miles away, but Grace was sure that she'd seen her soon after in Ross–on–Wye with a St. Catherine's uniform on. She would have forgiven Darren if only he'd said he was sorry, that he'd made a mistake.

She'd felt so clever back then, and so strong before Hope's birth, but it's all different now. She needs him so much that she's prepared to forgive him anything. She cuddles her baby and rocks her gently. She's sucking her rabbit's ear. She'll be asleep soon.

Grace remembers how she would spend hours daydreaming about Darren before he had even asked her out, and how she used to pretend that he was coming to see her when she knew he really wanted to see Leroy. She still daydreams about him, but her daydreams have become more passionate – the style of Jane Austen is no longer enough. She has now become acquainted with the works of such authors as Emily Bronte and Thomas Hardy and the smouldering desire expressed in such writing has ignited the sexual longing for him that was suppressed during pregnancy and for a time after Hope's birth. She has been inspired by the return of Angel Clare to Hardy's tragic heroine, Tess, in *Tess of the D'Urbervilles*. At such times she glosses over the novel's tragic ending. Of course, she still resorts to Jane Austen when appropriate. She's just finished reading *Persuasion* and is soothed by Captain Wentworth's return to Anne Elliot several years after a misunderstanding had arisen between them. Surely that could still happen with her and Darren, their misunderstanding could still be cleared up?

Sometimes when the doorbell rings, she starts up from whatever she's doing, wondering whether it will be him at last, coming back for her and their daughter. Or when she's expecting Joel on one of his visits, she imagines that Darren will come too. Does he even know where they live? Joel brings her money from him sometimes, not regularly and never a set amount, but there's never a note for her, never an acknowledgement of what the money is for.

She's relived the encounter with him in the hospital over and over again in the hope of changing what had happened. He would come in and say that he loved her, and he would show her the things that he'd bought, and then when the nurse brought Hope into the ward he would help to dress her in one of the tiny outfits. Instead of throwing that dirty envelope of cash at her, he'd say that they would go shopping together when he came back to collect her, and then they'd be together and he would look after them both. She shouldn't have greeted him so coldly. After all, he had come a long way to see her. She should have given him a chance.

She longs for Joel to give her more news of Darren. She hears snippets such as how he's teaching Joel to drive his new car, and how Darren is pleased with Joel's progress. She hears how Darren's gone up a notch and is mixing in very different circles, and rarely deigns to go into Eric's anymore now that he's given up the stall. But she never hears anything that matters. Joel's only left a little while ago, after coming down for Hope's first birthday. She recalls their conversations together. As is becoming more frequent, the main topic has been about Joel himself.

'That last Trade Fair at the NEC was great,' he'd said. 'After Theo had taken me to observe him ordering stock with our existing suppliers, he sent me off by myself for a while to hunt out some new things. I marked all the stalls I liked the look of in the catalogue and then Theo went back to have a look himself. He approved of nearly all of my choices. He says I have a very good eye. And my interior design course is going really well. I've even picked up the technical drawing aspect OK. And I've made quite a few friends at the class.'

Grace looks back on his enthusiasm fondly. Ever since he's found out about Theo being his dad, his confidence has blossomed. She's always wanted the best for him. He's been her best friend, and like a brother to her, ever since her real brother died. But they never seem to find time to speak of what she's doing, or how she's feeling. But why should anybody be interested in the dull routine of her existence: of how she has to hurry on and off buses with a pushchair in order to get Hope to the crèche before her college lectures start, of how she has to stay up late in order to finish her homework after she has finally settled her down, or how she sometimes gets into trouble over missed assignment deadlines and disappointing marks? Nobody seems interested in her life. Her parents have virtually cut her out of theirs, and as she's always in a rush to get home with Hope after her classes, she has made almost no new friends.

Her need for Darren is overwhelming her. As she does so often, she clutches their baby to her, fearful that she might somehow vanish – her only link to him. But Hope is very much here, soothed to sleep by a few kind and encouraging words, by getting what she wants, when she wants, always.

Her last words to Joel have been the same as ever. 'Be careful, Joel, and have a good journey. Text me as soon as you get home, won't you? And next time you see Darren, tell him that Hope and I would love to see him. Don't forget.'

# Chapter 6

## Be Careful What You Wish For

How do I get myself out of this one? This is almost worse than the situation I was in before Christmas. What's with these religious festivities? Here I am just before Easter, potentially saddled with a life sentence.

'I don't want to get engaged to Jess, Dad. Why should I?'

'I told you to be careful with that one, Darren. And to let her parents catch you in flagrante in their lounge like that was plain stupid. You must have known their views on such matters. "Not before marriage" if you can help it, but definitely "not before you're engaged". They're religious nutters, son. You must have known that.'

Of course I hadn't known that. How am I meant to know what goes on in their minds, what they get up to on Sunday mornings when I'm playing golf? I've failed to follow Dad's good advice, haven't I? I never bothered to concentrate on what was being said when I've been over there for Sunday lunch. I've never asked the right questions. I haven't 'listened, learnt or remembered'.

'But I don't think she's the one, Dad. She's not really my type. I'm sure there's somebody perfect for me out there somewhere, but Jess just isn't the one.' A get a sudden clutching pain in my chest as an image of Kaye flashes through my mind. I try to hold onto it, but it's gone.

'You told her you loved her, didn't you, son? That's what Jessica told her parents in your defence. That must count for something. Have you ever said that to any of your other girlfriends?'

'No, Dad.'

'Well, there you are then,' Dad says.

I thought I did love her at first. All that enforced abstinence over the first few months of our relationship had confused me. But she's really beginning to annoy me now, with all her great plans for our engagement party: telling me what to do, what to say, what to think, what to wear. And her sexual appetite is too much, even for me.

'She's the first girl you've really loved, Darren,' Dad's saying. 'Forget all the others along the way. They meant nothing. Take me and your Mum. She was the first girl I fell in love with. None of the others really counted, either before or after we got married.'

'But when I get married I don't want to need anybody else. That can't be right. Why did you need other people if you really loved Mum?'

'Well, she sort of "shut up shop" for years after you were born, Darren. She didn't seem to want me at all. She only had time for you. You were such a beautiful baby, and very demanding. It wasn't until we moved away from the council estate that I got a look in at all.'

'Oh, so it's all my fault, is it? How can it be my fault? That's just not fair!'

'That's not what I meant, son. In fact, it was you that brought us back together in the end. Children always do.'

246

I've had enough. How dare Dad blame me for cheating on Mum! I have to get away. I run upstairs and quickly pack an overnight bag.

'I'm going away for a few days. I don't know where to yet. And I'll be turning off my mobile. You'll have to make my excuses.' I give him one of my stares. 'You're obviously very good at that.'

I jump in the car and give Joel a call. There's nobody else I can talk to about this. 'Where are you, – Eric's? I'll see you in five.' I turn on the ignition and I'm off. Oh shit! Who moved the gatepost? That was close.

I'm in desperate need of comfort food. I order a latte and a couple of coconut macaroons and sit down next to Joel. I try to talk to him about all this engagement rubbish but he's not listening.

'You've got to see these,' he's saying. He's waving his mobile under my nose. 'Isn't she gorgeous? It was her first birthday last week. Not that you'll remember, of course.'

He's scrolling through all these photos that he took when he'd last stayed with Grace. She looks really hot. She's laughing, and doing all these ridiculous poses, her arms and legs shooting out all over the place. I like her new hairstyle – all wavy and flowing onto her shoulders, and she's had some blonde highlights put in. I wish I'd been there.

'Look at this one though. It's definitely my favourite.' My heart nearly stops. Grace is sitting down on a sofa with the most beautiful toddler on her knee. She's got a great mass of lilywhite hair and the most enormous blue eyes. And she's clutching the little rabbit I bought for her. These are the ones I should be with, not that annoying, stodgy Jess.

I have to see Hope. I have to see Grace. Grace was my first love, of course she was. Just because I never told her, it doesn't mean it's not true. She's the only one that's ever understood me, the only one who'd listen to me when I was annoyed with people who'd tried to make me look stupid or tried to blame me for things that weren't my fault. Nobody else has even come close to how special she was. And she's always been mine, not Joel's. I should have fought for her, not just let him take her like that.

'What is it between you two now?' I say. 'Do you sleep with her when you go and stay? Does her sister let you share Grace's room?'

'I sleep on the sofa, of course,' Joel says. 'Why won't anyone believe me when I tell them that we're just friends? She's only ever wanted you. I've never stood a chance.'

I feel hot and sticky and it's as if treacle's seized my brain. 'Then what was all that about you living with her, and having to creep about late at night and leaving early in the morning?'

Joel snorts. 'I wasn't actually sleeping in her flat. I'm not that brave – or mad – and anyway she would never have let me. I was living in her dad's store – you know – the ones by the lifts to the flats, on the ground floor. I had to clear out early just in case her dad needed anything from it before he went to work. My mum had gone off for a bit and I had nowhere else to go.'

I bite into my second macaroon. This one tastes even better than the first. 'Does Grace ever ask after me? Would she be pleased to see me?'

'She's always asking after you, but I never really know what to say,' Joel says. 'I don't think she'd like the sound of some of the things you get up to. I think her memory of you is rather skewed. But she's always saying she wants to see you.'

'Where's she living now? Give me her address. I've got to see her. And I'll get Hope a late birthday present. A Daddy rabbit to go with that little one she's got.'

So it's a year on and I'm rushing into the Mother and Baby shop again in the Shopping Mall. I'm programming the imperious 'Deirdre' with another Cardiff postcode and I'm on my second attempt to see Grace and Hope. *Please* let Joel be right about her wanting to see me this time.

'Do you really love me, Darren? You've never said that to me before.' Grace is lying in my arms, and looking straight into my eyes. She's stroking the soft, light coloured down that's gradually started growing on my chest since we were last together. Now she's rubbing her cheek across it and purring contentedly. I've been thinking about having it waxed, but I'll leave it for now. 'You are really here, aren't you? I'm not hallucinating? One moment I'm daydreaming that you're ringing the doorbell, and the next thing I know, there you are standing on the front step.'

'Of course I'm here, you ninny. And of course I love you. You're my first and only love. I suppose I was too embarrassed to say it before. I was only fifteen, after all.' I turn my gaze in the direction of Hope's cot once more, but she's still asleep. 'Why did you dump me then, Grace, if you weren't with Joel?'

She looks away for a while and doesn't speak. Then she whispers, 'I was waiting for you in your porch after the school outing, the one I missed because I'd felt sick. I'd brought round a pregnancy test for us to do together.'

'And...? What happened, then? Why didn't we do it?'

'You were with that Jenna girl. I heard what you were saying.'

Oh shit! I'm going to have to think fast. 'Jenna?' I say. 'What were we talking about? I don't remember any of this.'

Grace has that scared look of hers on her face. Surely she doesn't think I'm going to hurt her. Although eavesdropping is a bit much, isn't it.

'I can't remember the exact words, but she asked you how many girls you'd done it with – and was I the first? – and then she asked you to take her upstairs.'

I remain silent for a while, and put on a somewhat confused expression. Finally I answer her. 'It was an awfully long time ago now, and I can hardly remember her, but I think she'd come round to play that new game of mine, the one for the Wii. You remember, don't you, the one I'd got for my birthday?' I change my expression to that of bruised surprise. 'Surely you don't think she wanted to sleep with me? She certainly didn't want sex with me, Grace, I can assure you of that. In fact I can swear on Hope's life that she didn't.'

'I'm sure you were kissing her though, Darren, before you went in.'

'Well, maybe,' I say, 'but you know what she was like. She was always trying to flirt with me, and she wouldn't leave me alone that day. You should have been there, Grace. None of it would have happened if you'd been there.'

Hope is awake and standing upright in her cot next to Grace's bed. She's peering suspiciously at me through the bars. 'Dada,' she wails. She screws her face up really tight and lifts her arms up in the air. Before she has a chance to draw breath, I pull on my boxers, lift her out, and cover her with so many kisses that she's powerless to utter another sound.

'Take her a minute, Grace; I've got you both a present.' I dress quickly and rush out to the van to get Hope's rabbit. The

250

present I've decided to give Grace is still in its box, originally to be given to Jess at our engagement party.

I grab Hope back off Grace and sit her on the floor. She's clutching the little rabbit, so I prop the big one up against the side of the bed for her. 'Dada,' she gurgles, and points her lovely, chubby little fingers.

'I'm afraid it's probably a bit big,' I say as I slip the ring onto Grace's finger. 'I'd forgotten how small and dainty your hands are.'

My phone's ringing. It's Dad. I forgot to turn it off. 'Where the hell are you, Darren? I can't stall Jessica any more. I refuse to do your dirty work for you. You're on your own from now on.'

'I'm anything but on my own, Dad. I've just become engaged to Grace. I'm with her now, as it happens – with Grace and my daughter. I took what you said to heart, about first love and all that, about how children bring people back together.'

'Darren, is that you?' Mum's on the phone now. 'What's this about a daughter?'

'You'll just love her, Mum. She's the most beautiful creature in the whole world. She looks very much like me, actually – just like those old baby photos you keep showing me. Anyway, you'll see her soon. I'm bringing her and Grace back home for Easter. Make sure you get plenty of extra food in and get my old cot out of the attic. See you at the weekend. And get Dad to sort all that business out regarding Jess, can't you? I can't do anything from here, can I?'

I end the call. I want nothing to do with any of that now. That was all Dan's mess, not mine. And Jess will get over it. She's got her A Levels in a few weeks, and then she'll be off to Leicester or somewhere.

'Who's Jess?' Grace says.

'Oh, just a dog that belongs to a friend of Dad's,' I say. 'A slightly overweight golden Labrador, as it happens. I was meant to be looking after her for a while, but she just got too demanding. She kept jumping all over me, wanting me to play with her. It all got a bit too much for me in the end.'

'You're not really a dog person anyway, are you?' she says.

'Not at all,' I agree. 'Give me a slinky cat-like creature like you any day.' I go to tickle her, but she shrieks and grabs my wrists.

'No you don't, Darren O'Donnell! You know I hate that.' So I kiss her instead. This couldn't be better. I just love being good old Darren again.

# Chapter 7

## Joel Confronts his Confusion

Joel slips Darren's Mini into third gear as he approaches the last roundabout before he has to turn off the main road to Eddie's and Faith's bungalow. He's booked a caravan for a week on a campsite in Snowdonia and he's going to show Grace all the places he went to last year with Theo and his mum.

He's surreptitiously borrowed Jeannie's walking gear: her boots, anorak and rucksack. He can't imagine that she'll miss them any time soon. He'd been unwilling to admit to Theo and his mum who he was taking on this holiday, for fear of further questions about his supposed girlfriend, so he'd lied to them, saying he was going with a male friend from his evening classes. His true feelings for Grace are beginning to reveal themselves to him, and for the first time in his life, although looking forward to being in her company, he is nervous about them being in such close contact. But Darren had insisted that he borrow his car and take Grace off his hands for a while.

'Are you sure about this, Darren,' he'd said. 'Sharing a caravan is going to be rather intimate. She is your fiancée, you know.'

'Exactly, mate. That's why I'm letting you go. I trust Grace implicitly. She's not going to look at a runt like you when she's got me to look forward to, is she? Anyway, that two week holiday in Spain with Hope and her was a bit much, as it happens. I need a break, and Mum says she'll look after Hope while you're both away.'

Now that Faith's husband Eddie has come home on leave, after a long tour of duty in Afghanistan, he wants Grace and Hope out of the way for a while. He wants his family all to himself. Although August is not usually a suitable time for Joel to take time off work, this year is fine; Theo has agreed to it. Jeannie can help him out in the shop between her shifts at the King's Arms. She'll be losing her job there soon anyway. The place has just been taken over, and although reasons haven't been given, Joel guesses that the new managers have decided that she won't fit their new image. They're planning to give it a thorough make-over. All the dark brown wall panels are going to be painted a tasteful duck egg blue, the dark red walls transformed by several coats of cream emulsion and the wooden floorboards that are now covered with a ferociously patterned carpet will be stripped, sanded and polished. They'll no doubt be recruiting younger staff to go with the new decor. Anyway, Joel reckons that his mum's well out of it. She'll have more time to help Theo then, allowing him to catalogue his growing quantity of antiquarian books. He's got a new website, and is doing extremely well – so well in fact, that he's thinking of leaving the running of the shop completely to Joel, once he's finished his apprenticeship.

Joel slows down and parks the car outside Grace's local store. He'll buy them each a can of coke and a packet of crisps to consume on the journey. The temperature today is unseasonably low for August, with strong winds and rain, and his discomfort concerning the likelihood of prolonged periods alone in the caravan with Grace is returning. It will be totally different from when he stays with her at Faith's house. Grace is always up, dressed and attending to Hope by the time he surfaces, and he's always given the privacy he needs to get washed and changed. Heat rises from the pit of his stomach to infuse his face as he imagines possible scenarios happening between them, although he knows that they won't. Darren is quite right to trust them. He'd never try anything on with Grace unless he thought he had a chance, and, with Darren on the scene, of course he hasn't. And he wouldn't want to jeopardize his friendship with either of them. If only Grace had an inkling of what Darren got up to when he wasn't with her, then perhaps things would be different. Joel swears he would never treat her with such a lack of consideration. It was as if when Darren couldn't actually see her, then she didn't exist. The amount of girls that Darren has got through – in the last four and a half months that Grace and he have been back together – is phenomenal, even for someone who isn't engaged to be married. And Joel hates the way he's expected to accompany Darren on these jaunts.

Joel leans his head back against the driver's seat and relives the events of their most recent outing. His confusion over his sexual orientation is no longer an issue with him, and, thanks to Darren, he has had his first significant experience with a girl – only kissing admittedly, but quite enough to know that he is definitely not gay. Darren had just got back from his holiday in Spain and had come round to take Joel out.

'Late birthday celebrations mate,' he'd said, 'and for you passing your driving test first time while I was in Spain. That's definitely a reason to go out. And if you do the driving then I can drink can't I? We could go to one of those places I've been to with Mark.' They'd stopped at a rather dingy looking pub the *Sailor's Retreat* first, to tank up. Darren had said that the price of drinks in these clubs was exorbitant. The building fronted straight onto the street, and Joel had managed a perfect parallel park between two cars immediately outside the entrance. The interior was not very inviting, very little of the August sun was penetrating the tiny, small paned windows. Men in their twenties and thirties were standing around in the gloom – in groups or in pairs. Others were playing darts or table football. Joel had felt at least a dozen pairs of eyes turning towards them as they entered, scrutinising them in a way Joel had found disconcerting. Their stares were just too intense, too interested. He'd noticed a sign saying *Beer Garden* straight ahead.

'I still only look about fourteen, Darren. I'm getting out of here.' he'd said. Grace had cut his hair again recently and his eyes looked bigger and more innocent than ever. 'Just get me a coke as I'm doing the driving. I'll see you in the garden.'

He'd found himself a secluded spot at a table positioned against the boundary wall, heavily clad with honeysuckle. The flashy, yellow, hermaphrodite flowers hanging in large clusters were attracting moths seeking out their sweet nectar. He'd been allowing the heady fragrance of the surrounding blooms to banish his unease of earlier, when the door to the bar had opened and a man in his early thirties had come out and joined him at his table, moving the spare chair as close to Joel's as possible.

'Ah, so this is where you're hiding, is it? I'm Sam. My friend's chatting to yours at the bar, so I thought I'd take my chance. You've not been here before, have you? I'm sure I would have noticed a little cracker like you. You remind me of someone… I know! You look rather like that little lad that's just won a medal for diving at the Olympics.'

'Really?' Joel had said, unsure what to make of this unusual exchange.

'Believe me, you do.' Sam had laid his hand on Joel's knee before continuing. 'What are your plans for later? You and your friend could come back to mine, it's only round the corner. We could play some music… have a few drinks… see what develops. What do you say?'

It was all happening so swiftly that Joel had been unable to react. The pressure of the man's hand was increasing and Joel had tried to remove it with his own, only to find Sam's other hand encircling it. Joel's whole body had become rigid with revulsion, and he was frightened that his immobility was being read as compliance. And the strength of this aversion could not be mistaken for his lack of enthusiasm for the unattractive girls he'd been expected to kiss.

Then Darren had burst through the door without any drinks. He was frantically brushing at his shoulder with one hand, while continually flexing and clenching the other. His face had turned a livid red.

'Get up, mate. We're off. Now!' he'd said. 'I'm not drinking here. I'd rather pay the club's inflated prices any day. And as it's your birthday treat, you can have first choice of any *girls* we pull.' He'd glared at Joel's unwelcome companion as he'd said this. 'Not back through the bar, mate. We'll go through the archway. I've just decked somebody in there. You take the fit one for a change, when we've pulled. And as you're driving, you can have the use of the car as well. I reckon it's my turn to "take the dog for a walk".'

Joel shudders at the memory, taking a deep breath in and then releasing it slowly the way Theo has taught him to. Should he say something to Grace about Darren's behaviour with other girls, or is it none of his business? As he pulls up in front of Faith's and Eddie's bungalow, he sees her sheltering under the porch, her case beside her ready to go.

'It's so good to see you,' she says, getting in beside him. 'We're going to have such a good time, regardless of the weather. Anyway, it's bound perk up later on, isn't it?' She gives him a sisterly peck on the cheek and smiles. 'How are Darren and Hope?'

'Fine,' he says. 'Just fine.'

On reflection, he decides to wait for a more appropriate time to tell her. The last thing he wants to do is to spoil her holiday.

# Chapter 8

## Sophie Meets the Boys

Sophie manages to reach the shelter of the portico of the King's Arms just as the rain descends. It's sudden and heavy, accompanied by a biting October wind and her short, floral-patterned denim jacket is not enough to protect her. She huddles in as close to the wall as she can, avoiding the drips cascading from the ornamental pediment. From here she can see a family sitting around the table placed in the bay window jutting out onto the street. She sees a staff member placing their tea tray in front of them. The waitress is around forty, slight and alert with shoulder-length, light brown hair. But Sophie doesn't register her appearance. Her mind is elsewhere.

She takes the photograph out of her bag once more and peruses the face of the boy depicted in it, although she has already consigned to memory every detail of his face. She traces with her finger the length of his aquiline nose, then across his full, almost effeminate lips. She runs her finger across the thick fringe of hair that partly obliterates one of his large, brown, heavily lashed eyes.

Every Saturday for several weeks, Sophie has been tramping the streets of this town, ever since the letter and accompanying photograph arrived. The twice yearly letters from her birth mother to her adopted parents, via the adoption agency, have never been of much interest to her before. She sees no reason why she should be interested in the goings on of a woman who was prepared to hand her over to other people to bring up. So this boy was her brother, the child that her mother had decided she couldn't do without? She'd always loathed and resented him before she'd seen his photograph, but now everything has changed. She feels a strong affinity between them, it's love at first sight and she just has to meet him. She's aware that she's an impetuous and obstinate girl: in fact a difficult girl for her step parents to control. And she hasn't been honest about where she has been spending her time each Saturday lately. She's not mentioned that she's been making the three quarters of an hour coach journey in search of her brother. She has been able to tell from the postmark where he lives, but she has no address, so she's been in and out of the cafes and shops that a seventeen-year-old boy is most likely to frequent, but with no luck. She's decided that Saturday is not a good day to find him. Perhaps he has a Saturday job. But today is the Monday of half term and, although she's had no success so far, she feels more confident of finding him.

The rain has stopped as quickly as it began, so she ventures out once more onto East Street, walking west towards the river. A pale sun has emerged, making the once drab pavement sparkle with new life. Yes, she thinks, today is definitely the day for success. As she turns the corner into Broadway, she glances into the large curving windows of the Emporium – and there he is, standing on the deep window sill inside, tweaking the already immaculate display. She rushes through the front door just as the boy is stepping out of the window.

'Joel, it's really you. I've found you at last!' She throws her arms around the startled boy and grips him tightly. She's aware of him stiffening – offering resistance. She loosens her hold and places him at arm's length. 'It's Sophie,' she says. Her whole face is lit up with recognition. 'You must know about me, surely? Or were you too small to remember?' She's dropped her arms to her sides, dropped her head, her gaze. Her ecstatic mood has evaporated as fast as it has appeared. 'Perhaps no one ever told you that you'd got a sister.'

'Sophie?' the boy says. He's scrutinizing her from behind his fringe. 'My sister was called Zoe. I think you've got the wrong person. Anyway, you look nothing like me. You're blonde for a start.'

'My adopted parents changed my name. They didn't like the name Zoe.' She feels her elation returning, and she grabs his hands in hers. 'And why should we look the same? We probably haven't got the same fathers. And anyway, our mum sent me this.' She reaches into her bag and produces the photograph.

Joel's expression changes to match that of Sophie's. 'I remember this,' he says. 'My dad took it when we were on holiday. And of course, you're right. We can't possibly have the same father. In fact, mine doesn't even know you exist. Look, it's my tea break now. I'll just tell Theo I'm popping out for a bit.' Joel sticks his head around the stockroom door at the rear of the shop. 'A friend of mine's turned up, Theo. I'm just going to Eric's for my break.'

'Ten minutes then Joel. That's all.'

Joel grabs her hand as they leave the shop. He's almost dragging her around the corner into Broadway and she has to run to keep up. They enter a rather shabby little café and Joel chooses a table by the window.

'Two cups of tea and a couple of those shortbreads please, Eric,' Joel says to an elderly man behind the counter.

'New girlfriend Joel? Or is she *just a friend* like Grace?' Eric glances at Sophie and gives her a wink. Joel ignores him and leans over her to run his hand across the condensation blanking out the view of the river. Just then Sophie sees a tall, well-built boy walking past. Joel is out of the door immediately, exchanging words with him, turning and nodding his head in her direction. Then he comes back in, bringing his friend with him.

'An Americano please, Eric,' the boy says, and sits down opposite her, hooking his elbows around the chair back. He raises his head slightly, half closes his heavy-lidded eyes, and smiles almost imperceptibly before speaking.

'Hi, I'm Dan. Joel tells me you're the long lost Zoe, renamed Sophie. Your sixteenth birthday was just over a week ago – the 16$^{th}$ October, if I remember correctly.'

'How do you know that?' she says. She stares at him, hoping that the rise in her body temperature isn't showing too obviously in her face.

'Birth certificate,' he says. 'I was helping Joel trace you, as it happens, but we came to a full stop. So where do you live?'

'Oh, a village about half way between here and Cardiff,' she says. 'It's a bit of a journey by coach, but once I'd seen Joel's photo, I just had to meet him.' She turns to Joel and sweeps her long mane of wavy hair behind her shoulder to afford Dan the best possible view of her profile. She's aware that his right leg is stretched out under the table, so she manoeuvres her own so that their feet are touching. She makes sure that she doesn't glance at him. She won't even allow herself a quick peek. She intends to play it cool, to be the one in control. And she intends to have him.

She takes Joel's hand and gives it a squeeze. 'My adoptive parents don't know I've been searching for you. And I can't go and see our mum, not just like that, it's not allowed. Anyway, I don't want to see her, and you mustn't mention anything about us meeting. They'll only try to stop us. Does she ever mention me?'

'No, I'm afraid not. And she's not likely to now she's with my dad again. He was abroad when you were born. As I said, I don't think he knows about you.'

'It's like that, is it? That's why she kept you and not me. I wondered why, and now I know. I should have guessed. I was just an embarrassing mistake that our mum had to dispose of.'

'I'm not sure it was quite like that, Sophie,' Joel says. She's let go of his hand, and it sinks to his lap.

'Well, I don't care anyway. I don't need her at all. I'm living with my *real* parents, aren't I?' she says.

They sit in silence for a while, drinking their tea, exchanging glances.

'There's so much I want to talk to you about, but now that I've actually found you I can't think of anything to say,' Sophie says at last. 'Come and see me, and then we can tell each other everything. Here's my mobile number. But you can't come to my house 'cause the olds will recognise you.'

Joel drains his teacup and rises to leave. 'I'll ring you soon, but now I've got to get back to work. I've got to finish tidying up after doing my window display, and I've got a meeting with a rep this afternoon. I'll come and see you on Sunday, when the shop's closed. I love you, OK?' He puts his hand in his pocket and shrugs. 'Sorry Eric, I've come out without any money. I'll pay you tomorrow.'

After Joel has left, Sophie turns her attention to the boy who introduced himself as Dan. She sits upright, rests her elbows on the table and stares steadily into his eyes. 'Well, it was nice meeting you Dan, but I need to catch my bus home soon.' She remains seated however, showing no inclination to leave.

'Let me give you a lift in my car,' he says. 'I need to buy a very small relative of mine a present first, though. You can help me choose. I'm going your way anyway. I'm staying in Cardiff for a few days over half term. I was on my way there before Joel caught me.' He ostentatiously takes a roll of notes out of his pocket. He extricates a tenner and goes up to the counter with it. 'There you are, Eric, I'll pay for Joel's as well. Keep the change.'

'Thanks very much, Mr O'Donnell, sir,' Eric says, and gives Sophie another wink as she rises to leave.

Dan opens the door for her and lays his hand on her hip as he escorts her out. 'I'll come and see you on my way home on Friday if you like, Sophie – take you out.'

They head for the Mother and Baby shop in the Shopping Mall where, with Sophie's approval, Dan buys a smart brown winter coat with velvet collar and cuffs to fit a girl of eighteen months. Then, on the way back to where he's parked the car on Broadway, she offers no resistance when she feels his arm encircling her waist. Later, when he pulls up outside her house, she allows him to kiss her gently and slowly, exploring every part of her mouth with his tongue. He hasn't asked her whether she's already got a boyfriend and it hasn't occurred to her to ask him a similar question.

'See you on Friday,' she says. 'But ring me first just in case something's come up.'

He hands her his mobile and she enters her number. He goes to kiss her again, but she pulls away, laughing. She kisses her finger and lays it on his lips. 'Now off you go before I fall completely in love with you,' she says. 'See you on Friday.

And we won't tell Joel about us seeing each other. He won't want to share me just yet, will he?'

As she walks down the drive towards her front door she's aware that his car has not pulled away, so she very slightly exaggerates the swing of her hips. She contemplates the busy weekend ahead of her: a date with Dan on Friday, the rehearsal of the school play on Saturday followed by her usual date with Alex, and on Sunday she's spending the day with her lovely new brother Joel.

# Chapter 9

## Sophie's Journey with Joel

'Yes Joel, I'm waiting, and I'm absolutely freezing. Are you nearly here? The coach is awfully late. Ah, here it is. I'm so excited!' Sophie puts her mobile back in her bag and waves at the coach. She can see Joel at one of the windows near the back. He's waving too. She snuggles up to him on the adjoining seat and kisses him on the cheek. 'So tell me about Grace then. Are you in love with her? She must be pretty special if we're going all this way to see her on your only day off, and especially as she's the first person you're going to properly introduce me to.' She thinks of Dan, but that was completely different. He just happened to be passing by. 'Come on Joel, admit it. You're madly in love with her, I can tell.'

Joel shuffles in his seat and stiffens slightly. He extricates his hand from hers and rubs his fingers. 'Well I'm fonder of her than any other girl,' he says, 'but she's always been in love with Darren. They're engaged. They've even got a baby daughter.'

'A baby! They're a bit young, aren't they? I'm not going to have any until I'm at least thirty. I'm on the pill. I wouldn't ruin my future by trusting a boy to take proper precautions. I

266

don't want anything to spoil my chances of being an actress. In fact, I don't think I'd mind if I never have any children.'

'Well, of course the baby was an accident,' Joel says, 'and she's ruining Grace's chances of doing well in her A Levels. She and Darren were always top of the class when we all went to the same school. It's a real shame, and it's not as if Hope's a particularly nice child. She was quite sweet when she was really little, but now she knows she can manipulate people she's become an absolute pain. She's completely self-centred and demanding, just like her father. I know Darren's my best friend and everything, but there's things about him that Grace knows nothing about – and not just things that he's done in the past.' He's silent for a while, weaving his fingers in and out. 'He's not even faithful to her now they're engaged, and the bad thing is that she's got no idea. He's permanently on the pull when he's not with her. And I think he's just met someone else who he's going to keep on seeing, not just a one night stand, like the rest. He said I know her but he wouldn't tell me who though. He loves to keep me guessing. I didn't know that Grace and he had even been out together until after she'd had the baby. I sometimes think I should tell her what he's really like, but I can't. She's completely smitten on him… and I don't think she'd believe me anyway.'

'You definitely mustn't tell her,' Sophie agrees. 'She won't thank you for it. In fact she'll probably end up hating you. Remember the old saying about "shooting the messenger"? You've just got to be there for her when she finds out. It's like this play I'm rehearsing at school at the moment, *Sense and Sensibility*. Jane Austen. Have you read it? I'm the leading character, actually – Marianne. She's in love with this absolute bastard Willoughby who's got this other girl pregnant. There's this Colonel Brandon character who's in love with her, and who knows what Willoughby's really like, but he just waits patiently and picks up the pieces when Marianne finds out the truth. It'll be the same with Darren. He's bound to give himself away sooner or later and then you can step in and comfort her. She's bound to fall in love with you in the end, just like in the play.'

'Sophie!' Joel laughs. 'You're as bad as Grace. She lives her whole life believing sentimental rubbish like that. She was always wittering on like that when we were studying Jane Austen for GCSE. I only listened to her because I thought it would help me pass. It's all complete crap. What did Jane Austen ever know about "living happily ever after" anyway? According to Grace, she never even got married.'

Sophie pokes him in the ribs and smiles. 'Why are all boys so hideously unromantic?' she says, and grabs his hand again. 'Anyway, enough about Grace and Darren. I want to know all about you and your life, what I've missed out on all the time I wasn't with you.'

Joel's story about his early life – before his dad came back – comes in short, clipped sentences devoid of emotion, as if it had all happened to somebody else. The way he had to fend for himself while his – their – mother left him alone to pursue her own pleasures, horrifies her, and she feels her own rejection by this woman all over again. She remembers the initial confusion when, at the age of six, her mother had informed her that she wasn't her proper mother after all, that Sophie was adopted because her real parents had decided that they couldn't keep her.

'Your Dad and I had been searching for a little girl just like you for years,' her mother, who suddenly wasn't her real mother anymore, had said. 'We found you just at the right time. If we'd left it any later we'd have been considered too old to be parents. The Adoption Agency is very strict over things like that.'

From that day on, something had shifted within her. Instead of being a perfectly whole child, Sophie had felt like a doll abandoned on the shelf of a second-hand shop – the best on offer compared to the ones with a wonky eye or a damaged limb, but still not quite perfect. She had felt like an empty husk. Everything that she thought she knew about herself had been hollowed out and replaced with a tight ball of uncertainty. Although she'd been denied nothing up to this point in her life, her need to be noticed and approved of had spiralled, culminating during the infant school Christmas concert. Suddenly, she'd felt the appreciation of a whole roomful of adults. She'd been told that she had 'stage presence', that she was 'a natural'. She began to notice that the people she saw on television kept reappearing in different guises, and she started to invent different lives for herself. She found that she could quickly change her supposed emotional state to order. But she was aware that her feelings all came from a shallow place located in the very top section of her chest.

She turns her attention back to Joel. 'But you and your mum; you're alright now, aren't you? And what about my dad? Do you remember anything about him?'

Joel shakes his head. She has so many questions that lie partly formed in her mind, unable to find expression, and to which she knows there would never be answers. She's afraid that she's inherited too many of this unknown mother's genes, and that in her position she would act in exactly the same way towards her children. She too would make an irresponsible parent. She has certainly inherited her promiscuity. She thinks back on her own succession of boyfriends – perfectly nice boys, but for whom she has only ever felt mild contempt. Their need for somebody like her made them seem weak, and their inability to sense that she was constantly two-timing them, utterly pathetic.

But her date with Dan last Friday had aroused emotions in her that were as strong as they were unprecedented. The question as to whether they would make love had never appeared to be in doubt. He had parked in a sheltered back-road and had automatically reclined the front seats of his Mini, and his self-assurance had acted as an aphrodisiac. To Sophie, their activity had felt too soon and somehow wicked, but all the more exciting because of it. He'd apologised for the crush. He'd told her how much easier it had been when he'd had a van. He'd started to elaborate, and they'd ended up telling each other details of their previous experiences that she'd never thought of revealing to anyone before, and she'd found exchanging such confidences titillating. He hadn't seemed fazed by the fact that she was always busy on Saturdays with her school play rehearsals. In fact he'd seemed faintly relieved, saying that he had 'things to do on Saturdays anyway'. She'd not liked to ask him to elaborate. She'd suspected that he may be seeing other girls, and the threat of this thrilled her. But she'd hoped he wasn't in love with anyone. If he was going to fall in love, then it had to be with her.

She feels a hot and tingling sensation over her whole body as she thinks of next Sunday. 'My parents are going to be out all day,' she'd said, waiting eagerly for his reaction.

'Right! Instead of seeing you next Friday evening, I'll come over for the whole day on Sunday,' he'd said. 'I'll take you out for lunch, and afterwards we'll get to know each other properly.' She imagines lying naked with him in her bed – a level of intimacy she's never wished for with anybody else.

'Hey, are you OK, Sophie?' Joel says. 'Your hands have suddenly got very clammy. You don't have to be nervous about meeting Grace, you know. She's lovely. You'll get on just fine, and the baby won't get in our way. She'll be out with Grace's sister all day, thank God. You two have got a lot in common – Jane Austen for a start.'

Sophie laughs. 'OK, very funny. Just for that you'll have to bring her to see my show. My parents are coming to the opening night, so you can bring Grace on the Saturday evening. That ghastly Darren stroke Willoughby character she dotes on so much can stay at home and babysit for a change. It'll serve him right.'

# Chapter 10

## Darren Goes Off Grace

I lie on the sofa in my upstairs sitting room, my head on one arm rest, my feet on the other. Hope is lying on my chest, her face just above mine. She's grown so much recently. She'll be two in a few months. I can feel her soft breath on my cheek, and the gentle movement of her fingers as they play with the brightly coloured wooden beads threaded onto a thong around my neck. Why Grace insists that we both have to wear them I don't know. Some silly purchase in a tacky little gift shop she dragged me into on holiday in the summer. I'll take it off, or hide it under my sweatshirt, when I go out to play golf in a minute.

But first I must let Mum's lunch go down: lasagne, salad, apple pie. Everything's always homemade with Mum. She's an excellent cook, not like Grace. She's rubbish. How any of us would survive if we had to rely on her cooking I've no idea. She's sitting at the table by the window, catching what daylight she can while finishing her English essay for Monday. She's been really hacking me off recently with all this talk about when we're going to get married, where we're going to live next year when we're at Uni, what will happen if she doesn't get into one anywhere near Oxford. I don't even want to get married, and especially not to her. She's become so annoying. What's wrong with these girls once they've got an engagement ring on their finger? They become so proprietorial and controlling. Eight months with the same person is too much. I was with Jess for eight months and that was hell. Grace seems to have morphed into Jess, as it happens. In fact all the other girls I've ever thought I was in love with were just as bad, especially that whingeing Diane. Anyway, I don't want to be owned, or have to answer to anybody, not even to Sophie. But I don't think Sophie would ever be like that, not even if we were engaged. It's somehow different with her.

'Opie want Daddy froe!' Hope's crawling all over me, churning up my lunch.

'What do you want me to do, sweetheart?' I say.

'Daddy froe Opie.'

'Climb onto my tummy then.' She lies down on top of me and allows me to put my hands under her armpits, then I swiftly lift and straighten my arms above me as high as I can so that she's floating horizontally over me.

'Daddy drop,' she commands.

I let go of her for a second and catch her just before she lands on top of me.

'Daddy more.'

'Darren, don't do that with her, you'll make her sick. She's only just eaten. She should be having her nap now anyway,' Grace says. She's staring at me, accusingly. 'If she doesn't have a rest now she'll be in a terrible state later on. Your mum will change her mind about babysitting this evening if you're not careful.'

I don't really mind if she does refuse to babysit. I've seen enough of Joel this week as it is. Grace can go by herself for all I care. At least Sophie's safely out of the way rehearsing her school play this evening. I'm running a bit close to the wind choosing to see Joel's sister, but I can't help it. I'm completely mad about her. I nearly freaked when Grace told me that Joel had taken Sophie to see her the other week, but it seems nobody made the connection between Darren and Dan. And she didn't meet Hope, thank God. That would have completely buggered everything. It's great that Mum's suggested that Hope stays with us all next week. It'll give Grace a chance to get on with her assignment and I can do what I want with Hope without Grace sticking her oar in. But it means I'll have to take Hope with me when I visit Sophie next Friday on the way to Cardiff. That could be a bit of a problem. What if she calls me Daddy? I'll have to introduce her as my little sister, which means I'll have to train her to call me Danny before then. Lucky for me she's such a bright kid.

'Darren! Don't let Hope suck those beads. It's unhygienic. The paint will come off.'

'Don't suck the nasty beads, Baby. Do what Mummy says,' I whisper. I hold her close and stroke her lovely blonde curls, twirling them around my fingers. She smells all fresh and new in the little dress I've just bought for her. Grace has come over and is separating us. Hope is squirming in her arms, stiffening, ready to scream.

'Narty Mummy. Opie want Daddy,' she wails. She's staring plaintively over Grace's shoulder, her little arms outstretched to me. I've just got to have her, whatever happens to Grace and me in the future. Hope's mine by rights. She loves me much more than Grace. She never cries with me.

'For Christ's sake, Grace, let me have her.' I grab her back and carry her into the bedroom. She'll need a child's bed soon. She nearly managed to climb out of her cot yesterday. She's sucking her thumb now and looking particularly angelic as I gently lay her down.

'Now say "bye bye" to Danny, Baby. I'll be back soon,' I say.

'Bye bye Daddy,' she says.

'No: Danny, not Daddy.' I'd better start training her now before she meets Sophie. I can't have her fouling up my love life.

'Danny, no Daddy,' Hope says, staring very seriously at me. Her eyes have become very large and confused looking.

'That's right, Baby,' I say. 'Call me Danny, not Daddy.' She's such a clever little girl. She'll be fine with it by Friday.

This last month with Sophie has been the best ever. I knew we were soul mates as soon as I first saw her. I'm definitely in love this time. She never nags me like Grace. She never asks me what I've been up to when I'm not with her. She just enjoys the time we have together. I wish I could be with her the whole weekend instead of just Friday and Sunday evenings. I wish I didn't have to spend so much time in Cardiff with Grace. And when it's Grace's turn to come here it's even worse, especially if she decides to come up on the Friday afternoon coach. I can only see Sophie on Sunday then. But next Sunday will be great. We'll be spending the whole day together for a change – and part of the night. She's thought it all out. I'll make a show of driving off in my car, and then when her parents are safely in bed, she'll ring me and I'll leave the car around the corner and creep back. It's so lucky they live in a bungalow. It'll be a doddle letting myself in through her French window. I'll be able to stay until just before dawn and I'll still get plenty of sleep. I don't have any lessons first thing next Monday.

'Darren, do you have to come back from mine so early next Sunday?' Grace says. It's as if she can read my mind.

'I told you before. I've got a golf match that day. Anyway, I'll be getting to yours earlier than usual on Friday as I'll have Hope with me, remember. That'll make up for it. I've been thinking about all this toing and froing with Hope, as it happens. I'm going to ask Mum if we can have her here the whole time, not just next week. She loves looking after her and it would be much better for you. She'd be doing you a favour. You could really get on with your work if you were by yourself. You could finish all your homework on the Friday evening, and then catch the first coach on Saturday morning. It'll be great. We'll be able to spend the whole time together before you catch the coach back on Sunday afternoon. And you'll be able to see more of Joel as well. You and he can take Hope out on Sundays if you like, while I'm playing golf. And the bed's much more comfortable here than at Faith's, isn't it?'

She doesn't look completely convinced, so I kiss her – a long and lingering one that I've recently only reserved for Sophie. 'Right,' I say. 'I'm off to the golf club now, but I'll be back before you know it. And Mum can take Hope after her nap. I reckon I'll be feeling a bit frisky later before we go out. You can join me in the shower if you like. We can't do that in Faith's poky little bathroom, can we? It'll be so much better if you come here every weekend, you know it will.'

She's beaming now. 'Alright then, darling, I'll think about it,' she says. 'But you'll still come to me next weekend as we've planned and I'll keep Hope the following week as usual. But after that, why not? It sounds like a good idea. Don't be too long playing golf, will you? I love you.'

# Chapter 11

# The Real Marianne

It's Saturday evening in mid-December and the closing night of Sophie's school play. After a disastrous dress rehearsal on the Friday afternoon, the Friday evening and Saturday matinee performances have gone smoothly enough. Everyone has remembered their lines, the stage lighting hasn't failed, and none of the scenery has come crashing down – in fact they've had standing ovations.

Sophie sits staring at her reflection in the mirror of the girls' dressing room. The other members of the cast are all grouped around the door awaiting their five minute call. They're chatting together in a relaxed manner, but her nerves are alive and popping with a rush of adrenalin that she finds hard to control. She always feels this way before a performance, but she has learnt not to let it upset her. She knows that once she walks on stage and takes on the personality of her character, her fear and feelings of inadequacy will leave her and she will feed off the attention focused on her alone.

'Hey, Sophie! There's a couple of people to see you.'

She turns her head and sees Joel and Grace standing uncertainly at the half open door.

'Hi, you two. Come on in. Long time no see.' She hugs them in turn and laughs. 'Careful! Don't smudge my war paint. So Darren's finally let you off the leash, has he Grace?'

'I'm not seeing him at all this weekend,' Grace says. 'He's suddenly decided he's got too much school work to do before the end of term. He's never said that before. It must be because of his chances of being offered a place at Oxford. He reckons the interview he had last week went really well. It's all he can talk about. His mum's babysitting. She has her most of the time now anyway. He's lent Joel his car though, so long as he gets it back by tomorrow lunchtime. So Joel's coming back with me after the show.'

'That's great,' Sophie says. 'You must come to the cast and friends party after the show then. You can meet my boyfriend Alex.' She won't tell Alex that she's dumping him until later. She sees no point in spoiling the evening. Once the play is over she'll be spending her Saturdays with Dan.

Sophie smoothes her long tresses from around her face and ties her hair demurely at her neck with a ribbon that matches her dress. She's glad she'd held her ground over the green one. It suits her colouring much more than it would any of the other girls in the cast.

'What does she look like, this baby of yours?' she says. 'It's terrible, but I can't even remember her name. I'm sure she's lovely – just like you, I expect.' Sophie's not remotely interested, but she's developed an attachment to Grace and assumes that this is what a friend would ask.

'Yes, she is lovely, but she's nothing like me at all. She looks just like her dad. I've got a new photo of her on my phone, actually. Just a minute, I'll find it for you. Her name's Hope.'

278

Grace quickly scrolls through her photo library and hands her phone to Sophie. At first she can make no sense of what she sees. Staring defiantly out from the screen is a little girl identical to the one Dan brought round to her house just over two weeks ago, his baby sister who called herself Opie. She's even wearing a brown winter coat with velvet collar and cuffs, just like the one that Sophie had helped Dan choose on the first day they'd met, the coat he was buying for his 'very small relative'. So that was how it was. Dan was Darren – Grace's Willoughby – her fiancée described by Joel as 'always on the pull'.

Sophie holds the phone out in front of her for some time, although she has ceased looking at it. Her mind has gone back to last Sunday when Dan had spent the best part of the night with her. She'd only just remembered to deactivate the burglar alarm before he'd slipped into her bedroom through the French window. Her parents had taken so long to go to bed that night that he'd been shivering from sitting in his car, waiting for her to give him the all clear. But she'd managed to warm him up quickly enough once she'd got him into her bed.

'I love you more than anyone else in the whole world,' he'd whispered. 'I never want to be with anyone else. It's as if we're one person. I felt it as soon as I saw you. You felt it too, didn't you?'

At that moment, the strength of her connection with him had felt complete. She'd been sure that in a week or two they'd become engaged. But she'd been mistaken. To her mind, she was the real Marianne, not Grace. She was the one who was really being lied to.

'She's beautiful,' Sophie manages to say at last. Her voice comes out harsh and clipped, and she has to clear her throat. 'If she takes after her dad in looks, he must be pretty special.

279

You'd better watch out though; guys like that aren't always as nice as they look.' She forces a laugh. 'Now, I've got to get ready. Enjoy the play, both of you. And remember, Jane Austen always knows best when it comes to affairs of the heart and living happily ever after – whatever you might think to the contrary, Joel. And pay particular attention to Colonel Brandon. He's excellent.' She smiles a tight smile and dismisses them, turning to apply a touch more rouge. She feels an unknown emotion rising from deep inside that's draining her face of colour. She knows that tonight will be her best and most truthful performance yet. And she already has plans for tomorrow.

$$\approx$$

I'm on my way to Sophie's at last. I can't wait to see her. I'm felling particularly randy today. I haven't had any for a whole week, I must be losing my touch. I hope her parents have gone out already. I can't cope with coffee and polite conversation at the moment. My phone rings, so I put it onto speaker. It's her. She sounds rather strange. Even more animated than usual.

'Dan? Where are you? Are you nearly here?'

'Won't be much longer. About another five minutes. How did your show go? Did you "break a leg", or whatever the saying is?'

'It was fine,' she says. 'Standing ovations, flowers, the lot. But that's old news. I've got something much more important to discuss. Joel brought his friend Grace to the show last night. I'm sure you remember her. It seems she's engaged to someone called Darren. Does the name mean anything to you?' I hear a click.

'Sophie?' She's rung off. Oh shit, shit and treble shit! But it was bound to happen at some time. I should have told her, but I wanted to keep her for as long as possible. I wanted to keep her for ever. I don't know what to do. She hasn't given me any time to think.

I draw up onto her drive, and there she is, standing in her doorway, arms folded, her hair flowing out like a mane behind her as the breeze catches it. She looks like some magnificent wild beast, wounded but unbroken – defiant, proud, golden, like a Pre-Raphaelite beauty. An image of Millais' powerful painting *The Bridesmaid* bombards my mind, the one we saw in that Art Appreciation class with Miss Harris in Year 11 just before Grace humiliated me on my birthday. She still doesn't appreciate me on that score. How can she when she's still not been with anybody else? Not like Sophie. I can't possibly lose this creature because of somebody as naïve and mundane as Grace.

'Come on in,' she says. 'Mum and Dad are out. They won't be back till supper, so we can shout as loudly at each other as we like. You're invited to supper, by the way. Mum thinks you're a *wonderful* catch. She still can't get over how you brought your *baby sister* to see us. "Such a lovely young man, so considerate".' She laughs, but it comes out all metallic and hollow, like a kettle drum. I can't read her mood at all. She's jumpy, giggly, sneering.

'I should have told you,' I say, 'but I didn't know how to.'

'Oh, I don't mind about you and Grace at all. Not even about Hope.' Her voice rises to almost a scream. 'I do mind that you didn't tell me though. And I definitely mind about your being engaged. People who're engaged usually end up getting married and I can't allow that. If you ever do get married then it has to be to me. Do you understand?'

I don't understand at all, as it happens. She's standing there rigid in front of me, her fists clenched at her sides, her eyes staring open like large green stagnant pools, her face flushed. Then suddenly she rushes at me and starts pummelling my chest. She's crying now.

'What do you mean? Would you marry me then, after all this?' I try to hold onto her wrists but she pulls away from me. She's shouting and crying at the same time now.

'I might do. But not for ages, silly,' she says. 'And not until you've got rid of Grace. So don't go and propose to me just yet, will you? You'll be wasting your time. You can't possibly marry her you know. She's not your type at all. I'm the only person that really understands you. But I'm not going to be second best, the other woman. Absolutely not!'

I still can't get the drift of all this. Is she forgiving me, saying that I haven't done anything wrong, or what?

'Come here,' I say. I catch hold of her and pull her down onto the sofa. I kiss her, and she accepts it eagerly. In fact her response is more passionate than usual. She's almost devouring me.

'What can I do?' I say. 'I can't ditch Grace just like that. She won't let me see Hope. She's the only reason I'm with Grace at all. She's a pain. You know I'd much rather be with you.'

'Yes, I know that,' she says. Her anger has suddenly left her. She's snuggled into the crook of my arm and she's picking at a loose strand on my sweatshirt. 'Let me get this straight. Grace said that Hope's at yours most of the time at the moment. Your Mum's looking after her.'

'That's right,' I say. 'That's why I had to bring her to see you that Friday. I was taking her back to Grace. But now that she's got so much studying to do, Mum said she'd have Hope the whole time. Grace comes up for the weekend on the coach, although this weekend I couldn't face it and told her I was busy. And when she does come to stay, I try to fob her off onto Joel as much as possible.'

'That's perfect,' she purrs. 'Couldn't be better, in fact. At this rate you'll easily phase her out. Once she's out of the picture, it'll be difficult for her to get Hope back. The authorities are bound to give you and your parents custody, especially if you've been looking after her for ages. Grace is only a seventeen year old unmarried mother.' She gathers up a ringlet of hair and twirls it around in her fingers. 'And anyway, I'm sure Hope would rather stay with you, and the courts always take the child's wishes into account.' She's smiling now and dabbing at her eyes.

'Christ, Sophie! You've given this some thought. You're even more calculating than me. But you don't mind my seeing Grace while she's being "phased out"?'

'I don't see why. While you're shagging Grace, I'll be free to see other people as well.' She jumps up and rushes to the window, her back towards me. 'There's a guy called Alex in the cast who's hot for me, actually. He's a bit of a weed, but he'll do for a bit while you're busy. It'll be a laugh swopping notes.' She rushes back and joins me on the sofa.

'Right then,' she says. 'Now that's all sorted, let's get our kit off. We're wasting valuable time.'

'What, in here? What about your parents?'

'Oh, they won't be back for ages. What's wrong? Are you scared of being caught?'

'Yes, frankly,' I say. Memories of what happened with Jess rear their ugly heads.

'Come on then, you wimp.' She drags me off the sofa and into her bedroom.

283

'So you're advocating an open relationship, are you?' I say as I start to undress her.

'Exactly,' she says. 'But we both have to abide by the rules. You can only go with someone else when I'm not available, and vice versa. And we have to tell each other every last detail, especially the juicy bits.' She's fighting to get me out of my jeans. 'And most importantly, we're never to fall in love with anyone else – or get engaged. Understand?'

I cup my hands over her perfect boobs – just a handful each: no excess, no waste. 'Absolutely,' I say. 'Now get in, shut up and shove over, will you? And you'll have to invest in a double bed if you want me to keep seeing you like this.' I laugh. It seems that my luck's still holding out.

# Chapter 12

## Out of the Mouths of Babes

Grace sits on the edge of the sofa in Faith's living room, her packed case beside her feet. The February light penetrating the net curtains is pale and milky, casting an air of chill into the already colourless and sparsely furnished room. But Grace's mood is upbeat and expectant. Darren and Hope will be arriving soon, and after some tea they will be off on holiday with Lorraine and Ronnie. For the next few days they'll be a proper family. They're renting a timber lodge in a holiday park, with indoor swimming pools, sports facilities and a large playground for Hope.

She clasps her hands and rubs her fingers restlessly together. She wants to improve her relationship with her daughter; she's noticed a distancing between them. Although she's not a natural in the kitchen, she's made Hope's favourite fairy cakes for them to eat before they set off: chocolate with vanilla icing, sprinkled with hundreds and thousands.

She hears Joel and Sophie crashing around in the kitchen, laughing and chatting easily together. Faith has taken Dylan to visit his paternal grandparents for the half term week, and Grace's friends have taken advantage of this – Joel travelling down last night after his Saturday shift in the Emporium, and

Sophie arriving by coach this morning. They've all three just come in from a walk along the waterfront at Mermaid Bay, and Grace's cheeks are still tingling from the cold, brittle air. The girls had clung together like siblings as they'd gazed into the stylish shop windows and admired the unaffordable fashion items, and they'd whispered and giggled conspiratorially about the merits of their respective boyfriends, Darren and Dan, and who would be the most generous when it came to indulging them. Sophie had said that she couldn't wait to meet Darren, but had refused to allow Grace to show her any of the photographs of him that she has stored on her mobile.

'Absolutely not,' she'd said. 'I want it to be a surprise. But I'm sure he's gorgeous, Grace.'

Grace moves even closer to the edge of the sofa, her hands now clasped on her knees. As usual, she hasn't seen either Darren or Hope for a whole week. Darren had been gentler with her than usual last weekend. She had annoyed him less, and their lovemaking had been more lingering, almost wistful. It had seemed to Grace that he was going to miss her more than usual over the following week. She'd almost plucked up courage to tell him that she was pregnant again – by nearly three months – but yet again she'd left off giving him the news; she was unsure of how he would react. She wanted to savour this unusual moment of calm between them before a possible tirade of accusations and blame ensued. She would speak to Lorraine about it first – gauge her reaction to the notion of another grandchild. No doubt Lorraine would be overjoyed. Grace knew that Lorraine loved Hope as if she were her own daughter, and that Hope's love for her was reciprocated.

Grace shivers and pulls at the polo neck of her jumper, trying to make it cover her chin. A flickering and fading image of Hope has started to manifest itself in her mind's eye. She doesn't see enough of her. She's worried that Lorraine is unintentionally usurping her in her daughter's affections. But surely after this week on holiday together she'll be able to put this right? She tells herself to keep positive. Soon she'll be a full time mother to Hope. In four months' time, after she and Darren have finished their exams, they'll become a proper little family at last – just the three of them before the new baby comes.

The doorbell rings announcing Darren's and Hope's arrival, just as Joel and Sophie appear from the kitchen. Although Darren has his own key, he always indulges Hope by allowing her to broadcast their entrance first.

Grace feels herself shrivelling into the shabby fabric of the sofa. Hope has rushed in ahead of Darren and is clinging to Sophie's legs. She has not acknowledged Grace at all. She hasn't even glanced in her direction.

'Thophie!' Hope chuckles, and buries her face in the soft fabric of the girl's leggings.

As Darren enters the room, his bright and open expression changes to that of an inflexible mask. His full lips compress as he stares at Sophie, and he too ignores Grace. She tries to speak, but Sophie gets in first.

'Dan!' she says. 'I didn't know you were coming. And you've brought your little sister, my favourite little girl. I didn't even know you and Grace were friends, but then if you're Joel's friend… But you said you were playing golf today. What happened?' She extricates herself from Hope's grip and flings her arms around his neck. 'It's good though. You can give me and Joel a lift home later, after Darren and Grace have gone. We won't have to catch that horrid coach.'

Grace holds herself as rigid and cold as an ice sculpture as she watches Sophie attempting to kiss him. But Darren is flinching and turning his head away, the rest of his body staying as frozen as Grace's.

'Thophie love Danny. Thophie kith Danny.' Hope is dancing around the two of them, her arms in the air, skipping and twirling as if performing some tribal fertility dance. She has still said nothing to Grace.

Snatches of her time with Darren tumble out unbidden as Grace begins to understand that Darren, who Hope now calls Danny, is in fact Sophie's new boyfriend, Dan. She remembers the first time that Hope had started to call him Danny instead of Daddy. She had refused to be corrected. She'd been most adamant. *'No Daddy! Danny,'* she'd said. And then there had been Darren's rather uncharacteristic reaction when she'd told him. He'd been overjoyed, a few weeks earlier, when Hope had finally learnt to say it correctly, but he'd just shrugged and replied: *'Whatever. Danny's fine by me, if that's what she wants to call me.'*

Grace feels a great heat rising from deep inside her ice cold exterior, as doubts about him – those that she thought that she'd long since buried – jump up and dance before her, making her giddy, just as Hope is doing now.

She hears her old classmate Jenna giggling: *'What are we going to do then, Darren? ...you're the hottest boy I've ever seen, and I've fancied you for ever... Take me upstairs to your room.'* Echoes of the next day invade her ears, just before she and Darren had split up. She hears Joel's apologetic voice as they leave the café together. *'That Eric's got a one track mind. He's heard Darren shooting his mouth off about all his conquests so often that he thinks we're all the same.'* And she hears Darren's continual excuse of *'something's come up.'*

'Get out!' As she rises from her seat her voice erupts, her words burning and spewing lava-like from the fissures created by her clenched teeth. But they quickly cool and harden as she says, 'Now!'

'What's the matter?' Sophie turns to Grace.

'It seems we share a boyfriend, Sophie. You take him. I've had quite enough.'

Darren relaxes, his arm encircling Sophie's waist. 'It's true, as it happens. I was going to tell Grace after our holiday.'

'Just get out, all three of you, and leave me alone. Take Hope on holiday, Darren. She's been looking forward to it, but don't expect me to come too. Make my excuses to your parents. I'm sure you'll think of something believable, you've had enough practise.'

'But Grace, it's hardly my fault,' Sophie says. 'How was I to know? Can't I stay with you and Joel? You're my friend. I don't want to go with him.'

'Come on Sophie. She doesn't want you here.' Without anything appertaining to an apology or an explanation, Darren swiftly escorts the two girls out of the house.

≈

Joel stands at Faith's sitting room window and stares out, shielding Grace from what's happening in the street. He sees Darren and Sophie doing a triumphant 'high five' before Sophie straps Hope into her child seat in the back of Darren's car. She treats her more like a favourite doll rather than a little girl. She'll soon be tired of her, although he suspects that Darren won't; he will fight hard to keep her. Joel had somehow sensed that his friend was planning to ditch Grace, but to try and alienate her from her daughter in this manner was despicable, even for him. Had he actually coached Hope to act as the messenger of bad news? And he's horrified by his sister's behaviour. The scene now taking place outside makes it obvious that what has just occurred in the living room had been a carefully rehearsed act. No doubt she'd trained Darren up. He knew that Sophie was a convincing actress, but Darren's performance had been worthy of an Oscar. He wonders how long Sophie had been aware that she was dating Grace's fiancée. He wishes that he'd never met his wretched sister, much less introduced her to Darren that day. But, on consideration, he decides they deserve one another.

Joel watches them drive off before turning to Grace. She's sitting bolt upright on the sofa once more, her fingernails digging into her palms so hard that her knuckles have turned as white as bone. He gently uncurls her hands and rubs at the deep crevices she's made in the fleshy part below her thumbs.

'I knew he was going off me,' she whispers, 'but I never guessed he had anyone else. And Sophie too! I feel so stupid – I thought we were friends.'

'To be fair to her, Darren did introduce himself as Dan when they met. I was there. If only she'd told me she'd started seeing him, I could have put her straight. He's deceived her as well.' He can't bring himself to describe the scene of elation he's just witnessed. 'It's as Sophie said: how was she to know?'

'He can't steal Hope away from me forever, can he Joel? I shouldn't have ordered him to take her just now.' Grace starts to get up from the sofa and Joel catches her, holding her to him.

'They've gone already. And of course he can't keep her forever,' he says, 'especially if you're with a nice reliable bloke. An ugly little runt like me isn't much of a catch, but if it would help to tell people we're together…'

'What are you saying, Joel?'

'You must know how I feel about you, Grace. We can take things really slowly, in fact it can remain platonic between us forever if you'd rather. It's just that if it looks like you're not alone, it would stop that bastard…' He can't bring himself to say 'getting custody'. 'And now that you're pregnant again, the new baby will need a father, otherwise your mother will never speak to you ever again, will she?' He attempts a smile and holds her at arm's length and Grace's expression softens.

'You haven't told Darren about the baby yet, have you?'

Grace shakes her head. 'He's been so bad tempered and off with me lately that I haven't dared. I've been rather scared of him lately. In fact, if I'm honest, I've always been scared of him. I should never have taken him back. I'd forgotten what he was really like.'

Joel feels her relax into his embrace. 'I'm glad you haven't told him,' he says. 'Let's keep it that way. Have this one on me. It'll serve him right.'

'You'd really do that for me? You're not an ugly little runt by the way, Joel, as well you know. Haven't you heard that "small is beautiful"?' She pushes the thick strands of dark hair from his face and attempts to tuck them behind his ear. 'You remember when I cut your hair for you that first time, and I called you hot – or was it cool? And Faith's always fancied you. She thinks you're really cute.' She kisses his cheek, and he feels her tears wet his skin.

'Steady on. All this talk will make me as conceited as someone else I could mention. What do you say then? Shall we do it, announce to the world that we're an item and the proud owners of a growing lump?'

'Let's just take it slowly,' she says. 'I'd be proud to be your girlfriend though – a real one, not just pretend. Thank you, Joel. You're so lovely…'

291

'Well in that case, now that you've spent ages packing and repacking that bag, let me take it for you. Your carriage awaits. Or it will be in about five minutes if it's running to schedule. You're coming back with me for half term. I keep telling Mum and Theo that you're not my girlfriend, but they've never believed me. They'll love it. At last they'll be able to prove me wrong.'

He has said it at last; he's effectively told Grace that he loves her. He knows he always has on some level – first as a mother figure, then as a sister. But now his feelings are all-encompassing. The baby is due in six months and he's determined to marry her before it's born.

# Chapter 13

## The Reconciliation

'It has to be this one, doesn't it Mum?' Grace fingers the sheer jersey material of the ivory-coloured dress as she scrutinises herself in the freestanding, full length mirror that's taken the place of Hope's cot in her bedroom at Faith's.

'Absolutely!' her mum agrees. 'It suits you so well, and I love the cut. You hardly look pregnant at all. You look beautiful, Grace. And don't worry that it's the most expensive. Your dad and I are paying for it, as you know. Now, take it off and put it somewhere safe while I go and make us some tea.'

Grace starts to fold up the rejected dresses, ready to be sent back to the company specialising in maternity bridal wear that she'd found on the internet. But she's in no hurry to change out of the one she's decided to keep. Her mother is right; Grace has never seen herself looking so beautiful in her whole life. And no wonder – the dress costs £145. She's never considered spending that much on just one item of clothing before. She gyrates her hips, allowing the material below her bump to flow fluidly to her knees, showing off her slim, coffee-coloured legs. She prefers the ivory colour to pure white; it suits her complexion perfectly. She adjusts the modestly scooped neckline, and straightens the folds of material that emanate from it, allowing them to descend over her blossoming breasts to be caught beneath a matching ivory sash, just above the discretely disguised mound of her baby. The design gives her figure a feminine definition of which she was previously unaware.

Grace smiles as she remembers her mother's initial resistance when she'd phoned to ask for her help in selecting her wedding dress. 'It's a long way to come just for that, Grace,' she'd said. 'And anyway, I'm sure you know best when it comes to what suits you. And you've got Faith to help you.'

'Faith's no help at all. She just says they're all nice. I really want your opinion, Mum. I've got to make a decision soon. They're on appro and I've got to send them back in a couple of days. I'll have to ask Joel's mum Jeannie, I suppose.'

Grace's smile broadens as she recalls her mother's instant response to the mention of her future in-law. 'There's no need for that, Grace. Of course I'll come. It's my job as *mother* of the bride. And don't worry about the cost, we'll choose the one that suits you best. I've been putting some money aside recently darling, saving up for your special day.' The line had gone quiet for a moment before her mother had managed to resume her usual, unemotional manner. 'And anyway, I can fit it in around coming to see Faith and Dylan. I can't expect them to travel over here to see me every time, can I?'

Grace has now only a month to wait before her wedding with Joel. The date has been planned for early June, just after she has finished her A Levels. The baby is due in mid-August, and she wants to give herself at least two months leeway, just in case she goes into labour early, as she had done with Hope. She stops her folding and repacking and sits down abruptly on the bed. She had so much wanted her daughter to be at the wedding, but she has been persuaded out of it by both Joel and Faith. She knows that their reasoning had made perfect sense, but she's still unhappy about it. Hope was too young, they'd said: she'd only be two and a quarter and as yet her behaviour was too unpredictable. She was unlikely to be able to sit quietly during the ceremony without suddenly deciding that she should be the centre of attention and not Grace. And she would have to be chaperoned, but by whom? Lorraine spoilt her and was rarely capable of controlling Hope's outbursts. Darren was the only person who could manage her, but his attending her wedding was unthinkable. That fact alone had finally decided her, but it irks her to admit that he was still influencing her decision-making.

It has been three months since their separation, and Darren has only allowed Grace to see Hope on six occasions since then, on the weekends when she's been staying with Joel and his parents – and those occasions have had to coincide with when Darren was elsewhere. But each time she's visited her, she's been made aware of her daughter's waning interest in her. She's felt herself being relegated in Hope's affections from mother to that of an unnecessary and rather irritating aunt. Hope's resistance to her embraces have not gone unnoticed. She's felt her struggling to be put down; she's seen her head turned away from her in an attempt to find Lorraine.

She feels the volume of pent-up emotion building within her, ready to explode through her eyes and mouth. If only she could speak to another woman about the loss of a child. In theory, her own mother was the obvious choice, but she has never once spoken to Grace about Leroy after losing him. And anyway, she has made it clear that the subject of Grace's illegitimate daughter is off limits. Perhaps she could discuss her fears with Jeannie? She would understand; she too has lost a daughter to another family. But Jeannie has never mentioned Joel's sister. By rights, Grace shouldn't even know of her existence. She will just have to be patient. Everything will change after her wedding. Joel has promised her that they will win custody of Hope then, even if they have to fight for her through the courts. Faith agrees with him, and Grace respects her sister's judgement. She'd been right in her judgement of Darren and Joel.

'You're a sensible girl, Grace, and extremely fortunate,' Faith had said when she'd heard of her transferal of affections. 'You're doing the right thing, choosing Joel over that Darren monstrosity. I never warmed to him at all. He was just an arrogant poser. He didn't like leaving anything to the imagination, did he? The way he used to saunter around the house in just his boxers, thinking he was God's Gift, made me want to vomit. And he'd really begun to put on weight, which was hardly surprising with his sweet tooth, the great big lumbering lout. Dylan's nickname for him was the Honey Monster, which was spot on, especially when he'd grown that ginger-coloured stubble.'

'Faith, that's a terrible thing to say,' Grace had replied, but she hadn't been able to suppress a giggle.

'Well, it's true,' Faith had continued. 'It's like the emperor's new clothes. He made out that he was the centre of the universe and all you silly little girls believed him. No offence intended, Grace; after all, you were only fourteen when he first hit on you. But anybody can see that Joel's much the better person – trustworthy for starters – and definitely not up himself.'

Grace knows that Faith is mostly right, although she'll never concede that Darren was ever anything less than perfection physically. She's ashamed that she still gets that familiar lurching in her stomach whenever his name is mentioned. But she's not stupid. She realises now that a relationship built solely on lust cannot be sustainable.

Her mind goes back to the day of Darren's sixteenth birthday, when she was sitting by the stretch of river known as the rapids, thinking of her brother. Even on that day, nearly three years ago, her life with Darren had taken on the confusion and uncertainty that she had noticed in the water as she had watched it swirling back in on itself in the shallow rock pools. Her life with Joel would be like the flow of the river midstream: smooth and confident. Joel had no secrets that he was concealing in the undercurrents, she felt sure of that. From him she would not expect any sordid surprises. Leroy had still felt close to her on that day of the picnic, but now his presence has faded to a shadow at the corner of her vision, or a gentle, almost inaudible whisper cutting through the silence. He's a subject never mentioned by anybody. It's as if time has scabbed over the wound of their loss.

'Grace? Tea's ready.' Her mother is calling her from the living room, and as Grace enters she senses the sharp, tangy smell of lemon drizzle cake that her mother only bakes for special occasions. The thought of her mother bringing it with her on the coach, on her first visit since Grace moved away, touches her.

'Come on now, Grace,' she says. 'You'd better change out of that dress. You don't want to stain it before your big day. You look so lovely in it. You could dye it after the wedding. I'm sure with a few alterations you could wear it again after the baby's arrived and your figure's gone back to normal.'

'It's a boy, Mum. Joel and I decided to ask at the last scan.' Every day, since the reality of her growing bulge has started to manifest itself as a real person kicking inside her, she has been praying to a god she no longer believes in: *'Please let him be dark like me and Joel, not blonde and blue-eyed like his father.'*

'A boy? How lovely! Have you decided on a name yet?'

'Yes, we have Mum. There wasn't a contest when it came down to it. We're calling him Roy, out of respect to Leroy.'

'What a wonderful gesture, Grace,' comes the response, and for the first time since her brother's death she feels the warmth of her mother's embrace.

# Chapter 14

## It all Kicks off

Joel throws his jacket over the chair in the corner and places his rucksack on the one next to it. He has to keep a seat for Darren today. There are already two other people at his table. As is usual at this time in the morning in August, at the height of the summer holiday season, Eric's café is already three-quarters full.

Joel goes up to the counter at the back to order his breakfast. 'My usual please, Eric.'

The proprietor looks particularly harassed today. His assistant is nowhere to be seen, and he appears to have suddenly aged by at least ten years.

'No Benny today?'

'Given me his notice, Joel,' Eric says with a toss of the head. 'My own son too. But now that I'm retiring, he's no longer interested, is he? And I'm gasping for a fag.' He wipes the pearls of perspiration from his forehead with a damp teacloth. 'I'll bring your order over in a mo.'

'No hurry, Eric. I'm not working until 9.30.' Joel goes back to his seat to find a couple with a young boy asking how many seats at his table are free. One of the men already seated is shrugging his shoulders. Joel sits down quickly and starts rummaging in his rucksack, making sure not to catch anybody's eye. He picks out his diary and flicks through it, trying to look busy. He stares at the page announcing the date of his and Grace's wedding last month: a small, family only affair held in a Registry office in Cardiff. Grace had finally made her peace with her parents, helped by the fact that Hope – for the moment at least – was still living with the other side of her family and therefore not an embarrassment to them. And although Grace had been pregnant again on her wedding day, her parents seemed satisfied that she was settling down with a 'nice respectable boy'.

'Your order, Joel.' Eric leans over the little boy sitting next to the rucksack, and places a particularly undercooked offering on the table in front of him.

'Got any ketchup?' Joel is too late. Eric is already busy elsewhere, shuffling around on his flat, slippered feet. The place is filling up fast with the stallholders from the Saturday street market, holidaymakers from the campsite and the odd passing punter.

'Is that place taken, mate?'

Joel looks up from his breakfast to see Darren, all six foot three of him, standing in the aisle between the tables. Joel quickly removes his rucksack from the spare seat to allow him to sit down.

'My husband wanted that seat,' the mother of the little boy complains. 'He's had to sit right over there.' She's quickly silenced by Darren's steely stare.

'A cappuccino and a slice of your syrup sponge, when you're ready, Eric,' Darren says whilst preparing to sit down.

'Coming up, Mr O'Donnell, sir,' Eric calls from behind his counter. As usual, Joel is duly impressed. People still don't notice him the way they do with Darren, even though he is now an almost respectable five foot five, and hopefully still growing. But of course that's the reason why Darren likes to work with him. To people that don't know him he seems virtually invisible.

'Hey, you'd better zip your rucksack up mate, in case it gets knocked over.'

Joel looks down and notices that Darren has already put the package inside, so he quickly does as he's told.

'What do you reckon on our club's chances of being taken over by the Russians?' Darren is engaging the two strangers opposite in conversation, deliberately ignoring Joel.

'Something's going to have to change before next season, that's for sure. Otherwise we'll be bankrupt,' the burlier one of the two replies.

'Well, I reckon the coach is going to have to come up with something special straight away to get the team energised. If we lose any more matches, no one will want to buy us,' Darren says.

The little boy's father is leaning across the aisle from a seat at the next table, trying to have a conversation with his wife as Eric approaches with Darren's order.

'Actually, Eric, make mine a takeaway,' Darren says. Eric droops with resignation, and shuffles back to the counter to transfer the cappuccino into a polystyrene cup and the syrup sponge into a bag.

'Here, mate. Have my seat. I've just remembered I should be somewhere else,' Darren says to the inconvenienced husband. He rises and fleetingly turns to Joel, giving him a surreptitious wink before going up to the counter to pay.

Joel understands Darren's coded message completely. The drugs now sitting in his rucksack are to be delivered to the football club coach this evening before the start of the training session. Joel is used to Darren's little games, but is somewhat surprised that he's using such a device today. He thought he'd grown out of it. It was just like the old days when he'd liked to control him like a pawn on a chessboard, never giving him the chance to question or object to his decisions. It gives Joel a feeling of slight unease.

Once in the Emporium, Joel hides his rucksack as well as he can in Theo's stockroom before reporting for duty.

'Bright and early again, son,' Theo says. 'Actually, before you start serving, I'd like you to sort out that big order that came in yesterday. After you've checked the coffee tables and footstools over, could you concentrate on pricing the scented candles and incense sticks, please? The delivery notes are all out there.'

This suits Joel very well. He isn't really in the mood for talking to either Theo or their customers at the moment. After removing the bubble wrap from the small pieces of furniture, and satisfying himself that none of them is damaged, he takes his stool over to the stack of boxes at the back of the stockroom, near his rucksack. As he opens the first box of candles, a blast of exotic scents fills the air around him, entering his nostrils, relaxing him. He methodically ticks off each batch as he takes them from the box: a dozen each of Patchouli, Frankincense, Jasmine, Ylang-Ylang.

He'd already decided that this was to be his last delivery of drugs, even before Darren had told him it was. Darren was getting out as well, in readiness of going up to Oxford in a couple of months. Joel can't afford to get into any trouble with the police. He's taking his responsibilities as a married man very seriously, particularly now the baby is nearly due. Not that Darren is aware of the imminence of the birth, any more than he or Sophie had been invited to the wedding. Joel shuts the consequences of being caught with the contents of his rucksack from his mind. After all, nothing has ever gone wrong before, so why should it now?

'See you, later, Joel. Don't be too late. Jeannie's making us a shepherd's pie for supper. It'll be nice for the four of us to sit down together for a quiet meal before the baby's born,' Theo says, as he sets the shop alarm at the end of the day. 'We haven't seen enough of you since your mum and I have moved out of the flat. By the way, I'd like you to dress the main window again on Monday now that you've sorted out all the new stock, if that's alright with you.'

It certainly is alright with him. This is the job that Joel enjoys the most. Joel loves the shape of the window and the way he can climb onto the deep sill to create his displays. He will furnish it on Monday to look like a section of someone's living room. He'll use a couple of the new coffee tables together with one of those exotic Persian rugs that came in last week. His mind flies to the new table lamps, the bases shaped like elephants. He'll definitely include those. Not that he and Grace will have a living room like that. He prefers cleaner lines, nothing overworked or fussy. And once the shop is his as well as the flat, the stock will completely change as well.

The early evening air is misty, dank and chilly for early August. It's been raining on and off for most of the day. He pulls up the hood of his sweatshirt as he steps into the street. Bright pearls of light bounce in and out of the puddles formed by an earlier shower. As he turns the corner into East Street he catches a glimpse of the halo of light hanging in the haze, indicating the direction of the football ground about half a mile away. It's early to be turning on the floodlights at this time of year. He decides to head up East Street first, then turn right at

303

the Off Licence and vanish into the morass of side streets forming the original Georgian residential area.

As he approaches the corner adjoining Brewers Yard, Joel becomes aware of a dark-coloured car moving slowly along on the other side of the street, stopping in front of him, and then pulling slowly away again as he passes it. He turns the corner and is concerned to find that the car is still with him, slowing down and then starting up again. He feels vulnerable and exposed in this empty, rather narrow side road and he quickens his pace. He's sure that he'll feel safer once he's got nearer to the inhabited part of town. He won't stand so great a chance of being mugged.

Once he reaches the end of the back lane, he turns up a one way street displaying a 'No Entry' sign, in the hope of losing the car that's still creeping along behind him. This part of town has been laid out in a grid of parallel roads crossing each other at right angles, but when he reaches the next junction, there is the car, parked and waiting. Joel jumps quickly into the safety of the deep recess of a front porch. It has suddenly occurred to him that it could well be the police. A teenaged 'hoodie' carrying a rucksack would obviously be a target for them to stop and search. He has no idea what is in Darren's package; he's never been in the habit of touching any of them. His ignorance somehow makes him feel safer and that way there will be no fingerprints. He has become much more careful of late, now that he has so much more to lose. He hopes that it's only Class 3 – THG or some other performance-enhancing drug. He looks down at his puny form. Perhaps he can persuade the police that it's for his own personal use if there isn't too much of it.

What should he do? He knows he can't stay on the doorstep all night. He can hear the sound of the six o'clock news starting from inside the house. The owners may decide to go out at some stage and find him huddled there, pressed up against their front door, and the police would still be there, waiting for him around the corner. He can only think of two possible options. He could either post the package through the letter box, or ring on the doorbell in the hope of rushing in unimpeded and escaping through the back way. On reflection, the second option was a non-starter, and the first would enrage this Mark character and no doubt get Darren into trouble. There seems to be only one choice. He will have to walk out onto the street as nonchalantly as possible, and hope for the best.

He tries to think logically. Perhaps he's becoming paranoid. He's probably been imagining things. The car might not have been following him at all. It might not even have been the same one, and even if it was, it doesn't necessarily have to be the police.

He steps out from the safety of the doorway, and blotting everything from his mind except for that of Grace and their unborn child, he walks towards the corner of the street. The car has gone. He hurries to his destination as quickly as possible; he knows all the back ways by now.

It is not until he reaches what he assumes is the safety of the football coach's office that it all kicks off. They're not alone; the police have got there ahead of him. He's been set up.

# Chapter 15

## The Trial

Ronnie drains the last drop of beer from his pint glass and swills it around his mouth, trying to wash away the acrid taste left by the events of the day. He knows he shouldn't have had any more to drink, especially on a stomach almost completely devoid of solid food. One bite of dry toast for breakfast was never going to be enough, but Lorraine's fried breakfast had smelled too much of pig this morning. No doubt Darren had finished it for him after he'd left for work. And the liquid lunch at the Nag's Head before the case had been a big mistake. He couldn't go into the King's Arms because she worked there now, but of course, on reflection, she would have had the day off. The Nag's Head had brought back too many memories. Old wounds had been reopened, protective plasters had fallen off. He'd tried to push them under the table along with the empty crisp packets and misplaced beer mats, but to no avail. 'Choose,' she'd said all those years ago. 'Us or them. You can't have both.' Had he chosen well? Would he have chosen differently in hindsight?

'Ronnie! Save us those seats, will you? Another pint? Packet of crisps? Pork scratchings?' Sounds like Jim's voice.

Bile rises into his throat. He can't distinguish his mates who are approaching his table. They'll be having a swift drink after work before a round of golf. He prays that Bernie isn't amongst them. Ronnie looks at his watch yet again. Numbers blur in and out of his line of vision. Where's Darren? Still on the golf course? Friendly match with his mate Wills from school, to celebrate their A Level results. He's *got* to speak to him before he goes off to see that girl again. Ronnie had seen Sophie talking to Joel outside the Court House. He'd seen her throw her arms around Joel's neck. He'd heard what she'd called him.

He looks at Jim's two friends as they sit down at his table. They're pushing up, ignoring him. He's never really fitted in, has he? A social climber, that's what they think of him. That was all Lorraine's fault. Why had he stayed with her? To avoid scandal, retain social standing and respect? Where was the respect in that?

Bernie's not here. Ronnie hasn't done what Bernie would have expected from him; he'd wanted to make an example of Joel. What will he say when he finds out what's happened? Bernie had kept his side of the bargain. When Joel and all the other members of the drugs cartel were rounded up by the police on the same night, Darren hadn't been implicated. And over the last one and a half years, Darren's duties had been extremely light, as was promised. Apart from informing the police of the time and place of his meetings with Mark, he had only to carry on his job of the collecting and dispensing of his consignments of drugs in the usual way. He'd never been put into a dangerous or compromising position, and the only reason why his necessary cooperation with the police had been so protracted was that Mark had proved not to be a major player, and hadn't immediately led them to the top men. Ronnie wishes now that he'd refused to sit on Joel's case, said he was

307

too closely connected, but what excuse could he have given? Darren was in the clear, so why rock the boat, cast unnecessary suspicion by saying that his son was a friend of the defendant? But, of course that wasn't the only reason he should have refused.

He shivers as he remembers entering the courtroom this afternoon, a dingy space smelling of sweat, furniture polish and fear. The dark panelled walls had closed in on him and the chalky light transformed from the bright August sunshine by way of the dirty, high level windows had done nothing to lighten his mood. The room was packed and everyone rose as he and his colleagues entered. As he turned to sit, he saw Jeannie, sitting as close to Joel and his solicitor as she could. There was no trace of Theo though, thank God. Then he spotted Sophie, Darren's girlfriend, sitting right at the back on the opposite side of the room. What was she doing here? She must be a friend of Joel's.

Ronnie had run his hand through his hair and swept it off his face before putting on his reading glasses. He needed to examine the case notes. The people on the other side of the bench became a blur. Joel couldn't plead anything but guilty, of course. He'd been caught handing over the drugs. Money had been seen to change hands.

On the first adjournment, Ronnie had kept his head down as he'd left the courtroom, but on the second occasion he'd accidentally caught Jeannie's eye. From her hard, vengeful and protective expression, he knew what he had to do – but it wasn't going to be easy, not with Marjory Broadfoot on the bench with him. Why did it have to be Marjory? She was a Conservative with the biggest capital C imaginable, a 'pillar of the community', a fund raiser for countless worthy causes.

Someone Lorraine no doubt longed to emulate. He couldn't stand the woman.

'Right then, Ronnie,' she'd said. 'I reckon this one's done and dusted. He'll have to get some sort of custodial sentence for this. We can't be seen to be soft on drug-pushers.'

'Come on, Marjory. We all heard the mitigating circumstances. I think we ought to give the boy a chance.' Millie Pring, a scrawny, hawk-like woman with an oppressively floral-patterned skirt and sensible shoes was staring at them both as she'd said this. Good old liberal-minded Millie.

'Millie's quite right, Marjory,' he'd said. 'The boy clearly had a lesser role in this. He was performing a limited function under direction and he couldn't have had any idea of the scale of the whole operation. It's an isolated incident. He's had no previous convictions and he clearly showed remorse just now. Added to that, he's in full time employment, recently married and his wife's about to have their first baby. Everything fits with giving him a deferred sentence. What's the point in giving him a prison sentence? He'll only come out a real criminal.'

So Marjory had been outvoted and a major crisis in Ronnie's life had been averted. The potential headlines in tomorrow morning's paper had receded: *Local Justice of the Peace and Respected Businessman Jails Own Love Child.* Jeannie would have done it; what had she got to lose by telling the press? Theo had always known that Joel wasn't his. In those days Jeannie wouldn't look twice at Theo – not with Ronnie around.

He remembers that last night before Theo had left the country. It was his last night in England, and Theo had got so drunk that Ronnie had had to undress him and put him to bed. Jeannie had decided to let Theo have her bed as he would need a good night's sleep before going to the airport. The couch would be fine for them. Ronnie wouldn't be there for long anyway. He'd be slinking back to Lorraine before Darren woke up as usual for his 2.00am feed, regular as clockwork.

'Hey, are you alright Ronnie? How did the trial go?' Sounds like Jim, but he can't be sure. He puts a pint in front of him, and Ronnie takes a sip, restoring the thread of his thoughts.

Jeannie should never have made him choose like that, not then. It wasn't the right time. Any other time and his answer would have been different. He'd only ever married Lorraine because she was pregnant. If he'd met Jeannie sooner, Lorraine wouldn't have stood a chance with him. She was shallow, grabbing and a snob. She'd shut him out just after he'd married her, so he can't blame himself for looking elsewhere. With Lorraine, it was always 'not while I'm pregnant', 'not after I've just had a baby', 'it was such a difficult birth', 'not while I'm still breast feeding', 'I haven't got time', 'I'm too tired', 'I've got a headache'. On and on in that same wining voice, spoiling their son with all that attention, attention she should have been giving him. He'd decided to leave Lorraine – he really had – especially after Joel was born and definitely when Jeannie had become pregnant with Zoe. But that was before his accident at work. After that, Lorraine had started to take an interest in him again, fussing around him in hospital, nursing him at home. He'd side-lined Jeannie and she'd had to give birth by herself. Suddenly he'd found that Lorraine was the loving one while Jeannie had become complaining and tired. She was finding Zoe too demanding, just as Lorraine had found with Darren. Life with his two families was becoming impossible, but which one should he choose? Then when his health returned, the situation became clearer; he wanted to make a success of his life, build his own business. He realised he had a reputation to

310

maintain, and the possible scandal of him leaving his wife and family for a second ready made one, decided him. He could prevaricate no longer. How could he divorce Lorraine just then? When Jeannie gave him her ultimatum he hadn't had a choice, had he?

'Then you're not to have anything to do with us ever again, do you hear?' she'd said. 'I'll take your money, but nothing else. And you're to have nothing to do with the children or I'll tell everyone what a low life piece of scum you really are. It's your choice.'

But now he has to find Darren. 'Careful, Ronnie; you've spilt my beer,' someone says. 'Are you sure you're OK?'

'I need some fresh air. A cigarette,' he hears himself mumble.

Ronnie staggers out of the clubhouse, in and out of the groups of people congregating around the bar. No one acknowledges him. He's invisible. He stumbles around the side of the building, skirting the ornamental rockery filled with brightly coloured annuals. Repulsive! Garish! He can't stand the way they always arrange them in neat rows of alternating clashing colours. Wouldn't look so bad if they'd planted them in clumps. It's as bad as what Lorraine insists on doing in their garden. At least he's managed to kill off her hideous plaster gnome. He'd hidden it in the skip when they'd moved house.

Once round the back, he goes to light up a cigarette in peace but finds he's not alone. Darren's having a pee, aiming his flow high up the clubhouse wall like some competitive adolescent schoolboy.

'Why are you doing that here, son? What's wrong with inside? And why didn't you answer my texts?'

'No time, Dad. I'm late already. If I'd gone in the clubhouse I'd never have got out.' He cocks his head towards a narrow gap in the hedge. 'Short cut to the car park. Sophie wants me to get to hers by 6.30, and our match went on a bit.'

He approaches Ronnie who's starting to sink to the ground. He grabs him under the armpits and pulls him upright. 'You're absolutely hammered, Dad. What's up? Joel's trial go badly?'

'That's all fine, son. I sorted it. But you're not to see that Sophie anymore. Stop doing whatever you're doing with her, do you hear? It's illegal. Sexual Offences Act. Up to two years for that.'

'What the hell are you on about? She's sixteen – seventeen in a few weeks. Anyway, we love each other. We both felt it, as soon as we first met.'

'Of course you love her. She's your sister, Darren... half-sister. Joel's sister. Lovely little baby was Joel... so quiet and undemanding... so self-contained. Still the same – he's always managed to get on by himself. A survivor, just like me, eh? Not seen the resemblance, son? Not like you and Zoe. "Peas in a pod", you were, as soon as you were born. Always crying, wanting to be picked up. Prima donnas, the pair of you, just like your grandfather. I should have stayed with Jeannie then none of this would be happening.' Darren's grip on him has increased. He's started to shake him.

'What the hell are you on about, Dad?' Ronnie watches his son's expression turn slowly from confusion to comprehension. 'Why are you always spoiling everything, you complete bastard? I didn't know, did I? Anyway, if I didn't know, then I can't be done for it, can I?'

'That's right. But no more, do you hear? Just keep it in your trousers from now on.'

'Oh, just like you, I suppose? You're such a good role model, aren't you? "Listen, learn and remember", that's what you said. Well I've been taught by the real master – but all the wrong things.'

Ronnie sees his son's face getting closer as if in a distorting mirror. It's ugly with rage. He feels a gush of hot, sea salt breeze hitting him in the face and then he's suddenly unsupported. He hears footsteps crunching on pebbles, a swish of foliage parting… and then silence.

He's crumpling up as if he's been filleted. He's approaching a steep cliff. He's getting too close to the edge. A large rift is forming. He sees dark earth, overhanging. One more step and he's stumbling, setting up an avalanche of loose stones. He's falling over and over to the shore. Waves are retreating, leaving the flotsam and jetsam of his imperfect life exposed. He hears a thud, and then a thunder of water. Explosions of jagged white light appear, star-like, evoking childhood memories of strip cartoons. 'Pow!' 'Splat!'

# Chapter 16

## Darren's Bit of Good Fortune

I've got to get away from here, from Dad. He makes me sick. I've got to be with her just once more before I tell her. Actually, knowing her she'll probably think it's a laugh. I'd better turn my mobile onto *vibrate*, otherwise it'll be making a din all evening with Dad trying to get through. A text from Joel. That can wait. I know his news anyway.

At last I'm at Sophie's. She's leading me straight to her room. Her parents are out, thank God. I can't see them just now, not in the mood I'm in. Why I'm feeling so shifty I've no idea. None of this is my fault. How was I to know?

'How much do you love me, Sophie?' I say.

She puts on a silly theatrical voice. 'As much as I love myself: infinitely.' She laughs. 'Did I just make that up? It's rather good: very Oscar Wilde.'

'Enough to marry me if we could?' I have to know, even though it's impossible.

'Of course, my darling,' she says. 'And what's with all this "if we could"? We don't have to ask anyone's permission. We can do just what we like. I've got something to discuss with you about that, actually, hence all the hurry to get you over here. But that can wait for now.'

My mobile's going ballistic on Sophie's bedside table. It's still in vibrate mode and it's careering around over the shiny surface and crashing into things. Oh shit! The clock on it says 7.30am. We must have fallen asleep. I'm not surprised. What Dad said yesterday completely drained me. It's as if I don't know who I am any more. A brother and a sister and I never knew. It's unbelievable! The call's from home. I'd better take it. Dad can't do a thing. He can't prove who I'm with or what I've been up to.

'Darren?' It's Mum. She sounds tiny and very far away. 'Where are you, darling? You must come home. The police are here.'

'What's wrong, Mum? You sound terrible. Whatever's happened?'

'It's your dad, Darren. Oh, please come home. Please be quick.' She's becoming hysterical.

'Mum?'

'This is Sergeant Hampton, son. I'm afraid I've got bad news. Your father was found dead at the golf club first thing this morning. He was lying in the rockery round the back of the clubhouse. A member of the catering staff found him when he went out to the bins. He remembered him having one too many at the bar last night. It seems he went outside for a cigarette, tripped over and banged his head. Then he was sick and suffocated on his own vomit. It was all too late for him when he was eventually discovered. It was just a terrible accident, I'm afraid. No one's to blame. It's just a pity there was no one to look out for him when it happened.' The line goes quiet for a moment. 'You really must get back here, son. Your mother's in a terrible state.'

'Of course. Straight away.' I put down the phone and my whole body begins to shake. I'm unable to control the sobs that seem to tear through every part of me. I feel Sophie's comforting arms around me, clasping me close, trying to calm my tremors.

'Whatever's wrong?'

'It's my dad… he's dead.' Words I never imagined I would have to utter. My dad – my mentor, my guide, my protector – and until last night, my hero who could do no wrong.

'What on earth's going on, Sophie? Whatever's the matter with Dan, and more to the point, what is he doing in your bed?' Sophie's mother is standing at her bedroom door in her dressing gown, looking surprisingly intimidating. 'Your dad's downstairs making breakfast. I don't know what he's going to make of it all. We trusted you, Dan. We thought you were better than this.'

'Just throw me my robe won't you, Mum,' Sophie says, 'and I'll get up. Dan's just heard that his dad's died, so don't you dare start anything with him. And please go now and give him a chance to get up, will you? We've got some other news to tell you as well. Make sure Dad makes enough breakfast for all of us.'

I love her even more than ever. She's positively Amazonian standing there confronting her mum. She's like a lioness protecting her cub, her beautiful rich golden mane flowing down her back nearly to her waist. I've never noticed how alike we are before. The only difference is that she's not a coward.

We go downstairs to the kitchen, and her parents look at us sort of bruised and confused.

'I'm so sorry for your loss, Dan. Had he been ill for long? We'd no idea. It's probably not the right time to say this, but Sophie's mother and I are really not happy about your staying the night. What's this other news then, Sophie? I hope you're not pregnant.'

'As if! I'm not stupid, Dad. Dan and I are getting married, that's all. He proposed to me yesterday. That's why I let him stay the night. It's brilliant. It'll solve everything. You can't object to me accepting that place at drama school in Oxford now, can you? Saying I'm too young to leave home? I won't be all by myself now, will I? I'll be with Dan.'

'Sophie. My dad's just died. We can't do this now. It's not on.' I don't remember proposing. Surely I didn't. It was just a hypothetical question to boost me, after all those horrible things Dad was saying about me.

'You can't have changed your mind already. That's a bit quick, even for you. Anyway, I don't believe your dad dying should make any difference at all.'

She's unreal. And people have the cheek to say that I'm heartless and self-centred. But she's completely wrong; Dad's death makes all the difference in the world, now I come to think about it. Nobody else knows who her dad is; Mum certainly doesn't. And Joel's mum Jeannie won't make the connection. Sophie doesn't want anything to do with her, so we certainly won't be inviting her to our wedding. Marrying Sophie can't be any worse than anything else I've done, except for that business with Crunch. Up to two years, Dad said. That seems par for the course. The only other person that might twig is Joel, but he's easily dealt with. And anyway, even if it did come out one day, nobody knows that I know, so that's alright. Dad said so.

I give her a hug. 'Of course I haven't changed my mind. On the contrary. It just seems wrong to be thinking of our happiness at a time like this, that's all. We'll talk later, but I must go home to Mum now. She needs me.'

'You must stay to breakfast first. I insist,' she says. 'You haven't eaten for ages and you're not driving home on an empty stomach.'

The bacon does smell particularly good, actually, much better than Mum's... tastes better too.

'If Dan and I get married at the end of September, Mum, that'll give you nearly seven weeks to help me arrange it all. That's plenty of time. We'll have a marquee in the garden. It'll only be a small do, just close family and a few friends, say about sixty to seventy people? Your relations from Ireland will be invited of course, Dan, especially that cousin you're particularly friendly with – Dawn. We won't bother to get engaged. There's no point. It means nothing.' She looks at me and gives me a sly smile. 'You'll book the Registry Office, won't you darling?'

'Whatever you want,' I say. I clear my plate and get up to go. 'Right, I'm off. I've got a funeral to arrange.'

Poor old Dad was right. I really do have the luck of the devil!

# Chapter 17

## Darren in Oxford

Well here I am in Oxford at last, the 'city of dreaming spires'. Dad would have loved it here: the architecture, all the historic buildings. I've always imagined myself in a place like this – with all the shops, theatres, museums, clubs – and the river Thames of course. I think I'll take up rowing instead of golf. I'll row for my College; it'll help to hone my physique. I could even take up the guitar again, form my own group. And they've got an ice rink here. I'll get Mum to take Hope. She can start lessons straight away, get ahead of the game.

Everything's turned out just great. Nobody came forward and objected to my marrying Sophie last month. I was nearly shitting myself when they got to the bit about 'any just cause or impediment'. And I've still got custody of Hope. Grace and Joel have gone nice and quiet on that one for now. I was freaked out for a bit when I heard they were getting married, but now that he's got a criminal record that's definitely bought us more time. And time is of the essence. The longer we have Hope, the more likely she'll want to stay with us, especially if we spoil her. Good old Mum. She's been invaluable for babysitting duties. Renting our old house out and finding somewhere for us all here was a stroke of genius, especially somewhere with a granny flat attached. I can just see Mum at the Mother and Toddler group she's decided to join once we've settled in. The possessive way she's commandeered Hope and the pushchair just now, I'm sure she won't be letting on that she's only the grandmother.

Hope's looking around, pointing upwards and laughing. She's noticed the grotesquely carved stone heads placed around the guttering to the building we're passing. I pick her out of the pushchair and hold her up as high as possible.

'Look, Baby. Can you see the funny faces? They're called gargoyles. When it rains, the water flows off the roof and out of their mouths.'

'Garglies, Danny,' she says. 'Like you in the bartroom.' She makes a throaty noise and chuckles. 'I'm firsty, Danny. I want a drink.' She points at the nearest of the numerous cafes we've walked past this morning.

'We've seen better ones than that, sweetheart. Let's wait a bit longer.'

'No, Danny. Now!' She's pulling at my hair and struggling.

'OK, Baby. Everybody inside. Mum, Sophie, bag that spare table and I'll take Baby up to the counter to choose.'

We're pushing open the double doors to allow Mum to get the pushchair through when this really fit bird starts to come out. She looks familiar.

'Ryan,' she whispers. It's Kaye. She looks amazed and wistful, but there's no anger in her face.

I pass Hope over to Sophie. 'Back in a minute,' I say, and give her a wink. This will make her day. She keeps complaining that I'm not keeping up with her and that I'm in danger of becoming just another boring, faithful husband. She says she's much too young for one of those. *Remember what we added to our wedding vows: complete openness. I can't believe you haven't had anybody else at all. I'm having withdrawal symptoms. I need some juicy details. No secrets, remember'.* Actually, she's getting boring, always going on about it. And it's taking all the excitement out of having a bit on the side, now that she's made it compulsory.

I follow Kaye out. She's looking just as beautiful as she did three years ago. She's had her hair cut in this elfin style, all jagged and wispy around her face and ears. It sets off her enormous brown eyes to perfection. She's still just as slim, and her legs seem to go on for even longer than I remember. I noticed a little park a minute ago, so I lead her there in silence. We say nothing until we're sitting down together.

'Ryan, what happened to you? I waited and waited and you never came, and you stopped answering my emails. I decided that I must have made you up. My first term was hell. I nearly decided to drop out of Uni altogether.'

'I'm so sorry,' I say. I'm heartened to hear the soft Irish accent again. This Ryan character's a good bloke, I mustn't let him down. 'It was my father, you see. He had a terrible accident, just before I was due to come up. A fall from the tractor. Fractured skull in fact. He never fully recovered, as it happens. I had to defer my place here and run the farm for him – and for Mum and my sister Sophie. She was only just fourteen at the time and Mum was pregnant. You've seen my baby sister. We christened her Hope. But then my Dad suddenly died, and here we all are. We've rented out the farm; working on the land was never something I wanted to do.'

'Ryan. How terrible. You poor thing. Your poor family. I can see why you didn't contact me. You were too occupied with more important things to remember some girl you'd met on holiday. And your father having been ill for so long after his injury… it must have been a very serious blow to the head. A

321

cardiac arrest after sub-clinical seizures, I suppose. It can happen, I'm sure.'

'That's right. Clever girl.' I'd forgotten that she's studying medicine, but it seems that my story's feasible. 'You were important to me – of course you were – but after I'd left it so long I didn't think you'd be interested in me anymore.' I remember how impotent I'd felt as the date for our supposed reunion had got closer – how my anger and frustration had increased with only the inadequacies of Fiona and Grace to lift me. But that was all history and it seems I've got another chance.

'I assumed you'd found someone more deserving,' I say softly. 'No doubt you have by now.'

'There was somebody once,' she says. 'But it didn't last. He turned out to be utterly boring – and my mother just loved him, so that was it!'

'What will your mother make of me, do you think?'

'She'll probably love you even more, actually.' She laughs and her face lights up. 'What about you, Ryan? I'm sure you've had lots of girlfriends.'

'One or two,' I say, 'but nobody important. I become engaged at one time to the daughter of one of my father's friends. He owned the adjoining farm. We were going to amalgamate them at some time. But she didn't turn out to be the right girl, and when my father died we went our separate ways.' I put my arm around her shoulder. 'Do you remember what you said all that time ago, Kaye? How we'd be together properly as soon as we met in Oxford?'

She nods and blushes. 'It's something I've never stopped thinking about... But tell me, Ryan, did you keep up with the kayaking?'

'I'm afraid not,' I say. 'Not without you. We made a good team, didn't we? I needed you to encourage me. I can be a bit of a wimp by myself. But I'm thinking of taking up rowing. It's the obvious thing to do here.'

'That's great!' she says. 'You must come along to my club. I'll introduce you. I've become a cox. I'm hoping I might even be selected for the Boat Race next year.'

She's definitely my sort of girl. I think of Grace and Sophie and of their strange obsessions and interests. 'Tell me, Kaye, do you ever read Jane Austen?'

She looks surprised and says nothing for a moment. 'I'm afraid not. I only seem to have time for reading scientific journals. Why, do you?'

'Not at all. I was just checking.' I laugh and turn my face to hers. I kiss her, and my stomach lurches in a way I haven't experienced for years. It's wonderful. This time it must be the real thing. I imagine the sort of life I could have with Kaye – children, for one thing. I can never risk having any with Sophie. Perhaps I can follow Dad's example and run two families at once, but I'd do it more successfully and for much longer – perhaps even for ever. I tighten my grip on her and she snuggles her head onto my chest. I close my eyes and picture it all. I would never give Kaye up like Dad did with Jeannie. I could even marry her. I could change my name to Ryan by deed poll or something, or I could conveniently find out that Sophie's my sister and have our marriage annulled…

But I'm getting ahead of myself as usual. I must learn not to be so hasty. I've got my future to think of. I don't want to be surrounded by scandals when I'm in a position of power in the Government, the Cabinet, or as PM even…

'Ryan, are you alright?'

'Best ever,' I say.

'You still look so young, Ryan. Younger than me. And after everything you've been though…'

'Ah, but you haven't seen what's in my attic now, have you Kaye? Surely you remember that film that came out some time back – *The Picture of Dorian Gray*? Me and the Devil, we're very close.' I chuckle, and trace my finger around the line of her jaw. 'Now I must get back to Mum and the girls. I hate cold coffee, and anyway, I've promised to show them the sights. Here's my number. Ring me in a couple of hours and we'll meet up later tonight. Catch up on everything.' I give her my most engaging smile and get up to go. 'And I'm still on a promise, remember.'

As I look around me, I see that Matthew Arnold had got it all wrong. These aren't dreaming spires at all, but giant phalluses thrusting skywards, competing for the privilege of inseminating the universe. No wonder it's inspired so many people to achieve greatness. Tony Blair came here, and Margaret Thatcher, Bill Clinton, David Cameron… Darren O'Donnell? On reflection, do I really want the top job? I think I'd rather be a close advisor, be the power behind the throne. That way, when the shit hits the fan, as it invariably does, I'll be in the clear. No way do I intend to end my career as a sad old 'has been', forced to write numerous autobiographies or even worse, give after dinner speeches at Masonic functions.

And who am I really, anyway? I'm not just Darren O'Donnell. I see myself as a beautifully cut diamond, each facet polished to reflect a different image of myself. Sophie can't possibly be my soul mate. What's really left of her when she's deprived of a script? All I can see are shallow waters running across murky stones.

But she'll relish this scenario between Ryan and Kaye. She'll really appreciate the role-playing on my part. And she'll find it so romantic. I'll spare her the most important part though. She wouldn't enjoy it. It's none of her business, as it happens, and I'm still smarting over the way she cheated me into marrying her. She really forced my hand. What could I have actually said to her parents over breakfast that day when her mum had just caught us in bed? 'Oh, I can't marry her because we're brother and sister'? I don't think so. But I should have thought of something, shouldn't I? This sort of personal shit isn't going to look good if it ever comes out, however innocent I might appear. Incest is just the sort of crap people remember you for. Getting married to her seemed rather a laugh at first, and it was one up on Dad. I was still mad at him at the time, even though he had just died. But now I'm just like him, living with dark secrets. And Dad was quite right about my feelings for Sophie. It's only that GSA syndrome. That's what it said on the internet. It happens all the time when siblings meet and they don't know they're related, particularly if they resemble each other in some way.

But that's not the only personal shit I'm worried about. I'm still waiting for the knock on the door over that business with Crunch, aren't I? It's all good on the drugs dealing side. Mark and the rest of them are all locked up now, and none of them knew who I really was anyway. It all happened exactly as the police had planned it; everybody was rounded up on the same night as Joel. But I can't help worrying about what Inspector Wilkes said when I first met him – about how they were going to investigate the suspicious nature of Crunch's death when everything else was sorted. I've seen enough programmes on TV about cold cases being reopened to know that I may never be free of that one. And I've only got an alibi for part of that evening, when I was with Jess. There's no way she'll cover for me. Everybody said it was my fault when she got such rubbish results for her A Levels last year. Apparently they blamed me when she had to sit them again. Nothing's ever been my fault really, so why do people always expect me to feel guilty? But I am a coward, I have to admit, and because of that I feel ashamed that I've sometimes let myself down. And because of my cowardice, I'll always live in fear. My luck's bound to run out sometime.

I've suddenly gone off telling Sophie anything about Kaye. Anyway, even if I have to tell her something, I'm definitely not telling her everything. I've broken her cardinal rule about not falling in love, haven't I? Kaye's the best ever. This time it really is the real thing.

# Chapter 18

## Joel in Control

Joel relaxes into the soft black leather lounger and runs his fingers over the curve of the chrome armrests. He has positioned himself to enjoy the full panoramic view of the river from his open plan living room over the shop. The lights on the town bridge are on, great iridescent globes strung together like a giantess's necklace. The noise of traffic from behind the large Georgian sash windows is just a steady, soothing drone.

He feels rather like a giant himself right now. He has what he's always dreamed of: a proper family, consisting of two parents, and also the undreamt of added bonus of a wife and son. Grace has almost everything as well, he reckons. She seems more than happy with the turn of events in her life. She has achieved her 'happy ever after' scenario courtesy of Jane Austen. She's passed her A Levels and has just started an Open University degree, not in English Literature surprisingly, but in Psychology. It will take her about six years, but there's no rush, and it will give her plenty of time to bring up Roy properly. And her parents are talking to her again now that there's no evidence of her first child. But Joel knows that is clouding Grace's contentment. Once Joel and she had married, they had been sure that they would win custody of Hope, but now that

Joel has a criminal record for drugs dealing, he has been reluctant to take the matter further. He is loath to put her though a court case that will be heavily contested and which they are likely to lose. Anyway, he is quite happy as he is. Roy is perfect and more than enough for now. Roy's quiet contentment is the complete opposite of Hope's tantrums.

He wonders whether Darren had been privy to what was going to happen that night of the drugs raid. Had he known that he was sending him into a trap once he had entered the football coach's office? Joel had felt uneasy all day after his bizarre meeting with Darren over breakfast. Darren had long outgrown the game he'd played with him that morning in Eric's. On that day, it was as if he couldn't bear to look at Joel for shame.

Joel goes to the maple-wood console table that's placed against the back wall of the living area. He reaches into the central drawer, picks out his tin of hand rolled spliffs and lights one. Taking pot this way gives him a quicker relief from stress than baking it into a cake. He smiles. Poor old Theo. He'd been quite sure that it was the meditation that had done the trick. He inhales deeply, and as the herbal scent hits his nostrils, he glances in the mirror in front of him. He automatically drags his thick fringe of hair out of his eyes and looks more closely at his image. What he sees is a young Ronnie staring back at him, an image of the Ronnie that his mother had first fallen in love with nearly twenty years ago. Joel understands now why Jeannie had found it difficult to be always in her son's company, why she had so often felt the need to escape. He was, after all, a reminder of how she had been rejected. She had told him the truth about his parentage as soon as they had heard the news of Ronnie's death when there was no longer a need to keep it a secret.

'But why did Theo say he was my dad?' Joel had said.

'Because he's a good man, Joel. Don't you remember what he asked you that evening after we'd told you we were getting married? He gave you the answer you said you wanted to hear. He thought he was doing the right thing... which was more than Ronnie ever did.'

An unpleasant smell alerts him to look down at his spliff, which has burned down to the homemade cardboard filter. How much of it has he actually smoked? He pinches it out between his thumb and forefinger and throws it into the waste paper basket. Darren is right. It's a filthy habit and he no longer really needs it. He'll give it up when this supply of marijuana is used up. He ought to anyway because of his deferred sentence conditions. He has no intention of ending up in prison.

While he's standing up, he'll go into the nursery and check on Roy. He's babysitting tonight while Grace is off at her Thursday meetings. She's taken Joel's place in Theo's meditation class. He stares into the cot and experiences again the special feeling of love he gets each time he sees him. Luckily, he looks nothing like Darren, more like him courtesy of Roy's paternal grandfather, Ronnie. Joel feels a sudden light-headedness and sits down on the nursing chair he has had recovered to match the nursery's décor. He grips the sides of the armless chair as a pit of comprehension opens up beneath him. He's being rocked as if in a tiny boat on a turbulent sea. Did Ronnie love him the way he loves Roy? It's possible. It would explain the reason for his surreptitious glances, his gruff manner, his seemingly strange and arbitrary questions.

He feels that he has come to a T junction in his life. Which route will he take, the studied and sensible one now trodden by his mentor Theo, or will his natural inclination lead him onto more slippery, uncertain paths? Who will win the nature versus nurture battle? Will his genes prove to be more powerful than

329

his feeling of correctness? He had started out on the wrong foot, only thinking of how to protect himself, how to survive. He remembers how he had first held Darren to ransom, how he had exhorted money out of him week after week, capitalising on the other's cowardice. He recalls how Darren had said to him on that February day nearly four years ago, 'If anybody asks, I was here on the market all day, right?' He had detected the slight tinge of doubt in Darren's voice and he had demanded to know the details before he would agree. Before he could decide on the necessary price for his silence. Darren had appeared to him then like a factory reject: shiny and desirable in all its perfect packaging, but intrinsically faulty when unpacked. But he had still loved this strangely damaged boy, a confusing emotion then, but not confusing now. You always love your brother, don't you?

After glancing at his son once more, he makes his way back to the living room. He helps himself to another spliff on the way. The river is running high and fast now, the lights from the car headlamps twinkling and refracting in its multi-faceted surface like exploding stars. They morph into multi-coloured fireworks, banging and popping in his head.

Should he let Darren off the hook at last? For that particular piece of information – that of Leroy's fate – perhaps. But now he has another of Darren's secrets to keep, that of his incestuous marriage to Sophie. Joel takes another drag on his spliff. He's unable to control a slight chuckle. He's reminded of those books on Greek and Roman mythology that used to fascinate him when he first started working in the Emporium. He can imagine Darren and Sophie gazing into each other's aqueous eyes, as if gazing onto the surface of a stream. They would each put out a hand, but unlike Narcissus, who found his mirror image always to fragment and vanish, always to be betrayed by the surface of the water, they would find their alter ego. In fact, their parts as Narcissus and Echo would be constantly shifting, each in turn answering the other's need for an ego boost. 'Am I the greatest, or what?' they would ask each other in turn. 'Am I the greatest, or what?' would come the instant reply. But where was the harm? They deserved each other and their union wouldn't cause a problem to anyone unless they wanted to have children. By the time Sophie finally decides she wants to be a mother, there'll probably be automatic screening for foetal abnormalities anyway.

But he reckons that he deserves quite a substantial sum to keep quiet over that particular pearl. After all, Lorraine has inherited all of Ronnie's estate and once she has died it will all go to Darren and Sophie. Surely he, Joel, is entitled to something now, if he has to forgo his rightful share later on? Joel has always had an innate feeling for justice, as well as an inborn belief that knowledge is power and should be used to his advantage. And that money is his by rights.

Not that he really needs Darren's money anymore. And the secret that he has managed to withhold from Darren is worth any fortune he could possibly give him: that of Roy's true parentage. Joel has everything he wants. Theo has given him the shop now as well as the flat over it, and a new sign adorns its magnificent frontage: *Kitchen's Kitchens.* The Emporium has been transformed into a showroom for Joel's design consultancy and now that he's decided to specialise in kitchens, he has taken on Theo's surname as well. To Theo, Joel will always be his son, even though they both know the truth.

The Emporium is only one of the shops around here that has been transformed of late. He imagines Eric in retirement with his sister in Burnham-on-sea. What would he make of the new Wine and Tapas Bar that has taken the place of his café? Joel pictures the new awning outside the place, shading the row of tables and chairs set out to catch the best view of the river. Gone is the vision of seersucker and condensation. The place has been completely revamped. All the old mismatched pine tables and chairs have been painted. Even the chairs that Darren had knackered over the years by leaning back on them have been mended.

What had Eric said to him that day, the one that had turned out to be the beginning of the rest of his life? 'Don't worry, Joel,' he'd said. 'Something will turn up. It always does'. The thought of Eric's cafe has made him feel hungry, and his mouth has started to feel dry. He's getting 'the munchies'. He'll go to the kitchen in a minute and knock up a massive fry-up and a mug of tea Eric style... when he can be bothered to get out of his chair.

He reaches for the ashtray on the side table and stubs out the remains of his second spliff. He'll definitely give it up one day soon. He needs to have his wits about him now. He can't be too laid back. He has a commission to complete for his first client tomorrow. He pictures himself sitting at his drawing board in the window of his shop, right next to where the gigantic Buddha had sat on the day he'd first met Theo. He's left the Buddha where he is as a tribute to him. No one had ever thought of buying it. It was much too big. He can't help laughing again. Did Ronnie have any idea what he was doing when he chose his sons' names? Joel had researched their meanings when he and Grace were thinking of names for their baby. Of course, Darren means *great*. What else could you expect? But Joel is even better, and very appropriate considering the position his drawing board now holds, because Joel means *the one true God*.

He repositions himself in his leather lounger. He leans back with his hands cradling the back of his head. He stretches out and then relaxes completely. Everything is going to plan. His first premises command the best possible position; no one can miss them as they come over the bridge into town. And once this business has taken off, they'll be others, both here and elsewhere. He imagines himself expanding into other types of merchandise: lighting, fabrics, objets d'art. He intends to make a name for himself in this town. Who knows? Perhaps one day he'll even be Mayor? He can't prevent a chuckle. Once he had thought that Darren was the Main Man.